STRONG EMERGENCE

NELSON MANGIONE

Copyright © 2014 Nelson Mangione
All rights reserved.

ISBN: 1495949397
ISBN 13: 9781495949395

For my wife, Karol, who loves to read, For my son, Christopher, who loves to write, And for my daughter, Tiffany, who was never supposed to be able to do either

THE QUEST

It is words you seek,
Magnificent and true,
From a note to a doctor,
From an epistle to a king.

PREFACE

"The whole is more than the sum of its parts"

Aristotle

I

Wilmslow, Cheshire
United Kingdom
June, 1954

8:40 pm GMT

Alan stood naked in front of the mirror. The effects of twelve months of estrogen had altered his body in interesting ways, smoothing his skin, growing his breasts, and shrinking his testicles. At first he was angry at the jurisprudence that sentenced him to the injections. He was appalled at the humiliating disfigurement they were causing, but he had come to admire the changes, finding peace with his new-found gifts.

He ran his hand over his body, caressing the soft skin. The little chest hair he once had was now gone, and the touch made his nipples harden as he ran his fingertips across his nubile breast mounds. A tingle erupted in his groin. Funny, he thought, how hormones that were supposed to hinder his desire only emphasized them. True that it had become more difficult to obtain an erection, but that was just anatomy. His emotions and passions were stronger than ever.

STRONG EMERGENCE

His memories flew to Regis, and his heart skipped a beat. Today he would be seeing his friend for the first time in months.

Alan had met Regis at a visit to a café in Salford. He remembered it like it was yesterday. The maître'd had placed him at a two-seat table outdoors near the edge of the walkway. Within minutes, a tall, lithe, Frenchman plopped in the other seat as if conjured by magic. He was pretentious, bold, obnoxious, and gorgeous. A few glasses of Chardonnay later, the mustached Regis led the boyish professor on a moonlit stroll to an uptown flat for the evening of a lifetime. Now, two years later, Alan could hardly believe he was in Cheshire for the holiday weekend. He was planning to discretely stop by, hoping to avoid both the authorities and the paparazzi. Regis had promised him a surprise, and he had one for him in return. The thought of his visit made him tingle again, this time not out of lust, but out of pride and accomplishment. Alan's surprise was a discovery that might just change the world and, if he parleyed it appropriately, one that might just change his life too.

His musings were interrupted by the sound of the door chime. He quickly grabbed a pair of pajamas pants draped over his trouser stand and put them on. He contemplated answering the door topless. There was nothing wrong or illegal about that; after all, he was still a man. But what if it were not Regis at the door? What if it were his maid, or a neighbor, or the press? "Oh my, what a scandal!" he chuckled. Abandoning the notion, he found the accompanying night-shirt, threw it on, and wrapped himself in his evening robe as he scooted to the foyer.

He couldn't impede the smile growing across his face as he opened the door. It was indeed Regis carrying a bag of groceries and a bottle of Chevel Blanc Cote de Rhone, "Hello my friend!"

"Bonjour, mon amour!" Regis gaily answered back offering the wine, his face lit by the firelight tones of the sunset. Seeing Alan in his robe, he apologized politely with a touch of remorse and a slight frown, "Oh, Alaine, I am very sorry. I am here too early. Forgive me."

"Not at all! Come in! Come in!" Alan ushered his Parisian friend into his home, taking the wine in one hand and offering his other arm in an awkward embrace.

"Are you sure?" the fit, dark-haired, and well-dressed Frenchman inquired, "Do you wish for me to wait a moment?"

"No, not at all. I've been looking forward to your visit all day!" Alan's joy and elation were undeniable, and his smile was infectious.

Regis's demeanor changed. He was enamored by the sound of Alan's voice, a natural tenor, now transformed into something distinctly feminine, "Well, then, I shall!" Returning the smile and crossing the threshold, he changed the subject, "I tried this wine for the first time last week, and I thought of you. I know how much you enjoy French reds."

Alan admired the gift as Regis sashayed inside. He had been to Alan's home in Wilmslow once before, nearly eleven months earlier, but that had only been a brief visit. Still, the home seemed materially the same: fine furnishings hidden under semi-organized clutter, beautiful paintings hidden in dark corners, and dated upholstery in bad need of replacement. If he did not know firsthand, Regis would never have guessed the man had a housekeeper. "Your home is wonderful Alan," he politely lied, "Thank you for inviting me."

"Thank you, but your gratitude is unnecessary. You are always welcome. I am just so glad, after all this time and pretense, that you have finally come to see me."

Suddenly more serious, Regis turned to Alan, "Yes, I know. The cloak and dagger has been a bore but, trust me, it was necessary. If the authorities knew...," he stopped himself nodding negatively, "it would not have been good."

Alan reluctantly conceded that truth. If Mi5 knew what he had been up to, he would have been incarcerated, or worse. It was enough that he had sent the authorities into a tizzy chasing after acquaintances he made while on holiday in Greece. The hypocritical bigots were so concerned that he would betray a state secret to a gigolo or reveal an encryption algorithm at an orgy. But their small-mindedness blinded them to his true intentions: work on a discovery that would alter humanity's understanding of its place in the universe. "Oh, if they only knew," he thought with an inward smirk.

Regis quickly smiled a broad, jovial grin, "But enough of the past, we are together now!"

Taking the cue, Alan smiled and took his swain by the hand, guiding him gently back down the hall.

"My! My! Where are you taking me?" Struggling to hold on to the groceries and expecting to enter the bedroom, Regis giggled as Alan surprised him with a quick turn into the kitchen, "Oh, you are such a tease!"

Alan continued the playful banter, "I want to see what you brought me?"

"Oui, my surprise!" Regis set the bag down on the counter amid empty food boxes intermixed with newspapers and journals. He opened the bag and fetched the contents one by one, "I have brought all the makings for a supreme picnic: a fresh baguette... Jarlsburg Swiss from an excellent fromagerie near my home... Delicious apples..."

Alan smiled broadly, "My favorite! You remembered!"

With a flirting glance he continued, "strawberries ... with freshly whipped cream..." Regis could see his lover's growing excitement as he added, "and bananas!"

Alan took the bait, "What are we going to do with those?"

Regis laughed, "You will see! But first let's have some wine!" He could see a little boyish disappointment in Alan's face, "Boy, those hormones certainly did not have the desired effect, did they?"

"No, they did not," Alan dryly replied, understanding Regis's sympathy to his plight. The injections of feminizing hormones were ordered by the court, in lieu of imprisonment, after Alan was found guilty of a homosexual affair. The conviction cost him his career and his reputation and now he was left to work on his university grants independently. The judge assured him that the injections would "cure" him of his lewd and lascivious desires, but months after starting the weekly injections, he met Regis and his feelings were as familiar as ever. He was far from relieved of his passions and, truthfully, had no wish to be. They were part of his person the same as his heart and liver.

Alan allowed his anger to subside, opened a nearby drawer, produced a corkscrew, and began to open the wine.

Regis stood nearby. He watched as his boyfriend poured the elixir into two cut crystal goblets that he seemed to divine from nowhere. With a quirky flourish, Alan offered him the glass and raised his own in a toast, "To reunited friends and cherished memories..."

"And to forbidden love and new beginnings," Regis continued. They smiled, clinked their glasses, and enjoyed the taste of the '51 vintage.

"Mmm. That's very good," Alan pleasingly critiqued. He picked up the crisp baguette, took a luxurious bite, and then proceeded with a full mouthful, "And I don't know about you, but I'm famished."

"Well then, let's eat!" Regis had been enthralled by Alan from their first date. It made his purpose more painful, but he checked his emotions. Important work was still left to be done.

Over the subsequent hour, they sat at the kitchen table and enjoyed their in-home picnic, in complete privacy, away from prying eyes. To Regis's Jarlsburg, Alan added a smoked Gruyere, an 8-year-old cheddar, fresh barley crackers, boysenberry jam, and an assortment of fine Dutch licorice as they caught up on their lives and families. They reminisced about their first encounter at a pub outside Nottingham and jokingly speculated about the intentions of their Cambridge steward.

It was only after they had finished eating that Regis turned the topic of discussion to business, "I trust the money I have sent has been adequate?"

"Oh yes, more than enough. Most of my work has been conjectural, done with the mind and pencil and paper. What has been hardest has been the misdirection – pretending to study one thing when, in fact, doing something else entirely."

Such had been the case when Regis first approached him with his proposition, "I know you have lost your academic appointment and your government clearance, but I will continue to support your work, secretly, as long as I can take part in the glory and any financial gain."

Alan instantly accepted the offer, and to throw off the Scotland Yard as well as his compatriots at the University, he worked 15 hour days - 7 days a week. He budgeted the first part of his day to studying and producing scholarly work in the field of developmental biology. It was an interesting academic exercise, and he had even won some genuine praise for his work in the mathematical origins of biological structures. But his real pursuit, what consumed the rest of his time save for sleep, tending to the needs of the body, and an hour or so jog through town, was the search for a solution to the 'unsolvable problem'.

"I understand," was all Regis could say. "And progress? Your messages have been positive," he carefully added. He was referring to the system of communication they had devised. Once a month, Alan's part-time maid, Sonja, would find her way to a somewhat off the beaten track cafe in central Manchester. There she would join Regis for a cappuccino and, after breakfast, he would give her a gift to take back to Alan: gift-wrapped money and a love note or two. In exchange, Sonja would politely accept the box and offer 'Alan's best regards' in return. The words had a special meeting: code for 'steady progress being made'.

Alan had been waiting for the proper time to spring his own surprise, and now the time seemed ripe. He felt nervous energy charge down his spine. Regis, his amoretto, would be the first to hear – just as he had promised. He sucked in a characteristic hiss of breath and began...

"I believe I found it."

Regis understood at once and almost could not contain himself. "What? What do you mean *it*"?

"I have found a solution to the so-called unsolvable reduction problem." Regis was no fool and a scientist himself, but Alan feared that not even he could fully understand the discovery or its significance. Alan was not entirely sure he did himself. Nevertheless, he chose to press on. "The time-dependent Schrödinger equation is incomplete. I have shown that an even more general solution exists. More importantly, the math predicts that under certain circumstances an exception to Heisenberg can occur thereby avoiding wave collapse."

His last sentence was a bombshell. Regis had hoped beyond hope that Alan had made a breakthrough in Quantum Mechanics theory, the physics of atoms and the subatomic particles that make them up. Why else would Alan's housekeeper, after exchanging the monthly dispensation, arise and plant a moist kiss directly on Regis's lips and palm him a crumpled up piece of paper? At first he didn't know just what to think but then, with a grin and a gleam in her eye, Sonja answered the question asked by his face, "That's from Alan. He misses you and can't wait to see you again."

He read and reread his lover's message but not in his wildest dreams had he expected this.

Regis's mouth was agape, but he barely listened as Alan spoke of simplified probability density functions and algorithmic atomic state descriptions. All he could see was money. Alan's dream of a real thinking machine might come true after all.

"Now, don't ask me how big this could be," Alan continued, "but it will be fun finding out!"

"Oh my God, Alan, I cannot believe it. I don't think I fully understand it, but oh my goodness, this is incredible! I am so happy for you!" Regis's excitement was palpable. He had just won the jackpot. "This calls for more wine...much more wine!" Regis poured the last of their second bottle. The Rhone was long gone, and this was a varietal Gewürztraminer. It was a bit too sweet for his taste, but intoxicating nonetheless, particularly with his subtle enhancements.

With a knowing smile of Regis's erotic modus operandi, Alan downed the glass. "Would you like to see what your money has bought?"

Regis contained his excitement and allowed his curiosity to dominate, "Sure. I would love to."

Alan rose with Regis following. They stepped through the kitchen, into a dark hall, and finally into a back room that looked like a second kitchen. There, on a burner, sat a pot of tepid liquid. A distinct smell permeated the room.

"Are you cooking nuts in here? It smells like almonds," Regis inquired.

"No. That's cyanide you smell."

"Cyanide?"

"You're privileged. Only a few can smell it. I, for one, cannot. But not to worry, the recipe is quite controlled and only very small amounts of cyanide are produced. If not, we would both already be long dead."

Regis quickly glanced around the small room. Bottles of labeled potassium nitrate lined the wall, and jugs of distilled water and muriatic acid crowded the floor. In the corner lay a gas mask, circa World War I.

"Then what's the gas mask for?" Regis asked with a slight but genuine concern.

Alan chuckled. "Don't be alarmed. It's here for safety, yes, but mostly I use it to protect me from the hay fever. It can be wicked in the spring and fall."

Satisfied with his answer but after a small delay, the Frenchman pressed on with his second burning question, "Why on earth are you making cyanide?"

Alan answered by pulling a spoon out of one of the baths with a pair of industrial tongs. "Because I am trying to extract gold."

"I know a jeweler who can plate your entire cutlery for nothing," Regis joked with facetious angst. Alan could sense his friend's unease, "Come. I will show you the rest of the house, and then I'll explain."

They stepped out of the lab and closed the door. Interestingly, the door had no lock but, with the door closed, the smell of burnt almonds vanished. The next room down the hall was a lavatory followed by a back entrance into Alan's bath and bedroom. The room was moderately sized, nicely appointed, and fairly tidy given the remainder of the house. The tour continued through the parlor, past the underutilized dining room that doubled as a filing cabinet, his study stacked with boxes and books, and concluded back in the familiar kitchen with Alan explaining his suspicion for the quantum relativistic properties of gold's nature and apologizing for the mess at every turn.

"I can almost not believe it. You mean you can tell me why gold is gold?"

"Haven't you ever wondered why yellow gold is, well, yellow and not some shade of grey like just about every other metal: from lead to aluminum, from tin to iron, from mercury to silver – most are grey? Why not gold too? The answer is special relativity!"

"Relativity!? You mean like in Einstein? But I thought that has to do with space and time and gravity?"

"Yes. But I found a link to quantum physics – a link that combines computational theory with quantum mechanics and gravity at the atomic scale! The explanation of gold's color would be only a trivial success of a small part of the theory. The more profound implications will be considerably harder to work out. But if we can do it, the impact on humanity could be unfathomable!"

"Then how do you know you're right?"

"Because I have repeated and verified every step of the math and validated every assumption," the wine was inducing a cockiness that Regis found unappetizing. One thing was sure; Alan felt convinced. He certainly believed he had stumbled upon something.

"So who else knows?" Regis asked nonchalantly.

"No one, just like I promised. But I have called in some old favors and have gotten myself invited to a symposium in Amsterdam. Apparently there I'm still loved," Alan chuckled, the wine starting to get to Alan's head, "In the meantime, I'm writing a paper to *Nature*."

"This is truly so very exciting. There is no telling where this might go."

Suddenly Alan seemed a bit peaked. He yawned and stretched a bit. Regis poured the last of the wine into Alan's glass, but Alan stopped him, "I think I've had enough of that."

"Then how about something to eat?"

"Yes, maybe..." Alan foraged through the assorted fruits Regis had laid out earlier and picked out a fresh apple and bit deep into it. As the fruit hit his belly, his head subtly began to spin, "That did not help. I think I've had too much to drink!" he tittered.

"Then I think I'd like to see your bedroom again." Regis's voice was seductive and inviting.

Alan feebly smiled in return. The wine had taken its toll, and his heart began to speak against the advice of his body, "Yes, I think I would like that."

This time it was Regis taking Alan by the hand. Together, they walked past the study and parlor, through the foyer, down the hall and into the bedroom. Alan staggered twice along the way still clutching his apple in his free hand. Each time he was supported by his lover, giggling at each misstep like a girl experiencing love for the very first time. With Regis's help, Alan plopped into the bed. The professor smiled broadly, blew a few bubbles, and swayed to and fro. He wasn't up for much and finally appreciated his condition, "I'm drunk!"

"Yes, you are my sweet." Regis opened Alan's robe, exposed his pajamas, and gently pulled the garment down off his shoulders, "Let me help you out of this." Alan passively complied, and instantly, the robe was on the floor. Regis began to rub Alan's chest through his nightshirt. They both fell back on the bed in a passionate embrace, but within a moment, the kiss released as Alan fell into an inebriated slumber.

Regis stood over him for a second then positioned him properly on the bed, placing his head on the pillow and drawing the bed sheets up to his neck. He picked up the apple that had fallen to the floor. He sat it on the nightstand and then neatly folded the robe and placed it on a chair. He stood back and admired the scene; Alan lay restfully, gently snoring. Regis fought the urge to cry. He quickly found his resolve and focused on the task at hand.

Alan's surprise was not completely unexpected but its magnitude certainly was. It called for an unfortunate but necessary change of plans. Simple theft was not going to do. Regis's mind was swirling with possibilities but a simple solution quickly arose. But first he had to find his prize.

His first stop was the study. Papers and periodicals shrouded the desk and boxes of books were on the floor and on antique Queen Anne chairs that had been converted into tables. He scoured through the materials taking care not to overly disturb them, knowing that he had time to be meticulous and trusting that the narcotic-laced wine would keep Alan asleep for hours. He found notes on morphogenesis, books on quantum mechanics and the philosophies of Descartes and Locke, but nothing that was of interest to him.

He moved to the next room, the dining room turned warehouse, where stacks of books and boxes were everywhere. Dusty tomes, loose papers filled with barely legible script, and formal manuscripts from the likes of A. S. Eddington, J. Von Neumann and Bertrand Russell filled the cartons. The initially calm swindler began to sweat. He tore open box after box, pouring through letters and memos, frantically looking for anything even reminiscent of Alan's secret. He was beginning to think that it wasn't here or perhaps hidden in the basement or dashed away in a safe when he saw a lone case on an old buffet table set off in the corner. Forty-five minutes of searching had elapsed, and he controlled his expectations but let out an audible gasp when the contents were revealed. It was the mother lode. On top was the manuscript but alongside of it were the transcript for his speech, detailed notes, letters, diagrams, formalized proofs and a hand-scribbled journal; everything!

Conscious of his vocalizations, he hurriedly closed the box and stepped back into the bedroom. His friend still lay asleep, peacefully. Now the hard task lay ahead. He returned to his find and cautiously carried it to his car. With every step, he looked over each shoulder to assure no one was watching, but the night was quiet and still. He returned to the house. This time he ventured through the kitchen and into the lab. The experiment was still in progress. In the 8 quart pot was the single spoon covered in an inch of gently bubbling brew. He fetched out the spoon with the tongs and laid it on the tray. Knowing a bit more chemistry than he had let on, he donned the gas mask and some rubber gloves and opened a bottle of muriatic acid. He filled half of the pot, taking care not to allow any of the fluid to splash. He then opened a couple of bottles of the potassium nitrate and poured them into the acid. Immediately, the liquid began to violently churn. Leaving the door to the lab open, he hastily exited the house, carefully closing the outer door tightly. Quickly the house filled with hydrogen cyanide gas, the product of the acid and the nitrate salt. Within seconds of inhalation, Alan's cells became incapable of utilizing oxygen. His body, thrown into an anoxic state, convulsed briefly, regurgitated some of the wine and a bite of the apple, heaved a gasping breath and died.

In the safety of his Chevy, he set down the two chemical containers and removed his mask and gloves. He started the car and slowly began to drive away looking warily for any sign of eyewitness or passerby. There was no one. As he turned onto the street, he glanced back at the brightly-lit, charming, and unassuming home, and sighed, "Adieu, mon amant, adieu."

PART 1

"Only a life lived for others is a life worthwhile."

Albert Einstein

II

Present Day
Memphis, Tennessee
United States

9:32 pm CST

The three of them never saw it coming. A Friday night is not a Friday night unless you are harassing a down-on-his-luck, homeless, ex-roofer with a small drinking problem. At home, his mom called him Freddie, but on the streets, he preferred FlatTop, in honor of the style of his Afro coiffure. It was a week before Christmas; the temperature was down to just below freezing, and the stiff easterly breeze chilled the air even further. This was FlatTop weather: the perfect time to extract a little cash from those who owed him.

He stopped his Malibu a few feet from his target; a short, thin, middle-aged, bloke who had started a barrel fire to keep himself and a couple of street girls warm. They were standing in front of a former Woolworth's Five & Dime back in the sixties. Now it was a dispensary by day and a heroin house by night. FlatTop ordered his two enforcers out. One was a tall and muscular black man with east African features and the other, a Samoan heavyweight. The night was fairly quiet save for some distant sirens and tire screeches. He smirked to his posse. His prey hadn't even noticed their arrival. The bum was too preoccupied with the redhead. This was going to be fun, he thought. He motioned for the Samoan to take the flank. He didn't want the drunk to run; not that he couldn't catch him, but why bother.

Just then, the redhead glanced toward him. Her eyes widened and her breasts rose as she took in a breath. He loved this effect he had on people. South Memphis was his territory, and he knew the girl. She was a Clairol-dyed, ex-brunette, secretary turned street-walker, and he had enjoyed her before – on many occasions – often for free and against her will. He chuckled inside. Perhaps he would get to enjoy her again.

But it was the self-indulgence that would get the best of him. He was too busy planning his evening to notice the sirens getting louder and the rotor clack of a police helicopter in pursuit. Before he realized that the girl's wide eyes were not staring at him but at the screeching Integra that had turned the corner three blocks away, it was too late. Fate had different plans for him.

The sports coupe barreled straight for them with its engine in overdrive and a cadre of chasing blue and whites a hundred yards behind. FlatTop turned just in time to see the spectacle. He tried to move but his feet would not budge. He could hear the girls screaming behind him and the obscenities flying from the mouths of his men, but he was transfixed. The Integra swerved to avoid a Subaru as it entered the nearby intersection. The Subaru's driver tried to break, but the Integra's left edge clipped the Subaru's corner, ripping its fender and forcing a spin. The inertia of the Integra kept it moving forward, side-swiping a street post, before the adept driver regained control. The Subaru driver was not so lucky. He overcompensated his wheel turn causing the rotational energy to flip his car. The momentum sent the bumper and the left front tire flying like a patriot missile. FlatTop managed to glimpse the jagged chrome metal spinning through the air, decapitating the African before impaling the Samoan in the abdomen. Kind of funny, he thought. But he couldn't manage a smile either. He considered taking one last glance at the girl. Maybe she could get a message to his Mama. Maybe she could somehow tell his mother how much Freddie loved her. But then the tire crushed his skull. The force split his neck from the torso and propelled him through the air into the brick Woolworths' cornerstone ten feet away. Sometimes, fate has a sense of humor too: now FlatTop really was FlatTop.

"Oh my God, he just took out a car and nailed a bunch of pedestrians!"

The officer in the pilot seat of the Bell 206B Jetranger Memphis police helicopter circling overhead had 10 year's experience in the force and four years in the Marines preceding, but there was something about man's inhumanity that always seemed to bring out the emotion in him. It was that energy that was propelling the words out of his mouth, "Send EMS to the corner of Florida and Olive. Several injuries; probable fatalities!"

Dispatch was quick to respond. "Roger that Helicopter 2. Do you still have the target?"

The pilot looked to his co-pilot partner operating the cameras who nodded positively. The pilot maneuvered the helicopter into the driver's blind spot, high and behind, while simultaneously enabling his microphone and reporting, "Affirmative. We have quality visual and infrared."

Delta shift ran from 5 pm to 1 am at the Real Time Crime Center, acronymized RTCC, the Memphis Police Department's centralized crime data and dispatch post. According to its press releases, the RTCC was a high-tech, secure, secret, and continuously manned, command center where fifteen analysts and officers reviewed live video streaming from dozens of cameras, along with statistical reports and historical and predictive analyses, on 42 wall-to-wall monitors and some 20 workstations in a sleek, modern, softly lit, cool and comfortable, control room reminiscent of NORAD in the movie War Games. While not quite Mission Control, the RTCC more than lived up to the hype.

Lieutenant Jonathan Avery was in command when bank security notified the Center that an aggravated bank robbery with fatalities had occurred at the Federal Reserve Bank on 200 North Main Street. Avery had concerns the moment the call came in. At first he was amazed and amused at the stupidity of it all. I mean, who steals from the Federal Reserve. It's not like there are tellers or ATMs there. Sure, there's lots of money, but it's entombed in steel vaults, transported only under heavy guard, and surrounded by high-tech security cameras. But then his mood soured as he deliberated it further. The perpetrator had infiltrated the bank, escaped with as yet unknown booty, and killed two highly trained guards in the process. That didn't sound like the work of a crackpot or fool. He quickly deployed two patrol units to the scene along with a Crime Scene Investigation (CSI) and Felony Response Unit. There was also a helicopter patrolling the northern high crime neighborhood that he redeployed to offer air support. It turned out to be a wise move.

Within minutes, bank security submitted footage of the suspect's escape. He was a dark-skinned, fit appearing male, sporting closely trimmed hair and a full beard, running with an apparent sack of cash and brandishing a pistol. Another camera captured him climbing into a dark blue Acura Integra before speeding off. Warning bells deep inside his brain started ringing. He didn't have the look of the usual Memphis malefactor.

Moments later, a rolling patrol identified a car matching the description of the suspect escape vehicle. Avery authorized the pursuit and within seconds the chase was on. That was 10 minutes ago, and the suspect was still crisscrossing through the streets and back roads of the city at speeds upwards of 70 miles per hour. He briefly considered calling off his men in the interest of public safety but, instead, decided to consult with the Patrol Division 1 shift commander. Major Branson was responsible for the bank's district, and the Major had recommended continuing given the crime's severity. Guard killing wasn't cop killing, but it was close, and the Federal Reserve had never been robbed, a fact Branson was quite proud of. It was Avery's second wise decision of the night as now the action had resulted in multiple fatal casualties. He was sickened at the loss of life but, secretly, he was glad it wasn't him that would have to sit for hours Monday morning in front of inspectors justifying his decisions. Now that responsibility would fall to the Major.

The ground units had appropriately terminated their pursuit to render assistance, but the chase continued from the air as Avery ordered a second helicopter to join the first. Major Branson was quickly back on the line and this time, was acoustically angry. He had spoken to the bank's captain of the guard and relayed the essence of the conversation.

The bank guards were each shot in the head, execution style, and the assailant escaped not with money but with sensitive bank records including security codes and encryption keys. One of the guards was a retired Germantown sergeant and a friend of the Major's. Suddenly, this <u>was</u> cop killing – and personal to boot.

Branson's voice cracked. He not only authorized continued action but also directed additional units to shadow distantly behind the fleeing assailant and on parallel routes. The son-of-a-bitch wasn't going to escape; not on his watch. The Major was throwing the official pursuit policy into the wind. "In for a penny, in for a pound", Avery reasoned were Branson's feelings. The lieutenant was about to say something consoling when an unexpected tingle raced down the length of his spine accompanied by a foreboding sense of treachery and evil – like an ancient demon had awoken from a long and restless slumber.

He ignored the thought and got back to work just as a pang of indigestion erupted in the pit of his chest.

9:35 pm

The veteran nurse watched Dr. Paul Gudrun through the glass doors of the Baptist Memorial Hospital Emergency Room as he arrived for his shift. She liked watching him. He was cock-sure and lackadaisical but funny and subtlety pleasant on the eyes. He was nothing like the arrogant, egotistical losers she always seemed to find in her bed. He always wore baggy scrubs and oversized traditional doctor coats, but occasionally, she could catch a glimpse of his muscular back or firm biceps. Most of his colleagues found him mediocre and unimpressive, sometimes embarrassingly so; she felt quite the opposite.

    She fantasized about him often. Most girls drifted to his dreamy hazel eyes or his never-brushed dark red bangs, but she liked his hands. They were firm, strong and remarkably delicate. She loved staring at them while he tied sutures or manipulated small instruments. She imagined their touch on her body, and wondered if his stamina was as strong and gentle. The nurse had no idea of the vehicular mayhem happening across town but would not have cared even if she had; she was obsessed with Paul Gudrun. She wanted to know what he looked like under those scrubs...

what he smelled like...what he tasted like. But she would have to wait a little longer to find out.

She seethed.

He had found himself a bleached bimbo and the slut was monopolizing his time. So, she would have to do what she was supposed to do:

Watch and wait...

Wait and watch.

Abdullah Burja was driving for his life now. He jetted through traffic, dodging cars, turning corners sharply, first left, and then right. He had never driven Memphis roads before but had studied their detail thanks to Google Earth and had the help of a Garmon GPS suction-cupped to the dashboard. He glanced at his rear view mirror. His strategy had worked. The two police vehicles tailing him had stopped at the accident, and for the first moment, he could breathe. His mind began racing, searching for a solution to his dilemma. It would not take long for the authorities to find him again, and while he couldn't see a helicopter, he instinctively knew one was following. He trembled.

Hours before, at sundown, he had prayed to God for protection and success knowing the forces of evil were strong and his chances slim, but the opportunity was too great not to try. He glanced at the grey linen bag sitting in the passenger seat imprinted with the words Federal Reserve in black block letters. He patted the side of the bag as if to assure its existence as he weaved between cars and ran red lights. His could feel his heart racing and beads of sweat dribbling into his eyes as he prayed to Allah once again, this time for forgiveness: he knew the men at the bank and the people on the street were dead.

It had been difficult to get the document out, harder to betray his loyalty, and Herculean to escape the bank, and it was all for, at best, weakly incriminating circumstantial evidence. He sighed. It was not the hard proof that he had hoped for, but it was the best he could do.

Burja recalled the evening's events ruminating in his mind's gullet. He was at his computer reviewing his mission parameters when something about the login page triggered a memory. He wasn't sure where the thought originated, but it came from the recesses of his mind as if planted by an experienced farmer in the spring. He tried the combination, fully expecting a simple denial, but what happened even now he could not believe. The computer erupted in a fugue of information that first was incredible and then inconceivable. He and his holy brothers were being played the fool – sold out for money and power. The unholy alliance, certainly the brainchild of the evil one, was an abomination that demanded justice. It was blasphemy! It took him a mere second to reach his conclusion; this was a conspiracy that demanded exposure. Allah demanded it! But just as quickly, another realization dawned: Time was short, and he was expected to leave with his package soon. Luckily, that problem had an easy solution. He messaged his home office of a delay on the American end and then informed his local handler, blaming the matter on his home office. The ruse wouldn't hold long, and he knew it; he needed a quick solution. What he really needed was tangible evidence. He could try to access the site again, but that would not only be dangerous but unreliable. It would be easy to change or close the portal, and he would be exposed immediately. He needed something else, something more substantively convicting, but that would be easier said than done.

Numerous sophisticated security technologies protect the Memphis branch of the St. Louis Federal Reserve Bank including digital video monitoring, fingerprint biometric access, advanced software encryption, and a variety of intrusion detection systems, structural hardware fortifications and electronic sensor curtains. Abdullah knew simple theft would be impossible. Fortunately, a relatively low-tech solution presented itself. Weeks earlier he had read a brief detailing an exploitable vulnerability in the bank's Library Print Refuse Management System. If he couldn't get the proof out, maybe he could get the next best thing: scandal. Documentation might incite outrage and trigger demands for an investigation, he reasoned. That was the answer; it was a long shot, but the only one he could think of.

Despite the promise of a paper-less world in the electronic age, the truth was that paper usage was never higher, and the Federal Reserve was a major contributor. The reams of paper the bank generated daily required secure disposal and the responsibility fell to the Refuse Management

System (RMS) to dispose of all it, from sensitive documents to routine memos. The automated system consisted of shredders each fed refuse paper via conveyor belt from a series of secure holding bins. Designed to operate around the clock, the system had recently been placed under timed control as part of an energy conservation effort and no one seemed to realize that the trash holding bins were under simple lock and key. That was the vulnerability.

While Burja didn't have the permission to print a document, he did have authority to copy a document image and send it to the library to print. All documents processed this way required human review and certification for release.

With this in mind, he simply waited until the librarian had left for the day to act. Without an authorized recipient to validate and secure the hardcopy, the RMS targeted the printed document for destruction. It was then an easy matter to hack into the maintenance subsystem, program a shredder delay and defeat the locks. Unfortunately, Abdullah hadn't counted on his handler finding him rummaging through the garbage. Quick improvisation and lady luck saved his life – or was it something else. He continued his prayer – now for thanksgiving.

He allowed himself a brief smile of pride in his accomplishment but then reality awoke him as new lights and sirens joined the chase from behind. Surrounded and chased like a rat within a maze, the magnitude of his predicament finally struck. It was only a matter of time before they caught up to him. A new emotion erupted – one of fear: fear of capture and fear of failure. But there was a solution to his problem, a doorway to heaven, a tonic for his fear. It was waiting for him in the Integra's trunk. His prayers to Allah morphed again, this time for guidance. His knew his mission to Him was honorable and his cause just. It was in that knowledge that he placed his trust; the trust that God would light the way.

And then an epiphany materialized. He knew what he had to do.

IV

Tennessee is one of only eleven states with two or more FBI district offices. One is located in Knoxville, home of UT football; the other in Memphis, perennial top 10 metro crime haven.

The Memphis office of the FBI is responsible for a district that encompasses 54 counties in west and central Tennessee and extends as far east as Fentress County, a longitude east of Chattanooga. Since, 2001, defending the United States from terrorists, both foreign and domestic, has become the Bureau's primary responsibility. From defense against physical attacks and weapons of mass destruction to electronic warfare and cybercrime, the Memphis Joint Terrorism Task Force, an organization comprised of representatives from all levels of government, is tasked with the responsibility of investigating and preemptively repelling terroristic activities within its district.

While there is no FBI office in Nashville, Tennessee's state capitol, the Memphis office maintains a satellite there that assists the Memphis office with antiterrorism efforts, particularly in respect to internet-based crimes and attacks, through its own Joint Terrorism Task Force. Meetings between each of the task forces and related agencies occur regularly and quite often.

Special Agent in Charge of the FBI Memphis office, Phillip Oxmore, was on his way back from such a meeting, driven by his assistant, Special

STRONG EMERGENCE

Agent Tedder Stone, in his specially equipped Ford Explorer when he heard the news. The home office had a direct communication feed with both the Memphis police department crime unit as well as with Federal Reserve Security and the data and audiovisual streams from both sources were broadcast over the Explorer's speakers and dashboard computer screens.

The bank was located within the police department's jurisdiction, but its very importance to the nation's economic security made the incident an automatic FBI case – the treasury, not to mention the White House, would demand it. As a result, the FBI was notified of the robbery from the onset and already had obtained intelligence not even Memphis police knew yet: this was an inside job, a 21st century crime of international banking espionage, conducted by a foreign attaché of a so-called trusted ally. Oxmore knew their modus operandi all too well. He had served as a supervisory special agent on the joint cybercrime task force earlier in his career. There he had firsthand experience with the wide range of highly sophisticated technologies designed for the singular purpose of stealing American secrets: from social security numbers to passport numbers, from bank accounts to visa accounts, and from home addresses to email addresses. The perpetrator was likely a low-level diplomat that could hide behind immunity, a reluctant concession that made Oxmore's blood boil every time he thought of it. But this case was already different from most. This guy had to kill to get out of the bank, and not just kill one guard, but two. That did not sound like the work of a clandestine diplomatic operative. What could have been so important to steal to risk all of this?

His pondering was interrupted by the impassioned pleas of the police helicopter pilot describing the vehicular assailant forcing a church school bus into a fire hydrant.

Stone was first to break the silence, "This guy is a real dick!"

"He sure is" was the only utterance Oxmore could muster, but Stone's outburst managed a smirk on his face. Damn it was good to have an assistant with a sense of humor. He quickly flipped open his clamshell Droid and called his lieutenant, Assistant Special Agent in Charge Amy Peacock.

Amy hadn't been chosen by him. She was the pick of his predecessor and her tenure at the Memphis office predated his by almost a year. Rumors regarding the manner and cause for her appointment swirled throughout the break rooms of the Bureau and the moment he saw her he understood why.

Peacock was blonde, buxom, blue-eyed, and beautiful; the 4 B's of womanhood. Even in a masculinizing business suit, Amy had the physical properties that turned men's heads and drew their eyes downward. Phil saw 'distraction' stamped to her forehead and began the process of reassigning her immediately. But in as little time as it took him to reach his prejudiced conclusion, Amy changed it. It took one staff meeting for him to realize that she had a few more B's: brilliance, brains, and balls. Within weeks, she added resourcefulness, fortitude, judgment and honor. At first, Oxmore sought to protect her from lewd gazes and locker room banter but quickly learned that she used her appearance to her advantage, lulling her collegial prey into embarrassing and sometimes humiliating positions, earning respect in the process, and achieving results. Within months, his skepticism evolved to respect and then trust. Now she was cemented as his right hand and an indispensable part of his team.

"Peacock here," her North Carolina born twang was unmistakable.

"It's me," Oxmore instantly recognized her voice and knew she similarly did the same.

"So, I guess you're listening to this?"

"Has MPD asked us for assistance yet?"

"Not formally but I have already spoken to the Director. He wants us involved."

"That's no surprise. I want our own eyes in the air… and wake up Evidence Response. They are going to have a lot of work to do."

"MPD has already scrambled a second air unit and we've just got word that Channel 6 is spinning theirs as we speak. Are you sure you want to add a fourth helicopter to the mix?"

Oxmore understood her concern. Four aircraft in a tight airspace all in pursuit of a single target was a recipe for disaster, particularly at night.

But there was something not quite right here. He couldn't quite explain his apprehension, but it was there nonetheless, "We need to risk it."

"Understood."

"Have we heard any more from the bank?"

"Both men shot in the center forehead while kneeling."

"Executed?"

"He disarmed them first. Neither had their firearm holstered."

"So this isn't just a nut job or someone trying to finance a coke habit. This is a professional."

"I agree."

"Anything else?"

"Surveillance video got a pretty good look at his face. We've uploaded his image to the National Crime Database but, so far, nothing." Peacock briefly paused. "How far away are you?"

Oxmore looked over to Agent Stone who quickly turned his head to his boss in response, "About an hour."

"Did you hear that?" Oxmore spoke into the mike.

"Drive faster," Peacock prodded.

"Did you hear that?" Oxmore quipped back to Stone with a humiliating grin.

Tedder knew the pecking order well enough, but he didn't like it dangled in front of him. He should have known better but couldn't contain himself and whispered the words "Fuck her" to his boss in retaliation.

Unfortunately for Stone, this was exactly the reaction Oxmore was hoping for. He sardonically mouthed "Don't you wish you could" in return as he directed his attention back to his cell phone, "Call MPD and politely ask them if they need us and then call me back."

"Yes sir."

Oxmore slammed the phone closed and placed it into his shirt pocket laughing out loud at his aide's expense.

Tedder had no choice but to macho his honor back, "With all due respect, sir. When she rides my pole, I'll send you the sheets."

Oxmore's resulting guffaw almost triggered a seizure.

Tyler, Texas
9:42 pm

J.D.'s Auto Parts, a Tyler Texas institution for over 35 years, was about to close in 2008, a victim of the 'Great Recession', when it was bought by a hardworking family from New Jersey. Oscar Polenti, his three sons, and a host of cousins, nephews, and a couple nieces, saved the store from ruin and slowly restored it to its former glory. First labeled as a 'mob family' and later revered as a 'tight family' of workaholics, the shop's new owners had earned the respect of the community, and Polenti had found a bit of local fame, a seat on the Chamber of Commerce, and the ear of the mayor and city manager.

The store's success centered on the tireless work ethic of Polenti and his sons who kept the store always open, neatly stocked, and brightly lit. At least one of them could be found there day or night, tending to customers, keeping the books, and mopping the floors.

Old man Polenti was at the register ringing up Freddie Pierce's order. Freddie was a regular. He worked second shift and loved to drop by and pick up odds and ends for his hobby: piddling on his cars through the wee hours of the morning. Tonight was oil change night, and the counter was stocked high with Havoline.

Polenti saw his son Pete walk through the tattered curtain separating the shop and back rooms from the front desk. At first Oscar didn't think twice but then sensed the young man's presence. Polenti looked up. Pete looked tired. His shirt was wrinkled and grease stained, but he didn't have the look of someone who had worked for hours. It was more like the look of someone who knew he had many more hours to work.

Pete cupped his hand, walked up to the old man, and whispered quietly into his ear.

"We have a big problem in Memphis."

V

Memphis, Tennessee
9:46 pm

All eyes at the Memphis Police Real Time Crime Center focused on the chase. Two monitors devoted to live video feed, one from the hovering helicopter and the other from the front facing camera on the lead chase car, demanded most of the attention. A third screen displayed a city map with the positions of the suspect and a legion of pursuing emergency vehicles presented in real time. Next to it, a slightly larger display listed crime scene, escape vehicle, and subject descriptions along with a grainy picture of the alleged perpetrator. Finally, video feed from two representative news outlets: CNN and a local NBC affiliate played silently. Neither network had picked up the story yet – a luxury destined not to last.

Lieutenant Avery was watching the suspect race down Southern Avenue as it passed the stadium and headed toward the university. The suspect was slowing. "Maybe he was coming down from his high", he supposed. For whatever the reason, Avery had seen this behavior before. "He's getting lazy," the Lieutenant observed out loud, communicating to the other police officers manning their stations in the Crime Center,

"Have units 2 and 5 place tire spikes at the Highland intersection. He won't know what hit him."

But Abdullah Burja knew precisely what the police would try to do. He had spent years studying their tactics, learning their capabilities and reviewing their policies. He knew their weaknesses and their strengths and hoped his efforts would not be in vain. He continued racing down the avenue fully aware that the longer he stayed on this route, the more likely the police would try to corner or ambush him. He just hoped he could reach the intersection before then.

◆

Tyler, Texas
9:50 pm

Oscar Polenti was not his real name, and the young men who surrounded him were not his sons, but the cover worked well. Although not Italian, his ancient Hungarian and Greek ancestry gave him olive skin and dark hair. He handpicked his men to mirror his appearance, and the ruse had worked for years. Nobody seemed to notice the different body types, chin structure, or receding hair patterns each of them had; similar hair and skin color were enough.

He limped past the curtain into the disheveled storeroom decorated with stacks of assorted tires and workbenches cluttered with partially disassembled parts perfectly arranged to create the illusion of an ordinary business. He shuffled past stacks of old paint cans and walls of dusty boxes to the back of the room enjoying the smell of old rubber as he walked. In the shadows, he stepped through a door marked 'Private' and entered the dingy back hall, only then dispensing with the limp and the subtle crouch that went with it.

The hall opened to a small break room and a couple of cramped, rarely used offices but the real interest was the last door on the left. Originally, the room stored oil, kerosene, toluene and other flammables. The door was still marked with warning signs and was protected by a digital lock to dissuade the curious and the stupid. But the room no longer stored the toxins – it had a much more important purpose.

Victor Coombs, aka Polenti, punched in the combination and the electronic lock audibly unlatched. He entered the transformed storeroom dimly lit by the blue LED lamps of four server stacks lining the left wall, a number of computer monitors at the head of the room, and a small 20 watt lamp in the corner. The room was a miniature clandestine command center staffed by two men, each at their consoles, wearing headphones and intensely concentrating on the events unfolding before them. The change in ambient light was sufficient enough to get the attention of the man on Coombs' right. He turned to his boss and removed his headphone, but it was Coombs who was first to speak, "I understand there's a problem."

Technically, each of the men under his command had the same rank, but leadership qualities tend to float to the top and CIA Officer David Michael's had risen to Coombs' unofficial second. The other man in the room, Agent Ferdinand Gonzalez, recognized the question was not being asked of him and remained respectfully quiet as Michael's answered his supervisor, "Yes sir. We have a defection. One of our assets is off the rail. We've made him a criminal target and FBI and local law enforcement are in pursuit. We have full surveillance access."

"Is the situation contained?" The voice was concerned but controlled.

"I believe so, sir. The asset is isolated, and we have four teams in position surrounding the operations perimeter."

"Who?" Coombs tersely asked.

"Abdullah Burja."

"I knew that son-of-a-bitch was going to cause us a problem."

"Yes sir," Michael's agreed knowing full well that his supervisor liked affirmation. But Burja really was a problem, a much bigger one than his boss could imagine.

"What has he compromised?" Coombs asked.

"The Mediator."

"I'm confused. He already has access to the website."

"Restricted user rights, yes," Gonzales barged in, briefly pausing to brace for the outburst that was about to come, "But he hacked into the Administrator Portal with private credentials."

Coombs was still confused. The revelation was not what he had expected. A blown cover or a disclosed safe house, perhaps, but this was a bit incredible. Stunned, he continued with a run of instinctual questions, "What does that mean? Whose credentials?"

"He found the private web address," Michaels clarified, "and used an administrator's access code and password. We even think he may have obtained a copy of a document, or at least a few pages of one."

The gravity of the situation suddenly dawned on the CIA Station Chief and immediately he turned to Ferdinand Gonzales, his chief technologist, for answers, "What's our exposure? Is he still in?" Coombs continued feeling his anger rise.

"No sir."

"Hooray for bloody miracles!" For a brief moment, Coombs briefly relaxed, "How much did he get?"

"Enough."

Victor Coombs had a feeling he knew the answer but asked the question anyway, "So if he used an administrator's password, he must have had access to multiple compartments." The bleak expression on both of his men's faces told the answer even before either one spoke. "Probably all of them," Michaels finally answered.

"Shit," the old man muttered, "I just knew this was going to bite us in the ass one day." Coombs' frustration was now effervescent. "How the hell does this happen? I thought this thing was supposed to be unhackable! I can still hear that blonde bastard at division!" He was mocking now, "Don't worry Victor. It's an unacknowledged SAP with clandestine secure communication superior to NSANet. Bull shit!"

"I'm not sure anyone has figured this out yet sir," Michaels tried tactful reassurance but his chief was in no hurry to decompress. After a torturously silent moment, he blurted out, "Options?"

"Only one I can think of," Gonzales responded, "We should shut down the portal. That would give the Administrator time to determine the best course of action."

"We can't do that! The network would be disabled for hours, maybe days." Michaels objected, "We have too many vulnerable agents in the field, and there's an active transfer in progress!"

Coombs' scornful stare communicated his emotions and Michaels recognized the need to produce a viable alternative, "We could leave the site up and see if he tries again. If he does, we set up a trace. We might catch an even bigger fish."

Gonzalez was not so optimistic, "I don't know. We will be risking greater exposure if we leave it up."

The Mediator was the backbone of Project Quest, an ultrasensitive CIA Special Access Program, so secret that not even Congress knew of it officially. In fact, there were only fourteen individuals in the nation that knew of its existence and only four that fully knew its purpose and significance. Besides Victor Coombs, those included two confirmed by the senate and one sworn in on the steps of the capital every fourth year. The program was administered by a private, third-party but Coombs' unit was entrusted with the responsibility of directing domestic operations. Two different Presidents had made it clear in plain terms that compromise of the program was an eminent threat to national security. Although Quest had nothing to do with banks, securities or monetary policy, in every sense of the term, it truly was *too big to fail*.

It did not take Victor long to realize the decisions and implications were well above his pay grade, "I am going to need the Director's input here." Then he added, "And, I think it's time to introduce Mr. Burja to his 72 virgins."

Memphis, Tennessee
9:55 pm

Abdulla Burja's heart pounded as the sweat poured off his brow. In his peripheral vision, he could sense a growing number of pursuers, and in front of him, a Channel 6 news helicopter was coming into view. He began to doubt his plan. It was risky, and there was a good chance it would not work. The intersection was coming up. His mind raced, but he could see no other way. He prayed he could make the hard turn – he prayed their ambush would fail – he prayed no more innocents would be harmed.

The tension in the MPD Crime Center was palpable. Memphis was a big city full of miscreants perpetrating crimes virtually every minute of every day, but all attention was directed to the chase. Everything else was on hold.

The audio feed from his field officers boomed in Avery's earpiece, "We're in position, ready to deploy spikes on your command."

On the asset position monitor, patrol units 2 and 6 were brightly displayed, and the red dot noting the suspect was moving rapidly toward them. The distance was three blocks and closing, and Avery knew it would not be long now, "Stand ready. Range is 1000 feet. You should be able to see him any second now."

"We see activity ahead," the officer acknowledged. The vehicle was not in sight, but headlights were dancing in front of him blended with honking horns and screeching tires. He signaled 'stand by' to his partner just as the haze of a barreling, dark blue coupe came into view. Each officer positioned their hands on the deployment trigger as the leader communicated his status to the command center, "Visual contact."

"You are cleared to deploy," Avery ordered but a millisecond later, before the field officers could even process the command, the speeding Integra turned hard to the right into the preceding intersection less than 100 yards from the tire spike officer's location.

"Hell. He must have seen us!" The surprise reduced the professionalism of the police officer's screaming report but properly conveyed the essence of his assessment.

Immediately, Avery deduced what was happening as the dot moved off course, weaving south, away from the busier, seedier, business avenue, and into a more upscale residential district. "Abort! Abort! Pack up and redeploy."

Burja was pleased with himself again, but he allowed himself only a second of self-congratulation. He tried his cell phone once more, balancing it in one hand as he drove with the other, but again there was no signal. Although he should have expected no less from his enemies, the emotional energy of the moment diluted his judgment, and he frustratingly threw his useless cell phone into the passenger seat. Now all alternative options were officially exhausted. His destiny was set. This time he did not pray. Ten seconds later he made another racing, hard turn onto a busier road. In the distance, he could see colored strobes and beams of light slowly circling the sky. His target was in sight.

10:01 pm

The News 6 chopper cruised overhead with a good vantage of the action. The photographer was capturing exciting footage and the local affiliate had already preempted the previous headline with the breaking news. Even in Memphis, this chase was big. The pilot kept pace with the reckless assailant while the news anchor simultaneously dubbed over, dramatically detailing the high speed chase viewers were witnessing live. The reporter made mention of the many injuries and ambulances and did his best to sensationalize the robbery and shootings at the bank. All the while, the camera kept its focus on the car storming down a residential lane, weaving erratically through the traffic.

The reporter broke to a brief commercial, and with the attention shifted away, the pilot of the news helicopter changed the frequency, "Control, he has turned onto Getwell Road. He may be heading for the interstate." Inside the secret command center behind J.D. Auto Parts, Agent Gonzalez acknowledged while Coombs silently watched the action standing behind and between Gonzales and Michaels. Seconds later, Michaels interrupted the quiet, "The Director is on a secure line for you, sir."

Coombs touched a small switch on his earphone and was immediately connected to the Director of the Central Intelligence Agency. Coombs' boss was appointed D/CIA 16 months before the installation of the current presidential administration. Andrew Haas graduated from Berkley summa cum laude and had a JD from Yale and two advanced degrees from Johns Hopkins, an MBA and an MPA, but his real credential was his remarkable insight into the dynamics of the human condition combined with extraordinary analytical brilliance. The combination of talents made him ideally suited for his intelligence role and an almost indispensable advisor to the Director of National Intelligence and the President. The deference shown to him by his peers was exponentially magnified by his subordinates, and Victor Coombs was no exception.

"Yes sir," Coombs answered respectfully.

"Victor. I have been apprised of your situation," the Director began, "You appear to be taking appropriate measures. Regarding your request to disable the site or reinitialize the password database, I have already spoken to the DNI and apparently the Administrator has ruled out that possibility."

"That complicates matters."

"I know and I'm sorry, but our choices here are very limited. Accordingly, use all means necessary to secure the threat. Lethal force is authorized."

"Understood," Coombs acknowledged.

The director abruptly ended the communication with a brisk, "Good luck", and his ear piece quieted. The room became eerily still, and all three men looked forward, transfixed on the images displayed before them. Coombs took a moment to contemplate his instructions and meditate in the soft illuminated tones of the room. Once again, it was Michaels who interrupted him, "Sir. The target has turned again. It looks like he may be headed for a shopping mall."

For a moment, Victor felt contempt for his second's efficiency, attention to detail, analytical prowess and technical expertise. But the frustration was fleeting as Coombs quickly remembered who and where he was, quenched any empathic and sympathetic impulses, and internally applauded Michaels for his professionalism and tirelessness. "Excellent!" he congratulated and then ordered, coldly and almost gloatingly, "Position the teams and prepare to send in Recovery. I sense the end game approaching."

VI

10:05 pm

Ordinarily, the drive from Nashville to Memphis was quiet and relaxed. With unimpressive scenery and rarely any need for expedience, Phillip Oxmore often snoozed while Agent Stone daydreamed, but it was not an ordinary day, and no one was sleeping. Tedder was racing in at 95 mph, focusing on the road, adeptly negotiating traffic while Oxmore proactively alerted highway patrol to avoid a traffic stoppage. Although a simple flash of identification to a state trooper would clear them of any wrongdoing, they couldn't afford the time loss. Oxmore was listening closely to the MPD com feed when his cell phone began ringing. Once again, it was Agent Weikert. Hopefully, she had some good news.

"Phil, it's Amy," Agent Weikert began and then continued without waiting for a verbal handshake, "MPD has officially requested assistance and air support has just arrived on the scene. Death count so far is 6, two guards at the bank, 3 pedestrians, and one MVA. Several severe pedestrian injuries and about a dozen children from a school bus are being taken to the Med." Amy was talking fast, and her stream of consciousness quickly moved on to her next point, "MPD thinks he's high on Meth or something. They're very concerned about further injuries and loss of life."

Oxmore controlled his emotions. There was no room for them here. His desire to remove this predator from society was visceral but apprehending this man was going to require analytical prowess and cognitive dexterity. Like Bobby Fisher playing a game of chess, he was going to need forward thinking and anticipation of his opponent's next move; the only problem, this wasn't a game.

"Understood," was his simple response.

Weikert continued her update, "I have established an operations command at headquarters."

"Excellent. I want a direct link to me," Oxmore ordered then changed tack, "Who's flying?"

"Agent Marquis", Weikert informed. Charles Marquis was the regional Tactical Helicopter Unit (THU) commander and Oxmore's best pilot. She knew he would feel comfortable with Marquis in the air.

"Patch him through."

Within seconds, Weikert securely connected the helicopter to the truck, and live video images with a few second delay popped up on the Explorer's onboard video monitor. The view was a Memphis city nightscape — a mix of red and white lights flowing like corpuscles through the arteries of civilization. Oxmore could hear the helicopter pilot's voice garbled but intelligible surfacing above the engine noise and rotor throb.

"Do you have visual contact?"

"Yes sir," Marques responded, "That's him at the 12 o'clock. He just sped into a shopping mall."

"I see him." He was not hard to find, driving recklessly and insanely fast. Oxmore could sense the helicopter banking and then, suddenly, the camera image turned white, overcome by bright lights. Marquis quickly explained, "Wow, this mall is packed! It looks like some sort of fair or something. There are carnival rides here and everything!" A moment later, the camera readjusted, and Oxmore could see for himself.

Dellwood Village Mall was a southeast Memphis suburban shopping experience catering to the midscale market. Like most retailers, Christmas season was their busiest time of the year, and competition for customers was fierce. Anything that increased patron foot traffic was viewed as a positive from extreme sales to visits from Santa Claus, or, in the case of

Dellwood Village, a midnight madness winter wonderland festival featuring carolers, hot chocolate and kiddie rides. From every indication, the promotion was a success; the parking lot was full of holiday shoppers, families with young children, and grandparents enjoying the merriment.

"What's he doing now?" Oxmore continued his questioning simultaneously trying to decrypt the motivations of the fugitive driver. The floodlights kept overexposing the cameras making it hard to keep track of him on the screen.

"This is not good! There are lots of pedestrians here – lots of children running around. Whoa, he almost clipped one!" Marques continued his reporting, "He just turned in front of the Macy's..." There was a slight pause; "Hold up!"

Phillip never liked those words. He knew implicitly that Marques was only moving into a better position, but the lack of information, however brief, was unnerving. Fortunately, information was quickly forthcoming. It just was not what Phillip wanted to hear.

"He's heading toward the parking garage," the commander continued and instantly Oxmore deduced the eluder's strategy, confirmed moments later as the improving video revealed the driver exiting the safety of the lights and jetting toward the garage like a field sloth running towards his hole.

"Charles, I need you to keep topside. Stay vigilant and make sure he doesn't sneak out. Coordinate with Memphis Air Support and watch out for civilian air traffic," Oxmore commanded and, without waiting for a response, changed frequencies, "Memphis Command. This is FBI Memphis Division Special Agent in Charge, Phillip Oxmore, responding to your request for assistance."

Lieutenant Avery was quick to respond, "Thank you FBI. We appreciate the help. Our suspect has taken refuge in a shopping mall. We are concerned about a potential hostage situation."

Oxmore concurred and politely, but forcefully, suggested MPD converge on the mall and establish a perimeter. Avery acknowledged and severed the connection. Back at the Crime Center, the Lieutenant instantly ordered six patrol units to secure each lot exit and four more units to each side of the building. He had barely finished speaking when he felt the familiar burn of ingestion arising. He was just about to ask the Sergeant of the Day to spell him so he could run to the break room to fetch a couple of Tums when his cell phone began buzzing. He looked at his phone screen and cringed. It was the Major again. Now the acid was burning up his esophagus all the way to his throat.

Phil Oxmore called his operations center with words that were hurried but forceful. Time was of the essence if they were going to be successful, "Notify mall security and apprise them of the situation. Let them know they have a violent suspect in their mall and request remote access to their surveillance systems."

His coordinator acknowledged and then connected him to Agent Weikert, who, in turn, had just gotten off the phone with FBI Deputy Director Brent Taylor. Taylor was a 24 year veteran of the FBI and a longtime friend of Phillip's. Phillip first met the man when he was a grunt special agent in the Phoenix Division assigned to the drug trafficking unit. Brent was his supervisor, and they quickly developed mutual respect and a close friendship. Within a year, Taylor was promoted to Assistant Special Agent in Charge of the Little Rock Division, and he had skyrocketed from there.

"The DD is calling out SWAT? Isn't that a bit premature?" Oxmore reacted to Weikert's news, "Sure he's whacked out and might grab a hostage, but he's just as likely to pass out on a bench." Phil could sense Amy's unease and was trying to add a touch of levity, but she wanted no part of it.

"He's not 'whacked out'," Weikert started, and without waiting for Oxmore to respond, began to explain, "His name is Abdullah Burja, a Nigerian national with terrorist ties. He's part of a radical Islamic organization closely affiliated with African Al-Qaeda. I'm sending you his details." In seconds, Burja's demographic information and mug shot flashed on the dual screens. The photo portrayed a black man with short hair and a jet black, bushy beard. "He has supposedly never been to the United States before and is on the no-fly list. Prior to today, he was last seen in Sudan. He's listed as highly dangerous."

"If he has never been here before and is on the no-fly list, how did he get here?" Oxmore honestly but cheekily queried.

"That's a very good question. No one knows. But we do know what he stole: a hard drive containing highly sensitive cybersecurity data."

Oxmore was suddenly serious, "Now this makes more sense."

But his comment was a deceit and subconsciously he was even more apprehensive and confused. This was getting stranger and more volatile by the second. Phillip turned to Tedder, their eyes met, and Tedder knew exactly what his boss wanted of him – to get their asses to the mall.

10:15 pm

Abdulla Burja screeched into the parking deck in a waft of molten tire smoke and immediately began weaving his way up the ramps. He had studied the layout of the mall in detail for just this sort of contingency, but he never imagined he would have to take advantage of it. Oh, how Allah was good to him.

He sped to the third level following the signs to a mall entrance. The standard slots were filled, but a single vacant handicap space materialized, and he took it. With sweat pouring into his eyes and his heart pounding like a snare drum, he grabbed the bank sack and loosened the purse string. Inside was a large stack of papers. He discarded the first few superfluous pages and then found what he was looking for: a table of contents and an executive summary. He removed the pertinent sheets from the stack and pocketed them, leaving the rest. It would have been best to have it all, but he knew that was going to be impractical now.

With that done, he opened the glove compartment. Inside was a holstered Sig Sauer P226 pistol. He removed the gun. He assured the gun was fully loaded but without a round in the chamber. Then he stuffed the barrel into his waist belt. Wiping the sweat from his brow, he unlatched the trunk, quickly dismounted and walked hastily to the rear of the car.

The trunk was barren save for an overcoat and one other ominous article: a fully operational vest-type explosive belt. Burja quickly looked around. Given the number of cars and the hordes of people outside, there were remarkably few people in the garage and none nearby. He took this as a sign from God and quickly donned the vest and the overcoat covering it. Under the cloak of the coat, he took a second to disable the trigger. His mission crystallized in his mind; he could not afford a mistake.

Comfortable with his setup, he took a deep breath, and purposefully began walking toward the mall entrance. He took another look around. No one was watching him. "Foolish Americans," he thought. For all their talk of 'Homeland Security', 'Border Protection', and 'Counter Terrorism Task Forces', they were nothing but a bunch of lambs — easy marks for slaughter. With that conviction in mind, he pulled open the glass doors and entered the mall.

Back in Texas, Tyler Center was now fully operational. CIA Agent Sam Wade, aka Polenti's son Pete, was back from the counter after locking the front door and placing a 'Temporarily closed for restocking. Sorry for the inconvenience.' sign in the front window. He occupied the tactical positioning station along the right wall next to Agent Michaels. Moments earlier, Coombs had mobilized his full asset contingent: four assault teams and a cleanup crew.

"Where is Burja now?" Coombs question boomed above the radio chatter.

"Level 3 near the upstairs southwest entrance," Wade announced but then added, "But there is separation between the car and jacket signatures. It looks like the jacket is on the move."

"What's the jacket's status?"

It was Gonzalez's turn to enter the discussion, "I've tried pinging the vest with no response. He must have disabled it."

"He's inside the mall" Wade interjected.

Michaels turned to his supervisor with a puzzled expression, "What do you make of that?"

"Maybe he plans to do our job for us?" Wade contributed. Coombs dismissed the idea, "I doubt it. Burja is not an idiot. He's disarmed the jacket for a reason. He has something in mind. We need to take him down now. Have the cleaners locate the car and quickly sweep it. And, link in to mall security."

As always, Michaels was Johnny on the spot, "Already done."

The chatterbox had quieted for a few minutes, and Phillip was enjoying the silence. He peered out the window and could just begin to make out the glow of the metropolitan Memphis lights on the horizon. They were, at most, 20 minutes out.

The radio squawked, jolting him from his trance. It was Operations. They had Dellwood Village security patched through. Awakening quickly, Oxmore was back in the game. After a brief introduction and a description of Burja and his escape vehicle, the SAIC concluded with his standard warning, "I don't think I need to tell you that he's presumed armed and highly dangerous."

"Roger that," the guard acknowledged, "I am patching in our cameras to your network now."

Oxmore punched in video 2 on his keyboard and the helicopter images circling above the shopping center were replaced with images of a crowded mall filled with holiday shoppers. The views quickly rotated to different security cameras monitoring other parts of the building, inside stores, and even bathrooms.

"No one matching that description," the guard diagnosed but Oxmore was unconvinced, "Keep looking. He's there."

The images continued to scroll through various views: shopping concourses, department store aisles, break rooms, service corridors, loading docks, parking lots, and garage decks. Suddenly, the screen went black.

"What happened?" Oxmore demanded to know.

"Funny... The cameras are not working on garage level 3."

STRONG EMERGENCE

10:30 pm

Burja walked through the brightly lit mall adorned in sparkling colored lights and dazzling decorations of glittered topiaries, dangling streamers and banners in shades of red, green, gold, and blue. Overhead, gentle, melodious music played. It was a song he had never heard before, sung in words he could not understand. Beautiful yes, but irreverent. How insulting to God to celebrate him in this way, awash in the idols of glutinous commerce and wanton avarice. It was nothing short of blasphemy. He could feel his anger starting to rile but caught himself. This wasn't about religious differences or cultural divide. This was bigger than all that. He had to remain focused.

He strode briskly but inconspicuously. The weather was cold enough not to bring attention to his knee length trench coat and the shoppers and revelers were oblivious to his presence. He was amazed at the ease of it all. No one seemed aware of him. That was soon to change.

He spoke virtually no English and could read nothing at all. But he recognized his target – a Radio Shack electronics store – from the signage and red lettering. The store was fairly crowded with several browsers milling through the aisles and a couple of definite buyers at the checkout counter. The store, like the mall, was festively decorated with Santa Claus's wearing headphones, snowflakes dangling from the ceiling, and an elf holding an iPad.

"Ah. Exactly what I'm looking for," Burja thought, not in English, but his native African tongue. He pulled an off-the-shelf cell phone, one he recognized as having encrypted international calling capabilities, and pushed himself through the small crowd to the cashier who was busy checking out a customer.

In one fluid motion, Burja screamed aloud a cacophony of unintelligible words and slammed the cell phone down on the counter, pointed to it vigorously and then pointed back at the clerk, all the while swinging his arms back and forth in staccato movements.

Not sure of exactly what the man was angry or concerned about, he tried politely to diffuse him, "Sir I will help you in just a minu..."

Burja screamed out again, louder and angrier, interrupting the clerk mid word. He had no idea what the man had said, but his demeanor suggested pacification. He made his point clear, pulling out his gun, brandishing it at the clerk and then pointing the muzzle at his phone.

For a frozen second, no one moved, not the cashier, not the patrons, not even Abdullah Burja. And then the dark skinned Muslim screamed even louder, unintentionally spitting a few drops of saliva and breaking the spell in the progress. The clerk was first to recognize the store was being robbed and put his hands straight up in the air. The gentleman customer closest to the counter did the same and slowly backed away while a well-dressed, middle-aged lady, screamed faintly. Some in the store stood in shock; some raised their hands; others remained still. Outside the storefront, reveling shoppers noted the commotion and stopped to rubberneck.

Burja looked quickly around the room, waved his weapon, and screamed the only English word he knew, "Go!" The word was uttered gutturally, with a heavy accent, but intelligible. Again, each soul remained motionless, afraid they might misunderstand him. Unable to wait any longer, he holstered his weapon in his belt, drew open his coat, and flashed his vest with the explosives clearly visible.

In a flash, the reality of their circumstance registered to everyone present.

The male customer was first to comment, "Holy shit!" Immediately, the store was filled with screams and shrieks from the women and, suddenly, everyone in the store began stampeding out, yelling and waving their arms, frantically warning, "Get back, bomb!" The word bomb, screamed by running men and women in unison, marauded through the building like a flash fire, and soon the air was filled with Christmas carol drowning cries and screams as shoppers dropped their bags and ran for the exits.

The cashier tried to leave too, but Burja blocked his escape by redrawing his pistol and pointing the muzzle straight at the clerk. The young man's hands were still raised, and he began trembling, his heart pounding in step with his assailant, his face perspiring just as much.

"Tanna obarsa sauri!" Burja screamed. The clerk had no idea what the man with the gun wanted, but tried again to make peace.

"Hi, my name is Tom," the clerk offered and slowly lowered his hands and tapped his chest with his right hand and repeated slowly, "Tom. Tom. My name is Tom."

Once again, Burja screamed his unintelligible command. The clerk nodded no, shrugged his shoulders and pointed to his ears. Burja understood but was frustrated and infuriated. He needed to solve this problem quickly. Time was running out. He took his aim off of Tom and pointed his gun at the phone and then at the computer, vacillating his aim quickly, and garbling, "Go! Go! Tanna obarsa sauri! Tanna obarsa sauri!"

Tom finally understood, "You want me to activate the phone?" Burja continued his rapid aim alternating movements, spitting "Go!" over and over.

"Ok," the clerk conceded, "I'll activate the phone," and he stepped to the computer, logged in, and started typing.

Instantly, Burja realized the store clerk understood and was complying. He threw his hands up to the heavens in praise with a toothy grin and a yelp of praise, "Godiya ta tabbata ga Allah! Ya Gane!"

Praise God! He understands!

VII

10:47 pm

The FBI truck quickly pulled off of the interstate, traversed the two harried blocks of cars driving in the opposite direction, and pulled up to the armored SWAT mobile command vehicle (MCV). Oxmore and Stone stepped out and flashed their badges as armed SWAT officers descended upon them.

"Phillip Oxmore, FBI," he loudly asserted, "I am assuming command of this operation. Where is your commander?"

Captain Chunn stepped forward. Oxmore recognized Ian Chunn immediately. A year earlier they had worked together on a school riot mission and the experience had been a positive one for both of them. The two quickly exchanged pleasantries; Oxmore introduced Agent Stone and then asked for a situation report. With a nod, Chunn dismissed his men and hastily got the FBI agents up to speed as they walked toward the MCV, "The suspect is wearing an explosive vest and has taken a hostage inside a Radio Shack store on the first floor near the J.C. Penney," he apprized.

"What's your status?" Oxmore asked politely but firmly.

"We are ready to deploy as soon as we have sufficient manpower," Chunn answered as they approached Lieutenant Bob McCammon, Chunn's assault squad leader.

"What's it look like?" Chunn asked of his squad leader as soon as they were within earshot.

"We are just about set sir," McCammon replied as he looked at Oxmore inquisitively. Chunn recognized the expression immediately and answered before the question was asked, "This is Philip Oxmore, Memphis FBI SAC. He's in command."

McCammon and Oxmore simultaneously extended their hands and each shook firmly. "Nice to meet you sir," McCammon respectfully offered. Oxmore nodded in response and then questioned, "Do you have enough men to surround the store?"

"Enough for two elements," the squad leader answered with military formality.

"That should be enough. Position your shooters across the concourse and flank him with your assaulters. Guard for the escape and the wild shot and, remember, he's wearing a bomb and he's already killed several people today."

"Understood, sir."

Chunn listened and then subtly turned, speaking both to his man as well as to Oxmore, "We are not sure of his intentions." Without waiting for Oxmore to comment, he turned back to McCammon and finished, "Remember, our first priority is the safety of the hostage – then the suspect."

"Yes, sir," McCammon confirmed to Chunn with similar formality.

"Ok then, when you're ready, move out," On Chunn's words his man quickly moved into action.

Oxmore watched as the SWAT team deployed into the mall while streams of frightened and frantic mall patrons simultaneously began storming out. He ruminated Chunn's last words. They were mostly right. The first priority was the hostage, but he differed with respect to the second. Suspect safety was not priority two. No. Priority two was to get that hard disk. Priority three was to figure out what the hell else the son-of-a-bitch had done. Priority four was to figure out how he'd done it, and priority five was to figure out what he was planning to do next. In fact, he was pretty sure there were a few other priorities that, if he had a chance to think about it, would rank above 'safety of the suspect' on his priority top ten list.

In the Radio Shack, the clerk was hastily working to activate the cell phone. Burja's anxiety was growing, and he was visibly shaking, his belly secretly twisting in knots. He wildly waved his gun towards the computer, spun his free hand in a forward rolling circle, and yelled, "Ya tsaya! Ya tsaya!" The clerk muttered in response, "Yeah, I know, you want me to go faster. Do you have any idea how long it takes to set up a cell phone?"

The combination of internal chaos and external pandemonium made the recovery crew's job all the easier. Their role was to quietly enter an environment and remove all traces of an operational presence. The team was composed of two coed couples that looked more like a thirty something double-date than a covert operational unit. Caryn Fleet, the team leader, hated the term "recovery ops" but that's exactly what they were and they were extremely efficient, not only in their thoroughness, but their speed as well.

Within minutes of arriving on Level 3, they identified Abdullah's car. The vehicle was standard issue and surrendered to them with a click of a key fob. Caryn quickly found the burlap bag in the front seat, opened it, and instantly recognized that pages were missing.

While she was surveying the contents to determine exactly what was taken, her 'boyfriend' and the other couple busily swept the rest of the car; checked the trunk; used mirrors to look under the car; scanned for transmitters, computers, and other electronic devices; and wiped the car clean of prints. The only other finding was a pistol holster in the glove compartment and Abdullah's disabled phone. Caryn hid the holster, the phone, and the bank bag under her overcoat and the four of them slithered away as quickly as they had arrived.

Abdullah was pleased with the clerk's apparent progress and could not help but smile. Once the phone was activated, he would use it to securely contact his brother back home. Ishmael was well connected and would know what to do. Maybe this would end favorably after all. But in the next moment his fantasy was deflated. From the edges of his peripheral vision, he viewed soldiers scampering in crouched postures and taking positions around the building. He was surrounded and instantaneously knew it. Abdulla quickly moved behind the counter with the clerk and began yelling at him louder, "Ya tsaya!" Tom became suddenly more anxious and typed faster, pleading his case that he was working as fast as he could.

Burja was out of time and out of options. He now realized his every movement was being watched. They found him too fast and mobilized troops too quickly to permit any other explanation. He rapidly pointed the gun at Tom's head, and the clerk began to sob and plead. As subtly as he could, Abdullah pointed the gun back at the computer but this time slipped Tom the torn sheets of paper he had taken from the bank. He kept the transaction as clandestine as he could, passing the documents beneath the counter and trying to avoid eye contact while continuing his rants and violent gesticulations.

Tom briefly stopped his typing and looked at his oppressor quizzically. With sudden realization, he passively took the paper from his assailant and got back to work. He wasn't sure exactly what was going on but figured it would probably be smart to comply with a gun-waving lunatic strapped to a bomb.

Victor Coombs had men scattered throughout law enforcement and two of his best men were embedded in Memphis SWAT. Activating SWAT was his idea and, if he didn't say so himself, a stroke of genius. He could think of no better way to take Burja out.

The two men were part of a twelve-man advanced rescue team modeled after the FBI's Hostage Rescue Unit. Christos Sokolov, a Victor Coombs hand-picked expert-rated marksman and Chunn's best sharpshooter took a position on the lower floor behind a braided ficus tree planter with a Colt AR-15 assault rifle equipped with a high powered sight. Another shooter positioned himself at a different angle using the same weapon but was not part of Coombs' team. Both had a clear view of the terrorist and his hostage.

McCammon took the scout position behind an instant photo kiosk and quickly surveyed the store with his Monarch ATB high-res binoculars. The store appeared deserted except for the two men: the suspect, clearly agitated and anxious, bathed in sweat and wildly flailing his gun; and a hostage, scared and just as on edge, standing petrified yet typing wildly on his computer.

Sokolov was watching him too, but something struck him as odd; Burja was almost too wild. Was he high, manic, or psychotic, or was it something else? Just then the answer came. The suspect and the clerk had made brief eye contact before the African began screaming and pointing to the computer again. The sharpshooter wasn't fooled; he could tell a brush pass when he saw one.

Captain Chunn squawked in asking for a report.

The entire SWAT team was equipped with short range earpiece transceivers. The technology was sensitive enough to pick up a rifleman's whispers without the sharpshooter having to take his eyes off his prey. The only difference was that Sokolov also had a private, encrypted, and clandestine connection to Tyler Center that only Coombs and his team could hear.

"Team 2, what is your status," Chunn's squad leader queried of his flanking assaulter element. Team 2 had split in half with two men, each armed with M4 carbines, approaching from both directions and taking positions just outside each of the front corners of the store.

"We are in position, command. Do you want to try and get CNT in here?" McCammon asked, referring to the Crisis Negotiation Team, a specialized unit trained to defuse life threatening situations with verbal crisis management.

But before anyone could respond, another voice interceded. It was the Team 2B lead assaulter, "I'm close enough to hear the suspect... I'm not sure, but I don't think he's speaking English."

"What's he speaking?" Chunn asked somewhat incredulously.

"Arabic, I think."

Now it was team 2A's turn to speculate, "I don't think so, sir. It sounds African."

"There's no such language," McCammon corrected.

"Is there such a thing as African Arabic?" team 2B retorted back.

Chunn was listening to this all with Oxmore standing next to him. They glanced at each other with knowing grimaces.

"Cut the chatter!" Chunn harshly reprimanded. "CNT won't be much help if we can't communicate! Can anyone make out what he's saying?" There was no response.

"Maybe I can try calling him out with a bullhorn? He might speak some English." McCammon posited.

Time was running out. Burja knew it, and so did Chunn. "We have no time for any of that. What are my other options?"

McCammon exactly knew what his commander was looking for. "Team S, what is your status?" Team S – for sniper.

"I have line-of-sight on the target with relatively low risk to the hostage," Sokolov reported, "I can attempt to disarm or kill. What are my orders?" The question was directed as much to Coombs as it was to Chunn; both were listening to every word.

Chunn suddenly remembered something. "Can you identify the explosive belt?" he asked referring to the suicide vest Abdullah Burja was wearing.

Abdullah had instantly closed his overcoat the moment he recognized he was surrounded. He correctly surmised that police would recognize the belt and take precautions. He could only hope it would buy him the time that he needed to carry out his plan.

Knowing that he was not the only one who glimpsed the jacket, the sniper answered truthfully, "It's a wrap around low profile vest, probably C4 or other plastic. TNT is also a possibility."

The information was useful to Chunn. The use of plastic explosive and a low profile jacket rather than one using primitive triacetone triperoxide (TATP) suggested sophistication and confidence.

The chemicals needed to make TATP were inexpensive and easy to come by, and the explosive was difficult for dogs to sniff out making it the preferred choice for jihadists. But it had a price. The chemicals were highly unstable, hazardous to handle, and had injured almost as many terrorist bomb-makers as the victims they targeted. On the other hand, plastics were difficult to obtain and required a real detonator to work but were stable, discrete and, properly configured as this one was likely to be, considerably more powerful and deadly. It meant the guy was well funded, knowledgeable, and very dangerous.

"Can you see the vest trigger?" Chunn asked.

The trigger was obscured by Burja's coat. "Negative."

"Anyone with eye on the suspect, is the vest trigger in view?" Chunn called out to his entire team. No one responded in the affirmative.

Different explosive vests have different trigger mechanisms, something Chunn was well aware of. He knew that one advantage of TATP containing belts was their ease of detonation often executed with a simple light bulb whose glass has been broken. Plastics and TNT, however, required sophisticated detonators and potentially possessed safeties, semi-active triggers, and remote activation capabilities for the naive or cowardly suicide bomber. Those types were armed by depressing a button or squeezing a trigger but were not activated until the trigger was released. Shooting a bomber with that type vest effectively detonated the device as the dying terrorist released his grip. Since suicide vests kill and maim more by the scatter of the shrapnel contained within them than by the strength of the explosive concussion wave, Burja's vest could have been powerful enough not only to kill him and the clerk but injure or kill many of the SWAT officers as well.

Without knowing the specifics of the bomb detonator mechanism, Chunn had no alternative but to order his men to hold their position. Coombs had expected this complication as standard operating procedure demanded conservative action whenever innocents were threatened. He wasn't surprised to hear Michaels report, "FBI is choosing to hold and observe. They have chosen to wait for CNT."

But Victor was in no mood to wait. He knew Abdullah well; he had been a smart, resourceful and loyal asset. At least up until now. He was up to something, and whatever it was, it was unacceptable to the mission. Abdullah's lot was cast. "What is the position of our principal asset?" Coombs asked.

"Lower level with good vantage," Michaels quickly answered.

Seconds later the sniper's voice reported in, "Commander, the target is touching the hostage."

"As long the hostage's life is not being directly threatened, we hold. Is that clear?"

Michaels and Coombs stole knowing glances. That was not what Sokolov had said. "There are pages missing from the documents Burja stole. Could he have passed them?" Michaels questioned with hurried pace.

"Yes, sir."

"Those could be the papers, but it could have been something else," Gonzales truthfully added.

"Does he have a shot?" Coombs asked uninterested in meaningless speculation. He had all the information he needed.

"Do you have a solution?" Michaels echoed to the sniper.

Sokolov sniffed once.

"Stand ready." Michaels quickly paused and turned to his boss, "SWAT has orders to stand pat. We can't open fire in this situation without significant risk of exposure".

"Of course we can't," Coombs dryly replied and then turned to Gonzales, "Access the power grid to the mall."

VIII

11:02 pm

Outside of the building, Oxmore stood next to Chunn in the MCV. Communication feeds from the strike team members and visual recon from the mall security cameras filled the command vehicle's six monitors and Bose speakers.

"What's happening in there?" Chunn enquired out loud to Oxmore as they both watched the interaction of Burja and the clerk on the screen. The assailant remained anxious and impatient but was now smiling, and even the clerk seemed excited.

"It looks like he's activating a cell phone!" Chunn answered his own question somewhat incredulously.

"That's exactly what he's doing," Oxmore confirmed.

"But why? The mall is full of them." Chunn questioned himself again but Oxmore was way ahead of him. He realized the terrorist's goal the moment he arrived but was still trying to decipher the enigma. Although he was wearing an explosive belt, his objective was clearly not to blow himself up – he would have done that already; He was trying to communicate – but with whom – and about what?

STRONG EMERGENCE

The communication officer sitting at the console in front of them solved part of the puzzle. "The clerk looks like he is activating a Blackberry phone with secure international calling capabilities. It looks like he's about done."

"Can we intercept the call?" Chunn asked.

The officer was about to answer when the screens suddenly went dark; rifle shots rang out over the speakers, and loud yells bellowed out.

"What the hell!" Chunn was furious, "Stand down! Stand down!" he screamed over the intercom. He could hear the order to cease fire and hold position echo back followed by a dead silence.

"Who fired that shot?" Chunn demanded to know.

"Unclear sir!" was all his squad leader could answer, "But I think the subject may be down. There has been no detonation."

"Do you have visual confirmation?" Chunn immediately wanted to know.

McCammon peeked out from behind the kiosk and surveyed the scene. The blackout was brief as emergency lights quickly filled the darkness, but multiple shots had been fired in the interlude and now neither the clerk nor Abdullah were visible. In their place, pieces from the clerk's computer and behind-the-counter gaming gear were scattered everywhere.

"I don't see them," McCammon answered but another officer interceded, "I think I saw someone run to the back of the store."

Oxmore had been quiet, trying to analyze Burja's actions and motives, but finally spoke up, "He may be trying to escape through the service corridors."

Chunn agreed through his orders and actions, "All units, move in! Suspect may be trying to exit through the back. Exercise extreme caution! The vest may still be live."

Abdullah was beginning to see the end in sight. He knew enough about cell phones to realize the clerk was at the final stage of authorization. Then, suddenly, the store descended into darkness. He had expected some form of treachery and quickly changed levels, dropping to his knees. But his reflexes were not fast enough, and a rifle round penetrated his left shoulder eliciting a scream of agony and propelling the pistol from his hand. He clutched his shoulder as streams of blood began drenching his chest. He watched as the store clerk crouched into a fetal position in the corner of the cashier's counter while shots rang out propelling fragments of glass and plastic in every direction.

The emergency lamps were faint but offered just enough light to illuminate an exit strategy. He scampered back, keeping low, and headed for the back storeroom. From there, he reasoned, he might find an exit to the back halls and perhaps, an escape. Abdullah knew he was fooling himself. His options were very limited; he would not survive this.

Teams 2A and 2B each stormed in from each flank with their rifles in shoulder stock position. In the dim light, they proceeded quickly but cautiously looking down every aisle and around each kiosk. McCammon followed the assault team armed with his P226 pistol, keeping Sokolov to guard the back while sending the other to the mall exit to cover any possible escape route.

Moving in quick, sudden movements, the SWAT team moved deeper into the store and, within seconds, they amassed at the entrance to the back storeroom.

Abdullah made his way back through the service hallways, stumbling as best he could manage, trailing a line of blood. He passed doors to other businesses: a bakery, a lingerie shop, a newsstand; each door locked tight, bolted from the inside. He kept himself moving, venturing deeper into the eerie maze of halls illuminated only by the faint light of the emergency lamps. He was being followed. He could hear them. Voices began echoing louder through the hollow, concrete corridors. He pushed himself even as his breath became short, and the telltale lightheadedness of blood loss began to overcome him.

The Radio Shack storeroom was devoid of life and fairly empty, save for a sparse inventory of batteries, accessories, and laptop cases, but the door to the service corridor was open. The team immediately swarmed into the hall, first sweeping left and then right, while verbally communicating their positions in the dark environment.

McCammon methodically took up the rear, walking gingerly through the debris field that was made only worse by the advancing assault team. He walked carefully behind the counter to find the store clerk, Tom, still huddled in shock but with a soft smile of survival and gratitude on his face. Around the clerk were hundreds of shards of glass, and beside him, his assailant's gun laid harmlessly on the floor.

Tom still couldn't feel his feet, and his heart was still fluttering, but the exhilaration of the experience was beginning to set in. Wow, he almost couldn't believe it. What a story he was going to tell Jennifer and the gang at Matt's birthday party.

The sight of another police officer, not so scary in appearance, reassured him a little more, and he managed a faint grin. He was looking for the right words of gratitude to say, but his vocal cords were still off-line. His mind was still too preoccupied with his good fortune to process the object the police officer was removing from his pocket. It looked like a 6 inch long black hollow tube. He watched as the officer stooped down, picked up the terrorist's gun and twisted the tube on to the tip of the pistol. What was he doing? What was that? It kind of looked like one of those silencers you see on those crime TV shows. The excitement never turned to fear. The furthest it reached was a state of bewilderment as the officer raised his suppressor-equipped pistol, pointed it abruptly at Tom's gaping mouth, and pulled the trigger.

The young store clerk buckled without a sound. McCammon went quickly to work. His shirt was empty, but he found pay dirt in his right front pants pocket – four pieces of crumpled paper. He knew better than to read the contents but glanced at the title. The last thing he wanted was to retrieve a receipt for a stereo. There at the top of the first page was his prize:

Mission Statement: Project Quest

He quickly folded back the papers and pocketed them. He took the pistol, removed the suppressor, and let the weapon drop to the floor with a thud. Satisfied, he hurriedly made his way through the storeroom and into the hall to join his men.

The entire transaction was witnessed by Christos Sokolov, who provided a play-by-play report to Tyler Center. Now all that was left was to fabricate at least a semi-plausible explanation.

His breathing was beginning to falter, and the dull throb in his shoulder was becoming more acute, but Abdullah Burja pressed on. He was cautiously becoming optimistic. The caliber of the hall was getting wider. There was a good chance he was near the loading dock and a possible exit, but then the worst happened. The corridor abruptly ended, defended by a chained steel door. He tried the lock, but the chain was secure. Even a heavy duty bolt-cutter would take minutes to get through the door – minutes he didn't have. He turned briefly back. Perhaps there was another way. But the voices were getting louder, barking orders, and calling findings. He could hear their footsteps. There was no time.

"Allah, what can I do?" Abdullah cried out in a voice barely audible. And then the tonic of fear washed over him. Maybe this is what I was meant to do. Offer a diversion, a chance for the boy to make public the secret, a chance for the abomination of injustice to come to light.

Abdullah dropped to his knees and opened his coat. He had disabled the detonator by removing a battery lead and disabling the transponder. Restoring it would take only a few seconds. He adeptly enabled the detonator but reattaching the wire proved more difficult. His fingers trembled, and his vision began to bend. Surely God would give him the time he needed. The prayer was enough, and the lead snapped into place. He reached for the trigger, the red button of martyrdom that would begin his journey, but then – light. Intense light filled his eyes as the mall lights suddenly came on and in the ever so brief, disorienting moment, he held out the trigger and paused.

The shot that rang out was deafening, bouncing through the barren, concrete tubes, and followed by Abdullah's blood curdling screams. The shotgun had destroyed the trigger, blowing off the Nigerian's hand in the progress. He grabbed his stump, wailed in agony and instinctively fell back onto his haunches. Within seconds the wounded man was gang tackled and wrestled to the ground, each appendage secured, the agony in his chest and hand only exceeded by the horrible anguish in his mind. He had failed.

Voices screamed and intermingled as the SWAT team quickly worked to disable the bomb and search the subject all while the terrorist spat and yelled unintelligibly, thrashing in a growing pool of his own blood. Gradually, the man began to relax, the fight in his limbs easing to a tortured writhe.

The team 2A squad leader was the first to call in, "Command, we have apprehended the subject. He has suffered two serious gunshot wounds. He needs immediate medical attention!" Within seconds, a SWAT team medic kneeled by Abdullah Burja's side to inspect the damage. Bright red blood from the victim's wrist pumped from his transected radial artery in pulsing jets. The medic secured the blood loss with a forearm tourniquet as three officers held the screaming and writhing man in place while two others worked rapidly to slide the vest and detonator apparatus off. The medic surveyed the damage; the hand was gone, and there was a significant entrance wound in the left upper shoulder. Although the hand was gruesome, the shoulder was his bigger concern; the blood was slightly frothy suggesting a mix of air. He likely was suffering significant internal bleeding and needed emergency attention fast.

Moments later the back doors burst open, pulled off of their hinges from the outside, made possible by the muscle of a SWAT Cadillac Gage Ranger armored vehicle. Additional officers rushed in accompanied by a two man paramedic team rolling a stretcher and carrying a medical tackle box.

Phillip Oxmore, Ian Chunn, and Tedder Stone jogged toward the mall back service entrance stopping at the threshold of the officer-guarded, forcibly-opened, double doors. Abdullah was secured in 4 point manual restraint ten meters inside, his wailing now more of an anguished vocalization than true screams. Oxmore turned to Stone, "Secure the entire building. The whole mall is a crime scene!"

Stone acknowledged and began talking into his cell phone. Oxmore entered the hall carefully, dodging the splatters and pools of blood and tissue. He stepped up to the murderous suicide-bomber wannabe, moaning in a language he did not recognize. Swahili came first to the FBI agent's mind, but he had been to Kenya on an after-college safari, and after listening further, he was sure it was another language entirely.

Oxmore turned to the SWAT squad leader, "Did you find anything on him."

"No sir."

"No hard drive? No money?"

"Nothing except his clothes and the vest."

Stone joined up with them, and Oxmore turned to him for a second opinion, "What do you think?"

"I doubt he swallowed the hard drive," Stone answered in his signature, subtle sarcasm. "It must still be around here somewhere."

Oxmore was not in the mood. He was focused and clearly all-business, "Begin a systematic search: start in the store, under the counter, in the storeroom. Then find his car. Figure out his route. Where did he go? What trash cans did he walk by? What toilet did he use? Anything and everything. Got it!"

"I'm on it," Stone enthusiastically responded and then turned away.

Abdullah Burja continued to scream and babble. Oxmore looked up and called out to the mob of officers, agents, and emergency personnel, "Does anyone know what he's saying."

No one offered a guess.

Oxmore thought the language had intonations and words reminiscent of Arabic but still seemed African. He turned to Chunn, "Can you provide armed escort to the hospital? I want full security until we can question him. And we're going to need a translator."

"Fuck! You have got to be kidding me!" Coombs screamed. The mood at Tyler Center was decidedly downbeat, and Coombs' outburst could be heard even through the soundproofed walls.

Gonzales was the first brave soul to offer additional information, "It looks like he has been hit in the left shoulder and right hand. Both are likely non-lethal."

"Un-fucking-believable!" Coombs exploded. Almost violently, he turned to Michaels and acridly ordered, "Have all units fall back." Then with some clarity of thought, he switched gears to Plan B, "I want to know where that God damn ambulance is going!"

PART 2

IX

Poly-math *noun* \ˈpä-lē-ˌmath\
    Someone who knows a lot about many different things; a person of encyclopedic learning.

Origin: 1615-25 < Greek polymathés –

    Learned, having learned much. Derivative of poly + mathês or manthanêin, to learn.

Merriam-Webster

Memphis, Tennessee
United States
March, 1996

He was in the principal's office for the second time that week, seated across from Mr. William "Willy" Burns, a 350 pound, strict as a Jesuit priest, disciplinarian, who spoke with the gruff, marbled voice of Louis Armstrong. The office stank of stale air mixed with mildew and a touch of moisture. Piles of dusty books lined the faded walls and a disheveled oak desk separated the two of them cluttered with papers, reports and letters.

"So boy. What are you doing in my office again," he rebuked the auburn-headed, clearly out of place, freckle-nosed sophomore intentionally speaking in the common dialect of a southern-reared African-American.

"I don't know sir," Paul Gudrun honestly replied. He really didn't know why. All he had done was fail an algebra exam. And failure was not the exception for his school – it was the rule. Frayser High was not known for producing National Merit Scholars. It was a harsh, suburban Memphis school remarkable more for its gangland reputation, school yard violence, and soaring teen pregnancy rate. The students were 98% black, 2% white and 100% poor. Despite the sustained bull market, record-low unemployment, and giddy consumer confidence, the children of northern Memphis remained in abject poverty. Years later the school would earn the Title 1 designation for special funding consideration as part of George W's No Child Left Behind Act; it would be too late, and not enough.

To the casual observer, the teen was apparently no different than any of the children, other than being white in a virtually all black school. He was medium height and of medium build with the highly toned musculature of an athlete but not exceptionally so. Girls knew him more for his ability to help them finish their homework or cheat on a quiz than for his looks. Both of his parents drew social security, and his family lived in a doublewide in the CountryView mobile home community. Like most of the students at Frayser, he was on meal assistance and much of his clothing was courtesy of Goodwill. He appeared to be just like everyone else. So when he flunked the test, he had anticipated a reaction, but this wasn't it.

"Mrs. Murray told me you failed her math test!" Burns continued from behind his burly, salt-and-pepper, nest of a beard, "and Mrs. Murray says you've never failed one – ever!" Without waiting for the boy to answer, the principal kept up the assault, "Is there something wrong with you boy?! Are you on drugs?!"

"No, sir," Paul answered lazily, somewhat annoyed and sheepishly.

"Then is something happening at home? Is your daddy doing something to you that he shouldn't?" Burns pressed.

The boy straightened up in his chair. His demeanor changed from irritated to defensive, "No sir!"

"Then what is it? I heard stories from all your teachers last year. You were setting the curve in chemistry and teaching Mr. Johnson some history. They were betting on you being valedictorian in a couple years," then with added emphasis, "Not anymore!" Burns kept it up, "And Coach Fry told me you were his best athlete – said you could be a future Olympic star and Coach Merrell called you his three-point phenom! Now you can't even dribble the ball!"

The principal was on a role and beads of sweat were beginning to stud his balding forehead. He was not quite yelling but was speaking with loud, emphatic emotion and had moved to the edge of his seat, "We know what you're capable of, and you better get straightened out. Are you letting gangsters get to you?"

For a moment, the student became genuinely concerned for his principal's health. Were those veins popping out on his neck? Was he going to have a stroke? What could his blood pressure be? He couldn't wait any longer. He had to settle the man's nerves.

"Gangsters? Do you think they're worth my time?" the teen dryly responded.

Immediately Burns was disarmed. He couldn't help but chuckle. "No boy. No, I don't suppose they are," he snorted with a gurgled laugh then tried a different strategy. He paused a moment, rubbed his beard and continued his reprimand slower, 20 decibels softer, an octave lower – and in standard English, "You know, Paul, Miss Kirby really appreciated the help you gave her last semester. She never said what you did for her." Burns paused a moment waiting for a response. None came. "But she told me she misses your visits."

The principal stared deep in the student's eyes, hoping for a reaction. Getting nowhere, he decided to take a chance, "Do you know what a *polymath* is?"

"No, sir," Paul lied.

"Go look it up!" the principal yelled. He had never felt so defeated, "Now get out of my office!" He pointed to the door in an unmistakable gesture, signaling the end of the meeting and the student's instruction.

Paul Gudrun rose from his chair. He quickly reasoned the principal's motivations. His school was constantly in turmoil and had a tendency to make the news for all of the wrong reasons: Boy attacked by gang members sent to local hospital – Frayser drug use tops county – freshman girl caught with firearm. Despite the fact that Frayser High School was effectively overwhelmed, Burns was under tremendous pressure to show progress and perhaps parade a victory or two. He knew the principal was counting on him to be one of those success stories.

As honestly and sincerely as he could muster, the boy answered, "Sir, I promise you I'll try to do better. I will make you and Frayser proud!" He stood and extended the principal his hand. Burns was impressed and took it, shaking briefly but with vigor. Releasing the hand shake, Paul turned to walk out of the room. As he did, Burns completed his benediction, "I expect better things from you now on, you here!"

The teen turned his head and looked back over his shoulder, "You will sir. I promise." He continued walking forward, turned the knob to the door, and stepped through the threshold into the administration hall, satisfied with his deception. He knew the truth was Frayser wasn't ready for Paul Gudrun – maybe soon; but not yet. It had taken a while for Paul to come to that conclusion, and it wasn't the locker room taunting or the walk-home beating that convinced him nor was it his PSAT perfect score or his winning bicycle kick soccer goal. It was the look in Laura Kirby's eyes when he told his English teacher she was pregnant, and the child was not her husband's. The truth had come to him spontaneously – in the middle of class – from where he had no idea, but he implicitly trusted the source.

After class, he approached the proper lady. His intentions were therapeutic, but the revelation incited fear in the young woman's heart: fear of humiliation, of blackmail, of marital ruin, of destitution and loneliness. He helped her turn the fear into comfort but not without time and pain – hers and his. He could have withstood the bullies' mocking and heckling, but not her tears. No, the old Paul was frightening and dangerous. The new Paul was keeping quiet, playing dumb, and blending in. Much to his principal's chagrin, the strategy was working like a charm.

For a moment, Paul contemplated his future. It was more like a vision. It only lasted a second and was as mysterious and chilling as it was strangely compelling. In that instant, his future unfolded before him and his purpose became clear. Only the route remained mysterious. All that he was sure of was the importance of remaining subdued, quiet, dull, and almost invisible – stealth in a world that valued physical prowess and intellectual might. It was a life many inner city youth naturally lived, but strangely, he knew he was different.

He paused and prayed as he offered his sacrifice, exhaling as he accepted his purpose in the grand design, and humbly accepted his lot, content with his decision to act unwitting and unaware. As he continued his walk through the commons, he couldn't help feeling sorry for Mr. Burns: The only thing the principal wanted was success for Frayser High, accolade for himself, academic achievement for his students, and a district championship or two. Paul Gudrun wasn't sure what was in store for the school, and his principal possessed the energy and passion that would eventually earn him a promotion and a few honors. But what was clear was the simple reality that student achievement awards at Frayser were going to be difficult to come by.

He certainly wasn't going to be earning any.

X

Memphis, Tennessee
United States
Present Day

11:20 pm

The senior paramedic climbed up into the cab of his ambulance and started the engine. He could feel his adrenaline surging. Moments ago he and his partner had stormed into a crowded mall service corridor with a team of SWAT soldiers and subdued a terrorist caught before he could carry out his plan. The man was shot twice, and they had arrived to find him groaning in pain and shouting in tongues. Someone said the language wasn't Arabic, but it certainly sounded like it. Regardless, he and his partner quickly bound the right hand, shot virtually completely off, and then directed their attention to the profusely bleeding left shoulder. After slowing the hemorrhage with a pressure dressing, they hoisted the wailing fanatic on to their gurney and jogged back to the ambulance. That was moments ago, and now his partner was tending to the wounded man in the back along with one of the SWAT officers providing security. He could still hear the man screaming.

STRONG EMERGENCE

He took a moment to take in his surroundings. Police officers dressed in riot gear surrounded the ambulance, scampering like ants in an ordered chaos. One officer stood in front of the vehicle with his hand raised signaling stop. Clearly he was being instructed to wait. He looked to his left and immediately understood why. On each flank, hummers were joining him with a full contingent of SWAT team members with their rifles at the ready. He had seen many things on his fourteen years of emergency services duty. He had even been a part of a few riot actions and SWAT deployments, but he had never had armored police escort to the hospital. Clearly what was happening was momentous, but the gravity of it all was just beginning to sink in.

Out of the rearview mirror he could see an FBI special agent, easily identified by the large, bright white letters spelling out "FBI" on the back of his jacket, speaking to the SWAT commander. It was clear who was in charge; one was barking orders, the FBI agent, the other nodding in acknowledgment, the commander.

The special agent was not very tall but was imposing nonetheless. He exuded confidence and authority and his decision-making was quick and crisp. Even more impressive were the actions of his men. Their responses were much more than the obedient conduct of a subordinate officer or loyal servant; they were more like those of a child acting to please his highly respected father. So when the FBI special agent turned to him and gave the order to get to the nearest, capable hospital, there was no question he would give the matter thorough consideration.

Ordinarily, major trauma victims were taken to Regional Medical Center affectionately referred to by Memphians as "The Med". It was the area's major trauma center, an academic hospital complete with in-house 24/7 trauma surgeons, a burn center, and a dedicated closed head and spinal cord injury unit. It also had a long history of treating the rich and famous, and in fact, was the hospital that had attempted to revive Elvis. The alternative was Baptist Memorial, a smaller, level II trauma center on the city's east side. It did not have any of the high end resources of The Med, but its proximity to the city's crime laden neighborhoods provided Baptist Memorial with its share of stabbings and shootings. And the truth of the matter was, Muhammad or whatever his name was back there, did not have very severe wounds. Sure his hand was grotesque but it was almost certainly unsalvageable and would require simple amputation. The shoulder was the bigger deal. The man was probably bleeding into his thoracic cavity and would need a thoracotomy and possibly a sophisticated shoulder reconstruction, but that was certainly within the wheelhouse of the surgeons at Baptist. And Baptist had another advantage. It was only 12 minutes away. Regional was almost three times further even with lights and sirens. In the end, the decision was simple. Baptist Memorial it was.

11:26 pm

Oxmore returned to his sedan with Stone left behind to coordinate the mall search and evidence recovery unit. He watched as the ambulance was waved onward, racing toward the mall exit intersection, sirens screaming and lights pulsating in a luminous rhythm of red and white. Oxmore climbed in and started the engine. Within seconds, the heads up display located his position as well as those of the ambulance and SWAT units. Two teams were rolling with them, and two had already gone ahead, one to prepare the hospital, the other to secure the route.

On the radio, the voice of the ambulance driver blared, "Baptist, this is EMS 6 transporting VIP emergency trauma, heavy escort, GSW right hand, left shoulder, moderate blood loss, BP 110 over 68, heart rate 92, right radial tourniquet, left shoulder hemostasis currently adequate, I.V. 18 gauge left antecubital, normal saline at 250. We're 11 minutes out; maximum security requested." Phil sighed. The Memphis district had its share of excitement during his tenure and the years since 9/11 but nothing like this. On the surface, the crisis seemed averted but his heart rate told him his subconscious did not agree; his conscious didn't either.

STRONG EMERGENCE

11:30 pm

Interventional radiology is a busy department at most hospitals, and Baptist Memorial was no exception. The day had seen a vertebroplasty, two cerebral angiograms, two peripheral angioplasties, and five biopsies: three of the prostate and one each of the lung and liver. Amber Chase was in the dimly lit fluoroscopy room, diligently logging in the day's work and shutting down the equipment, unaware of the stealth figure creeping up behind her. With the whisper quiet motion of a feline predator, the dark form pounced unto her unsuspecting flanks with two fingers each angled just beneath her rib cage accompanied by a very loud and boisterous "Boo!"

Amber squealed as Paul howled in delight even as she swung around and delivered a playful but powerful punch to his left shoulder. He cried out in mock pain as he rubbed his shoulder with a toothy smile. She smiled back at him in similar mock anger as she scolded him for scarring her.

"I didn't realize I was so scary," Paul jokingly retorted. Dr. Paul Gudrun was a third year attending emergency room physician at Baptist. To the casual observer, he had come a long way from skid row and his days at Frayser High but his road had not been easy. His old high school principal would not have been proud. He had struggled through medical school, muddled through residency, and was a likeable, barely competent playboy on a career track to nowhere. Amber was a former Miss Tennessee, fifth year staff radiology nurse that should have been well out of his league. She didn't feel that way.

Their paths had never crossed meaningfully until a Halloween party the prior year had brought them together. Unbeknownst to each other, she had dressed as a sexy police woman and he as an escaped convict. The combination sparked playful banter that evolved into overt flirting, intimate conversation, a moonlit stroll, and an eventual kiss. The evening ended there, but there was no question the officer had gotten her man. He was enraptured immediately and the following day the wooing continued with a proper dinner date and late night jazz. It wasn't long before they were a couple, quietly dating, hoping to remain invisible and trying to keep one step ahead of hospital administration. There were strong rules against on-the-job fraternization.

The flirting done with, he spun her around and held her close to his chest, tight enough to feel her breasts against his own. He gently but passionately kissed her and their tongues interlocked. He held the kiss and then repositioned and embraced her again releasing her briefly to run his nose along her cheeks. Her scent was intoxicating. He took a moment to nuzzle the locks of her blond hair while erotically running his tongue into her ear. The effect he had on her was primal. She tingled in anticipation when he was near, drawn by his musky cologne, enjoying the comfort of his strong hug. He rubbed his hands along her shoulders playing with the edges of her bra strap as they entwined again. As they kissed, his hands slowly drifted downward toward the small of her back until his fingertips began to caress her bottom. His left hand was positioned to cup her buttock, and his right hand was about to slip inside when, suddenly, the romantic ambiance of their softly lit hideaway was dashed by a bright light and a brash voice.

"What the hell?" thundered through the room, and Paul half expected rain to start falling. The voice emanated from Ophelia Roberts, an experienced, well-educated, slightly overweight, ER nurse proud of her Afro-American heritage. The scowling look on her face communicated a cross between a mother's displeasure with her unruly children and a police officer about to write a citation. Paul and Amber quickly released, and Paul simultaneously smiled and blushed as Amber worked quickly to straighten her scrubs and hand-comb her hair. Ophelia was quick to press on as Paul braced for the worst, "Does this place look like a cheap hotel to you?"

"Hi Ophelia" was all Amber could frailly muster as she frantically tried to primp herself, "I was just finishing up for the day."

"It looked more like you were just starting!" Ophelia's rampage continued with a heavy-laden, ebonic accent, "This is X-Ray not X-rated!"

"We weren't doing anything," Amber responded but the scolding continued.

"Girl, have you met the new CNO yet? Let me just tell you. She's a Type A bitch with a chip that would just love to make an example out of someone like you."

"We get the point Ophelia," Paul irritatingly interjected.

"Do you? What do you think the ER director is going to think when he hears about this? I can see the 'Disciplinary Hearings' now."

Paul was starting to get angry, "Yes Ophelia, I said we get the point!"

"You're not going to tell anyone about this, are you?" Amber pleaded.

"I don't have to. They're cameras everywhere in this hospital!" With a condescending glare, Ophelia looked up and pointed. In the corner of the room, a small video camera peered down on them.

Without a further word, Paul gently directed Amber out of the room and into the radiology work area past Ophelia who guarded the threshold like a roman centurion. As the two walked past, Ophelia's hypocritical arrogance was uncontainable, "At least have the common sense to do it in the bathroom!"

"That's gross!" Amber instantly critiqued.

"Yeah, whatever."

Paul decided to end the conflict by changing the subject. Ignoring the bully, he turned to Amber and refocused on what was truly important, "What are you doing tomorrow tonight?"

"I am going to the deli, pick up some groceries, and make you a candlelight dinner."

"Sounds delicious!"

Ophelia was not amused. "You are going to do this all in front of me?" she emphatically questioned.

Amber was gentle and somewhat demure but had her breaking point. She returned her answer with an icy stare and an almost guttural utterance, "I'm going." She then turned her back and walked away heading toward the radiology break room.

Before she could get far, Paul called back to her, "I can't wait for desert!"

Amber looked back to Paul and winked, flashed a sultry smile, and continued her walk adding a not-so-subtle sway to her walk. The effect was not lost on either Paul or Ophelia, and it took only a millisecond for the doctor to feel an audible discharge of air from the bitch, "You are one piece of work!"

"Come on Ophelia, you know you love me," Paul responded with a boyish smirk hoping to disarm her with humor.

"You want a date with me too?"

He tried again, "You are way too much woman for me!"

"Yeah. Yeah."

Feeling the need to end the senseless debate, Paul resorted to the ageless tactic of retreat, "I need to get back to the ER."

Unfortunately for Paul, his chosen route was directly into Ophelia's waiting ambush. With a haughty cock to her neck, slightly pursed lips, and an arrogant tone, she pounced, "Yes you do. That's why I came looking for you. Redmond wants you. They just called a code Trauma. 'Should be here any minute now."

XI

11:36 pm

Tedder Stone walked gingerly through the devastated electronics store, trying hard not to disturb anything but even walking required tiptoe agility and careful planning. He scanned the scene, looking for anything of value. Glass and wood fragments intermixed with store inventory were scattered everywhere. Supposedly in all this there was a hard drive. Finding it was going to be harder than finding the proverbial needle.

Tedder peered around the corner of the checkout desk and found what he had hoped not to see but knew was there, the crumpled form of the cashier slain in the prime of his life. Another agent had already found the man, dead from an apparent gunshot wound. On the floor by his feet lay a Sig, by all measure the terrorist's hand gun, with one round of spent ammunition. He gently turned the young man onto his back, taking care not to overly disturb his position or otherwise do anything that could potential destroy biological evidence or hinder the investigation. The boy was Caucasian, in his twenties he surmised. The mode of death was obvious: a gunshot wound through his blackened mouth. The round was powerful and blew out the back of his skull. Only a trickle of blood streamed down from his lips, but grey matter floated in a pool of blood beneath him.

He quickly ran his hands along his chest and pants pockets and pulled out a thin leather wallet and set it on the countertop. He ran his hands down his trousers from his belt downward including his groin and buttocks; thoroughness demanded it, and there was no need for modesty. He found a ring of keys then directed his attention to his socks and shoes and finally to his collar and sleeves. Satisfied with his search, he turned back to the counter and was about to open the wallet when his cell phone rang. The tone was characteristic, but he instinctively peeped at the caller ID panel anyway. It was Oxmore.

"Tedder, it's me. What have you found?" Philip was multitasking, his body driving automatically, trying to keep up with a convoy of racing emergency vehicles while his mind relived the incident at the mall.

Tedder Stone began his report, "We found his gun, one round discharged. And there is one other casualty, the store clerk; it looks like Burja shot him right in the mouth."

"In the mouth?" Oxmore was flabbergasted, "Are we sure it wasn't friendly fire?"

"I don't think so. The clerk was down low behind the counter when he was shot, and the wound looks point blank to me. There's a Sig on the ground about two feet from the victim, and I think that's what the perp was packing at the bank." Stone was referring to the bank surveillance footage, and his recollection was correct. He then finished, "And I don't see any other weapons."

"One round fired means he used another gun at the bank."

"Or he reloaded." Stones counter-theory made Oxmore take pause. After a few seconds, another question popped into his head, "Why would he kill that boy?"

"He's a terrorist. Does he need a reason?"

Philip's mind was reeling. The case had officially evolved from the unusual, to the strange, to the unfathomably sad. He decided to change the subject once again, "Did you search the victim?"

"Yes. There's no evidence of a hard drive, thumb drive, or any other storage device. He had a wallet and car keys on him." Stone retrieved the wallet from the counter, opened it, and scanned the contents, carefully pulling out the driver's license, "Driver's license identifies him as Thomas Linton, age 20." He rifled through the wallet carefully, card by card, inspecting each carefully, looking through the money pouch for a piece of paper, a card, a note, anything that could be a clue. In the card holder, he found a single picture of an attractive, platinum blonde girl. Finding otherwise nothing of interest, he continued his itemized report, "a credit card, a couple of gift cards, a university ID card...."

Compartmentalization, the defense mechanism that helps protect the psyche of doctors, nurses, relief workers and law enforcement, briefly failed him. He had a college age son too and, just a few days earlier, had encouraged him to find a winter break job to help offset tuition. He suspected the young man's father had done the same thing. A lump briefly formed in his throat, but he fought it off. He continued his report, "a picture of a pretty young woman, probably a wife or girlfriend, and 13 dollars."

Oxmore kept the conversation moving, "Nothing on or under the counter?"

Stone directed his attention to the counter. The surface was in complete disarray and essentially barren save for the register. On the floor, a shattered iPhone was lying face up. "I think I found the cell phone Burja was trying to activate. Hold on..." Without touching it directly, he took a pencil from beneath the counter and pressed the activate button with no luck. "He apparently never did."

"Anything more?"

"I don't see a hard drive anywhere but then again it's a Radio Shack. There's technology everywhere."

"What about the car?"

"We found it but it's empty."

Unfortunately, he had nothing else to report. Oxmore picked up on it immediately and changed his line of questioning, "Have you looked at the surveillance films yet?"

"We are pulling those up now, but the power failure knocked out the cameras," he remarked knowing full well that was an unacceptable answer.

"Find that hard drive!"

"Yes sir". And with that brief charge, Oxmore hung up leaving Stone and his crew to start working on the haystack.

Something told him there would be no answers at the mall, but protocol demanded due diligence. As soon as the line cleared, Oxmore made another call, this time to Agent Weikert.

Amy Weikert was quick to answer.

"Have you found a linguist yet?" Phil asked.

"Yes. Her name is Alesha Deng. She's from the Counterterrorism Behavior Analysis Unit. She's supposed to be an expert in the languages of Africa and the Middle East."

This was good news and Phil's emotion was evident by his speech, "Bring her to the hospital as soon as you can and can you do me a favor and contact hospital administration. I am going to want to speak to security as soon as I get there."

"I already have. The CEO and his team are going to meet you in the lobby". Amy's efficiency was unmatched, and Phil complemented her for it.

They mutually ended their call and Phil now directed his complete attention to the road. The sky was grey, and flurries were starting to fall. As he followed the headlights in front of him, he tried to put the day's jigsawed events in perspective and mumbled to himself his quick conclusion, "This is some mixed up shit. And I thought I was going to be in bed by now."

11:40 pm

Paul walked into the emergency room. It was bustling with more than usual activity, and several security officers were huddled near the ambulance entrance. He nonchalantly walked behind the work counter where quite a few nurses and physician assistants were huddled. Rumblings of SWAT teams and CNN bubbled above the banter of nervous excitement. Paul was intentionally private, and publicity, in any form, was something he tried to avoid. On the other hand, he abhorred an information vacuum and the shift charge nurse was someone Paul could traditionally count on to correct that anomaly.

Paul strolled up to her and two other murmuring nurses and casually enquired.

"Code Trauma," was the charge nurse's terse reply. Her demeanor reflected the same anxiety everyone else seemed to share.

"Yeah, but what's all the commotion?"

"I'm not sure but security got here moments after EMS called in the code. It's some sort of VIP. Rumor has it; it's a suicide bomber!"

One of the male nurses chuckled. "More like a non-suicide bomber," he hacked and all the women could do was shrug. Suddenly, a loud voice blared over the intercom, "Code Purple."

Paul overheard one of the new hires asking, "What's a code purple?" but before anyone could answer, Dr. Eric Redmond, the Emergency Chief of Service entered the department. Dr. Redmond was chief attending but spent more time in his office than seeing patients. He was a typical hyper-achiever with a powerful intellect; impatient, demanding and often crass demeanor; and a touch of hyperactivity. The nurses hated him, the residents feared him, and the patients never saw him, but he was detail-conscious, aggressive, and a stalwart of efficiency and management. In other words, the hospital loved him.

Paul kept his nose to the grindstone and kept his distance from Eric, taking care to avoid his boss's limelight and trying hard to remain as mediocre as possible. For over a year, the strategy of contemptible neglect had materially worked, and Dr. Redman had left Paul alone. In a split second, the streak ended.

"Hey, Paul, where have you been?" Redmond asked, clearly both anxious and a little irritated.

"Hi Eric, I went to radiology for a coffee," expecting that the notoriously awful brew in the ER kitchen and the reputation of the radiology break room cappuccino machine would be sufficient explanation.

"Yeah right, but did you get some?" Redmond rudely asked, taking Paul somewhat by surprise and offending the brood of eavesdropping nurses.

Paul chose not to legitimize the question by answering, but Redmond kept talking as if he had never said a thing, "We have the national evening news coming in to trauma 1".

"What?" Paul curiously questioned.

Once again, the overhead intercom blasted, "Code Purple; Code Purple; this is not a drill!"

"Lockdown?" Paul quizzed again, this time raising an eyebrow. He clearly was out of the loop and never felt comfortable unknowing.

Redmond answered taking a victorious glee in intimidating his subordinate, "The Code Trauma is a terrorist. He tried to blow up a mall. Apparently he has severe right hand and left shoulder gunshot trauma. He's coming in with SWAT escort... and FBI". Paul controlled his emotions. "We are going to put him into trauma 2. Make sure we are all set."

Paul seemed distracted, and this time, it was Redmond that was in the dark, "Something wrong?"

Without hesitation, Paul answered, "I don't like terrorists." After a brief pause, Redmond retorted with a condescending and authoritative smirk, "We treat them just like everyone else."

Paul kept his opinions private. His boss was an idiot and an ass but a predictable one. He took a deep breath and swallowed his pride. He still had an eight hour media circus to look forward to.

11:42 pm

The hour was getting late, and the Memphis traffic was beginning to thin, but the route was taking longer than expected. Phillip continued to machinate over the evenings events. Things just did not make sense. He was going over it for the fourth time and contemplating possibilities when the phone rang. Once again, it was Weikert.

"Yes, Amy. What do you have for me?"

"Hold on to your hat! We just got some more intel from the NSA on our friend. Burja's not just a suspected terrorist; he's the real deal. We have certified voice transcripts with him talking to Kashmir Al-Mijarad, a top-ten lister and the suspected leader of North African al-Qaida. He's from a predominantly Muslim, non-English speaking town in northeastern Nigeria. According to CIA, he has been implicated in a number of definite and suspected terror related activities in Mombasa and Kampala and may have played a role in the 2007 Somali conflict. He may also have played a role in the recent Boko Harem abductions. He also was apparently a good friend of Fazul Abdullah Mohammed who headed East African Al-Qaida until he ate a bullet. NSA believes Burja could be the leader of a bona fide al-Qaida cell right here in the U.S. with significant operational knowledge. They think it's likely that other cell members may try to extricate or assassinate him."

Oxmore digested the information, but it didn't help. The incongruities were overwhelming, and the skepticism finally surfaced. "Amy, this makes no sense."

"What makes no sense?"

"Just think about it for a minute," Phil began and the words just came pouring out, like the waters from the sluice gates of an overflowing dam, "A high ranking Al-Qaeda terrorist who speaks no English comes all the way to Memphis to steal financial data that we can't find. That, in and of itself, sounds like the setup for a bad joke – but wait – it gets better! He kills some bank guards, drives like a lunatic, dons a suicide vest, and walks into a crowded mall full of Christmas shoppers. But instead of blowing them to Jesus, he takes a store clerk hostage and tries to get him to activate a cell phone!" His voice was now pressured and increasing in both pitch and amplitude. "SWAT arrives to save the day but just when it looks like things might settle down, the lights go out courtesy of the ghost of Christmas present, shots are fired, and we're left with a dead clerk and a wounded suicide bomber wannabe…"

"He finally did try," Weikert interrupted.

"And why do you think he did?"

"Because he didn't want to be captured…"

STRONG EMERGENCE

Oxmore echoed back "Because he didn't want to be captured." Phil paused but then continued sarcastically, "Why, I don't know 'cause he's singing like a canary! We don't know what the hell he's saying, but boy, he's saying it."

"Maybe he's psychotic or cursing us to hell."

"Maybe, but I don't think so. He was trying to make an overseas phone call. He was trying to communicate with someone. Maybe now he's trying to communicate with us."

At that moment, the hospital came into view followed a couple hundred yards later by a brightly lit sign with the word EMERGENCY in bold, block, white letters printed on a red background above the hospital's name and logo. The lead SWAT humvee slowed and turned the corner following the sign towards the ambulance porte-cochère protecting the double glass door entrance to the emergency room. The ambulance followed a few seconds behind and the trailing Humvee a few seconds behind the ambulance. Oxmore didn't follow the convoy but instead took the subsequent turn into the visitor's parking lot. He had the feeling he was going to be there for a while.

XII

11:47 pm

Paul chose to watch from the glass door to trauma 2. Redmond was standing halfway between Paul and the ambulance entrance, directing traffic. "What an inflated ego", Paul mused, "the only possible explanation is a very small dick." Suddenly Paul's cell phone rang. He glanced at the caller ID display. It read 'Snow Bear'.

It was Amber. His heart skipped a beat as he remembered how she got her pet name. It was last winter, and he had surprised her with an after Christmas trip to Breckenridge. She had never been skiing before, and he went all out renting a luxury chalet decorated with roses, Belgian chocolates, chamomile bubble bath, and a bottle of Dom Perignon. The first morning he awoke early to check out the trails. Fresh powder was falling, and he loved watching the sun rise over new fallen snow. When he returned he found Amber standing outside waiting for him. She was dressed in at least 5 layers topped with a fur parka that was already covered in fine snow dust. Just her rosy cheeks and a few stray locks fluttering in the wind were visible. He couldn't help smiling at her. Clearly she had not understood the ski trip dress code. That night they made love on the

STRONG EMERGENCE

Turkish rug in front of their rustic fireplace. He still remembered her silver blonde hair sparkling in the firelight. He called her his Snow Bear for the first time, and she responded to him with a deep, passionate kiss. He could still smell the aroma of her perfume …

His memory was interrupted by another buzz of the phone. He answered it as two policemen joined the security guards, both with their hands on their sidearms. The terrorist was here.

"Hey, Snow Bear. What are you up to?"

"I'm driving home thinking of you, Baby. It was kind of fun getting caught by that old bat, don't you think?" Amber mused.

"Old bat? That phrase went out with 'Leave it to Beaver!'"

"Well, you know I'm kind of old-fashioned?"

"Yea, sure you are." Paul liked the banter and knew she did too. It was playful sparring. She was spunky and smart not to mention drop dead gorgeous. What she saw in him, he did not understand. "So, it's going to get busy here in a second. What's up?"

"I was thinking. I've got the day off tomorrow. Instead of dinner, how about coming over to my place for brunch after you get off and who knows, maybe I'll have a little desert for you like I promised?"

And she was as hot as a firecracker. Damn he was lucky. "I'd love too!"

At that moment, the glass doors to the ambulance emergency entrance opened and Paul could hear the commotion outside. This was going to be a three-ring circus. As much as he wanted to be with Amber – *really* wanted to be with her – he knew he was going to have to be on his toes. Duty and attention were expected now. Anything less would be inappropriate, and the intense media exposure could present other hazards. He would have time for her later.

"Hey honey, I have to hang up. I have a sick patient coming in the door," Paul blurted out. EMS already had the patient inside, and it wouldn't be long before he was in the room. Already a nurse was opening a trauma cart, and a respiratory tech was preparing a ventilator in case the patient required intubation. Soon the entire room would be crowded in a swirl of frenzied activity, all with the intended purpose of saving a life.

"That's OK," Amber replied, "I'll be waiting for you." Then she added playfully, "Maybe with a surprise or two."

"Sounds good. I can't wait!" he responded sincerely. With a click, he knew that she had hung up. The phone dimmed, and he pocketed it in his scrub shirt. Seconds later the gurney turned the corner powered by the paramedics with Redmond at the side. He could see the injured man flopping and screaming in agony, his mangled wrist stump and over-saturated shoulder dressing splattering droplets of blood through the air with every writhe. At first Paul thought he was blabbering in gibberish but it became quickly clear he was speaking a different language.

"Zai iya gane?" the injured man cried out.

Was that Hausa he was hearing? Paul almost could not believe his ears. Hausa, a language originating among the tribal peoples of Niger, is the lingua franca of north-central Africa spoken by some 43 million people, mostly Muslim, from Burkina Faso to Sudan, but Paul knew it was extraordinary to hear it anywhere else. He had first heard it as a child.

Yusuf lived four doors down from him. He and Paul were middle school best friends. Yusuf and his family had emigrated from Nigeria in 1990 during an attempted coup by a regiment captain and his junior officers. His father had been the captain's personal physician. When it became clear that the revolution was failing, Yusuf's father reluctantly fled the country with his family in close tow. It turned out to be the right decision. Within the subsequent months, sixty-nine men, including his captain, were executed, some quietly, others by impalement upon stakes foisted in town centers.

Paul remembered how his friend recalled coming home from school one cloudy afternoon. His father was standing at the door and told him to empty his backpack and stuff it full of his best clothes. He mother was inside, frantic, and his older sister was crying. Yusuf remembered wanting to take his toys and tell his friends goodbye, but his father refused. He hadn't been home five minutes when his father ordered everyone to the family car, a '78 Impala in bad need of repair. They drove through the night to Port Harcourt and smuggled themselves out of the country aboard a merchant oil tanker.

In Nigeria, Yusuf's father was a respected doctor tending the ruling elite, in America he was a butcher at the local Piggly-Wiggly. He spoke no English, and so Hausa was the language of the house, more specifically, a single-wide trailer where Yusuf lived with his parents and sister. Paul spent a lot of time there. They studied well together, his mother made the most delicious native curry dishes, and his sister, Tanesha, was a stunning beauty. Paul began to hear as much Hausa as he did English and was quick to pick it up. Two years later Yusuf moved to Detroit, but his childhood friend's language had been ingrained forever.

It was less than twenty feet from the ambulance entrance to the threshold of trauma 2, one of three exam and treatment rooms reserved for the sickest patients: victims of heart attack, motor vehicle accident and violent crime. Within moments, Abdullah was wheeled into the room surrounded by nurses, technicians, and pharmacists. The paramedics were busy blurting report to Redmond who immediately took charge, "He took a rifle shot to the right hand and left shoulder. We bound the shoulder but had to tourniquet the wrist. His blood pressure was 124 over 72 when we got him on board, but his heart rate has been steadily rising. His last blood pressure was 110 systolic." The taller paramedic, breathlessly paused as the gurney was rolled in and brought alongside the permanent stretcher already in the room. Two of the staff nurses moved alongside the bed and in one swift move pulled the draw sheet, along with the patient, from the gurney to the stretcher.

Redmond began blurting orders as the room began to twist in a whirlwind of activity. Simultaneously, one nurse was placing a blood pressure cuff on the wounded man's right arm, another was placing electrodes on his chest, another was using special garment scissors to cut his pants off, and a respiratory tech was replacing the paramedics' portable oxygen with hospital supply all while Abdullah was still conscious and moaning, "Zai iya gane?"

Paul moved to the foot of the bed and felt the femoral pulse. It was weak and racing, and beads of sweat were starting to form around Abdullah's lips, both clear signs of falling blood pressure and impending shock. Redmond recognized it too prompting Paul to enter the fray and call for a stat femoral line tray setup. The patient needed better IV access, and the femoral vein was large, accessible, and away from the commotion at the head of the bed.

As the automatic blood pressure cuff confirmed the obvious, Redmond called for an emergency blood transfusion. The words propelled the blood bank technician into action like a lit fuse on a bottle rocket.

Despite his dwindling pressure, Abdullah continued to cry out, partly in agony, partly in a vain effort to communicate, "Zai iya gane? Zai iya gane?" Redmond looked up, his own adrenaline clearly rushing through his body, "Does anyone know what he's saying?"

Paul suppressed the urge to answer. He had been doing it for years, playing dumb, avoiding the questions, dodging when he ought not to know, darting when he should know, salting with the occasional brilliance, peppering with simple errors so that in the end, he had crafted an illusion of an average man, a doctor, but an average one nonetheless. He could have explained away his fluency as an academic hobby or even tell the truth and recall the story of Yusuf and his family. After all, he choose the medical profession as a cover for a reason. It was easy to hide his intellect there. But questions might follow, questions followed by more questions, questions he had no interest in answering. The risk was too great to get any more involved than he already was. As unusual a situation as the one before him presented, now was not the time for revelations. No, he would keep his knowledge of this man's language a secret, locked in the vault of his mind, safe and warm amongst all of his other secrets. He focused instead on reading body language – that anyone could do, "I think he's scared and wants to try and tell us something."

"Zai iya gane? Don Allah! Ya taimake ni!" The word 'Allah' perked everyone's ears, but it was the technologist at the head of the bed who was first to comment. "Well, I know what Allah means," he opined with a Tennessee twang and a soft chuckle. "He must be speaking Arabic," added the young, plain-faced nurse tending the fluids and the high-tech Medtronic infusion pumps that were forcing them into the patient.

"It's not Arabic," spoke a voice among the hoard of people, all official: additional nurses, pharmacists, technicians, administrators, security, social support staff, and clergy that had accumulated just outside the door to Trauma 2. Paul felt a moment of relief. Maybe someone else could translate and relieve him of the moral struggle that he was enduring because Paul understood the foreigner, the alleged terrorist, completely. Zai iya gane?

STRONG EMERGENCE

Don Allah! Ya taimake ni! Can anyone understand me? Please! Someone help me! Even though the man was a terrorist, one intending to blow up a suburban mall crowded with holiday shoppers, he was still an injured human, and Paul could not easily dismiss his obligation to render assistance on that basis, much less his own selfish needs to maintain appearances. Unfortunately, his relief was short lived.

"I speak Arabic fluently and it's definitely not Arabic." The voice came from a lab technician Paul had never met, "It sounds African. He kind of looks Nigerian." Abdullah's skin was cafe-au-lait brown, and his lips were thin despite being obscured by his unruly beard, features clearly more middle eastern; yet his physique was chiseled, muscular and lean, features clearly more African. The technician continued, "Maybe Dr. Tinibu can understand him."

Paul did know him. Dr. Bangtane Tinibu was a radiologist and chief of staff. He was Nigerian, but Paul knew he spoke Igbu and not Hausa. Igbu is the language of eastern Nigeria while Hausa is spoken virtually exclusively in the north. He recalled a conversation Bangtane was having one day around the lunch table in the doctor's lounge. One of the physicians had expressed wonder that the Nigerians were able to function, do business, and effectively govern despite having three discreet languages. When the question was asked, "How do they communicate?" Bangtane's raucous laughter bubbled as he recounted the Nigerian solution, "We speak English!" No, Dr. Tinibu would be no help at all.

The terrorist's voice began to falter as his blood pressure steadily declined, but his pleas remained the same: "Zai iya gane? Don Allah! Ya taimake ni!" Can anyone understand me? Please God! Someone help me! Paul did his best to focus on the task at hand. The cuter, petite, strawberry blonde nurse had set up his Mayo stand and opened the femoral line kit for him. He quickly donned the sterile gloves and began prepping Abdullah's upper thigh with antiseptic precisely over the spot he had earlier felt the pulse. Seconds later, he began numbing the skin reciting, "This is going to sting a little bit," knowing full well that his patient could not understand him. Just then, a realization struck Paul. This man really knew absolutely no English! If he knew any words: hello, goodbye, even yes or no, certainly he would have used them by now. Even if he was intentionally avoiding speaking English on some foolish principled ground, Paul could not fathom him holding to such a conviction in his condition, severely injured and pleading for understanding. How strange. Paul was calculating the possibilities, simultaneously placing the guide wire into the femoral vein when Abdullah suddenly tried to sit up, finding a source of energy no one expected. Redmond quickly held down his shoulders futilely exclaiming, "Don't move! He's almost done!" Paul did his best to secure the injured man's groin, but he continued struggling, crying out in pained anguish, "Don Allah! Ya taimake ni! Ya na da maganar rai da mutuwa!"

The words caught Paul off guard, and he couldn't help meeting the eyes of his patient. His empathetic gaze betrayed him, and Abdulah recognized it immediately, smiling through tears and praising Allah. "Ka san ni!" You understand me! Paul took every effort to fight the temptation to confirm the suspicion, but Abdullah pressed his opportunity, knowing his consciousness was fading and his time short, "Ya na da maganar rai da mutuwa!" The words rang through Paul's head once again, this time complete with a spinal shiver. Ya na da maganar rai da mutuwa! It's a matter of life and death! Then as if knowing now might be his last chance to get his message out, Abdullah began to recite:

Ka nemi,
mai girma, gaskiya ne,
daga wasiƙa likita
daga wasiƙar da sarki

Then, with one last surge of might, he looked at Paul squarely, drool pooling around his lips, and uttered, as close to a scream as he could muster, "Ka san ni? Ya na da maganar rai da mutuwa." Do you understand me? It's a matter of life and death. Redmond was oblivious to the purposeful intent of the man's pronouncement, but it did not escape the eye of the petite, young, pixie-faced nurse. "Do you understand what he is saying?" she asked. In his mind, he issued her a touché for her observation, but kept his demeanor intact, thinking how unwise those who underestimate the intelligence of a person based on their stature, youth, gender, or color of hair.

STRONG EMERGENCE

"I have no idea," he lied – partially. In fact, Paul understood every word but it was the meaning that made no sense to him. As he began to contemplate, the shiver returned, then transformed into a sensation of dread mixed with unexpected curiosity as another revelation overtook Paul, one even more disturbing, the stark realization that the man before him was dying, and not because of a couple of gunshot wounds.

XIII

**Saturday Morning
12:10 am**

Phil Oxmore walked into the main hospital entrance to find Ben Caruthers, the hospital CEO; Keith Ware, the COO; Tanya Morone, Director of Emergency Services; and Frank Scaglione, Chief of Security all waiting for him in the sparsely occupied, nicely decorated, lobby. Across the street, the local Fox News affiliate van had just arrived. They properly and politely introduced each other, joked about the witching hour, and then Mr. Caruthers gently ushered the group down the hall toward the emergency room, outlining the recent renovations and touting the 'Top 100 Hospital' honor the institution had recently received. Victor listened politely for a couple of minutes but then he changed the conversation abruptly to business.

"May I ask for an update on our suspect?" Oxmore asked knowing that the hospital had legal restrictions as to the extent of information they could provide.

Tanya was the first to speak up, "He's suffered significant injuries and may be going into shock."

"Will he be all right?" Oxmore's concern was genuine.

"Based on their initial assessment, the doctors are optimistic," Marone added clearly unaware of the most recent developments.

Oxmore debated the extent to which he should confide in the hospital administration but quickly concluded that he needed them as an ally, "The man is a high value target. He may have information vital to national security."

Caruthers was defensive, interpreting the agent's statement to imply they were incapable of treating or protecting the man, "I assure you that our doctors and nurses are doing everything possible to help him. I have supreme confidence in the capabilities of our trauma team."

"I am sure the staff of your excellent hospital is more than capable, sir." Oxmore was trying not to sound placating or condescending, but he was doing a poor job of it, "But we have reason to believe that he was not working alone and that others may try to either free him or kill him." Oxmore was calm but forthright, "I have placed men around the perimeter of the hospital to hopefully prevent any mischief, but the risk is still significant."

Scaglione, the hospital security chief and a retired army master sergeant, was quick to reassure, "The hospital is already in lockdown. All exits are secure, and we are already actively monitoring the entire facility."

"Excellent. Additional backup is in on the way but, for the short term, it's just us."

"No problem, we've got it." the security chief confidently answered. Oxmore found the bravado a bit annoying but chose to let it lie.

Oxmore turned to Caruthers, "In addition to any nasty ideas this guy's friends might have, you're bound to be bombarded by media and gawkers, nut cases, and anybody else looking for their fifteen minutes of fame. My suggestion is that you keep the doors closed, avoid the cameras, and answer any question with the loosest of generalities."

Oxmore answered a flurry of questions, and when he was confident that he had satisfied all of them, he turned back to the CEO, "We are going to need an office space of some sort, not big but private and preferably close to the action."

"There is a small conference room right down the hall," Caruthers offered.

"That should do. Has the suspect said anything?"

Marone chimed in, "He's been talking up a storm, but nobody understands a word he's saying!"

Oxmore was comfortable with everything he heard and with the demeanor and professionalism of the staff. Sure they were scared and clearly out of their comfort zone – but not too far. He decided that it was safe to share additional intelligence, "I have a team on their way in with a translator. We will need to speak with the suspect as soon as he is able."

"We'll make sure to put them through as soon as they arrive," Ware assured.

As if startled awake from a deep sleep, their heads all turned in sudden unison to the sound of yells and screams from the far end of the emergency wing. There, a crowd of clinicians and staff were standing outside of an exam room. Oxmore knew the answer but asked the question anyway, "Is that our man?"

The response from the others came almost humorously in unison, "Yep."

Abdullah Burja's burst of energy exhausted, his head collapsed back on the pillow as flashes of light formed at the edge of his vision. Despite a wave of nausea forming in his abdomen, he focused on what had to be done, exposing the travesty that threatened everything. He had killed many men in his life and knew that he now too had been killed, just not yet. It was too late for him to do much good but maybe the American could help. He had to trust; he had to try. As a starship captain directing all energy reserves to the bridge, he channeled all his strength to his voice, "Dari da ashirin takwas. Casain takwas. Dari guda. Goma."

STRONG EMERGENCE

At first Paul could not make out what he was saying. Then it became clear that the words weren't words at all but numbers. 128, 98, 100, 10. Abdullah kept repeating the numbers over and over, his voice fading to a drone whisper.

"Pressure is down to eighty!" the vitals nurse reported, "Pulse is now 140. Rhythm still looks sinus." Paul took the opportunity to interject, "I'm not sure this is all trauma related. Let's get a quick echo to look at his heart!"

"Good idea," Redmond added. The sonographer, waiting amongst the spectators just outside the door, pushed her way through as Paul finished the last suture on the femoral line. She positioned her Acuson 2000 sonograph to the right of the patient, immediately booted the machine, and began taking images as the first unit of emergency O negative blood was being hung. Pallor was overcoming Abdullah, and he was now frankly diaphoretic. The fight in his muscles were long gone, and his skin was starting to cool. Still, with every neuron, every cell, every mitochondrion, committed to his singular task, he continued in nothing more than a whisper, "Ga shi a ƙarƙashin halata ɗakin littattafai."

"Look in the law library? Is that what he just said? He must be delirious now," thought Paul as the sonographer placed the probe on Abdullah's chest. The image appeared on the monitor instantaneously, but the result was unexpected. "Oh, that's not good," muttered Redmond. The man's heart was normal in size but contracted uniformly feebly.

Redmond quickly looked up to the hallway, "We need an ECG stat!" he called out and then appended loudly and with emphasis, "And get cardiology down here now!"

The stat call for cardiology blared on the overhead hospital intercom system.

Through all the commotion, Burja continued to groan, "Ya na da maganar rai da mutuwa. Ga shi a ƙarƙashin halata ɗakin littattafai..." It's a matter of life and death. Look in the law library. The ECG technician stepped to the right side of the bed with her smaller rolling cart, temporarily displacing the physicians and nurses, and adeptly placed the ECG leads on the patient while the sonographer completed her exam. All the while, the words incessantly flowed.

"What the hell is he saying?" Redmond's adrenaline-laced frustration was mounting, "Where the hell is Tinibu?"

Another voice spoke up, "He was already here. He says he's speaking Hausa, whatever that is, and doesn't understand him. He went back upstairs to find someone he thinks might be able to translate."

"That's just terrific!" Redmond facetiously retorted, "Where's cardiology?" As if conjured by magic, Drs. Patel and Witherspoon raced in, the hoard parting to make way for their arrival.

Vanzant Patel and Rick Witherspoon were both first-rate interventional cardiologists. Patel graduated from Emory via the University School of Jakarta and was Chief of Cardiology; Witherspoon hailed from Washington University in St. Louis and was Director of the Cath Lab. Together they were the dynamic duo of the hospital's heart care team and Redmond could not have been happier to see them.

Patel was first to enter the fray just as the technologist ripped the freshly printed ECG off of the machine and handed it to Redmond who, after a quick glance, handed it off to Patel who agreed with the computer's interpretation printed at the top of the tracing: sinus tachycardia. Left bundle branch block.

The sonographer interrupted her almost completed exam and recalled her previously captured images as she gave her grave report to the cardiologists.

"We need to get him to the Cath Lab stat!" Patel interrupted. Witherspoon then opened his iPhone and dialed the lab and his chief technician answered the call, "We need the crew down here in the E.R. right away, and we need to prep for a balloon pump now!"

Patel pressed the paramedics for additional historical details, as all physicians do, particularly when rendering a consultative opinion or assuming care responsibility while Witherspoon managed the Cath lab staff, and Redmond kept the nurses hoping, aggressively up-titrating the medications, demanding frequent vital updates, and reviewing the results of the emergency blood work drawn earlier. Meanwhile, Paul took the opportunity to listen more closely to the dying terrorist whose utterances now were nothing but a feeble murmur, "Ga shi a ƙarƙashin halata ɗakin littattafai. Ya na da maganar rai da mutuwa!" Look in the law library. It's a matter of life and death!

And then he added two more words...

"Hakika, Allah"

And he continued repeating them over and over, "Hakika, Allah. Hakika, Allah," until his consciousness finally faded into oblivion.

Hakika, Allah.

Truth, God.

XIV

2-Trifluro,4-dimethyloxohexyl,6-dibenzyl-N-pyridone, also known as LSX, is a synthetic metabolic poison and closely guarded secret of modern chemical warfare. It acts by potently and irreversibly binding to ubiquinone, permanently inactivating it and rendering it useless. Ubiquinone, more commonly known as Coenzyme Q10 and the same supplement sold over the counter in health food stores and supermarkets everywhere, plays a unique role in the electron transport chain, the mechanism by which all living cells in the body generate energy. The depletion of ubiquinone results is the quick inhibition of cellular energy generation. Cell death, followed by organism death, quickly follows.

LSX, short for 'Lethal Substance 10', is a molecular mimic. Its chemical signature is remarkably similar to cholesterol. Only very sensitive and expensive technologies like high resolution mass spectrometry can reliably detect it thus making it the perfect tool for the assassin who does not want to appear to have killed. But, unlike several other agents known to science that act similarly, LSX is a large molecule that does not easily cross the blood-brain barrier, the natural biological shield that helps to protect the central nervous system from attack. The effect is a slower, conscious death that appears more natural but is less useful, particularly when haste is prudent. Fortunately, it is a limitation easily overcome by administering a large enough dose.

It's funny how fortunes can change in a couple of minutes. Moments ago, abject failure turned to near triumph with the news that Team I had reported success. It was Christos Sokolov's idea. Just before leaving the mall, McCammon, at Victor's command, had managed to delay the ambulance long enough to allow Sokolov time to board the ambulance disguised as SWAT security. Cristos Sokolov wasn't just a sharpshooter; he was well versed in the assassin's trade craft. He was aware of another valuable attribute of Lethal Substance – its compatibility with opiates. Sokolov had managed to slip the unwitting paramedic a vial of LSX tainted morphine. One vial was effectively deadly, but he would have preferred to have administered two. Unfortunately, the occasion to inject the second dose never arose.

"Sir, I have Agent Sokolov on a secure com line," Michaels blurted out to Coombs standing right behind him.

"Do you have good news, Agent?" Coombs asked over the radio via his headphone mouthpiece. The question was a formality. He already knew the answer and was preparing his team for a victorious cheer. Unfortunately, he was about to be disappointed.

"Mostly," Sokolov responded and with the word, Coombs' chest slightly deflated, "One vial of toxin was delivered with high confidence but there was no opportunity to deploy the second."

Although less impressive than he expected, the news was still positive, and congratulations were appropriate, "Good work," Coombs commended.

"Sir, there is a problem. He is still conscious and yelling out," Sokolov added, "There is no indication that anyone understands him, but he is trying desperately to communicate."

Coombs knew good and well exactly what the African was trying to do. He chose not to emphasize it, "Maintain close surveillance."

"Roger that." With a click, the secure connection was severed.

"It's a good thing he doesn't speak any English", Michael's muttered.

"How long?" Coombs asked turning to Wade.

Sam Wade inferred the meaning of his boss's question, "Hard to say. The response is very variable with only one diluted dose but given his weakened state, I'm guessing a half hour, more or less."

Thirty minutes was too long to wait for Abdullah Burja to die; too many things could go wrong. Unfortunately, there was little Coombs or anyone could do about it. The breach needed resolution, but secrecy was an even greater priority. Cautious patience was the most prudent course.

"We need to sit on this closely gentlemen," Coombs announced and then tapping Agent Michael's shoulder commanded him directly, "I want two teams in close with full support. This is a dangerous situation, and we need to tidy this up quickly. No loose ends. We need technical tie in to the hospital and linguistic support."

Like usual, Michael's was one step ahead, "Already working on it."

Memphis, Tennessee
12:40 am

"He's fibrillating!"

Paul wasn't sure who screamed it, but he instantly stopped what he was doing and looked up. Within seconds of his last utterance, the organized waves of electrochemical energy normally driving Abdullah's heart electrically degenerated into chaos. The telemetry monitor told the story. The electrocardiogram, normally depicting a regular pattern of electrical pulsations now revealed a low-amplitude, erratic scribble reflecting what was functionally happening in his heart; the muscle was quivering ineffectively and pumping essentially nothing. Abdullah Burja was in cardiac arrest.

"Quickly, get the back board underneath him. We need to start CPR!" Redmond screamed, but the team was already initiating cardiac resuscitation protocols instinctively. Paul's assistant dropped the gauze pads she was holding for him and reached for the defibrillator pads while the male nurse at the head of the table placed the base of the palm of his right hand on the terrorist's sternum, gripped his hands together with fingers intertwining, and began chest compressions. A third nurse pulled the crash cart toward the patient, ripped open the seal, and opened the drawer exposing a selection of life saving medications.

Almost instantly, the patches were attached to the dying man's chest and connected to the defibrillator. The machine confirmed ventricular fibrillation and Redmond quickly and appropriately called for a shock.

The nurse manning the defibrillator complied, programmed the machine, and pressed the charging button as she anxiously echoed the doctor's order. An audible tone, crescendoing in pitch, tracked the buildup of electrical charge within the capacitor until the digital readout displayed 150. "Clear," she yelled. Up till then, Paul was observing the action and reviewing the attending's orders and the nurses' responses for accuracy while still contemplating the significance of Abdullah's last words: Truth, God. What possibly could this man possibly have been trying to tell him? He moved back just as the electrical energy discharged from the defibrillator propelling Burja momentarily off the bed by the violent contraction of his chest muscles. The monitor took a second to reset, but it became quickly clear the shock had been ineffective.

"It's still V Fib," the charge nurse blurted.

"Quickly! Shock again!" Redmond loudly commanded. Once more, the nurse professionally complied.

The rising drone of the defibrillator again filled the room and, for a second time, Abdullah endured the furious convulsion. But this time it worked; chaos was replaced with order. The ECG abnormalities persisted, but it was a stable rhythm, and for a split second, there was a communal exhalation – an anomie – that was just as quickly replaced with a deadening exhortation by the male nurse at the head of the bed, "There's no pulse!"

CPR was restarted, pausing only momentarily to position the backboard beneath the dying man, and then seconds later, paused again to allow the nurse anesthetist time to intubate him. Voices in the room collided in a dissonant noise of orders, counter-orders, clarifications, and confirmations: "Open fluids at wide open! ... Give one milligram of IV epinephrine stat! ... Do you want to give atropine? ... Continue CPR.... Pulses with compressions... 0.4 mg of vasopresin..." The drone continued. Eric Redmond's bellowing voice dominated at first but was then crowded out by the authoritarian shouts of the cardiologists. Paul remained silent; there was little else he could add. Instead, he offered the femoral line sideport to the IV nurse infusing the volume of saline Dr. Witherspoon had ordered, and silently replayed the last words of the dying man in his mind, "It is a matter of life and death. Check the law library. Truth. God." There were other words too, vague and cryptic, something about searching for words: words from a doctor; words from a king. The implication was both mysterious and unsettling.

"I have a pulse!" The words came from the respiratory therapist at the head of the bed who was squeezing the bag valve mask with one hand while simultaneously feeling for a carotid pulse with the other.

Rick Witherspoon clamored for levophed, a drug reserved for people clinging to the edge of life, "If he's got any chance, we're going to have to get a balloon pump in him right now!"

A member of the Cath lab technologist team, standing at the door and watching the action, chimed in, "The Cath lab is ready Dr. Witherspoon."

With those words, the ER staff began to transition the resuscitative equipment for transport. A portable oxygen tank was placed on the bed along with a portable monitor/defibrillator while the bed was simultaneously pulled away from the wall. In seconds, the mob began propelling the gurney slowly toward the door of the examining suite and into the hall.

"Better get air-evac flying," Patel called back over his shoulder as he pushed the trailing IV pole.

Eric and Paul stood quietly in the hall as Patel, Witherspoon, and the entire cardiopulmonary/anesthesia/pharmacy/nursing entourage raced down the hall toward the cardiac catheterization lab. Burja had a pulse, a left bundle branch rhythm, and a blood pressure of 65 systolic on maximum dose levophed. The cardiologist's plan was to insert an emergency intraaortic balloon pump to hopefully stabilize him well enough and long enough for transport to the Med. He couldn't explain it, but Paul instinctively knew their efforts were for naught.

Eric broke the silence, "What do you think?"

This time Paul thought honesty might just be appropriate, "It doesn't look good."

Eric agreed and added, "I'm going to go to the cath lab and see if I can be of any assistance. Can you cover the ER?"

Paul said sure. He knew that Eric just wanted to be involved in a big case. This was sure to make the news, maybe even interviews on national outlets, and that was always where Eric wanted to be. As Eric Redmond smiled and started quickly walking off towards the cardiac catheterization suite, he turned and asked Paul, "Hey, do you mind writing the note? It's important that it be thorough."

"What a piece of work", Paul grumbled. Redmond was running off to the action and leaving the grunt work to him. Paul just nodded and turned back to the ER, now suddenly quieter and less crowded.

Tyler, Texas
1:08 am

"Team 1 is reporting in," Michael's announced to the team at Tyler Center. There was quiet in the CIA command post as Coombs and the others waited for the word, "Burja went into cardiac arrest but they were able to revive him."

"That won't last," Ward dryly added with a touch of cruel arrogance.

"What's his status now?" Coombs asked ignoring the crass remark.

"Unconscious and on his way to surgery," Michael's quickly answered.

"Are they sure Burja didn't pass on any information?"

"He apparently tried to. He was conscious throughout and very verbal, but there is no evidence that anyone could understand what he was saying. They had several people try to interpret but none could. The FBI interpreter apparently didn't make it on time."

"Speaking of interpreters, where's ours?"

"He just arrived," Gonzales interrupted directing Coombs' attention to him.

"Good. I want him to review all the hospital security footage we have. We need to know if Burja said anything he shouldn't have," Coombs emphatically ordered and then added, "This needs to be done carefully.

Make sure he destroys nothing and leaves nothing. FBI needs to think nothing has been touched."

Gonzales answered with his eyes and an almost imperceptible nod. He was fully aware of the stakes; Project Quest was a category 1 special access program demanding the highest level of secrecy and deniability and had authorization by the President to invoke covert action if necessary in order to accomplish its mission including unrestricted action within American borders, something the CIA was legally prohibited to do. Failure would cost them their careers and maybe their lives. Already, several men were dead and countless laws broken, and he was about to break another. He remembered having been told that things might get messy but after months of complacent operation, everything now seemed to be exploding at once. The best chance he had for personal survival was a quick resolution to the crisis. With any luck Abdullah Burja would soon be dead and his secret dead with him. He took a shallow breath and called in the interpreter.

XV

Memphis, Tennessee
1:13 am

Paul grabbed a pen and sat at the desk overlooking Trauma 2. The chart was open to the ER physician's encounter note. He began diligently jotting down the evening's events, but the words of the terrorist and his mysterious presentation careened through his mind on a runaway train of consciousness: What had just happened? The event was almost surreal. Why was my patient dying? Certainly not from a couple of relatively minor gunshot wounds. Was he poisoned? And what was that jibber he was babbling? It was almost as if he was trying to tell me something. Did a dying man pass me a secret? A secret of life and death? That's just what I need, another secret. Perhaps I really should go to the authorities. But could I afford to do that? Would they believe me? Maybe the better part of valor is to ignore it happened...

He tried to finish the note, but the words kept reverberating through him like the clang of a monastery chime. He moved on to documenting the physical exam but his mind kept wandering. The numbers combined with the instruction to look under legal archives seemed straight forward, he thought. After a moment's indecision, Paul's curiosity drove him from the comfort and safety of the emergency room. He abandoned the hospital chart, stood up from the desk, and walked past the receptionist and towards the doctor's lounge. No one seemed to notice.

The lounge was devoid of life. Everyone was standing at the desk or looking out the window at the police and the scores of reporters, paparazzi, and the casual curious amassing beyond them. The room was small in size compared with the main lounge two stories above. While it had a small television, a counter refrigerator and a nice sofa, it lacked the full buffet kitchen, desert bar, and big high-definition flat screen of the main retreat. It did, however, have a couple of personal computer workstations. Paul settled behind one of the computer kiosks and logged in generically. He recalled the numbers the terrorist was reciting: 126, 98, 100, 10 and immediately understood their significance. He took in a deep breath and began to type: http://126.98.100.10. Within seconds, the four-digit Internet Protocol or IP address, the number used for identifying and localizing any device on the Internet, found a server and located a web page.

Paul wasn't sure what he was expecting to find, but he halfway expected to see a "no network available" message or perhaps a governmental or referential website or maybe even a blog. He didn't expect to see the homepage of the International Poetry Society, a site dedicated to the "global interchange and development of modern poetry", or so the logo professed. Paul chuckled. This had to be a joke. Maybe he had heard the numbers wrong. He was about to close the browser when another pang of curiosity drove him to explore the website instead.

The page was professional, brightly colored, and ornately styled. He scanned the text. The left bar promoted coming poetry related events, competitions and seminars, the right bar listed several resources for the aspiring and professional poet alike, and the center frame showcased various works, poets, and their anthologies. As he was scanning the page and musing lightheartedly at the variety of poetic styles, a particular set of pieces caught his eye, not for its beauty, sophistication, or style but because he had heard it before – recently – paraphrased in Hausa: *The Quest* and *The Temple*.

The words in Hausa were disjointed and disorganized, but in English were poetic:

NELSON MANGIONE

The Quest

> It is words you seek,
> Magnificent and true
> From a note to a doctor,
> From an epistle to a king

He felt the shiver again. Suddenly, the ranting nonsense of the terrorist was becoming less nonsensically ranting. Juxtaposed with *The Quest* was another poem, the font and page positions identical, the subliminal message clear, both meant to stand together as a set:

The Temple

> Designed by the creator
> Like one in rome,
> Dedicated to an author
> Who never won a pulitzer,
> For his writing
> That changed the course of history,
> Commissioned by a man
> Who did the very same thing,
> Surrounded by gifts
> From a future mortal enemy,
> It is the southernmost point
> Of a recumbent cross,
> Whose center is a tribute
> To the father of us all.

Both *The Quest* and *The Temple* were clearly more than poems; they were puzzles, one directed to a form of content, the other specifically describing a place. If some of what the terrorist said was meaningful, then perhaps most if not all of it was too. He said, "look in the legal library". Perhaps the website had a legal library. He looked at the menu bar. The first thing that caught his eye was a language option box in the upper right hand corner. It was set to English, likely because that was the default language of the computer he was using. He clicked on the box and scanned the options: English, Spanish, French, German, Swiss, Portuguese, Chinese and Japanese, but also Arabic and – there it was – Hausa. Like in the childhood game, it was clearly the one that did not belong.

He selected Hausa and the page rapidly refreshed in identical style but with text entirely in Hausa. The translation was good but imperfect – clearly the effort of an automated translation program. He scrolled down to the poems. There the poems sat entirely as the dying man had recited them. What was the significance of all this? He reverted the language back to English and directed his efforts back to the home page. There was no reference to a library, but there was an "about" tab. He clicked on it. The submenus included a listing of offices. The main office was in Lucerne, Switzerland with satellites in New York City, Dubai, and Shanghai. He looked for the name of a president or director, but there was none. There was also nothing indicating a legal department or library.

Then it dawned on him. Sometimes legal disclosures are grouped with copyright notices and official matter at the bottom of the web page. He quickly scrolled to the bottom. There, at the very end, was a simple line in a small font:

Home - Mission - About - Legal - Copyright

Could this be what the dying man was talking about? He clicked on the Legal hyperlink, and a new page loaded. It still contained the logo of the International Poetry Society, but the page was more austere and official. It warned that access to the legal archives was restricted to library personnel. The page then asked for a user name and password followed by warning against unauthorized access and copyright infringement. Paul easily saw through the smoke. This was all a rouse – a smokescreen – to hide the true intention of the site. It asked for a user name and password. Paul knew exactly what was required:

User Name: Truth
Password: Allah

The poetry website vanished and was replaced with a security web portal that quickly downloaded an in-memory applet and started a secure web session with a service called The Mediator. Paul's initial gestalt was that he was looking at some sort of social networking site —and it was – of the most bizarre variety. The center panel was essentially a day planner listing names and locations of various drop points and parole exchanges, the sign/countersign used by agents to identify themselves to each other. Was he looking at some sort of "terrorist web site"? He scrolled down the list to today's date. There, with a Memphis location tag, was the name Abdullah Burja. He clicked on the name, and a new window opened to display a passport photograph of Paul's patient. The photo depicted an austere but vivid image of a man capable of terror in contrast to the anguished, pleading and broken man Paul had treated in the exam room only moments earlier. He read the dossier:

> Abdullah Burja. Born: November 18th, 1984; Birthplace: Sokoto, Nigeria; Citizenship: Nigeria; Domicile: Khartoum, Sudan; Member: Boko Harem sect; Associations: Mali al-Queda, al-Shabab Somalia. Implications: Lagos UN bombings, 2007, Niger kidnappings, 2011; Handler: Mahmud Hamza al-Sudani; Role: Courier

So that's who he was – a North African terrorist, but it was the last word that caught his eye: courier. What was he carrying? Information? He clicked on the name of the handler. Handler, Paul knew, was slang for an intelligence agent's contact or supervisor. It wasn't a word usually associated with a homicidal jihadist and hinted that Burja might be more than he appeared. A second later Mahmud Hamza's profile displayed on the screen:

> Mahmud Hamza. Alias: Abu Tariq al-Shuli, Ibrahim Abdullah al-Masri, Muhammad Musa Slahi Al-Shuli; Born: April 19th, 1975; Birthplace: Khartoum, Sudan; Associations: Egyptian Islamic jihad; Handler: Saif al-Adel.

STRONG EMERGENCE

Paul recognized al-Adel. He had recently viewed a documentary on the War on Terror. Al-Adel was a vicious terrorist that few Americans had ever heard of. He participated in the 1981 assassination of Egyptian President Anwar Al Sadat, the 1998 United States embassy bombings in Africa, and in the days following the death of Osama bin Ladin, Al-Adel was purported to be the acting leader of al Qaeda. Later, that honor was awarded to Ayman al-Zawahiri", bin Laden's lieutenant and spiritual advisor. But al-Adel remained a high-ranking member of al Queda. He clicked on al-Adel's name and was simultaneously confused and stunned. There was al-Adel's picture, similar to the one he had seen in the video. Next to his name was his personal information:

```
Saif al-Adel (Arabic: سيف العدل)
Birthplace: Cairo, Egypt. Birthdate: April
11, 1963.
Associations: Egyptian Islamic jihad, Majlis
al Shura of al-Qaeda
Domicile: Esfahan, Iran. Amadgah Street
```

Paul could not believe what he was reading. Adel was living in Iran?! The man indicted for embassy bombings in East Africa; a known member of the Majlis al Shura of al-Qaeda, a military and intelligence trainer of radical extremists in Afghanistan, Pakistan, Yemen, and Sudan; Al-Qaeda's likely second in command, and an FBI top ten most wanted was living on some street in Iran's third largest city! Wow!

Paul gathered himself and returned to the main page. He regained his bearings and relocated Burja's name on the parole list. The accompanying date was the day before yesterday, and a quick glance at the computer's clock told him it was well after midnight. The rendezvous point was listed as Escoses, Mexico and the parole phrase was in Hausa:

> Hello my friend. It's a beautiful day in Mexico.
> Welcome to Monterrey.

And the counter phrase was:

It's a great day for a drive.

His contact's name was Obi Hondora. He clicked on the name, but this time, the result was unexpected: fascinating but unexpected. Obi Hondora was CIA, and not just a low level drop agent; he was part of the Special Operations Group, the paramilitary arm of the special activities division of the CIA responsible for all means of covert combatant action throughout the world. Next to his picture was Obi's partner, a broad-jawed Caucasian male.

He quickly traced Obi's administrative tree. He worked out of someplace called "Tyler Center" under the command of Victor Coombs. He clicked on the Coombs hyperlink and the right side of the page expanded to reveal a list of names — names of not only American officials but also key members of British, French, and German authority. The list read like a Who's Who of Western government. He followed the chain of Coombs' command: to the Director CIA, to the Director of National Intelligence, to the...

Paul's was interrupted by the creek of the lounge door. He looked up to see Redmond walking in the door apparently oblivious to his presence. He had seen enough and immediately felt it best not to divulge what he had discovered. He hurriedly logged out, accessed administrative rights to the computer, and began to erase his tracks. Finishing, he peaked around the corner. Eric's eyes were turned away, focused on the televised news reports of a thwarted terrorist attempt in Memphis. The screen was split between a young reporter sternly broadcasting from just outside the hospital to live video from a helicopter circling over a shopping mall surrounded by dozens of emergency vehicles. Paul took the opportunity and slipped away from the computer and into the empty bathroom nearby. After a short interval, he stepped out with wet hands and a paper towel and addressed Eric directly, "Hey boss, I thought you went to the cath lab?"

Redmond looked away from the television slightly startled but quickly regained his composure.

Trying to remain cool and nonchalant, Paul continued his line of typical physician banter, "So what's the status of the terrorist? Did they get the pump in ok?"

"He's dead," Redmond declared without emotion but the news struck Paul squarely, "He coded again before we could even get him on the table. We worked on him for twenty minutes but couldn't get anything but an agonal rhythm. Patel just called it a little while ago."

The news impacted Paul like a nuclear bomb and the fallout of understanding began to rain down upon him. Abdullah was dead because he knew too much. And now, Paul realized, he did too.

XVI

1:18 am

Agent Gonzales was sitting in one of the small, dank offices outside of the Tyler command center and had just finished briefing the interpreter on the station chief's orders when the harried call came in to him over his secure Bluetooth, "Gonzales, I need you back at your station!" The voice was David Michaels' but he wasn't his usual subtly conceited and overtly self-serving self. The mystery was quickly solved. "We have another Mediator breach!"

"Have you started a trace?" Gonzales immediately began diagnosing.

"Affirmative. Initial localization is East Memphis. I need you here quick!"

The conference room the CEO had selected was perfect. It wasn't overly big, but it was right next to the emergency room. It had a round desk suitable for conducting a small meeting, a workspace with secure Ethernet and landline telephone connections, and plenty of electrical outlets. It had been a long time since Phillip Oxmore had tried to setup a command post singlehanded, and he was making slow progress. He had just assembled his local secure network hardware and was booting his laptop when he was interrupted by Tanya Marone, the ER director he had met earlier. She knocked gently on the door and somewhat cannily poked her body through.

"Come in," Oxmore politely offered.

"I'm sorry to interrupt you, but I have some bad news," Marone solemnly reported and then with genuine consolation proceeded, "Your suspect has died."

Outwardly he made sure to suppress any emotion but in his mind he screamed "Damn" with his loudest inner voice. He had really wanted to interrogate the bastard. Circumstances surrounding the evening were bizarre at best, and he was hoping for answers, but now Burja was dead. Flatly he managed a "Thank you." Tanya nodded in acknowledgement and was about to extricate herself when Phillip suddenly remembered something, "By the way, did you ever manage to find someone who could understand him, get a story from him – next of kin – anything?"

"No," but then Tanya followed with a morsel Phillip could seize upon, "But one of our doctors recognized the language he was speaking. It's called Hausa."

"Never heard of it."

"Me neither. I guess you know it only if you speak it in your Hausa."

She giggled at her own silly joke. Sophomoric, dry, and often inappropriate humor was Phillip's trademark, and he couldn't help but crack a grin. Tanya smiled back.

"Thank you," Phillip obliged himself. For a split second, he admired her form. In the dim light, she was quite pretty.

"I will let you know when the other agents arrive," Tanya added breaking the spell.

"That would be great." Phillip watched as she closed the door behind her. The hour was late. He sighed deeply wondering if he would think she still looked good in the morning. Given the investigation that was about to follow and the amount of paperwork he was looking at, he groaned at the reality that he was probably going to find out.

His contemplation was once again interrupted by the bells of his cell phone. It was Agent Stone.

"Hey, boss. Are you private?" Stone started before Oxmore had a chance to say a word.

"Go ahead."

"No news yet on the hard drive. We've scoured the mall and looked at all the available film. So far not a damn thing."

"And the boy?"

"CSI has finished processing the scene and the body's on its way to County."

Phil had known Tedder long enough to read between the lines: The mall was a bust.

"OK," Oxmore resigned, "Leave Chunn in charge and have him coordinate the clean up. Then come to the hospital. I need your help here."

1:38 am

Earlier, Victor Coombs had stepped out of the command center to greet his interpreter, Richard Hunt, a Cambridge-educated linguaphile he trusted and had worked with for years. Afterwards, he had retreated to his private, ultra-secure office to make an off-book phone call, but now he was back at the Tyler Center helm demanding a full report.

"Breach lasted 9 minutes and 12 seconds from 1:16 am to 1:25 am," Gonzales began, "Localized to the Baptist Hospital intranet web proxy."

"Baptist Hospital? Are you sure?" Coombs asked incredulously.

"Yes sir. With certainty," Gonzales sternly confirmed.

"Could it have been Burja?"

"No, he died while the connection was still open," Michaels interjected.

Coombs' frustration began to mount again as he scratched his neck and disgustedly commented, "The bastard somehow got a message off to someone." Once again, victory danced just out of reach like a teasing seductress, but he quelled his anger and quickly refocused, "Do we have a lead?"

"Unfortunately, the web proxy provides some anonymity," Gonzales informed.

Coombs' chagrin was palpable, and he grimaced as his mind concluded its assessment and course of action, "We have a much bigger problem here, gentleman. We are going to need more boots on the ground; we're going to need to tunnel into hospital security – and we are going to need covert FBI interface – and we are going to need it now!"

"Yes sir," the three of them said almost simultaneously.

Within a few seconds of Marone's departure, Oxmore was on the phone. The operator answered on the second ring and quickly patched him into hospital security. Scaglione answered and cooperatively agreed to begin pulling up Emergency Room security video footage for review. Phillip had just hung up when another knock on the door startled him. He half-hoped to see Tanya's smile again, but this time it was his assistant Amy Peacock walking in followed by a tall, lithe, stylish black woman.

"There you are," Amy declared, "They said you were in a conference room, and the door says 'Staff Lounge'."

Oxmore looked up. He was tired and was not interested in her vapid excuses. He needed help. "Where the hell is everybody?"

"In route. They should all be here shortly," She answered. It was obvious he was not in the mood for levity, so she went right to work. "I have someone I want you to meet," she continued, "This is Doctor Alesha Deng, Professor of Afro-American Studies at the University of Memphis. She is an African language specialist. She's also BAU-1." Weikert was referring to Behavior Analysis Unit 1, the team from the National Center for the Analysis of Violent Crime tasked with analyzing and assessing terrorism threats from a behavior-based perspective, "She's part of the African Counterterrorism Rapid Response Group."

Phillip stood up and walked straight to the imposing dark-skinned beauty. With a broad smile and an outstretched hand, he introduced himself, and after dispensing with a polite introduction, he proceeded to ask the only question that mattered, "Do you speak Hausa?"

Paul excused himself from the doctor's lounge and a depressed Redmond; word had already come down from administration: No Interviews. But Paul felt no better. He wasn't melancholy but instead stewed in a mixture of confusion and amazement. He now had a name for his patient: Abdullah Burja. He felt the little yellow warning light blink in the back of his mind: This was too crazy. And it was potentially dangerous. He needed to stay out of it.

He somehow managed to imperceptibly stagger his way back to the nursing station. Along the way, he concluded a simple solution: Ignore everything, get back to work, and keep the nose to the grindstone. He had used this technique many times before with success. It would work again.

Oxmore, Weikert, and Deng huddled around Oxmore's newly configured workstation as security feed from the ER cameras began streaming in from the security office. The images were slightly grainy but more than adequate to see faces and gestures, but the audio was more disappointing. Not only was the sound quality poor but the overlapping chatter and multiple concurrent conversations made discerning individual voices difficult. Fortunately, their subject was speaking a different language.

"It's not a middle eastern language. It's definitely African and could be Hausan," Deng quickly determined but then frowned, clearly uncertain of what she was hearing. The scene was graphic. On the gurney, a black muscular man writhed in pain as a cadre of swarming nurses removed his clothing, attached ECG leads, and began to insert IVs into his arms. A doctor at the head of the bed was clearly directing the team and simultaneously tending to the dripping shoulder wound while another physician was performing some kind of surgery on the man's upper leg.

Deng was becoming progressively pessimistic when, suddenly, the patient sat suddenly up on the stretcher and screamed a clear phrase, "Ya na da maganar rai da mutuwa!"

"There you go," the interpreter cheered, "That's definitely Hausa!"

"What did he say?" Weikert was anxious to know.

"He said 'It's a matter of life and death'."

"It's a matter of life and death?" Amy echoed quizzically.

"Alesha, can you make out anything else?" Phillip redirected.

"Something about 'Understanding'. He's asking if anyone understands him," Deng answered but then her triumphant smile began to wither.

"Anything else?" Oxmore pressed.

Alesha Deng was momentarily silent. "He's muttering now. It's hard to make out what he's saying." Burja's words were obscured by the loud commands and bustle of the trauma team. "Maybe if we could clean up the audio," she posited.

"We will definitely do that," Oxmore offered, "But for right now, anything that you can give us maybe very helpful."

The professor refocused. "I think he's praying. Or maybe reciting something. I'm not sure," she started.

"Can you make out any more content?" this time it was Amy that pressed. Alesha did her due diligence and listened intently, trying to hone in on Burja's voice while excluding the others. What she heard sounded nonsensical.

"I'm hearing something about doctors and kings and now he's reciting numbers!" Deng reported somewhat grudgingly. She knew that answer would be of no help.

"I've got some good news!" Fernando Gonzales exclaimed suddenly. The surprise almost jarred the coffee cup Coombs was sipping into his teeth, but he didn't care. He needed some good news.

"What do you got?" Coombs felt Gonzales' excitement and wanted to magnify it. He could tell his team was getting tired, and so was he.

"We've localized the computer responsible for the breach. It's a generic account in the ER doctors lounge!" Gonzales enthusiastically reported.

"Good work!" Coombs responded, already calculating the possibilities.

"He must have communicated with someone in that emergency room – someone with access to the doctor's lounge and the hospital computing system. That can't be too many people."

"No, it can't be." The room quieted with Coombs' deadpan directive, "So let's go find the son-of-a-bitch!"

XVII

1:50 am

"Dr. Gudrun, have you finished the John Doe's chart?" The question jarred Paul to his senses. He looked up to see the ward clerk holding up Burja's unfinished paperwork. Without a word, Paul placed the clipboard he had in his hand back in the chart rack and sheepishly walked up to her.

"Sorry 'bout that." he pouted with a grin. He took the papers from her and sat back down to finish his note. He continued where he had left off, but his mind had different ideas. What exactly was that website he was viewing? It clearly had advanced security. Could it have been a hoax or some kind of game? That was not out of the question but seemed unlikely given the site sophistication and the dead terrorist in the cath lab. No, it definitely seemed to be some form of clandestine communication tool, and based on the limited glimpse he had acquired, a communication tool between the West and the Arab world. Was this some sort of 21st century Hot Line? Paul wasn't sure that was it either. The Hot Line was something created in the hopes of it never being used. What he saw was a vibrant, active interface for the coordination of exchange.

But "exchange of what?" was the real nagging question. For that Paul had no answer.

The two FBI agents and the interpreter poured over the video, running it back and forth, trying to glean anything more than they already knew. Abdullah Burja rolled into the ER just before midnight, writhing and yelling, in what Professor Deng now revealed was a passionate plea for understanding followed by praises to God and what seemed to be prayer. He said nothing threatening and nothing 'terrorist like'. There was no tirade of jihadist condemnation or religious entreaty. There was no declaration of innocence or demands for justice. There was no revelation of plot or admission of guilt. Even more disappointing, there was nothing about a hard drive or money or anything else relating to the bank heist, the mall takeover, or the dead store clerk. All they had was a bleeding, dying man murmuring chants filled with numbers and nonsensical phrases in a room full of health care workers working hard to save his life. There was no overt evidence of foul play yet it was clear the doctors could not understand why the man was dying. Intel had received warning of a credible threat to the terrorist's life and the three naturally turned to the possibility of assassination, but the questions just seemed to mount up: If he was killed, why? If he was killed, how? Unfortunately, the room was full of people with the expertise to pull off a killing, and he had received multiple injections and IVs. With that line of investigation exhausted, they began to review who in the group might have been an associate of Burja. The sonographer looked Indian. Could she have been Pakistani? Several of the nurses and a respiratory therapist were black. Could one have been African? They were getting nowhere fast, and the room had fallen silent as footage played over once again for the countless time. Then Amy suddenly saw something the others had missed.

"Hey, did you see that?" Weikert asked knowing full well the others hadn't.

"What?" Oxmore's ears perked up.

"Alesha, did you say Burja is saying 'understand me' here where he sits up and looks at this doctor," Weikert continued.

"Yea, and?"

"Look at the doctor!" Amy explained, "He looks at Burja just before Burja's outburst." Weikert took control of the computer and rewound the video slightly. "Look, the doctor looks at him right after he says 'Ya na maga....whatever....'"

"Ya na da maganar rai da mutuwa!" Alisha corrected.

"It's a matter of life and death," Oxmore looked uninterested and ambivalent but he was listening to every word.

Just then, the conversation was interrupted by Oxmore's cell phone. It was director Taylor.

Oxmore answered with a curt but venerable salutation. He respected Brent as both a wise boss and a trusted friend. Oxmore excused himself and turned away to take the call privately.

"I heard the suspect died?" Taylor began.

"Yes sir. We had no opportunity to interrogate him and so far we have been unable to recover the hard drive. We're combing through the hospital security footage now but so far nothing." Phillip chose not to share their new found suspicions of one of the doctors. The surmise was much too premature.

Taylor continued, "Top brass is highly concerned about this. They believe Burja was involved with something big – perhaps 9/11 scope or maybe even bigger. There is almost universal consensus that he was assassinated."

"Really? Should I order an autopsy?"

"Don't bother. It doesn't matter how he died. All that matters is who killed him. Figure that out and we'll know more than we do now."

"Still, an autopsy might help..."

"I've already ordered a forensic autopsy. If he swallowed that hard drive or shoved it up his ass, we're going to find it!"

Oxmore stayed silent. He wasn't quite sure how to respond to that. Mercifully, Taylor kept talking, "They should be there within the hour. In the meantime, I'd like you to start interviewing the staff. Find out what you can. Interview everyone. Start with the doctors."

STRONG EMERGENCE

Oxmore felt a shiver run down his spine, "Why the doctors?"

"Why not the doctors?"

Oxmore wasn't sure quite how to respond to that either. Taylor's tone was harsh – almost condescending – definitely atypical. Once again, he kept quiet. The order to interview the staff was reasonable but to begin with the physicians was almost too coincidental. It was almost as if... His mind halted mid-sentence. He wasn't going to give in to fatigue-born nonsense. He shrugged and then finally responded with a simple "yes, sir" almost not hearing the Director requesting to be kept informed and then hanging up.

◆

2:11 am

The coffee in the ER nurse's kitchen was rancid, but Paul welcomed the treat. Although, he had decided earlier to set the matter aside and get back to work, rumors were circulating that the FBI might want to talk to the staff. He wasn't quite sure what to make of the news and was struggling with how much information to divulge if asked. He figured a cup of Joe might clear his mind.

Frankly, Paul expected the FBI to have an interest in him. He was at the bedside and was witness to everything, at least until Burja was wheeled off. They would be interested in his opinion of why he died. Frankly, so was he. In fact, his mind had not stopped swirling with the facts: Abdullah Burja, an apparent Nigerian terrorist, had apparently robbed a bank, eluded escape, suffered injuries in his capture and ultimately died from the wounds. There was no evidence of foul play, but his wounds were not fatal. Then why did he die? Before he was shot, he was running through the mall. Wasn't that was the paramedic said? How could he be running anywhere with a heart that weak? And why wasn't he in pulmonary edema if his illness was due to an acute insult. But then again, if his demise was due to a sudden deterioration of a chronic process, then there should have been evidence of that. There wasn't. The only explanation was a process that would cause severe myocardial dysfunction accompanied by profound venodilitation that would defend, at least in the short term, pulmonary edema. This theory fit the facts and explained the dropping blood pressure. Unfortunately, no natural process did that; the conclusion was inescapable.

Paul stepped out of the kitchen and found an emergency room abuzz with nervous energy. There were only a few patients waiting to be seen, but there seemed to be an out-of-the-ordinary anxiety in the air.

"What's up?" Paul asked.

The plain-faced nurse spoke up, "Mr. Caruthers was just here. He told us the FBI wants to interview each of us. He ordered us to cooperate fully. Dr. Redmond volunteered to go first."

A respiratory tech chimed in, "They think this guy was part of some sleeper cell that was about to pull off something big. They want to find out if anyone saw or heard anything."

Paul was only half listening as he watched an obvious FBI agent escort Redmond into the conference room. The nurse and the technologists recounted the event to themselves while other nurses anxiously and intently listened as if learning fresh, juicy, gossip. Every few minutes or so, one or the other looked back to Paul for confirmation but Paul was only partially engaged. If the terrorist was killed, who killed him? How was it done? Clearly it was some novel poison, but why? Was he killed to prevent him from reciting that poem? Was he really a modern day man who knew too much? His stream of consciousness was interrupted by Tanya Marone, who had walked up to him unnoticed.

"Dr. Gudrun. The FBI has requested you next."

Paul nodded subtly in acknowledgment. He had already decided to simply tell the truth. If asked, he would answer.

2:26 am

Victor left the command center again leaving Michaels in charge. Gonzales successfully penetrated the hospital firewall and piggybacked into the FBI-Security interface; Wade tracked the suspect hardware, and Brandon

Hunt, the Cambridge interpreter, reviewed the security video footage and the FBI assessments.

"So what do we know?" Michaels asked of the three huddled up in the back of the command center.

Wade was first to speak. "We have identified the access machine. It's a Dell workstation in the ER doctor's lounge – one of only two. We remoted in, but the device has been swept clean."

"But we do have good news," Gonzalez interjected, "The lounge is apparently restricted to physicians, nurse practitioners, and physician assistants. There were only four physicians who were involved in the case. No NPs or PAs were present, and only one other practitioner was even on duty during the time of the breach."

"That doesn't matter," the interpreter interrupted, "We know who Burja communicated with."

Michaels, Gonzales and Wade all stared quietly at Hunt. It was Wade who recovered first from the stunning pronouncement, "Who?"

"The ER doctor at the foot of the bed."

2:40 am

Paul stood outside the conference room turned FBI command post and watched as Redmond exited and walked right past him.

"Piece of cake," Redmond gloated, "They just want to know what happened."

A voice from inside the room called Paul's name. He turned and began to walk toward the room door, convicted in his decision to reveal everything if necessary. Just as he was about to enter, a second agent guarding the interior of the room caught his eye. He felt his spine chill again as his little brain warning light switched from a blinking yellow to a violently flashing bright red. He had seen his face before – from the website – the man next to Obi Hondora. Robert was his name; he recalled. Robert "Bob" McCammon.

XVIII

2:41 am

Phillip turned to Tedder as Redmond walked out the door. "What do you think?" he asked.

"He's an arrogant ass. He knows nothing but he will fall over backwards to do anything we ask him to," Agent Tedder Stone's response rolled off his tongue.

Oxmore nodded in agreement. He was about to pick up the dossier on their next interviewee when he saw Deng and Weikert entering the conference room through the back door.

"Can we have a moment with you privately, sir?" Amy was more formal than usual; coworkers and MPD SWAT were in the room.

"Be quick," Oxmore tersely obliged. The four of them stepped out into the hall with Stone guarding the door keeping an ear on the conversation and an eye on the room.

"OK," Phillip's impatience was subtle but evident.

"We optimized the audio as much as we're going to be able to," Weikert began.

"And?"

"He is reciting something about seeking words that are great, from a letter to a physician and from a letter to a king. We're not quite sure what to make of that yet. But then he starts reciting some numbers."

"I remember you mentioned that. Can you make them out?"

"He is reciting a string of discrete numbers, not one long number... Then he's basically whispering. There is not much else audible."

"I don't see the significance of any of this," Oxmore responded.

Then Weikert added, "We didn't either. So we entered the numbers into Google and got nothing. But then I decided to try the FBI cyber database."

"It's late. We have a crowd to interview. Cut to the chase," Oxmore's impatience was now palpable.

"It's a website! The International Poetry Society!"

"What?" Oxmore didn't understand.

"That's what we said!" For some reason, Weikert sounded almost giddy.

Stone was only half listening to the conversation when he noticed a dark-red headed, medium build doctor entering the conference room. Without regard for their confused blabbering, he interrupted the three of them, "The next one just came in."

Paul walked into the room and sat at the conference table. A stenographer was seated to his left and next to her was a video camera that seemed to be recording. She was a pleasant, grandmotherly type who informed Paul that Agent Oxmore and his staff would be with him in a moment. The officer Paul saw at the door stood quietly behind them. Paul gambled and stole a glance at him, offering a sheepish grin in the process. It definitely was McCammon. He was dressed in Memphis police SWAT gear but seemed out of place. Paul saw through the smoke immediately: he wasn't MPD and this interview was about much more than just a debriefing. His conclusion was inescapable. Somehow they knew he was the one who accessed the database. This changed everything; the truth would not be forthcoming now.

Oxmore and Stone quietly walked in and sat at the conference table across from Paul. Weikert and Deng were both about to excuse themselves when Amy suddenly recognized Paul as the doctor in the video. She quickly motioned to Dr. Deng to stay in the room, and the two of them quietly took observation positions against the far wall.

Stone began the interview, "My name is Agent Tedder Stone, and this is Agent Phil Oxmore, both of the Memphis FBI office. Thank you for agreeing to speak to us." Paul nodded, and Stone continued, "This is not a formal investigation, you are not a suspect, and there is no alleged crime. The purpose of this meeting is to obtain a better understanding of the circumstances surrounding tonight's event and to determine whether or not a breach of national security occurred or whether a threat to homeland security remains. You may have heard that your patient tonight was a dangerous terrorist. What you heard was correct. His name was Abdullah Burja. He was a high-ranking member of al-Qaeda, and we believe ..."

Paul was barely listening. This was all bullshit, but he nodded in deference and tried to appear anxious and concerned.

"... The entire conversation is being recorded by transcription as well as video recording. Do you have any problem with that?"

"No."

"Then let's begin. Can you state your name?"

"Doctor Paul Gudrun."

"Address?"

"400 Broadmore Court, suite 210, Germantown."

"Date of birth?"

"August 1st, 1979"

"Can you provide a quick biography?"

"What's to say? I was born in Memphis and lived my whole life in west Tennessee except for college in Arkansas. I went to UT Memphis for both medical school and residency, and I've been here ever since." He went on in detail answering a battery of questions about his family, his first appointment and subsequent career moves, and his latest opportunity at Baptist. The line of inquiry then changed to a chronology of the night's events.

"What were you doing when Mr. Burja arrived?" Oxmore asked. He and Stone were tag-teaming the questions.

The following ten minutes were filled with droll and mundane questions regarding the details of where he was, what he saw, what he did, what he heard, and what he suspected or may have surmised. Paul recognized the line of questioning was merely a technique to magnify fatigue and induce complacency. He kept his guard up and was prepared when the meaty questions finally arose.

"Now if I may take a different line of questioning that may seem strange but I assure you this is necessary." Now it was Oxmore asking the questions. "Did you personally know Abdullah Burja?"

"Of course not!" Paul did not need to act surprised for that one.

"Do you speak Hausa?"

"What's that?" Paul was now wide awake. The lions were no longer circling. They were looking to pounce.

"Did Abdullah Burja give you anything?"

"Like what?"

"Papers, notes, money, a computer disk, a thumb drive, anything?"

Paul nodded in the negative, "No."

"Ok, Dr. Gudrun. Thank you for your time." Paul pushed his chair back and began to rise. "One last question though before you leave," Phillip lingered for a moment before asking, "Are you familiar with the International Poetry Society?"

Fortunately, Paul was expecting this question from the beginning. "Never heard of it," he abruptly answered then inquired, "Is that all?"

There was a moment of awkward silence that Stone quickly filled, "No. That's it." Paul was not going to belabor the separation nor give them an easy opportunity to ask any more questions. He quickly stood tall, turned and walked out the door.

Oxmore, Stone and the team took a brief coffee break. "That's the doctor from the video earlier," Weikert whispered.

"Yes, we know!" Stone jabbed. He didn't have many opportunities to trump Amy, but Phil was all business, "So what do you think?" he asked.

"I'm not sure. My gut says he's lying."

"I agree. I think he is too." The words came from Jim Neighbors, who had just walked in behind them. Jim headed up the Memphis office cybercrime unit and was Oxmore's chief investigator. His knack for sniffing out the truth was unmatchable. Jim had suffered every Gomer Pyle joke imaginable in his 34 years of life but was one of Oxmore's most valuable players. Twice he had been offered promotions to the national security branch, but each time he refused to avoid relocating his family. He was the most decorated member of the Memphis team and had more honors and awards than anyone else in the office including Oxmore himself. He had a whopping 42 cybercrime arrests to his name, had directly infiltrated and disrupted 3 different terrorist cell networks, and had directly and almost single-handedly exposed a WMD plot on American soil that could have taken tens of thousands of innocent lives. That plot never made the headlines but earned Neighbors his highest honor: the President's Award for Distinguished Federal Civilian Service. He opened up his iPad and pulled up the Emergency Room security camera footage while simultaneously talking, "I've reviewed the audio and the video, and I've had a chance to talk to the interpreter."

"You have my attention," Oxmore was not patronizing.

"I'm fairly sure that the ER physician you just interviewed was the contact."

Jim's convicted statement surprised Oxmore, "Why?"

Neighbors pointed to the screen, "When everyone else is busy doing something, he is glancing at the subject frequently." He then quickly advanced the video, "And then here, when he's whispering, he's looking straight at him. Do you see this glance when the subject says 'do you understand me?' And then again here…" Jim kept scrolling through example after example, "And then here…" After a few more clips, he clicked off the tablet and directed his attention to his boss, "Those are definite tells – no doubt about it."

"So, Dr. Gudrun is lying when he says he doesn't understand Hausa?" Phillip clarified.

"My guess is that he understands every word."

Police officers directed Paul away from the conference room as several staff members corralled him, pelting him with a barrage of questions. One of the faces was Rick Witherspoon who nervously smiled at him. Paul responded in kind. The questions flew around him from all sides: What did they want? What questions did they ask? He answered simply and honestly while secretly questioning himself in his mind's voice: Did they believe him? He wasn't in custody. Was that a good sign? He excused himself and walked back to the ER where Redmond and his harem of nurses were holding court.

"Hey, Paul. How did it go?" Redmond asked with a playfully arrogant smirk on his face.

"No sweat," Paul lied but his fatigue was fairly obvious.

The ER Director took an uncharacteristic modicum of pity on Dr. Gudrun and offered him a quick break. Paul decided to take him up on the offer and stepped outside the quiet-for-a-moment ambulance entrance. With Burja dead, the reporters had all gone home and so had most of the police. Only a few blue and whites and one SWAT humvee remained. He reflected on the evening's events in the crisp night air and felt himself tremble. Was he shivering or was this something more? Was Burja really killed? Was his life in danger too? He looked at his watch: 3:20 am. His shift was over at nine – not a moment too soon. He reaffirmed the futility of worry and resolved to let events naturally evolve. Perhaps work therapy would be good. He took a deep breath and walked back inside.

At Tyler Center, the voiceovers from the interview with Dr. Paul Gudrun had been intercepted and processed, and the five of them were huddled up in the dimly lit and cramped room to discuss their findings. The interpreter stacked the transcription printout together and then handed it to Coombs who quickly read through it.

"So, he denies knowing Burja or anything he's saying," Coombs summarized.

"He's lying," the interpreter finished.

Coombs agreed, "But the question is why. Who is this guy? We've already determined he's not ours right?" Wade nodded in the affirmative as Coombs kept talking, "Then whose is he?" The room fell eerily silent. Victor filled the void, "I want a full BI on him – and I want it now!" BI referred to 'background investigation', the systematic and comprehensive discovery and analysis of an individual's personal history. Paul Gudrun had spent the majority of his life trying to sustain a low profile and avoid scrutiny. Now the full resources of the United States Intelligence Services were about to test him.

XIX

3:32 am

Paul gazed at the threat board: the list of patients awaiting care in the emergency room, their room number, whether or not they have been seen by a physician yet, and a brief one to four word description of their problem. After the early evening excitement had waned, the emergency room was back to business as usual with a twenty minute queue in the waiting room. It never ceased to amaze him how there always seems to be more people in the ER at four in the morning than at four in the afternoon.

The electronic medical record had not yet found itself to the Baptist ER, a fact Gudrun found refreshingly quaint. He pulled a paper chart and walked in to see an older man, a regular, "frequent flier", alcoholic who has had a plethora of medical problems, including endocarditis from severe dental caries, cirrhosis complicated by bleeding varices, and tobacco abuse that left his skin thick and cracked. Today he had conjunctivitis. He treated the patient, but the memories of the night's events intruded: the web page, the incredulous possibility of a secret pact de detente between Al-Qaeda and the West that ascended to the highest echelons of government, the possible assassination of an alleged terrorist, and the concern that his curiosity might have exposed him. He dismissed the thought. Idle speculation and wanton worry were valueless. No one had arrested him. That had to be a positive. He took a deep breath and refocused. The best thing he could do to diffuse suspicion was to get to work. For some reason though, he couldn't shake a nagging question: Just what was Burja trying to tell him?

Victor Coombs was back in the control room hovering over Gonzales and Michaels. If this doctor really was their man, he wanted him taken out sooner rather than later. But there was still a problem; there were too many unanswered questions. His musings were mercifully interrupted by his IT chief.

"The chatter is very encouraging," Gonzales blurted out breaking the silence, "it looks like FBI now suspects Gudrun too."

"Excellent," Coombs replied, "Leak out that Burja was killed with a topical cardiotoxin."

"Sir?" the request surprised Gonzalez. Revealing agency tradecraft was not something routinely done.

Coombs' eyes answered the challenge.

"Yes sir," Gonzales acquiesced and diligently began typing on his keyboard.

"Sir, I have an incoming call for you. It's Langly again," Michaels interrupted, and without waiting for an order, put the Director of CIA through to Coombs' earpiece.

"Victor. It's Drew."

"Yes sir."

"We've looked at this guy, Paul Gudrun. He seems to be pretty clean. Are you sure he's the one?"

"He's our best and only lead at this point," Coombs explained, "And now FBI is looking into him too."

"Squeeze him then and see what you get."

"Just how do we go about doing that?"

"There is a deep asset already inside at the hospital – a sleeper."

Coombs was genuinely surprised, "Really?"

"Her handle is Marti Gras. She was installed years ago by my predecessor for reasons I don't know, but I think she may be able to get very close to him."

"Ok," Coombs really had no other response to the revelation but was pleased and certainly willing to take advantage of it, "Can you activate her?"

"I've already assigned you as her case officer. I'm sending her codes to you now. Keep me informed." With that command, the Director hung up leaving the control center once again in complete silence.

Paul walked out of ER room 7 and quickly scribbled a note: 68 year old, severe cirrhosis secondary to alcohol and hepatitis C, purulent conjunctival discharge, oculus sinister, multiple prostitution contacts, queening-type cunnilingus behavior, probable gonococcal conjunctivitis, gentamicin ophthalmic solution ordered. After quickly treating a young kid with swimmer's ear, he walked into the next room to see a woman experiencing severe abdominal pain. He assessed the patient while simultaneously thinking about the poem: *The Quest*. Perhaps he was going about this all wrong. Maybe he was meant to hear that message. Maybe he was meant to decipher it. He used his cell phone browser to make a quick keyword search, but it only took him a second to realize the futility of the method. This was a puzzle; one that was going to require brilliance to solve.

4:06 am

Oxmore's phone rang. It was Deputy Director Brent Taylor again. "Are you secure?" The question only regarded the privacy of their surroundings. Their phone systems enjoyed NSA grade telecommunication encryption technology ensuring the digital safety of their conversation.

"Yes sir," Oxmore looked over his shoulder as he issued his assessment.

"Burja was assassinated," Taylor dryly informed him.

Oxmore was incredulous. He had been looking for a contact, a brush agent that Burja may have somehow passed the information he stole to. He wasn't looking for a killer.

Taylor explained, "We have been in contact with NSA and the NTTF," referring to the National Security Agency and the National Terrorism Task Force, two agencies responsible for monitoring communications and countering terrorism respectively. "Burja was killed by a potent cardiotoxin. Somehow, he infiltrated a secure network zone inside the Federal Reserve and hacked into the NSA subnet. NTTF believes his intent was not terrorism but theft and transfer of highly classified information to an unknown operative. The robbery was just a cover up."

Oxmore completed the paragraph, "And Burja might have been killed to conceal his contact."

"Exactly."

The information wasn't surprising. His team had already deduced much of it. The Deputy Director was only providing confirmation. Still, he remained uneasy.

"Do you have any idea who the killer-contact might be?" Taylor questioned.

"Dozen's of people: SWAT, EMS, hospital personnel. Hell, Burja might have poisoned himself!"

"That's not what I asked," Taylor had a knack for drilling through the flack.

"We do have one lead," Oxmore finally confessed, "His name is Paul Gudrun. He's one of the emergency room doctors who took care of Burja when he first came in. We think he may have been at least one of the contacts. There may have been more."

"I don't think I need to tell you to make this investigation your highest priority, Phil. Use whatever agency and local law enforcement means necessary to sort this out ASAP."

Taylor's voice was pressured. Oxmore understood and with a "Yes sir" hung up the phone.

The woman was a middle aged, obese, hirsute Hispanic woman. Her abdomen was distended, and she was clearly in pain. Dr. Gudrun quickly determined epigastric and right upper quadrant tenderness, diminished bowel sounds, and diagnosed probable cholecystitis. Simultaneously he convinced himself to embrace the revelation of the poem's meaning: It's more than just a poem; it's a puzzle, but what does it mean? What's the solution? The answer lies in words, but what kinds of words: a book, an essay, another poem perhaps, a lyric or catch phrase like smile, you're on candid camera or life's a bitch? Or maybe it referred to a reference: a dictionary or encyclopedia or body of law. Didn't Abdullah say something about look under legal archives? Or do words refer to something religious like the word of God? Perhaps words refer to an opus of religious writings like the Bible or the Koran or the Apocrypha. Certainly those texts would all be considered magnificent and stirring.

Paul ordered a CT scan, blood work, and an abdominal ultrasound, jotting his note as he went. He glided into another room, pulling the chart off of the wall rack. A young boy had injured his wrist falling out of bed, and his mother was frantic. He examined the boy, determined a hairline fracture in the scaphoid and decided he needed a wrist splint. His mother asked if her son was going to get an X-ray. Paul explained that it was unnecessary, but the mother insisted. He strolled out and wrote: healthy 8 year old, probable hairline fracture, left scaphoid. Neurotic mother. X-ray left wrist.

4:49 am

Oxmore assembled his team in the small staff lounge turned mobile command center. Around him sat Stone, Weikert, Deng, and Neighbors.

"I've just gotten off the phone with the Deputy Director," Oxmore started.

"And?" Stone impatiently asked.

"Abdullah Burja may have been assassinated."

"One less terrorist," Stone commented with a smirk and based on body language, the rest of the group seemed to agree.

"Yes, but unfortunately, he was in possession of sensitive information that he may have passed on before he died," Oxmore retorted, "Our last witness, Dr. Paul Gudrun, is now a formal person of interest."

"Really?" Now it was Weikert who was chiming in?

"Yes, that's straight from the Director," Oxmore confirmed and then added, "I want to set up a monitoring command post in security. We are going to track this guy's every move. I'm not quite sure what his game is yet, but we need to figure it out." Oxmore turned to Chunn, "We are going to need MPD support too."

"You've got it," Chunn enthusiastically offered, "I've arranged for Lieutenant McCammon to supervise internal security, and I have an additional unit in route to fortify the perimeter. Right now, all of the media attention is on the mall. That should help."

Oxmore turned his attention back to Stone, "We are getting a DOJ order to wiretap his cell phone. In the meantime, we need to track any calls that he makes, and find as much as we can about him: demographics, friends, family, hobbies, interests … the works. Let's go." With that final charge, the meeting ended, and the purposed scurrying began.

5:02 am

Dr. Gudrun's next patient was a beautiful young woman complaining of pain in her chest, specifically her right breast. She was wearing a gown that opened in front and proceeded to explain to the doctor that she awoke with pain after she had been partying all night with her girlfriends. She opened the gown, exposed herself and pointed to a spot in her right breast, near her areola. She was stunningly gorgeous; her full breasts sat tenderly on her petite frame with an almost imperceptible natural sag. Dr. Gudrun didn't notice. He inspected her skin from multiple angles looking for a zone of discoloration, but his mind was processing: from a note to a doctor, not a doctor's note, and what kind of note, a letter, a clinical note, a musical note? And what kind of doctor? – A physician, a PhD, a chiropractor, a homeopath, a witch doctor, a love doctor?

Paul asked her to recline and then lightly passed his fingertips over the surface of her soft, smooth, skin feeling for the 'onion skinning' alterations in the surface texture characteristic of certain breast cancers. All the while, his mind was parallel processing.

And from an epistle to a king. An epistle is a letter too, like a note, but with special significance, like a religious communication, the most famous being the epistles of Paul in the New Testament. But those epistles were not to kings, they were to churches in Rome, Ephesus, and Philippi. Even his letter to the Hebrews was not to a king.

Paul's exam was meticulous, gently massaging the woman's breast, searching for a mass, scanning slowly away from the painful spot. Now her eyes were closed, her fear was gone. The turgor of her nipples firmed and the skin of her areolas began to wrinkle. Paul's fingertips reached the zone of tenderness, but the pain now seemed less intense, almost pleasurable as she gently bit her lip, struggling to suppress an urge to moan.

… And is king here a reference to the King of Kings, Christ Jesus, as the proximity to the word epistle suggests, or does king refer to a real king, King David perhaps, or maybe another historical king, Charlemagne, or Henry VIII, or Macbeth or perhaps a modern king, King Hussein of Jordan or maybe a mythical king like Arthur?

He then inspected her nipple, giving it a gentle squeeze, looking for an abnormal discharge of blood. She released a gentle hiss from between her lips; she could not help herself. Paul apologized and asked her if it hurt. She said no, and her cheeks started to flush from embarrassment. Paul remained oblivious as he directed his exam to the opposite breast.

… Or does king refer to a proper name? Martin Luther King was the obvious first choice but could it refer to another king: Nat King Cole or Larry King or Rodney King?

She felt the blood flowing to each of her nipples and parted her eyelids just enough to see the skin of her areolas turning a shade darker, and deep wrinkles forming on her hardening skin. She could even see the little bumps, the glands of Montgomery, becoming more prominent. Her abashment mounted as a familiar sensation began to arise in her groin.

… Or perhaps king is a metaphorical reference, like to the King of Rock, Elvis Presley; or the King of Pop, Michael Jackson; or the King of Soul, Otis Redding. Or maybe it's a business name: Smoothie King, or Mattress King, or Burger King.

Finding nothing of significance, Paul abruptly finished his exam and pronounced her well. She opened her eyes, returning to reality, sad that it was over, but elated that she was fine. Ordinarily modest, she made no effort to cover herself, blissfully unaware that her chest was bare. He told her that she could get dressed, speculated that she had unknowingly bumped herself, then reassured her that it was nothing to worry about. He looked away and pulled out a prescription pad. It was only then that she sat up and drew her gown closed.

She scanned his hands – no wedding band. She summed up his body – firm, muscular – like a gymnast – and tall, at least six feet. She concluded that he must work out and was very handsome and smart, with soft, gentle hands, and a doctor no less. She was pretty and she knew it, even sexy. She liked the feeling he gave her. Paul wrote out a prescription for high dose Naprosyn but the pain in her breast was now completely gone. "Maybe she could catch herself a doctor", she mused. She gently threw back her vivid jet black curls over her shoulder, and almost not believing she was about to do something so brazen and reckless, allowed her gown to gape open exposing her swollen breasts with her nipples still fully erect. She reclined ever so slightly back. Paul placed the prescription on the chart, gave her the proper dosing instructions, and admonished his patient to follow the medication instructions precisely. Then abruptly he walked out of the room with her chest still exposed and heaving and her mind still lost in fantasy. She remained in her seductive pose until a disheveled older man shuffled by the door ogling at her with a broad toothless smile. Paralyzed by the mortifying peep show she was unwittingly giving, the young woman temporarily froze until an excruciating moment later her visceral humiliation drew out a pitiful shriek just as the door mercifully swung closed.

Paul walked out to the doctor's workstation. The child's X-ray was on the computer screen, and the adjacent radiology report confirmed the hairline fracture in the left scaphoid. He was about to sign off on an order when a familiar voice called out to him from exam room 6.

"Paul, I need a favor," it was Redmond suturing a forehead laceration.

"I forgot my watch in the call room. It was a gift from my wife, and you know how things have a habit of walking away around here. I don't want to lose it. Do you mind running at getting it for me? I'm going to be tied up here awhile."

Paul agreed and left the ER heading to the call room wing. At first he was a little perturbed; work therapy was helping him focus but, on the other hand, another break might be just what he needed.

The small Baptist hospital security office was dark and overcrowded. Moments earlier, Oxmore, Stone, and McCammon had commandeered the office and shoehorned themselves in behind Security chief Scaglione and one of his officers. The five of them were transfixed on the video monitors. Displayed on the center screen was their principal subject: Dr. Paul Gudrun.

"Anything unusual so far," Oxmore asked.

"Not a thing," Scaglione answered.

"What options do we have available?" Stone asked.

"We have cameras throughout the facility and guards at each exit," Scaglione affirmed.

"And I have plain-clothed officers circulating," McCammon added.

Phil Oxmore was pleased. "Ok. Let's see what he does."

X X

5:34 am

Although "The Med" was the major teaching hospital of the region, Baptist ran its own smaller but highly regarded Osteopathic residency program. On any given night, over two dozen physicians in training where housed *en résidence* in the hospital "on call" to tend to the nocturnal needs of the hospital from tending to critically ill patients to ordering sleeping pills.

The call rooms were on level three past administration and the laboratory. Paul looked at his watch. It was just after five thirty in the morning, and the business offices were still closed. He walked past them to the call suite. The Physician Residency Suite, as it was officially called, consisted of a common room with couches and a television, a library with a connected meeting room, and a small kitchenette with a microwave. The room was flanked by a men's shower on one side and a woman's dressing room and shower on the other. Beyond the showers were a bank of dorm room like sleeping accommodations, each room big enough for two bunk beds and a small desk. The men's section was Spartan in decoration, cluttered with pizza boxes, disheveled linens, and orphaned socks. The back wall was completely in common with administration and therefore had no windows, but that didn't keep the men from adorning the walls with posters.

STRONG EMERGENCE

In times past, those might have included Playboy pinups but now were limited to Sports Illustrated swimsuit and Maxim pictures along with sporting events and Harley Davidson posters. In contrast, the women's side was chic. Their shower was more like a boudoir with vanity space, plush dressing areas, and full length mirrors. The sleeping accommodations were in common with an exterior wall permitting windows, albeit frosted and semi-opaque, and their side had a private exit that spared women with fresh styles from having to endure the humidity of the showers.

Attending physicians in many hospitals had their own private call rooms and the same was true at Baptist, but the rooms were still part of the call suite, the only difference being a slightly larger space and an in-suite bathroom. Paul entered the suite by using his RFID pass card. He knew that it not only allowed access but recorded his identity as well.

The common room was deserted. The television was off and the lights were muted. That was not completely surprising. By 5 am, interns were expected to be pre-rounding and residents getting breakfast. Still there always seemed to be a few stragglers in the suite, but none were there today. He took a moment to check out the library. It too was vacant, and the adjoining conference room was dark. He thought there was something a bit curious about all this but redirected his attention back to his task.

He walked through the common room and into the men's shower taking care to avoid slipping on the wet floor. The vacant room stank with a musty smell of mildew mixed with body odor and the stench of an unflushed commode. He wasted no time, and proceeded into the back hallway. The hall led to a row of six call rooms, all with their door wide open. All except for the one at the end. The attending call room was always kept locked.

5:39 am

"Where's he gone?," Oxmore inquired as he looked up from his cell phone and saw Doctor Gudrun was no longer in the emergency room. Amy

Weikert had been updating him on Paul Gudrun's background investigation. So far, he seemed to be exactly as he appeared: an overworked emergency room physician, qualified but ordinary, single but sleeping with a coworker, comfortable but not rich, charitable but not churchgoing. He had no warrants, no arrests, and a remarkably unremarkable FBI dossier.

"He just left the ER and headed to the call rooms. He went inside a couple of minutes ago. There are no cameras inside," Scaglione reported. The center screen was focused on the call suite entrance.

Oxmore shrugged, "We are going to have to fix this oversight."

"Are there any other exits?" McCammon inquired, trying to redirect Oxmore's wrath.

"This is the only door to the common room and the men's side has no other exits. There is a second women's exit through the showers, but he doesn't have a key to get in there," Scaglione informed.

"Well, for now, let's keep an eye on every possibility," Oxmore ordered.

Tedder smirked, "I'll keep an eye on the women's shower!"

"Yeah, I'll bet you will," Phil sarcastically muttered, and the others snickered in unison.

The attending call room had a physical lock with an old fashioned steel key. Paul used it and entered the call room, turned on the light, and stood face to face with an HK tactical pistol equipped with an AWC sound suppressor. His shock was evenly balanced between the long gun and the black, southern nurse who was holding it.

"What the... Ophelia?" Paul was bewildered beyond comprehension.

"Who are you?" Ophelia questioned.

"Ophelia, you know who I am?" Paul smiled expecting some sort of dark humored gag.

"Cut the crap, Gudrun." Her voice was different. Her southern accent was gone. "What did Burja tell you?"

Suddenly a rush of serotonin-laced, adrenaline-spiked realization poured down upon him. This wasn't a practical joke. This was a real gun pointed at his head, and she was looking for information. He had underestimated the situation and the depth of his involvement.

He spied the environment. The room was narrow, flanked by two sets of empty bunk beds separated by a four foot wide passage. Ophelia stood five feet from Paul, her arm stretched out, the long barrel of the silencer less than two feet away from his nose. Behind her was an open medical kit on a pressed wood desk. She was still wearing her nursing scrubs and in her left hand held a silver tipped syringe. Her intentions were clear before she overtly stated them.

"Make this easy or make this hard. Your choice," Ophelia commanded. Her ultimatum was all that the confirmation he needed.

With ballistic suddenness and before Ophelia's brain had even registered movement on the part of the good doctor, Paul's left arm swept up and out, deflecting the weapon and ripping it out of her weakly gripping hand. Ophelia subconsciously reacted by lunging forward as if to magically summon her weapon but Paul remained still. Then pulling his left hand back hard and rotating his hips counterclockwise, he generated maximum rotational acceleration as he extended his right arm in a rapid, fluid motion that delivered maximum force to the black woman's lower jaw. The sudden rotation of her scull coupled with the lagging inertia of her brain stretched the cortical supporting ligaments, transiently shut down her brainstem, and knocked her out.

Paul stood there for a moment as he watched Ophelia reel into the desk and then crumple to the floor. The syringe she was holding bounced off of the right bunk and landed harmlessly on a pillow. He left it there. His heart raced as he took a deep breath. Transient bewilderment and confusion was quickly replaced with a sense of betrayal.

He had known Ophelia for well over two years. She had started at Baptist not long after Paul had come on staff. She was a good two decades older but within weeks they had developed a lighthearted platonic relationship of back and forth playful teasing that became contentious only after he and Amber began dating. Paul dismissed Ophelia's change in behavior to protective jealousy. For months, she had become increasingly shrill but this was entirely different. The coworker he had known for years was someone else entirely. Even her voice was different! His mind raced through a field of questions: Who was she? How was she involved with Burja? Was she really trying to kill him? Answers were not readily forthcoming, but two deductions were obvious: first, he was being watched and, somehow, Redmond was complicit either by stupidity, coercion, or bribery; and second, Burja's secret really was a matter of life and death, and now *his* life was in the balance. At that moment, a tragic realization struck. Someone else was in mortal danger too.

The unconscious nurse was still wearing her lab coat with her RFID name badge. He unclipped the badge and quickly moved out of the room closing the door behind him. He rapidly advanced back through the showers and into the common room. Fortunately, there was still no one there. He knew the outer door was under camera surveillance, and the only other exit was through the women's dorm which, unlike the men's, were secured with a gender-specific lock. Apparently, there was no fear but only fantasy of a woman traipsing through the men's room. He took Ophelia's badge and swiped the electronic panel. With a soft click, the door unlocked, and he opened it gently.

The door opened into a feminine dressing room with open storage lockers and a cushioned center bench. After scanning the room and assuring it was clear, he carefully walked in allowing the door to close behind him gently. The room was sizable and L-shaped. He continued forward thankful that the room was empty but as he turned the corner he heard a sound he hoped not to hear – the sound of cascading water; someone was taking a shower.

"Something is wrong. He's been in there too long," Oxmore observed.

"Maybe he decided to take a shit." Tedder's crass humor again induced a chortle in the room, but Phil wasn't laughing, "Is there any security at all inside?"

"None," Scaglione answered swallowing a laugh.

McCammon suggested that he casually send in a couple of his men, and Oxmore agreed. The contingency had not been completely unexpected, and McCammon had a team on standby. Confirmation of success was necessary, and if there were any uncertainty, his responsibility was to clarify it.

He peered into the shower room and carefully walked in keeping light-footed. To the left was a row of five showers, and across from them were a line of benches. Beyond the showers and through a narrow archway, a sizable boudoir with vanities and chairs was visible. In the corner of the expansive room, he spied his prize: a rack with assorted ladies scrubs next to the door to the outer corridor.

He continued to move forward with slow, purposeful steps. The showering woman was in the fourth stall away from him. The others were empty. As he continued in he realized another problem: the shower curtain was clear plastic; He would be seen immediately. He inched further trying to glimpse her identity. Maybe if he knew her, he could make a tawdry pass in case he was discovered. That was clearly a solution of last resort but infinitely preferable to her yelling rape or pervert.

He was in luck; he recognized her. Her name was Deidre Locke. She was a third year medicine resident who had rotated through the ER just a few months earlier. She was spirited, sexy, and Paul had gotten along nicely with her. Plan B would work well if necessary, but that wasn't the good news. She was immersed in the shower with her head thrown back and her eyes closed. She hadn't seen him. Paul recalled that she was on an ICU rotation meaning she had just finished a 14 hour shift without a break. She was dead tired. He continued slowly walking, watching her as she ran her hands through her brown hair, taking care to keep from casting a shadow unto the stall.

Suddenly the room was filled with music and Paul froze. She was singing! At first, he was sure she saw him, but Deidre kept her eyes closed, enjoying the hot water cascading over her scalp. He used the time to admire her form. She was stunning: athletic but not thin nor overly muscular, with long, trim legs, an hourglass figure, a plump, firm bottom and an unexpectedly large, natural bust. She could have been a model. The boy in him wanted to linger, but the man knew better. As she began humming her second verse, he resumed his trek and increased his pace.

Paul reached the dressing area beyond the showers and quickly reviewed the scrub selection. There was a fair variety of tops and bottoms. He chose a pair of pink scrubs and a floral jacket and quickly stripped hoping that neither Deidre nor anyone else would pop in on him. The worry was for naught. He changed lightning fast, put a bouffant scrub cap on, and donned a lab coat that was draped on a nearby coat hook.

He admired himself in the mirror after wadding up a handful of scrub caps into fake bosoms. The coat was small, and he would have made a horrid drag queen, but he knew the ruse would only have to last long enough to fool the video-monitoring guards. He took a big breath and headed toward the exit.

◆

6:02 am

Two of McCammon's officers wearing hospital security uniforms approached the call suite front entrance. The lead was Sgt. Kirkpatrick. A 5 year veteran of the MPD SWAT, he had led his assault Team 1 at the mall, but it was the other man McCammon desperately needed to get inside. Christos Sokolov had specific orders. In the event, Marti Gras failed, responsibility for threat containment would fall on him. Either way, this ended now. His orders were explicit.

Kirkpatrick opened the door, and the two slithered inside. The space was empty.

Immediately they slid their hands to their pistols and began systematically searching the suite. Kirkpatrick directed his partner toward the library while he inspected the kitchen. Sokolov had no problem following his instruction. He knew where Dr. Gudrun was – dead in his call room. He was in no hurry; they would find him soon enough.

Christos played it up walking into and through the library to the darkened conference room. He turned on the light, and as expected, the conference room was barren. He took a moment to check in as he turned off the light and headed back through the library to the common room. A moment later, Kirkpatrick announced he was proceeding to clear the men's room. Sokolov was right behind him.

Paul opened the door, this time with Deidre's badge, and nonchalantly walked out into the hall. Paul knew the location of every surveillance camera in the hospital. One was in the corridor ceiling only twenty feet away. He turned walking toward the camera making sure to keep his head low. The back entrance to the blood bank was just beyond the camera. Once again, he used Dr. Locke's badge and ducked inside.

The blood bank was staffed by two technicians. Fortunately, both were focused on their work and neither recognized a disguised Paul walking in. He quietly strode passed them and into the pathology lab. Once again, he entered unnoticed. The lab was busy with technicians processing early morning specimens, looking through microscopes, and typing on their computers. He turned down a back hallway lined with small physician workrooms and found the unoccupied office of the Assistant Director of Anatomic Pathology, a simultaneously brilliant physician and a bombastic egotist who loved to give residents, colleagues and administrators self-touting tours of his lab. Paul had been a patron on more than one of those tours and knew his office well. The pathologist dressed impeccably, kept a neat office, and always had extra supplies on hand, facts Paul hoped to take advantage of.

Tedder was first to notice the back door to the Physician's Residence Suite had opened, "Someone is coming out of the women's locker room."

"Who is she?" McCammon asked. The primitive disguise was successful. Tedder had his eyes focused on Paul's fake chest, and McCammon was fooled by the feminine scrubs and surgical bonnet. Of course, McCammon was also fooled by something more. He was fully expecting a woman to walk out that door. It was the planned escape route for Marti Gras. Unfortunately, he had not been briefed on the sleeper's appearance, so the white skin caused no concern. They followed the girl briefly and watched her enter the blood bank.

"That's Dr. Locke," Chief Scaglione confirmed, "She's a senior medicine resident. She was the only other one inside." Almost immediately, the photograph of a beautiful, tall, white woman emerged on the computer screen. The form on the black and white, somewhat grainy, video monitor was close enough and Oxmore accepted the conclusion. There was no reason to question the evidence. Just then, their concentration was interrupted by Kirkpatrick's scouting report. They were about to enter the showers.

Inside the office, Paul found exactly what he was looking for: a better-fitting physician's lab coat, a hospital computer, and a short stack of sterile surgical kits sitting on a bookshelf. He sneaked inside, removed his floral jacket, cap and falsies, and donned the coat. He then directed his attention to the computer.

All computers in the hospital were linked via the hospital's intranet – including hospital security – a fact Paul learned eight months earlier in humiliating fashion. Within a few hours of his first torrid tryst with Amber in a surgical supply room, Paul received a call from Security Chief Vito Scaglione. Vito discretely invited him into his office to 'show him something', but Paul had already deduced his intentions. What he wasn't prepared for was the quality and graphic nature of the images Scaglione's video cameras had captured. He worried for a moment that Vito's motivation might be financial but was relieved when the conversation turned to a gentle warning to avoid prying electronic eyes. That night, Paul hacked into the security subnet and familiarized himself with the hospital security system, the closed circuit televisions, and the camera control systems. From then on, Paul made sure the hospital cameras were always pointing in a different direction when Amber and he were together. Who would have guessed that expertise would come in handy for another reason?

Paul logged in using workstation emulation, altered camera angles, deleted command codes and changed the password. As the computer rebooted, he pulled one of the surgical kits off the shelf and unceremoniously ripped it open. Reality had already struck him; he was going to need help to get out of the building. Inside the package, he found what he was looking for: a bone marrow biopsy needle.

Bone marrow biopsies are one of the few procedures pathologists perform on living patients. In order to diagnose bone related disorders such as leukemia, the pathologist uses a special instrument with a cylindrical blade known as a trephine to bore a hole through the bone to obtain a core sample. The tool Paul grasped in his hand was 6 inches long. It was made of thick, hard steel alloy with a large blue handle grip and a razor sharp tip. It wasn't an ice pick or switchblade, but it would do.

Paul pocketed the biopsy needle along with a pair of gloves and a scalpel, snapped on Ruiz's name badge, walked out of the office making sure he wasn't noticed, and sauntered confidently through the clinical lab.

Paul's plan was to slither out the front lab entrance and head for the crosswalk that linked the hospital with the physician and staff garage next door. The alternative was to take the stairs down to the loading dock. The crosswalk door was probably guarded and locked, but the loading dock would fare no better. Paul knew he had to act quickly. It wouldn't take long for his pursuers to realize their ambush had failed. He kept his head down and made a choice. He walked out of the lab and headed straight for the crosswalk.

Christos Sokolov checked out the shower stalls while Kirkpatrick inspected the adjacent toilet room. They rejoined at the entrance to the back call room hall, the looks on each of their faces communicating that nothing had been found. Sokolov took the initiative and turned to the left inching closer to the attending call room while Kirkpatrick continued the search to the right.

Sokolov reached the end of the hallway and waived for Kirkpatrick to join him. He opened the door, but it was Kirkpatrick who was first to see the collapsed body on the floor. Christos initially smiled internally but then suddenly realized the fallen form was not a white man but a black woman.

"Man down!" Kirkpatrick yelled through his collar tip radio transceiver.

The words reverberated through the security office. "What?" Scaglione took a moment to process the plea but instantly the others were on edge.

McCammon instantly called in backup while Stone asked for confirmation of identity, "Is it Gudrun?"

Sokolov quickly answered the question moving in to tend to the injured woman. He needed to communicate the catastrophe implicitly, "Negative!" he started, "It's a black woman. She looks like she might be a nurse. There's been a pretty good struggle, and she's not moving."

The news hit McCammon in the gut, but Oxmore and Stone were faring no better. "What the hell?" Tedder Stone exhaled.

"Where's Gudrun?" McCammon shouted over the radio, his agitated concern obscured to everyone except Sokolov.

"There's no sign of him," Kirkpatrick exclaimed. As McCammon was about to order his men to continue the search, the hospital intercom blared overhead.

"Code Blue, Third Floor, Physician's Residence. Code Blue, Third Floor, Physician's Residence."

Now it was McCammon who was cursing in frustration, "Who the hell did that?!" In the confusion, Scaglione's assistant had called the overhead hospital code for a cardiac arrest.

"What?" the assistant reacted to the question, "A woman is hurt!"

Oxmore understood the young man's actions. This was a hospital where lives were meant to be saved, but this was in all likelihood a crime scene and their target of surveillance had disappeared. He had been silent up until now and when he spoke the others were suddenly quieted. His first command was to McCammon, "Have one of your men secure the scene and send the other one to continue the search." He then redirected his attention back to the Director of Security, "Find Doctor Gudrun, Mr. Scaglione!"

XXI

6:22 am

Christos Sokolov watched Officer Kirkpatrick leave. He had immediately seen the syringe on the bed but had said nothing. Now that his partner had left to find Doctor Gudrun, Sokolov left the side of the unconscious woman, grabbed the syringe carefully and inspected it. It still contained a full five milliliters of pure LSX.

Marti Gras had failed spectacularly. Gudrun must have somehow surprised and disarmed her. "How miserably incompetent", he seethed. Now he would have to pick up the pieces and finish the job. Sokolov chuckled to himself, partly in contemptible disgust, partly in poor taste: the agent lying before him was black, black in both skin color and operational designation. Unfortunately for her, she was the first mess he was going to have to clean up. The nurse was still breathing, but the risk was too great to allow her to survive. They simply couldn't afford to make the same mistake with her that they had made with Burja. He also knew time was short and soon the room would be crowded with doctors and nurses. He picked up the syringe and turned the woman's head to the side exposing her sternocleidomastoid, the prominent branching muscle that outlines the side of the neck. He aimed for the base of the muscle where the two lobes separated and injected the syringe. He saw just a speckle of blood, enough to know that he was in the jugular vein, and quickly emptied the syringe.

The sudden pain caused Ophelia's eyes to open. She stared at Sokolov speechlessly, and he took a moment to render a sardonic apology. He completed his brief pre-mortem eulogy, then stood and hid the medical kit and syringe behind the corner desk.

Ophelia released a gentle moan and began to stir. Although still in a haze, she was slowly becoming conscious of what was happening to her. Emotions and memories were swirling inside her pain-filled head: anger, resentment, remorse, fear, dread, disappointment, and worst of all, regret. The distillation bubbled out as a grunt followed by a whisper-soft "son of a bitch".

"Now, now. That's no way for a well-trained operative to speak," Sokolov sarcastically responded kneeling back down beside her. Even though she was technically on his side, he had a job to do. Besides, he couldn't deny his sadistic tendencies; he was having just too much fun, "Yes, I am a son of a bitch. But you, ma'am, still have a duty. Tell me what Gudrun told you."

Another "son of a bitch" was the only satisfaction she would give him. Then her eyes twittered closed.

Kirkpatrick ran through the suite frantically. He looked back through the call rooms and in the shower stalls but instinctively knew Gudrun wasn't there. Dr. Gudrun must have used the women's key card to get into the ladies locker room, he deduced. It was the only place he could be. He swiped the security master key and stormed through the door, drawing his pistol as he rushed through the empty room. As he turned the corner, he came face to face with Deidre Locke. Her towel was wrapped around her hair, and she was wearing nothing else. His embarrassment was equaled only by her unbridled scream. He quickly turned away, apologized and asked if anyone was with her. Only then did he register the magnificent feminine form he had just seen.

"Of course not! Who the hell are you?" she screamed.

"Memphis PD. We're looking for Doctor Paul Gudrun. Is he here?"

"Doctor Gudrun? I'm alone in here!" The disgust dripped from her lips. At that moment, her nude mental image evaporated – it was the moment his mind realized he would never see it again.

Paul exited the lab into a corridor of activity. Residents, nurses, respiratory therapists, and other hospital personnel were racing, some in a fast walk, and others in a full sprint, towards the call suite. It was easy for him to slip into the stream, even in pink scrubs. A nurse and a couple of the residents recognized him but did not give him a second thought. An ER physician responding to a Code Blue was not unusual. Paul had no intention of making it to the code though. He fell back and when the flow turned to the right towards the Physician's Residence, Paul turned to the left and headed towards the crosswalk and the parking garage. He had taken the time to disable the crosswalk corridor camera. If he had to take out a guard, he didn't want to have it on film.

Paul turned the corner, hand in his pocket clutching the large biopsy needle, fully expecting to see a burly officer guarding the door. He was pleasantly surprised to find the exit unmanned but not surprised to find it locked. Although the door would not open for his key card, or Deirdre's or Dr. Ruiz's, something told him it would open for Ophelia's. Paul swiped Ophelia's card and, as expected, the electronic lock unlatched. Once outside, he broke out into a jog. Even though he was outside of the hospital, he knew he was not out of the woods. His car keys were useless; his vehicle was parked outside of the Emergency Room, surrounded by police, and almost certainly under watch. He was going to have to arrange alternative transportation.

Scaglione's assistant had worked security at Baptist alongside his boss, Frank Scaglione, for nearly eight years. He was fully aware of the capabilities and operation of the hospital's security system. He was the chief technician and Scaglione's go-to troubleshooter, but something was wrong and nothing he tried seemed to make much difference. "The computer's not responding," he finally shouted in exasperation.

"What do you mean?" Scaglione asked, not yet fully understanding the magnitude of the problem.

"I can't get the camera angles to change!"

At just that moment, Kirkpatric's exasperated report blared over the intercom, "Gudrun is not in the call suite! The only one here is Dr. Locke!"

"Dr. Locke? I thought she left ten minutes ago?" McCammon asked.

"That wasn't Locke! It must have been Gudrun – in a disguise," Stone deduced.

With sudden clarity, Oxmore suddenly realized that something was indeed terribly wrong. Nothing at all was making any sense; he needed to gain control. "Lock down this building! All exits! No one in or out!" he commanded.

"The control system has been hacked. Nothing is working!" the technician screamed back exasperatedly.

"Scaglione, we need those cameras!" Oxmore screamed.

The room began to bustle as the Director of Security tried valiantly but vainly to reset the computer. At the same time, Agent Stone worked his way behind McCammon and edged toward the door. Tedder Stone's eyes met his bosses but no words were needed. He knew what he wanted: to find Paul Gudrun. Stone silently nodded just as Scaglione pessimistically mumbled, "What we see is all we're going to get."

Tedder raised an eyebrow at the comment and struggled to restrain a condescending sneer. All Phil could do was nod his head in disgust.

6:26 am

Paul bolted across the pedestrian bridge, entered the stairwell and careened down the stairs four and five steps at a time using the handrails as gymnasts would use parallel bars. He reached the bottom level and considered making a run for it, but instead chose a different strategy. He needed a car, and he knew the one to take.

Redmond wasn't just an arrogant ass and a brown-nosing Judas; he was as cheap as a Hollywood boulevard souvenir stand. Obsessed with gas mileage and value per mile, he drove a 1995 Honda Civic, world renown as one of the easiest vehicles to steal. The car had no significant theft deterrent system and was easy to hotwire, a point Paul had made to him many times. But Redmond was blissfully heedless. He only drove the car from his garage in River Oaks to the garage at the hospital and only parked the car in the doctor's restricted parking area. In fact, he always parked in the same place – next to a 7 series BMW. He figured if thieves were going to break into anything, they would target the BMW. He was about to find out how wrong he was.

Paul burst out the parking deck door and walked quickly to Redmond's car simultaneously scanning his surroundings. The garage was deserted. He removed the scalpel and surgical gloves from his coat pocket and transferred them to his pants. Finally, he took out the biopsy needle and placed it on the roof of the car, removed his coat to wrap around and protect his hands, grabbed the needle, and positioned himself beside the driver side door. He carefully placed the needle in the right lower corner of the window. The needle had a sharp tip designed to bore through solid bone and a large blue handle to allow the operator to grip it firmly in order to focus maximum force on the needle tip. With constant pressure, he pushed firmly. The glass was no match for the needle, and it quickly shattered. The sound reverberated remarkably softly. With his protected hand, he swept the broken glass out of the door frame, reached inside, and unlatched the door.

We have another problem," Scaglione's security technical assistant added, "Outgoing communication lines are down." While voice communications within the facility were conducted by old-fashioned land line and short wave radio, extra-facility communications were decidedly more advanced. Voice was transmitted via a secure VOIP network. In the era of health care privacy, even telephonic conversations could potentially expose confidential patient information. As a result, the hospital employed an encrypted Voice-Over-Internet-Protocol communications network. Unfortunately, now that system also appeared compromised, "I'm going to reset the router. That should work."

His words were interrupted by Agent Sokolov dutifully reporting in, "We've identified the woman as Ophelia Roberts. She is apparently one of the ER nurses. There are several people here now, and that seems to be the consensus."

"Can you give us a status report?" Scaglione asked.

"The doctors are working on her but it doesn't look good. They're doing CPR."

The report was interrupted by Oxmore's cell phone. It was Stone, "He's not in pathology – or the lab – or the call suite. I'm extending the search."

"This is too strange. How do we lose a fucking doctor?" Oxmore's patience was failing.

"No clue but we'll find him," Stone confidently responded as he hung up the phone.

"Make sure to keep the environment as secure as possible," Scaglione ignored Oxmore's phone tirade and continued his conversation with Sokolov, trying to maintain decorum, unaware of the covert agent's sinister motives.

"He's not using his passkey or Dr. Locke's, or Mrs. Roberts," the security assistant interjected and then added, "Interesting..."

Oxmore picked up on the word immediately, "what do you mean?"

"Ophelia didn't use her passkey to enter the call suite."

"Then how did she get in?" Scaglione asked.

"And what was she doing there?" McCammon added. His question was intended to distract suspicion; he knew the answer.

Oxmore nodded his head in dismay, "this is just too damn bizarre!"

The intercom blared again. This time it was Kirkpatrick. "He's nowhere to be found on the third floor," the officer reported hurriedly, "He may have changed floors. There's also no one guarding the exit to the physicians parking deck."

The FBI SAIC was starting to lose his patience with Vito Scaglione. "I thought you said the exits were all guarded!" he shouted. Scaglione could do nothing but shrug.

"Has anyone exited that door?" Oxmore was now directing his questions specifically to Scaglione's assistant.

"This is strange. It's hard to tell. There's a mismatch between the badge counter and the door lock counter."

In that instant, Vito Scaglione noticed something, "There's no video camera on the garage crosswalk."

"Is there video in the garage?" Oxmore asked.

"Ordinarily yes, but they have all been disabled."

"That's too damn convenient," McCammon commented.

"Agreed. We need to secure the whole campus – including the garages," Oxmore bellowed, "and we need to do it now!"

Paul quickly wiped the glass off of the seat with the lab coat, sweeping the chards to the pavement and away from the floorboard. Sufficiently satisfied, he dove under the steering column while releasing the handle on the seat positioning lever to give himself more room. Under the column, the ignition apparatus was guarded by an access cover secured by a couple of screws.

Paul used the biopsy needle like a screwdriver and rammed it hard along the edge of the cover, prying it open. The plastic flimsily gave way and the panel popped off with a crack. Behind the cover, the ignition wires were bundled by a wiring harness. He deftly freed the wires: two red wires, a brown one and a couple of others.

He reached into his pocket for his surgical gloves and scalpel. He donned the gloves and then went to work. Scalpels, while sharp, were not meant to cut wire and would dull quickly. He had to work efficiently. He isolated both of the red wires. One was the primary power supply for the ignition switch; the other was the connection for the vehicle's electrical circuits. He bent each one and with a quick movement, spliced them both.

He quickly stripped the wires a couple of centimeters and twisted them together. He would have preferred to wrap the splice with electrical tape, but he didn't have the luxury. He then directed his attention to the brown conduit, the ignition wire. In similar fashion, he carefully cut and stripped it, this time only about half an inch, then touched the brown wire to the spliced red ones.

With a spark, the car started. He pumped the accelerator with his free hand to rev the engine while securing the wires so that they wouldn't short against the car frame. Breathing huskily he pulled himself into the driver's seat. He didn't have much time. He shifted the gear into reverse and pulled out of the parking space, turning the wheel hard to the left as he did, barely watching for anyone behind him.

The car lurched into drive, and he headed for the exit ramp. His mind was racing. He contemplated a variety of options in the event the garage exit was guarded or he encountered a roadblock. He forced the remainder of the glass on the driver side window out with his left elbow while he drove quickly but smoothly with his right hand. To the casual onlookers, it would appear as if the window were simply rolled down. To enhance the illusion, he lowered his passenger side window as he turned toward the exit. He hoped it would be enough.

6:32 am

"Come on man! We need SWAT to lock down this hospital now!" Oxmore screamed. Scaglione was a bumbling idiot and he had struggled to remain kind, but his patience was now officially gone.

"Nothing seems to be working!" Scaglione reacted exasperatedly.

"Get me Chunn on your cell phone," Oxmore commanded but McCammon was already dialing before the words were out of Victor's mouth.

Chunn's cell phone answered, and before pleasantries could be exchanged, McCammon blurted out, "Sir. It's Bob. We've had a security breach, and the rabbit is in the wind! Agent Oxmore wants the entire perimeter secured. Cover all exits including the garages." As he spoke, he kept his thumb firmly depressing the volume control of his iPhone. The maneuver instructed his specially programmed phone to record the conversation and then transmit the audio file to Tyler Center. This insured that his words would not only be heard by Commander Chunn, but by Victor Coombs as well. Nothing was going according to plan. He was going to need reinforcements – and he was going to need them quickly.

XXII

Tyler, Texas
6:43 am

Once again Gonzalez was taken by surprise. It was the second time in the past 10 minutes that a Michaels' superlative had startled him. This time it was news that Sokolov had terminated Marti Gras. He wasn't sure how he felt about that. Sure she had been critically compromised, and the agent was just following protocol, but he still felt a knot of fear deep in his abdomen. The stakes they were playing for couldn't be more apparent – and so was the penalty for failure. He had been flat footed all night and knew it. Sleep or no sleep, if he was going to live he was going to have to step up his game.

Gonzales only half-listened as Agent Michaels recanted the gory details. Paul Gudrun had uncannily managed to turn the tables on an F-6 deep cover agent. That fact itself was nothing short of incredible.

F-6 was started as a byproduct of the Vietnam era Phoenix anti-Vietcong counterinsurgency program. When Phoenix's human rights abuses came to light in 1971, the program was officially scuttled, and F-6 arose from its ashes in the wake of the scandal. After the war, F-6 was rejuvenated in response to the Iranian Hostage Crisis as an ultra-deep and ultra-black no-tool-off-the-table counterespionage program. It was so off-book and undocumented that virtually nothing was known about them, even among the intelligence community; nothing except rumors of the extensive training and development of its operatives. F-6 had played legendary but unofficial roles in the Gulf wars, Afghanistan, Grenada, Mogadishu and the ongoing Mexican drug war. "That must have been Marti Gras' duty", Gonzalez thought. It was the only logical explanation he could think of for why such a valuable asset would be stationed in a hospital, but then again, what better place to hide a deep cover agent. Amazingly, now she was dead at the hand of a purported ER doctor who had somehow managed to overcome her. Was it luck, or were they all just grossly underestimating the good doctor. It was obviously the latter; Gudrun could not be as he appeared.

Michaels and Wood were murmuring, but Gonzalez managed to block them out. He focused on his computer. His commander would be back in a moment demanding answers, and he was going to be ready for him. Coombs had asked for a detailed background analysis of Doctor Gudrun and Ferdinand had found something: Gudrun appeared to be an all-American professional – all but for two glaring discrepancies.

Firstly, despite a thorough search of Memphis hospitals and the surrounds, Gonzales could find no primary certification of Paul Gudrun's birth. When he was fourteen, his mother applied for and received a birth certificate for Paul but prior to that there was no record of one. Gonzalez knew there were many possibilities for this: Paul's parents were quite poor, and he could have been delivered at home or in the back seat of a car for that matter, but still, there would have been documentation. Maybe he was adopted, but if so, how could such a poor couple adopt, and where were the adoption documents?

But even more interesting was Gudrun's work history. After graduating from college but before starting medical school, Paul Gudrun took two years off to "see the world". According to his medical school entrance essays, he backpacked Europe, did South American mission work, and sailed through the Caribbean. Interestingly, none of his work during that time was independently verifiable. Attempts to contact the relief organizations were unhelpful. None of them kept volunteer records. Gonzales processed the obvious conclusion: Gudrun had gone off the grid for two years – plenty of time to be trained, radicalized, or weaponized.

The cackling had ceased and for a moment the room was eerily quiet. Feeling a modicum better, Ferdinand Gonzales took in a deep breath and prayed for Marti Gras, the woman whose real name he did not know and for her family whose questions would never be answered. In that brief moment, a pall of comfort descended on the Tyler Center technical officer, and he suddenly felt a rush of contentment and clarity of purpose; all was going to be just fine.

But then just as quickly, the peace vaporized, pierced this time by the stern look of Victor Coombs as he crashed through the control room entrance. Ferdinand knew what Coombs was going to say before he said it, "Talk to me, Gentleman." This time he was going to have answers for his boss.

Memphis, Tennessee
6:50 am

Victor Oxmore assembled his team back in the conference room. Bob McCammon, Ian Chunn, and Vito Scaglione joined Amy Weikert, Alesha Deng, and Jim Neighbors. Oxmore surveyed the room. Tedder Stone was noticeably absent, but Oxmore was in no mood to wait. Lack of sleep and an empty stomach combined with a series of unsolved mysteries and a visceral hatred of failure had set his fuse of anger and frustration. But it was the disappearance of Dr. Gudrun that triggered his smoldering eruption, "Ok, I want to know what the hell just happened here?" Oxmore growled. The echoing silence was off-worldly. Only Vito Scaglione was courageous enough to speak.

"We lost him."

"No shit!" Neighbors scoffed.

Bob McCammon's heart was racing. Oxmore was staring straight at him, and he knew the FBI Special Agent in Charge held him, not

Scaglione, responsible for Gudrun's escape. Oxmore was not officially the boss, but that didn't matter; he and the Police Director were close friends. But Oxmore could only take his job. If he didn't solve this problem, Victor Coombs could take his life.

"We'll find him," McCammon reacted to Oxmore's nonverbal question, "He's got to be hiding around here someplace."

"What's your name?" Agent Weikert asked with slight condescension.

"Bob McCammon, ma'am."

"Never underestimate your suspect, Mr. McCammon."

McCammon wanted desperately to leap across the room and bitch slap the clueless princess but suppressed the urge and with great restraint answered politely, "Yes, Ma'am."

"Could he have gotten out of the building?" Oxmore asked of the room loudly and with a glaring scowl.

"I don't think so. We had all exits blocked," Chunn answered, hoping to diffuse the situation.

"Are you sure? At least one exit was unmanned?"

"We had teams stationed in the ER, at the main entrance, employee entrance and loading docks."

"How about the garages?"

Scaglione clarified, "The doors to the garages were sealed as were the doors to the physician's building and radiation therapy."

"Could he have gotten through a locked door?"

"I have teams searching the entire grounds, and so far they've found nothing," Chunn replied.

"But you're not answering my question," Oxmore wondered loudly again, his exasperation starting to resurface, "Could he already be off campus?" Phillip was almost screaming.

Chunn answered calmly, "Possible, but not likely. The building is on lockdown and heavily guarded. On top of that, there is less than a twenty minute period from when he was seen exiting the call rooms until we quarantined the entire campus including the garages, emergency exits, doctor's offices, and accessory buildings. That's not much time."

Before Oxmore could respond, Tedder Stone rushed in panting and brandishing his cell phone.

"Nice of you to make it Agent Stone," Oxmore's displeasure was palpable.

Tedder Stone apologized with a gasp and tried to catch his breath while waving his Droid, "I've been on hold for ten minutes waiting for a Verizon supervisor to release Gudrun's cell phone records."

"You rushed all the way down here to tell us that?" Weikert smirked.

Tedder could have shot a zinger back at Amy but decided to keep his powder dry. He had important news to convey and little breath to do it, "I think the nurse may have been murdered."

The entire room was stunned, but only Weikert verbalized her astonishment, "What?"

"Her jaw was broken, and it looks like she was punctured in the neck with something. The doctors noticed blood on her neck when they started performing CPR," Stone answered matter of fact but a bit breathlessly. He had just run down three flights of stairs to join the rest of them, "It will be awhile before CSI processes the scene, but it sure looks to me like a homicide." The room was quiet as he took a quick breath, just long enough to complete his next two sentences, "It looks like it just happened – fresh blood, fresh everything. And there's no sign of Gudrun."

"It looks like Doctor Gudrun's Person of Interest Status has been upgraded," Jim Neighbors grumbled.

"Are you saying this woman was killed by Doctor Gudrun?" Scaglione asked with a combination of facetious sarcasm and utter disbelief.

"He was the only one inside. Other than the naked lady doctor," Stone observed with a smirk. Krikpatrick's embarrassing encounter had already made the rounds.

"And someone, presumably Gudrun, sneaked out disguised as Doctor Locke," McCammon compounded.

"As crazy as it sounds, Mr. Scaglione, we were following him for a reason," Oxmore added more calmly and conciliatorily than he had been previously, and Vito quietly conceded with a submissive nod.

"Could there have been anyone else inside?" Weikert asked. Amy had no desire to draw suspicion from Doctor Gudrun. She just detested hasty conclusions, and there was something about the entire evening's events that just seemed odd. In fact, the more she thought about it, the more the whole thing was downright fantastic: A bank robbing terrorist passes information to a doctor, and now the doctor is on the run after killing a nurse? They couldn't make this stuff up in Hollywood!

"Not that we know of," Scaglione answered but then conceded the computers had been tampered with.

"So what's the motive?" Weikert pressed, taking over the line of questioning.

For the next several minutes, Phillip quietly listened to his team bat hypotheses and theories back and forth. Blackmail, public disclosure, professional ruin, collusion, and intimate rendezvous were all discussed with varying degrees of support and detraction, but Alesha Deng was not participating. Tiring of the discourse, her mind began to wander to the night's earlier events: Burja's experience in the ER, her assessment of the audio logs and Jim Neighbor's independent confirmation, the peculiar website, and the dying man's crazy mumblings. Then an idea popped into her head. She quietly retreated from the group, sat down discretely at a computer workstation, and logged onto the Internet.

The subject matter shifted to alternative possibilities including accident and self-defense, but Gudrun's flight from the scene was incriminating. Amy and Vito each offered alternative, less damning, explanations, but each was effectively dismissed by Tedder and Jim. Ultimately, Agent Stone summed up the indictment, "The only thing that makes sense is that she said something or had something on him that he didn't like, and he killed her for it. Two people died here tonight, and Dr. Gudrun appears to be the common thread."

Tedder Stone's proclamation was interrupted by a gasp and a boisterous noise. Alesha Deng had found something. "This is weird," she exclaimed.

Deng had everyone's attention, "Remember that webpage we talked about earlier? – The International Poetry Society?" Everyone stood by motionlessly listening, "When Burja was on his death bed, he was muttering some words that sounded like nonsense – like he was delirious," She continued excitedly, "But he wasn't! He was reciting a poem – a poem that happens to be on that webpage!" She then took a deep breath and began to recite it herself.

NELSON MANGIONE

**It is words you seek,
Magnificent and true
From a note to a doctor
From an epistle to a king**

The recitation quieted the room. Deng had made a connection, a very significant one. Phillip felt the truth down to his core, but he couldn't make sense of it. He looked to Alesha hoping she could help, expecting she would have an answer. She didn't.

"Hey! Hey!" Tedder interrupted unceremoniously. He was talking into his cell phone, "I'm going to put you on speakerphone so that my boss can hear you. Say again what you just told me."

The speakerphone filled with a new voice. It was the cell phone provider's regional security supervisor, "The phone in question is no longer functioning. The last call was made 28 minutes ago. At the time, localization tracked the phone to Walnut Grove Road moving west."

Chunn could feel Oxmore's stare drill straight through his head.

"Who was the call made to?" Stone asked.

"The number is registered to a land line at 400 Broadmore Court, suite 210."

"That's his condo," Amy whispered in Phillip's ear.

"Any idea what the content of the conversation was about?" Stone was directing the conversation.

"No, but the whole call only lasted 23 seconds. Right after that, the cell signal was lost."

"Thank you very much," Stone thanked her and was about to finish the call when Neighbors spoke up loudly, "Excuse me ma'am, Jim Neighbors here, FBI. Can you access his phone internet cache and see what web sites were recently visited?"

There was a slight pause and then the woman answered, "The last activity was a Google search at 3:58 am."

"What was searched?" This time it was Phil Oxmore doing the asking.

"Four words... Note, Doctor, Epistle, King."

"Son-of-a-bitch!" Stone exclaimed.

Phil Oxmore turned to Agent Weikert, "Put out an APB then contact Martin. Have him activate SWAT. I want them boots on the ground at this address ASAP!"

7:00 am

Traffic was heavy and moving slowly, but most of it was traveling in the opposite direction. Paul drove aggressively but not recklessly. He wanted to avoid attracting any more attention than an open window on a freezing December morning already did. Fortunately, it was not snowing but that was little consolation. He turned the car's heat on high hoping it would help; it didn't but neither did it matter. His mind was not focused on the weather.

The night's events were bursting from neuron to neuron across the landscape of his mind like a New Year's Eve fireworks display. But there was no celebration. He had watched a captured Middle Eastern terrorist die slowly in his care in what was certainly an assassination. Then a woman that he had known for years, a maternalistic nag who he had nevertheless respected as a fellow colleague and a good nurse, tried to kill him.

He ran the chain of events over and over again: Burja, supposedly a terrorist, was captured and injured. He was brought to Baptist Hospital where he was killed, most likely poisoned. Before he died he revealed a cryptic secret and though Burja's mannerisms suggested he knew he was dying, his awkward recital of the poem in Hausa made it clear the African Muslim had no idea what he was talking about. Maybe he was taught to recite it. Or maybe he just knew it was important. Nevertheless, Paul felt certain Burja was killed for it and now, somehow, someone had figured out that he was the secret's new repository. All the energy he had expended to remain discreet for all this time had gone for naught, and his curiosity to solve the riddle had been his undoing. Paul kicked himself for his impatience. If he had only waited awhile, he could have curbed his curiosity safely and completely anonymously using a variety of methods. But he couldn't help himself, and now he was paying the price.

Paul deduced something else: there was more than one group interested in him. The FBI agents, Stone and Oxmore, seemed to be typical police, but there were others after him too, people who wanted him dead. It wasn't too hard to figure out whom. The International Poetry Society was a front for a secret espionage network. He wasn't entirely sure what he had uncovered, but it certainly appeared to be a network of operatives at the highest levels of government in both the West and the Arab world. Perhaps he had viewed some form of clandestine diplomatic channel. Maybe it was some sort of spy-counter spy network. Or perhaps there was something more sinister going on. What did Burja say? *It was a matter of life and death.*

Traffic was starting to clear up, and he was driving closer to the speed limit. He would be there shortly and would have to be quick. It would be foolish to believe they weren't already tracking him, hoping to spring a trap. Paul wished he could call ahead and warn her. Unfortunately, he had destroyed his cell phone earlier. He knew it would be a liability; the tracking and locating capabilities of modern devices were almost frightening. Still, he had taken the time to make a single phone call. Although much of the data on his desktop computer in his apartment was encrypted, he couldn't take the chance. He was going to need to pull every trick in his book to get out of this, and his computer held too many secrets.

The call had been brief. When the computer connected, instead of screeching with a modem handshake or giving a droll pre-recorded message, it simply remained quiet and listened. He entered the nine digit code, and the computer beeped twice acknowledging the instruction had been received and was about to be executed. A second later, Paul permanently hung up the phone. He threw it out his open window and down hard on the pavement, watching it shatter into dozens of fragments through his rear view mirror.

But that was all so trivial. What was important was her. He just hoped she was home.

PART 3

"Turing believes machines think, Turing lies with men, Therefore machines do not think."

Alan Turing

XXIII

Saturday
Lucerne, Switzerland

2:02 pm, CET (7:02 am CST)

Each winter, for seven years, the University of Lucerne sponsored a Nature of Being Conference on ontology, the study of what it means for something to exist, and each winter, for seven years, the conference's organizers asked Professor Dr. Alexander Nef, PhD, MSBA, MSc, permanent visiting professor from Oxford in the department of Theoretical Philosophy, to proctor a one day mini-symposia on Emergence, the branch of complexity theory that tries to explain how some things occur inexplicably or surprisingly from their constituent parts, like the perfect geometric patterns formed within snowflakes from simple ice crystallization or the robust diversity of biological evolution arising from the apparent simplicity of random mutation and natural selection.

    This winter had been no different except the organizers chose to run the lecture series before the holidays rather than after the New Year hoping to catch more participants looking for a way to combine an academic

STRONG EMERGENCE

meeting with a ski trip with their kids. It seemed to work. Attendance was up, and it seemed few people cared about the timing – during Hanukah and so close to Christmas.

Dr. Nef watched as the small lecture hall slowly refilled after the lengthy lunch break. Most of the participants were graduate students or academics in other fields; Emergence had wide implications in a variety of disciplines from business to the humanities and from the sciences to technology. Nef himself came from such a non-philosophical background. He had studied physics at Cambridge before pursuing two different master's degrees, one in information theory and another in business analytics, before settling on Philosophy. But it was specifically the Philosophy of Emergence that settled his academic wanderings. Emergence provided the basis for his doctoral thesis and dominated the subsequent decade and a half of his existence, both in academia and out.

He adjusted his wire-rim glasses and ignored his abdominal rumbling. He always chose to forego lunch on teaching days. He hated lecturing on a full stomach but today, for the first time in a while, he second-guessed his decision. His students were glassy eyed, disengaged and already a few minutes late. He wondered if even one was truly listening; he wondered if even one truly understood what he was talking about.

The first hours of the symposia, and the last six hours of his life, were dedicated to defining the philosophy of Emergence and discussing its various types. He started with definitions and history but spent most of the morning discussing the notion of Weak Emergence, the idea that some phenomenon in nature and society seem to arise without a clear connection to the basic principles and laws of nature that serve as their foundation. He used the example of cellular biology: While the laws of chemistry and physics precisely define how molecules form, they don't readily account for the coordination of literally tens of thousands of molecules and their interactions necessary to drive even the simplest cellular organism. In that sense, he argued, the complexity of life *emerged* from these basic biochemical principals.

The early didactic lectures were followed by a "working lunch workshop". Small groups had the opportunity to explore Weak Emergence through simulated gas computer programs that created works of art and complex dances. They also played with evolution simulators that created interesting "beings" through digital mutation, genetic recombination, and natural selection. Dr. Nef walked from table to table, answering questions, sipping unsweetened tea, and avoiding the buffet. He kept a perennial fantasy that he would find a protégé, someone who was as excited about Emergence as he was. He was still looking.

Now, after a brief recess, the afternoon session was about to begin. Nef watched as the returning attendees slowed to a trickle. The afternoon was reserved for his favorite topic but he knew his listeners were mentally somewhere else: on the slopes, at the bar, or in the spa. But now, for the next three hours, he was going to have the opportunity to spark fascination and wonder in the minds of his students one last time: the science of complexity was about to enter the metaphysical. He was going to introduce concepts outside the realm of simulation and scientific inquiry. Behind them was the relatively simple idea that there were things in nature, so complex, that it was difficult to see how they developed from their constituent parts. Now they were going to ask the hard question: Are there things in nature so complex as to be impossible to derive from their constituent parts – was there such a thing as *Strong Emergence*?

Professor Nef had pondered this question since his honors undergraduate years at Princeton. His musings and notions became a source of great academic interest throughout the 'Complexity Community' and also the punch of a few anecdotes. Originally meant to be a joke, Nef later embraced the tag line for the university's organization web page:

The University of Lucerne
More Than The Sum of its Faculties

Aristotle recognized millennia ago that the whole was more from the sum of its parts, but Nef believed there was the possibility of something more – something much more – that humankind could be exponentially more than the sum of our parts and that technology was the key to advancing the human condition. Some in the Emergence field felt consciousness was strongly emergent, incapable of reproduction from the basic laws of physics. It was the domain of something else – something beyond the ordinary – something other, perhaps holy – something clearly not yet understood. The professor had no use for the metaphysical; he was certain machine consciousness was possible. It was an obsession that drove him to near madness before he was rescued by a knock on the door from an attorney for the Rothschilds, the three century family of business moguls that made, spread, and hid billions of dollars, first throughout Europe, and then throughout the rest of the world. He allowed himself to relive the surrealistic memory: the thin Frenchman in a tailored suit, the offer to run a private and secret Strong Emergence research lab for one of the Rothschild's wealthiest subsidiaries, the ungodly remuneration package that would keep him and his family luxuriously comfortable for generations. He sighed and began his lecture.

Two paragraphs in, his cell phone buzzed. It was a special, characteristic vibration that always seemed to make Alexander chill. The small screen displayed two words: Come home. It was a text from his lab – a place that had indeed become like a new home to him. Meant to sound warm, loving, and longing, the concise message had a deeper meaning: something momentous had happened. Either it was a breakthrough or a disaster. He would have to wait to find out.

Nef politely interrupted his talk, unwaveringly canceled the remainder of the seminar, gave a trite and obviously hollow explanation for his actions, and unceremoniously left the room. In the hall outside, an escort was waiting for him – a thin Frenchman in a tailored suit.

XXIV

Memphis, Tennessee
United States
Saturday

7:27 am

While smaller and less frequently deployed than local law enforcement SWAT, FBI SWAT teams are highly specialized tactical crisis response units specially trained for high risk target capture, rescues, security, and anti-terrorism action. Phil Oxmore had assigned special agent Chris Martin as Memphis FBI SWAT team leader the previous summer on the advice of Amy Weikert and couldn't have been more pleased. Chris was built like a stone fortress. In fact, rumor circulated that he had once subdued a suspect with his imposing physique alone. Phil hadn't doubted it for a minute. Martin's lieutenant, Andre Jones, was an ex-marine special operator. While he didn't have Martin's stature, what he lacked for in size was compensated by his ability. He was part of the DET1 project in Afghanistan, a marine special operations detachment, and went on to receive advanced operator skills in close quarter combat, breaching, and tactics. It was expertise that was about to be tested.

STRONG EMERGENCE

Memphis FBI SWAT was small and consisted of two Elements, each a five man team consisting of a sniper, two assaulters, a rear guard, and a leader. Agent Martin directed the first unit from a grassy berm about 50 feet above the small parking lot adjacent to Dr. Paul Gudrun's luxury apartment complex. While Germantown didn't enjoy quite the same posh, "home of the Memphis elite", status it once had, the neighborhood was still lavish and their residents quite wealthy. With its clay tennis courts, fully equipped workout facility, day spa, indoor Olympic-sized swimming pool, sunning decks, climbing walls, and a Caribbean-inspired lazy river, the Residence at Broadmore was quite impressive. The parking lot was crammed with Mercedes and Jags, and Martin had already spied two gorgeous brunettes walking their dogs. It was a fitting address for an unattached bachelor physician with money to burn.

Jones commanded Team Two from a van on a nearby side street waiting for orders. He anticipated a *Sneak and Peak*, the unofficial euphemism for a clandestine deferred-warrant search for the specific purpose of obtaining intelligence. The tactic was specifically legalized under the Uniting and Strengthening America by Providing Appropriate Tools to Intercept and Obstruct Terrorism act of 2001 better known by the acronym USA PATRIOT or the Patriot Act in common parlance. Title II authorized these special intrusions but prohibited the seizure of evidence thereby skirting the protections of the 4th amendment. The driving motivation of the law's sponsors was to create law enforcement tools in the interest of thwarting terrorism. In reality, the majority of Sneak and Peaks were directed against the drug war. This would be a rare case where the law was being implemented in the spirit for which it was intended.

While Jones waited, Martin viewed 400 Broadmore, Suite 210 through his binoculars. No one seemed to be home. He reported in and Weikert authorized the sneak-and-peak as expected. Martin confirmed the order and disconnected the call. His next communication was to Jones. It was show time!

The Element Two leader ordered his van in motion. It turned the corner driving straight for Gudrun's apartment. Martin's sniper took aim of the apartment door while the rest of his element was on their haunches.

The van stopped in front of the building and Jones' element filed out with military precision.

Martin observed from his perch. So far so good. No sign of resistance. Jones reached the door first with his sniper providing cover and the assaulters and rear guard protecting the flanks and back. Ordinarily they would knock and announce themselves but Weikert's orders were to remain covert. He went to work quickly on the door. The real challenge was the dead bolt. Jones took a small flat-tipped tool reminiscent of a standard screwdriver and inserted it into the lock giving it a slight turn to the left. The tension wrench created a tiny ledge inside the tumbler. Holding the wrench carefully with his left hand, he inserted a pick into the keyhole with his right hand and began lifting the pins carefully listening for a soft click signifying that the upper pin had fallen into place on the small ledge created by the wrench. Within a minute, he systematically pushed each pin into its proper position and opened the lock.

The lower lock was a simple spring latch that opened quickly with the aid of the wrench alone and in seconds the door popped open. The living room was dimly lit, but that did not impede the SWAT team. Within seconds, the five men swept into the sprawling condominium, assault rifles raised, and systematically began their detailed search room-by-room, announcing their movements and search progression to each other through their secure intercom headsets.

Paul Gudrun's suite was impressive. The focal point of the two story living room was a stacked stone fireplace. Tile floors led to a gourmet kitchen with stainless steel appliances and emerald green granite. Gudrun lived well, but oddly, the suite was spartanly appointed. The condo had the look of someone who had overbought and was now too cash-strapped to buy anything else. The dining room was empty save for an expensive chandelier dangling from the ceiling, and the living room furnishings consisted of an old oak wall unit with a relatively small flat screen television, a cheap couch and what looked to be a thrift store coffee table. There was nothing on the walls, on the floors, or on the shelves.

Jones listened through his earphones to his team members clearing each room as he walked into the countertop-barren kitchen and carefully opened the refrigerator. He had been surprised before by body parts, dead babies, volatile chemicals, and cultures of anthrax. Experience had taught him caution, but this time all he found were some unopened condiments and a bottle of water. His disappointment was disrupted by the voice of his sniper calling out to him from the next room.

Jones walked into the small and dark guestroom. His sniper and an assaulter were huddled over a cheap, battered, pressed-wood office desk in the back corner. On the furniture sat a Dell desktop computer. It was the only thing in the room.

Almost immediately, Jones was struck by both a pungent, metallic smell and a grating, high-pitched, whirring sound. It was the sound of grinding and the smell of burning metal. The computer monitor wasn't running Windows. Instead, the screen was blue with a single, white line border. Jones had seen this once before, in a college History of Computing class. It was a DOS based program. In the left upper corner were a couple lines of text:

Disk Destroyer 2.0
Extirpation in Progress...

"What does Extirpation mean?" The assaulter verbalized what Jones and the sniper were thinking.

"The computer is self-destructing!" Jones immediately concluded.

"Unplug it!" the assaulter screamed.

"Watch out, the computer may be rigged!" the sniper yelled back.

The assaulter ignored the warning, dove under the desk and unplugged the machine. Despite his efforts, the computer continued to run powered by an onboard UPS. Jones and his two officers watched helplessly as the monitor script changed to read: Extirpation Complete. A second later the disc whirring stopped and the computer rebooted itself.

"Is there any chance of recovering any information?" Jones' sniper looked to him for an answer and all he could do was shrug. The Dell logo disappeared and was replaced with a single line of white text:

Non system disc, Press any key to continue.

Jones' assaulter verbalized his assessment, "Uhh... I don't think so."

Paul Gudrun pulled in to Amber's apartment and looked around. The building and the adjacent parking lot were quiet. The apartment building was on a modest hill and she was on the 7th floor with a panorama of the surrounding homes. He parked in the lot facing the view. Below him and down the hill was the road and on the corner stood a small preschool daycare. Children were playing in the yard and he could hear them cackle from inside his car. He would have loved to admire the idyllic scene but he had no time. Instead, he burst out of his car and walked spritely toward the building entrance. He entered the code Amber had given him, opened the door and walked inside. He chose the elevator, itching and pacing as if he had to empty his bladder as the lift lumbered upward. At the landing he raced out, darted to his lover's apartment and loudly knocked.

Amber opened the door with a mixture of surprise, wonder and amazement. She imagined he was surprising her with a romantic morning delight but Paul's words spoiled the mood.

"Come on, we need to get out of here!"

She laughed, clearly thinking this was a joke, "What?"

"No time for explanations. Come on quickly, get your shoes on."

Amber was only wearing an oversized t-shirt and panties. "You want me to go out like this?" she twirled around showcasing her lacy white thong but Paul rushed into the room ignoring her sultry advance.

"Put on some pants quick. We need to be out of here in three minutes. Do you have any cash?"

Paul's voice was pressured and suddenly Amber was worried, "What are you talking about Paul, what's going on?"

"We need to get out of here right now!" Paul was clearly flustered and spoke in hushed, low pitched tones.

Amber's concern began to transform into fear, "What's going on Paul? You're scaring me!"

"No time." He ran into her bedroom, opened the dresser and pulled out a bra and a pair of old running sweats. "Quick, put this on. We need to get out of here."

"Paul, I'm not going anywhere. I need you to tell me what's going on?" Her voice increased in both pitch and volume. She was getting angry.

With a look of determination, Paul looked directly into the eyes of his beautiful girl, "Do you want to live?"

Amber's emotions fluxed from consternation to fear to anger to sheer terror. Overcome, she began to tear. Paul encouraged her trust and promised to explain everything in time if only she would dress. Amber reassured slightly, began moving more hastily. She even revealed the location of her emergency cash, stashed in her closet in one of at least fifty shoe boxes. It was a puzzle that would have frustrated any burglar.

Paul looked out the window. So far the coast was clear but that wouldn't last. It wouldn't take long for his pursuers to figure out he wasn't going back to his condo. Amber walked out, dressed, with her hair pulled back into a pony tail. Even disheveled as she was, she was stunning. He took a split second to admire her figure and then, just as quickly, pulled her out of the apartment by the hand.

Less than a minute later they exited the building into the frigid but bright morning. Amber was in a sweatshirt but Paul was wearing only the scrubs, his adrenaline keeping him warm and vigilant. Paul rambled towards his car almost pulling Amber behind him. She didn't know how to feel: was this a put on or for real? Paul had purposely left the Chevy running not wanting to risk a stall or failed restart. He opened her door and tucked her in. She decided to humor him and buckled. He ran around to the driver's side, jumped in, shifted into reverse and began moving back.

"Now tell me what the hell is going on Paul!" Amber wanted answers.

Paul intended to explain but his attention was drawn to a vehicle speeding towards the car from his left. Instantly, he sensed another one racing towards them from the right. Paul quickly analyzed their velocity and deduced their intentions. Instinctually, he threw the transmission into gear. The car jolted forward over the concrete parking stop scraping on the undercarriage. The front of the car impacted the barrier hedge as the back wheels jerked over the block. The hedge was small and gave away suddenly as the car began accelerating, almost sliding, down the hill toward the road.

The two chasing vehicles caught unawares by Paul's nimble action rammed head onto each other in a plum of wafting smoke and shattered glass. Paul admired his quick thinking but the self-adoration was short lived. A third car was waiting for them at the bottom of the hill.

Paul turned on to the access road and headed for the intersection. It didn't take him long to see another vehicle giving chase. Paul tried to focus. He raced through the side street intersection and headed for the main road leading to the interstate. It was Saturday morning but there was still a fair amount of traffic and it was getting heavier. He ran the first redlight and turned on the busier thoroughfare doing his best to outrun the closing black Mercedes and to simultaneously placate Amber's screams.

He ran another intersection before the traffic became soupy and then finally came to a stop. Paul could see the sedan behind them. They were only about eight car lengths back. Amber was hysterical but Paul ignored her. They were in a tight spot and he needed an exit. Fortunately, one presented itself.

"Amber, quickly get out!"

"What?"

"Get out of the car!" Paul opened his door and bolted out running towards her side. She was still buckled in, scared, petrified, and stunned into inaction. He opened the door, unbuckled her belt and wrestled her out of the car.

Amber drug her feet as they ran forward, through the stopped cars, sprinting toward a sparkling black-on-chrome Iron 883 Harley motorcycle. The Harley driver weighed two twenty easily and sported a long scruffy beard and a riding suit that hadn't been washed in months. Paul looked over the motorcyclist's shoulder, pointed skyward, and grimaced, drawing the driver's helmet-less head back in bewilderment. With the man momentarily distracted, Paul pivoted his hips and swung his left foot in a roundhouse kick that landed squarely on the burley man's thick jaw knocking him off of his motorcycle and sending him tumbling to the asphalt. The bike landed on its side with its engine still running. Paul adeptly pulled it up and climbed quickly onboard with Amber watching, paralyzed in udder shock.

She finally sucked in a breath, "You just knocked him out!"

"He'll be all right. Come on, get on board!" Paul screamed.

"Not until you tell me what the fuck is going on!" She screamed back.

"Not now Amber, please," Paul pleaded, "Get on the bike! I said I promise I will tell you everything." Out of his peripheral vision he could see men jumping out of the Mercedes. He wasn't completely sure, but he thought he could see at least two carrying firearms. "Come on baby. Please for me!"

Amber reluctantly mounted the Harley with Paul's help. It was not until then that she noticed the three men running toward her, each with pistols in hand, the closest about 25 yards away. In her mind, she wanted to scream "They've got guns!" but her mouth wouldn't move. She instinctually communicated by squeezing Paul's waist for dear life. He read her mind, popped the clutch and ballistically accelerated. As he weaved through the traffic, he could see the agents scamper in his rearview mirror, one calling in back-up, another stumbling back to the car, but he didn't care. Escape was his first priority. He revved his bike and headed for the interstate.

XXV

7:39 a m

Chris Martin walked into Gudrun's suite with his rear guard by his side. The residence was just as Jones had described it: striking crown work, crystal chandeliers, travertine tile, and remarkably little furniture.

"Hey Martin, you got to check this out." The voice was Jones' echoing out from the master bedroom. Martin walked in to find his lieutenant staring into a virtually empty closet. Only a few shirts and a pair of slacks were hanging. Most of the dresser drawers were empty too. Only one had underwear and a few pair of socks.

Martin had seen enough and reported in to Weikert, "Gudrun's not here and it doesn't look like he's been here in a while. The place hardly looks lived in. I'm thinking he moved in with someone else, his girlfriend, maybe. He might just use the place when he's on call."

"He's an ER doctor. He doesn't take call," Weikert sarcastically corrected.

Martin did not process the comment, "We did find his computer but it was running a wipe program when we arrived. We tried to save it but I'm not optimistic."

"Ok. I'll get us a formal search warrant to confiscate the computer. Pull out immediately. He still might show." Weikert was getting tired and her fatigue was inducing unrealistic optimism.

Paul wove his motorcycle past the asphalt trucks that were holding up traffic and raced toward the interstate on-ramp. He opened the throttle and jetted ahead of every car on the highway. He could feel Amber's arms clutched around his neck, holding on for life, her screams buffered by the wind. He quickly looked behind him. There was no sign of the sedan or any other pursuers. He kept up the pace, ignoring the instinct to relax, certain they were still following them. He looked back once more, this time back and up. There in the sky trailing behind him at nearly a 45 degree angle was an EC 135 Eurocopter.

Paul took a couple of glimpses. It was a news helicopter; he could just make out the Channel 6 logo. To the rest of the citizens driving the roads of Memphis, the air patrol was reporting on road traffic and the various crime stories of the day, but Paul knew differently. With each glimpse, the helicopter maintained its angle but was dropping in altitude.

Paul pulled off the interstate and headed for Shelby Farms Park, the largest urban park in West Tennessee. He had intended to use the 4800 acre park all along but now the need was greater than ever. He turned his head again. The helicopter's altitude was less than a thousand feet and closing.

Paul drove the motorcycle into the park over the Wolf River Bridge and turned off road onto a dirt trail that doubled back underneath the overpass. As soon as the bike was engulfed in shade, Paul gripped the front brake tightly, decelerating sharply. He leaned forward, keeping the bike balanced. Amber felt the rear wheel of the motorcycle lift off the ground and, for a moment, she thought she was going to die. But Paul kept his balance, adjusting the break tension until the bike reached a 55 degree angle but no further, taking care not to lock the tire or over-rotate. The added weight of Paul and Amber's combined mass quickly slowed the cycle and brought it to a stop, abruptly dropping the rear wheel back onto the dirt.

With the motorcycle finally at rest, Amber found her voice. "O my God! O my God! You could have gotten us killed! Get me off this God damn thing!" She screamed. Her yells began to ramble with intertwined nervous laughter, "Who are those people chasing us? When were you going to tell me you could drive a motorcycle like that? Were you a stuntman?" Paul listened to her holler but silently hoped to defuse her rage by slowly maneuvering the bike around. This tempered her briefly but the ruse ultimately failed and she began railing his arms against his back, demanding to dismount, now angrier than ever.

Against his better judgment, he relented. Almost immediately, the petite, gorgeous and ordinarily demure southern belle began screaming sailor-blushing obscenities, "You prick-sucking ass hole! What in the God damn fuck is going on?! What the hell are you doing?! I asked you a question! Who, the fuck, are those people chasing us?!" She didn't wait for an answer. With a frustrated, boisterous huff, she threw up her hands and started to storm off.

"No baby. Stop, please!" Paul pleaded, chasing after her. Instinctually he cried out, "Please, Snow Bear!" Desperate, his voice cracked as he begged her to stay and hear him out. The beseech worked, at least for an instant. She stopped and turned around, her arms crossed, her right hip thrust forward, her tone dripping venom, "You've got thirty seconds."

Paul took a deep breath. He hadn't been too honest this far but he was going to have to offer at least some measured truth. Amber was too smart to fall for anything less. Besides, he wasn't sure exactly what was going on either, "Those men chasing us with guns aren't cops. And that was no accident at the apartment. Those cars were meaning to ram us." He paused, allowing her to process the morsel before moving on, "Do you hear that helicopter?" Amber looked up, listening. "That's not a police helicopter and if you peaked out and looked at it, and please don't, but if you did, you would see it's got a Channel 6 logo on it. But it's not Channel 6 either."

"Then who the hell are they?"

"People that want us both dead – well, me primarily, but you're a loose end. They'll want you too. I'm sure of it."

"Dead! Why?" Her anger was clouding her rational mind. The gravity of Paul's words had not yet sunk in.

"Haven't you been watching the news?"

"No!" Amber could see genuine concern in Paul's eyes. She had been more angry than scared but now the emotions were beginning to reverse.

"Remember that 'Code Purple' Ophelia was telling us about when you left last night?"

"Yea," she was getting a bit sheepish now.

"His name was Abdullah Burja, an Al-Qaeda terrorist. He was in our ER, shot by a SWAT team trying to blow himself up."

"So?"

Paul could hear the helicopter getting louder. He had hoped they would take the bait and start searching the acres of pine forest surrounding them but instead they were circling right overhead. He figured he had only a couple minutes.

"Burja died. I think he was a double agent. I think he was poisoned by someone who was trying to keep him from passing on information."

Amber rolled her eyes, "So, what does this have to do with us?"

Paul decided to come clean – at least partially. "Before Burja died, he gave that information to me."

"To you?"

"Yes, and now those people who killed him are after us."

"What people? Who are you talking about?"

"CIA I think. Or something like that. Or maybe Al-Qaeda – or Hamas – or God knows who."

"Oh my God! What did he give you?"

"Does it matter?" Amber recognized the helicopter engine getting louder. "Yes, they are right over us."

"Why? What do they want?"

"They want to pin us down until their ground team arrives?"

"Ground team?"

"Yea, the ones who tried to ram us and shoot us on the freeway. We probably only have a few minutes until they're here and we're dead."

Amber's lower lip quivered. The anger was now completely gone – replaced by abject fear. Her eyes watered, silently asking her next question, "What are we going to do?"

He read her mind, "I'm not sure what the next move is baby but whatever it is, I need you to follow me. Ok? I need you to do what I say. I'm not going to let anything happen to you."

She nodded, speechlessly, fear taking over. She heard him say "I love you", but she could not respond. All she could do was nod.

Agents Michaels and Victor Coombs were directing the orbiting helicopter outfitted to resemble a civilian news service. Agent Caryn Lund was commanding the Eurocopter and the pilot, Brent Stokes, was her 'husband' from the mall. She kept the Center well informed, "They're under the bridge. They must have wrecked. They stopped way too fast."

"Are you sure they didn't make it into the forest?" Michael's knew the answer to his own question.

"No. It's wintertime. Good visibility on all of the trails and nothing on infrared," Lund's answer was the expected one.

Victor interrupted the pleasant conversation, "Agent Lund, this is Agent Coombs. We need visual recon. And if they are still alive, we need to correct that."

"Are you sure, sir? This is a busy road. And we're supposed to be a news helicopter."

"So, go get the story." Coombs' order was loud and clear.

XXVI

8:02 am

Phil Oxmore gave his team a short break after hearing of Martin's disappointing report. It has been a long night, and everyone needed the rest, he included, but there were still political duties to fulfill.

On the hour, Phil Oxmore joined Baptist East's Chief Executive, Ben Caruthers, and his COO, Keith Ware, into the hospital's administration lobby. He had hoped to meet up with Tanya Marone as well but had no such luck; it was her day off and she had already been sent home. Phil thanked them for their hospitality and service, praising the security team and taking the time to answer a few questions about staff member and well-respected physician, Paul Gudrun.

"Any news yet on Dr. Gudrun's whereabouts?" Ware started.

"Not yet but we have an APB out on him. We'll find him." Oxmore's practiced conceit was effective, neither of the administrators doubting the FBI's capabilities for a second.

"Do you really think he killed Ophelia?" Caruthers asked.

"It appears that way," Oxmore flatly answered.

Caruthers dropped his head in melancholy, "They've known each other for years."

"Yes, but I don't think you would say they were friends?" Ware corrected triggering a chief executive chuckle Phil found interesting, "Adversaries more like it. She always seemed to be harassing him about one thing or teasing him about another." Caruthers jumped in laughing, "Yeah, she did root over him like a mother hen, didn't she?"

A second later, Vito Scaglione unceremoniously barged in, interrupting the chief's jocular reminisce, "There you are Agent Oxmore."

"Please call me Phil." Oxmore took the opportunity to take a step back from the cacklers.

"Yes sir, we have completed our security diagnostics..."

"And?" Phil Oxmore was trying to be polite but all he could think of was "here we go again. Another run of bumbling bombast from the hospital's Barney Fife."

"There were two breaches," Vito answered, oblivious to Phil's derision. "One came from inside the hospital. It originated from a console in one of the pathologist's offices. The breach correlates with the time we believe Dr. Gudrun was in the lab but there is no direct evidence of that. However, the hacker reprogrammed the cameras and locked out changes. Those are things Dr. Gudrun would have needed to do to facilitate his escape. But I'll tell you this, if it was him, he has a whole lot of technical expertise I never knew about. He knew just what to do."

"And the second breach?"

"It occurred at 4:34 in the morning. For a five minute period, all security data in the entire facility was wiped."

"Wiped?! You've got to be kidding! By who?"

"That's the real interesting part. The hack was external. Whoever did it penetrated all of our firewalls like butter."

All of a sudden, Vito Scaglione had become Columbo.

Michaels, Gonzalez, Wade and Coombs were all huddled in the hot, cramped control room monitoring the chase. Coombs was not leaving anything to chance. He had his best cleanup team descending to a kill. Hopefully, Gudrun had wrapped the motorcycle around a pole. But if he hadn't, Coombs wanted Lund to finish this. Agent Sokolov was his most versatile and ruthless asset but Caryn Lund was an equally talented shot, particularly with the rifle.

They listened as she positioned herself with the butt of her M4 Carbine in the angle of her shoulder, her back supported by the frame of the aircraft. Stokes continued his steady dissent as she relaxed, slowed the rhythm of her breathing, precisely positioned her cheek in the stock, and tested her view through the rifle's EOTech holographic weapon sight. As the shot window approached, she released the safety and positioned her right hand carefully on the pistol grip with her trigger finger waiting patiently on the guard.

Paul listened closely. The rotor sounds were slowly getting louder and the vector of the sound was progressively moving in front of them. He concluded that the helicopter was descending; physics required it and Paul had expected their move. Human nature was impatient. Their pursuers would want visual confirmation of their situation.

Paul turned to Amber who had repositioned herself back on the seat behind him. She was petrified. He looked at her lovingly and spoke with his eyes, "It's going to be alright. I know you doubt me, wondering whether or not you should trust me or just give yourself up. Baby, know that I love you." She managed a miniature smile, the best she could produce. The sound of the helicopter clack was drowning out the traffic noise or, more likely Paul believed, onlookers were stopping to watch the spectacle unfolding before them. He calculated the helicopter's rate of dissent; the skis were less than 10 feet above the surface of the overpass. Swirls of dust and fine pebbles began to pelt the two of them, driven by the action of the spinning blades. Amber covered her eyes but Paul was focused on the task. His timing needed to be perfect. He started the motorcycle engine and looked over his shoulder to his beautiful girlfriend one last time, "Are you ready?" She nodded ever so slightly then buried her head into his back.

Agent Lund readied her weapon. The helicopter was seconds before revealing her prey. She could see the remnants of the motorcycles trail cutting through the gravel. Suddenly, a deafening roar overcame the oscillating beat of the helicopter. She recognized the sound a microsecond too late. Timed perfectly, Paul accelerated the Iron 883 straight for the Eurocopter.

Lund saw the blur but so did the pilot. She fired the M4 but his instinctual reaction to pull up drew the shot high missing Amber's shoulder by an inch. Lund tried to recover but immediately knew it was pointless. In less than a second, the motorcycle had raced beneath them, slid onto the dirt path, and headed back toward the street.

Agent Stokes tried to compensate by rotating the chopper 180 degrees but the effect was more dizzying than useful. By the time Coomb's crackerjack sharpshooter regained her aim, the motorcycle was gone.

The silence in the Tyler Command Center was tomb-like and Gonzales could literally feel Victor's breath on his neck. Gonzales was first to comment, "He's smart."

"He's fucking James Bond!" Wade yelled back.

Michaels ignored them both and focused on his radio, "Reacquire the target. Where is he headed?"

"We're coming around now," Lund answered as she tried to regroup, "I see him. He's back on the road. It looks like he's heading for the interstate. We might be able to get off another shot."

"Negative. Risk is unacceptable. Maintain surveillance and await ground support," Michaels ordered. Taking the initiative, he changed channels, "Team 3, what is your status?"

"Screwed! We're stuck in traffic!" McCammon quickly and exasperatedly answered, "Gudrun roundhouse-kicked some poor bloke to get his motorcycle. The man's out cold and now the cops have called in an ambulance. We might be here for awhile."

"Well, now we know what happened to Marti Gras," Wade mumbled beneath his breath.

Gonzales felt a whiff of moist heat. The sensation was followed by the sound of a short snort and a grumble reminiscent of distant thunder.

"What about the others?" Michaels continued his interrogation.

"Teams 1 and 2 wrecked. An agent is down. And you will be happy to know the FBI is here."

"Your plan?"

"I don't have one. As soon as we regroup, lick our wounds and find alternative transportation, I'll check in."

Before the conversation had ended, Gonzalez felt his neck suddenly cool. Without a word, Coombs had left the room.

XXVII

8:12 am

Agent Caryn Lund was visibly angry. She hated being played the fool. The wily doctor and his nurse lover were tragic pawns in a grander game and she had initially pitied them, but not anymore. She now had active kill orders and had been outfoxed and embarrassed. Coombs had been giving her the rookie slack, but she was no longer a beginner and this prize was too big to lose. Her anger hid her deeper fear of the consequences failure might bring. The thought just made her angrier.

They had pulled up to 2000 feet and were following the motorcycle and her two riders driving westward on I-40. They were driving fast but comfortably. Either they believed they were in the clear or were hoping they would blend in with traffic. Either way, they were sadly mistaken. She watched as they sped off onto Poplar Road, drove about a mile, and turned into a commercial parking lot. The building housed a coin laundry and a restaurant. The motorcycle pulled in front and Lund watched as the riders dismounted.

At Paul's direction, Amber followed him into the Ms. Lu's Wash-a-mat. She had felt a rush of excitement at the park. She heard the gunshots and saw the gunman in the helicopter and the thrill of escape was exhilarating.

She had never had felt more alive! But now fear and foreboding began to erupt again. The place was empty except for a hopelessly obese black woman folding clothes in the back corner. "What are we doing here?" Amber wondered out loud, and Paul was quick to answer, "I'm hoping to throw them off the scent for a few minutes. They're smart though. We're going to have to be quick."

The two scampered to the back of the laundry down a row of vacant washing machines, into a service hallway, and through a wooden door. It was the back entrance to the restaurant.

The cafe was dressed in dark paneling and sported a nautical theme. The tables were made of partially burnt oak and the walls were littered with fake pirate memorabilia. The little light that emanated from the boat lanterns was obscured by a thick waft of Marlboro smoke. Amber instantly felt out of place. Most of the clientele were gruff, tattooed black men wearing wifebeaters. There were a scattering of disheveled and wrinkled white bums and a couple of Mexicans camped out in the corner, but there was not a single woman there. She watched as plates of scrambled eggs served on chipped plates with mugs of oil slick coffee were served to men still nursing their last draft beer. She wanted to stop in her tracks but Paul's confidence kept her going. Any hesitation was erased by the next words she heard, her boyfriend and the bartender exchanging familiar bro-talk like Paul was a regular. In fact, he was.

Two years earlier, Paul had walked into Captain Cadillac on a whim. The greasy spoon by day, tavern by night was also a full service Internet cafe with ten Windows 7 workstations, three Mac Pros and two Linux boxes. They offered printing, fax, and copy capabilities along with access to Microsoft Office software, games, a variety of internet browsers, and ten beers on tap. Although the offerings were comprehensive, most of the patrons used the computers to gamble and view porn. The owner didn't care and Paul knew well enough to keep quiet. The truth was he only cared about one thing – anonymous access to the Internet. No one asked him any questions and he returned the favor in kind.

"That smells good," Amber truthfully uttered. She was hungry.

"That's not what we're here for," Paul oddly answered, "I will get you a proper breakfast later. I promise."

Paul plopped in front of a Linux workstation and started the Firefox browser. In seconds, he logged in to his specially configured server housed at a collocation center in St. Louis. He chose the city for a reason. In common hacker parlance, Paul was a wizard well-versed in all manner of deep magic. In other words, he had programmed special software safeguards, anonymous remailing systems, and cloaking technologies into his server to mask his activities. But in the event the machine was ever compromised, he wanted no direct connection to him.

Amber watched quizzically as Paul began typing at a speed a court reporter would envy. A series of computer windows filled with foreign jargon and symbols popped like fireworks on the screen. She wanted to ask a question like "why are we here?" or "what are you doing?" but thoughts were having trouble translating into words. Things were happening too fast and her emotions were in continuous flux. She was angry enough to leave him yet scared to death and she was confused beyond belief yet strangely curious. She finally decided on a question but before her vocal cords could vibrate the screen changed once again. She recognized the webpage logo instantly. It was a FedEx site.

This demanded a question change. "FedEx?" Amanda asked.

"I'm getting us a job. You are going to work in the sorting room and I'm on the flight line."

Amber had no idea what the hell he was talking about.

8:49 am

Oxmore walked into the dimly-lit conference room to find Alesha Deng typing on her laptop, Jim Neighbors prostrate on the floor, and Tedder and Amy both asleep on a bench. Phil had encouraged his team to take a rest and regroup after Dr. Gudrun's escape but this was not what he meant.

Phillip took a millisecond to absorb the scene. Amy's back was against the wall and Tedder's head was in her lap. How on earth Tedder managed to find his way onto Amy's embrace, he could only imagine. But now he was snuggling up to her bosom and snoring like a drunken swashbuckler.

Phil looked unbelievingly at Alesha who shrugged her shoulders and whispered, "All three were beat and decided to take a 10 minute catnap."

The atmosphere and her words reminded his mind that he needed sleep too but Phillip pushed the urge away. Critical developments had just come to light and there was no time to rest. "Wake up!" he bellowed, "We've got work to do!"

Neighbors popped right up to his feet, "Sorry sir."

Amy instantly awoke too, realized Tedder was on her lap, and roughly pushed him off causing him to slide gracelessly to the floor. She stood bolt upright making full eye contract with a smirking Neighbors. Her eyes pierced through his brain. She was not amused but he sure was. He continued grinning as he pointed to her chest. She quickly realized her blouse was agape, sufficiently so, that Tedder's head had been in perfect position to admire the view. Ignoring Jim completely, she rearranged herself just in time.

"Alright people, rise and shine! I'm glad somebody is getting some sleep. No more nursery school. Some serious shit is going down here and I need everyone's head in the game," Oxmore's profanity was uncharacteristic and rapidly seized everyone's attention.

A cacophony of soft "sorry sirs" filled the room.

"Scaglione just told me that the hospital's computers were hacked twice. Once by Gudrun and once by someone else. Someone outside the hospital. Someone who happened to erase Ophelia Roberts' entry into the resident's quarters moments before she confronted Gudrun. Someone with very sophisticated capabilities. Someone able to cover their tracks – even from us."

The room was silent. Oxmore scanned the room. He had already reached the natural conclusion but wanted independent confirmation from his team. He expected the revelation would come from Amy or Tedder, or perhaps Jim. Instead, it was Alesha who was more awake than the rest.

"The CIA is here."

XXVIII

Jungfrau Region
Bernese Oberland, Switzerland

3:49 pm, CET

Located within the eastern Bernese Alps, the Aletsch glacier is the largest, longest and deepest glacier in all of western Eurasia. The glacier is supported to the east by the Gross Fiescherhorn and Gross Wannenhorn mountains and on the west by the Aletschhorn. The northern boundary of the impressive landscape is bounded by the spectacular Eiger, Mönch and Jungfrau peaks, three of the most superlatively scenic and iconic mountains of the high Alps. Immortalized in art and literature, the famous north wall is an epicenter of alpine tourism and a favorite destination of mountain climbers and outdoorsman alike.

Regardless of the circumstances, protocol demanded silence until within a secure communication environment. Professor Nef wasn't there yet. The flight from Lucerne to the Lauterbrunnen heliport was quick but marked by moderate turbulence, not unexpected given the unpredictability of winter alpine weather, but the short train to the Kleine Scheidegg train station was serene. Even through the overcast mist and light snow, the beauty of the valley and the ride up through the village of Wengen and into the mountain heights offered a stunning panorama of the Jungfrau massif. He never grew tired of the views. If all went as usual, he would reach Kleine Scheidegg shortly and then quickly board a waiting train on the Jungfraubahn headed south.

In 1894, the Swiss industrialist Adolfo Guyer-Zeller envisioned a train station at the top of the Jungfraujoch, the natural saddle between the Jungfrau and the Mönch. It took sixteen years, the deaths of six men, and the burrowing of a tunnel through Mont Eiger for his vision to become a reality. The rail line would come to be known as the Jungfraubahn carrying sightseers and thrill seekers to the famous Jungfraujoch station, the highest altitude railroad station in Europe, with magnificent views of the Aletsch glacier and the Bernese Oberland below.

Unlike the typical passenger summer trains that might transport upwards of 8000 visitors a day to the observation terrace, observatory, ice palace, and restaurant at the "Top Of Europe", winter trains carried fewer visitors. But on this day, the weather was particularly poor, and this train was carrying mainly freight and fresh water. There were only seven passengers in the front car, 5 men and two women. None were tourists. Everyone on the train knew each other. No one said a word.

Nef could feel the train slowing as it approached the Eigergletscher station. There, if he were headed to the Jungfraujoch, the train would continue on through the Eiger tunnel, stopping at two other viewing stations built within the mountain before terminating at the top. But he and the others were not going that far. Ordinarily, only adventurists, skiers and Eiger north wall mountaineers disembarked at the Eigergletscher station, but this group was here on business.

The professor stepped off the platform into the 10 degree, overcast, late afternoon. There he was met by a white-haired, rotund, German speaking rail conductor who escorted Nef and the others into the tunnels below the station.

In 1939, days after the Nazi blitzkrieg streaked across Poland inaugurating World War II, the Swiss leadership finalized their plans to expand the national redoubt strategy, a defensive plan to retreat the army into the mountains in the event of a German attack. Fort de Dailly, a massive subterranean complex of gun turrets, 75mm cannons, and open artillery positions protecting the Saint-Maurice valley was expanded and new fortifications were built to defend the strategic passes at Saint-Gotthard and Sargans.

At the same time, the financiers were establishing their own redoubt strategy. Switzerland had amassed significant wealth in the interwar years and no matter the outcome on the battlefield, there was strong conviction to deny Hitler the spoils of war. Shortly after the fall of Paris, gold and other treasure was moved from Geneva to points south. Officially, the gold was split between the newly built fortresses guarding the Gotthard Pass and banks within the midlands. But it was decided early on that a special ultra-secret hiding place was needed for the Swiss national reserves. Code-named Fort De Berne, or just Berne for short, it safeguarded the nation's wealth through the World War and the Cold War that followed. Although most of the redoubt was no longer classified nor in use, Berne was the only remnant of the twentieth century Swiss military mountain fortress chain that was still secret and had never been decommissioned. But it no longer kept Swiss gold, jewels, rare art, or currency. Instead, it now hid a treasure significantly more valuable. Alexander Nef was one of the few people who knew or who had ever known the real name or the exact location of the Swiss National Monetary Redoubt: Untereigerbasis. The Base Under the Eiger. And the professor was about to walk inside.

Memphis, Tennessee
8:57 am

The helicopter circled above the building watching for an escape on foot, but Gonzales had already deduced their plan. He pulled up the architectural schematics. There were no utility tunnels or other modes of escape. There had to be another reason they were there and washing clothes and having breakfast were not it. The answer had to be communication. Sure enough, the building was serviced by a T1 line. He began immediately to hack in. He was a wizard too – a wizard of black magic.

While Gonzales was working hard on the ground, Lund remained vigilant from the air. Her mood had calmed. She had just gotten word that Sokolov and Reynolds were about to leave the apartment complex and would soon be in route to intercept. She took in a deep breath, sighed and was just about to report in when she noticed activity below: Gudrun and Chase were getting back on the road. She had no clue what they had been doing there and could have cared less. She directed her pilot to pursue and watched as the motorcycle turned south on Mount Moriah Road and headed once again for the interstate.

Stokes kept his altitude while she established a private connection to Tyler informing Coombs and company of their target's movements. The ground team had been redirected but was still several minutes away. She was about to order the chopper in closer when a grimace from Stokes directed her to don the headphones. She could instinctually feel her mood changing, even before she heard his words, "He's heading for the airport. We are going to need special emergency FAA clearance to enter the airspace."

Coombs and the rest of Tyler Center were already on the channel and could hear the pilot.

"Not a chance. Air 1," Michael interceded, "You're not the police. Your Channel 6, remember? Stay clear. We'll wait for ground. Can you still see him?"

Agent Stokes answered in the affirmative and gave a play-by-play description of the target's movements while Agent Lund kept quiet, watching as the motorcycle turned left, then right, before finally settling into the FedEx SuperHub complex on the grounds of the Memphis International Airport.

9:14 am

Oxmore was surprised by Deng's assessment but shouldn't have been. She might have been called in to translate Hausa, but she was part of the FBI's Behavioral Analysis Unit and experienced in the modus operandi of the intelligence community.

"That would explain many things," Agent Neighbors was beginning to see the picture too.

But Amy Weikert still doubted, "The CIA doesn't act within the borders."

"You don't really believe that, do you?" Tedder condescended. Amy didn't show it, but she tacitly agreed. Still there were so many questions, "So, if CIA is responsible here, then what do they want with Gudrun? Is he one of theirs too?"

"He certainly has skills," Stone retorted.

"Maybe he's opposition – or a DA," Neighbors offered.

"A double agent? Doubling as a doctor and a what? How much intelligence do you think runs through a Memphis ER?" Weikert's mind was still reeling. There were too many inconsistencies.

"Maybe Burja passed Gudrun something and they want it?" Neighbors deduced.

"You think they were working together? Maybe that's what the nurse was trying to get?" Tedder asked, "You think she was in on this too?"

"Are you kidding? She was snuck in!" Neighbors and Stone were on a roll.

"Wow. So, maybe she was really confronting him."

"More like trying to put the squeeze on."

"And he turned the tables."

Agent Weikert interrupted the duet, "Why are we so sure this is a Langley op?"

"By law, the CIA leads all covert operations," Deng contributed, "unless the President says otherwise."

"Besides, this has Special Activities Division written all over it," Neighbors added, referring to the division of the CIA's National

Clandestine Service, responsible for covert political influence and paramilitary operations, "No one else could have pulled this off. Not even the Brits or the Russians – certainly not some Al-Queda cell."

Oxmore weighed the comments and understood them. If true, what was happening here was highly organized and official, directed from levels of authority well above his, in fact, either implicitly or explicitly, with Presidential approval. The evening's events were finally beginning to make sense, including his conversation with Assistant Director Taylor.

"Damn!"

Her boss' superlative startled Agent Weikert and stunned the room, "What?"

"I need to make a phone call."

XXIX

9:19 am

Oxmore needed some fresh air. He walked through the eerily quiet emergency room, passed the nurses desk that had been ground zero for the preceding evening's pandemonium, and walked out the ambulance entrance's double-glass automatic doors. The air was dry and crisp with virtually no wind. Phil gazed up at the remarkably clear star-studded winter sky, took a deep breath followed by a fog-laced exhale and dialed Assistant Director Taylor. He felt his heart racing. He hated confrontations, especially with his superiors. After vapid pleasantries, Phil dove right in, "So, when were you going to tell me that there was a third party here, Brent?"

"I'm not following," Taylor dryly answered.

"Why is CIA involved?" Oxmore was clearly annoyed.

"Now I understand the question. It's need to know."

"Don't give me that, Sir! People have died!"

"I understand that. Your priority is to locate and apprehend Paul Gudrun as a matter of national security. And you need to do it before more lives are lost."

"Why? Is he a terrorist too?"

"If that helps you feel better, yes." There was a momentary pause before the Assistant Director gently clarified, "Bring him in Phil. That comes all the way from the top."

Phil sensed the conciliatory gesture, but he was dead set on finding how deep the rabbit hole went, "The Director?" There was silence. "The White House?" More silence. "So, am I going to have CIA help here?"

"Believe me, they have the same orders you do."

"I doubt that."

9:23 am

Paul hacked his name on to the FedEx authorized parking list as a visitor. It was enough to get him past the entry guard post, but that was the easy part. He pulled in to the employee parking lot and double-parked the Harley. Amber was full of questions and Paul began to brief her while they briskly walked over the pedestrian bridge toward the checkpoint entrance, "Don't look up now but our eye-in-the-sky is still following us and pretty soon they're going to be more of them." Paul was almost jogging, but Amber was keeping up, listening intently to his every word. "We need to lose them."

"But this place is crawling with security!" Amber huffed still not completely buying what was going on.

"That's why I stopped at the restaurant. FedEx's security is highly sophisticated but it's all driven by a complex computer network – and all networks can be infiltrated."

"Hacked, you mean."

Paul gave Amber a knowing play-along look as they slowed down and strolled up to the guard post. A thirty-something prematurely graying FedEx Security Specialist pulled them to the side away from the other employees passing through turnstiles that led into what looked suspiciously like airport security. Paul had practiced his pitch in his head and offered the guard a plausible explanation: they had just gotten hired and were directed to check in and get their name tags. The irritated man mumbled something about not being told of new employees as he checked his computer and asked their names.

"Paul Gale. And this is Amber Paige," Paul lied.

Gudrun's hack was successful. Not looking up from his console, the security specialist acknowledged finding their files and then began reciting an orientation Amber was sure he had given countless times before. He explained the need for a badge holder and where to get it, the location of the uniform shop, the time clocks and break room and the personnel office. Minutes later, he handed them the freshly printed badges and watched closely and they progressed through the metal detector and bag screening station.

He kept an eye on the couple as they walked into the complex. He wanted to make sure they were following his directions, and he sighed in relief as they entered the right building through the right door. "You couldn't be too careful these days", he grumbled. As they left his view, he began to fume. He had worked at the SuperHub for over three years, and this was the first time he hadn't been notified of new hires at shift change. His supervisor was going to get an earful.

Eigergletscher Station
Jungfrau Region, Switzerland

4:31 pm, CST

The professor separated from the others after clearing a guard checkpoint and passing through two heavy steel doors separated by a hundred meters of serpentine, cold, and dimly lit galleries carved into the mountain

It wasn't until he passed through the third door that his loneliness was checked by the familiar face of Dolf, his trusted executive assistant. Alexander greeted his friend warmly, and they each traded greetings ranging from critiques on their travels to news of the family. The professor rationed the idle conversation for precisely one minute before changing the substance to business, "So, is this good news or bad?"

"Something interesting is happening in America," Dolf quickly answered, his demeanor both charged yet quizzical.

"Really? Tell me. But I'm freezing. Tell me on the way to my office," Dolf responded, shivering and rubbing his black gloved hands together.

Dolf answered by walking, "Three subjects have spontaneously and randomly interacted, actually collided would be a better word."

The professor practiced silent patience. This was not particularly notable news, but he had known Dolf for years and there was surely something more. His assistant did not disappoint. "All three have exhibited very interesting emergent behaviors and two of the three were completely inert until twelve hours ago."

"I'm listening."

"Subject One was a Nigerian, raised by a shoemaker, and grew up in the town of Damaturu in northeastern Nigeria. He became radicalized as an adolescent and for a time was affiliated with Boko Haram but was recruited by Project Quest about three years ago. We were not involved, interestingly enough. He was a Team B, Compartment Alpha transport currier for the Project, but had never exhibited any behaviors and was certified inert, observation status F, shortly after joining the Quest. That is, no behaviors until today. He transformed first, about fourteen hours ago."

Dolf had Nef's interest, "Go on."

"Unfortunately, he broke and went off the rail and had to be removed," Dolf continued, "Subject Two is an American physician. He was raised in a ghetto just outside of Memphis, Tennessee in the armpit of the country. Unlike Subject One who never showed any promise, he was very interesting as an adolescent but then stalled and has been fairly inert ever since although he was able to achieve a professional degree. He has had Observation Status E for the past twenty years."

"So you are saying he is not inert anymore either."

"Since interacting with Subject One, he has now begun to demonstrate some very interesting behaviors that are highly suggestive of early transcendence. He transformed less than 9 hours ago."

"Really? And I'm assuming all measures are being taken to bring him in for verification."

"Yes sir. Several assets have been deployed. It's only a matter of time."

"And the third subject?" Nef inquired.

"He's a soldier – an American paramilitary operative who we've been watching closely for some time. He was raised by an upper middle class Boston family, transformed as a youth, and is one of the few that are Observation Status C. He has consistently scored high in aptitude across the board but has never achieved pre-transcendence or anything close. But now, he has been tasked to track and capture Subject Two and has been showing some improvement."

"Ah, now there's some good news," Nef sarcastically reacted, "Our best prospects are the least impressive!" He tried to remain polite, but his frustration was beginning to mount, "Is there a common denominator amongst the late bloomers?"

"Perhaps. Both Subjects One and Two accessed the Mediator just moments before transforming." Dolf could tell his boss was surprised. "We can't explain it either. Those programs are not related, are they?"

Nef feinted ignorance, "Not to my knowledge."

"Should we take this upstairs?"

Nef contemplated the request as he pressed the button to summon the elevator. "No. Not yet. We need more information. Determine the nature of the Mediator connection." The door to the elevator opened and Nef kept talking as he boarded, "And let's make Subject Two our little American project. Keep him under close watch until Subject Three can bring him in. I will be in my office."

Alexander exhaled as the door closed in front of him, and the lift began to ascend. He remembered the day the Administrator approached him with the two poems and the instruction to post them prominently on the International Poetry Society web page. He had always found the poems mysterious and never believed for a moment that the title of the first one, *The Quest*, was coincidental. Project Quest had been the code name of Operation Mediator from its inception. But the professor hated puzzles and had never really given the poems much attention. Perhaps he should have.

Memphis, Tennessee
9:35 am CST

'He hacked FedEx!' Gonzalez clarioned, breaking the silence of the somber Tyler Center, "He's penetrated their security!" Without a word of explanation, he began furiously typing on his keyboard. The keystrokes were interrupted by an intertwined flurry of mouse clucks with the purposeful intent of emulating a cell phone GPS signature and placing the phantom phone outside the FedEx entrance. It only took a few more clicks to make a phone call and only a couple of rings for someone to answer.

'911. What's your emergency?'

Gonzalez rigged the speaker so everyone could here, "I need the police right away. And an ambulance. I just saw a man get run over right in front of me!" Gonzalez was virtually screaming.

"Calm down sir. Police and paramedics are on their way. Explain what happened."

"A guy on a Harley and his girlfriend ran over a homeless man right in front of me," Gonzalez tried his best to sound as harried as possible, "I got out to help and the man pulled a gun on me. Told me to get back in the car or he'd shoot. Then he sped off. It looks like he went through the FedEx gate. They just let him in!"

"Is someone attending to the pedestrian?"

"Yes. Someone is now. He's conscious but doesn't look good. You gotta send help quick!"

"Help is on its way. Can you describe the man and the woman on the motorcycle?"

"White guy with dark red hair and a wild, crazy look on his face. The woman had blonde hair. Neither was wearing a helmet. They went right through the FedEx gate! Please send police fast!"

Gonzalez hung up and turned to see both Michaels and Wade staring speechlessly and with their mouths slightly agape. Victor Coombs broke the silence with a single word, "Outstanding."

Tiring of the solitude and starting to chill, Phil headed back into the hospital, this time walking into the main hospital entrance. Hours earlier, he had spied a boarded up cafeteria. He hoped they would be open by now. Some bacon and eggs sure sounded good. His mouth was starting to water at the thought but was quickly quenched by the sight of an anxious Tedder Stone walking quickly toward him.

"Just got word from Jones," Tedder was breathless again, "They're at the girlfriend's apartment. Witnesses saw her and a man matching Gudrun's appearance drive off in a Honda Civic with a broken window. He wrecked a couple of cars in the process and then abandoned his in traffic. There's one casualty, and another man was trapped. Highway patrol just pulled him out."

"Where is he now?" The breakfast was no longer on the SAIC's mind.

"He jacked a motorcycle and got on the interstate. We've notified MPD. And there's something else..."

"What?"

"Neighbors wants to show you something."

9:40 am

Lieutenant Avery was in Major Branson's drab office nursing a cup of 2 hour old coffee. He had gotten precisely four hours of sleep before his home phone disturbed his erotic dream. She was a tall slender Swedish bikini model. Now an overweight, pock-faced Major Branson walked in with a stout, muscular, prematurely wrinkling Commander Chunn right behind him. He couldn't even remember what the model looked like anymore. He was just glad he had popped that Prilosec before walking into the precinct.

"Thank you for coming in this morning, Jon. I think the faster we can get the details of last night's events down on paper, the better," the Major began abruptly.

"Just as long as I'm not here Monday morning," Avery joked. The truth was he had been reading the first responder reports and the eyewitness testimony since he arrived, and there were more than a few inconsistencies. There was probably no way he was going to avoid the Monday morning review.

"Where is McCammon?"

"Still stuck in traffic," Chunn answered regurgitating what dispatch had told him. Avery, for his part, was glad Chunn had chimed in. He had spent the last half hour researching, trying to make sense of the night's crazy events, hoping to anticipate his boss' every question. That one hadn't been one of them.

"So, what do we know?"

"Both of the guards were shot in the head, execution style," Avery began, suddenly more comfortable. That was a question he was expecting.

"Do we know anything about the shooter? Any idea how he penetrated security?"

"FBI says he was a high value terrorist. What we know is he got in posed as an armored courier."

"What?"

"He walked right in. His partner has attested that it was the first night he had ever worked with the guy. Swears the guy knew the gig and had all the appropriate credentials. According to a witness…"

"The only guard that lived, by the way," Chunn dramatically inserted.

Avery gave a quick nod to the Commander in agreement, then continued, "As soon as the shooter got inside he started screaming in Arabic. Then, he made the guards get on their knees and began putting slugs in their heads one at a time from behind." As soon as the words were out of his mouth, he realized his insensitivity. "I'm sorry sir. I forgot one of those men was your friend."

The major started fuming, "You're not the fucker who killed him."

"How did that guard get so lucky, I wonder?" Chunn tried to change the subject.

"Says he was next but at the last moment the lunatic suddenly pulled up and ran off."

Avery stopped talking and there was a prolonged silence.

Branson was not impressed, "Is that it?" and his lieutenant nodded in the affirmative, "He just let him go? And was disguised as a federal courier?"

Avery nodded again.

"That's about as believable as I once fucked Brittany Spears."

The joke broke through Ian Chunn's professional veneer, and he guffawed, "I agree!" He almost could not stop laughing. "I had to listen to this guy rant and rave for an hour. He didn't speak a lick of English. There's no way he was employed officially as a monetary courier!"

"So the other courier was lying. Why?" Now it was Avery trying to make heads or tails of the situation.

"He had to be in on it," Chunn deduced.

"So, we'll need to pick him up. Then what happened?" Branson kept up the pace. He wanted to go home too.

"We appropriately initiated a pursuit. There were four fatalities at one intersection, several injuries, and ultimately the suspect died in custody at the hospital," the lieutenant answered.

"There was also one other related death," Chunn added, "A young store clerk was apparently killed at the mall by the suspect."

The Lieutenant was running on empty, and his temples were pounding. Coffee or no coffee the couch was starting to look mighty good. Only the burning indigestion was keeping him awake. Then he remembered something. Something the FBI agent, what was his name, Agent Stone had written in his report. The terrorist's gun. The one the boy was killed with...it only had one spent round. So... either the terrorist used another gun to kill those guards... or he wasn't the one who killed them!

XXX

Memphis, Tennessee
9:40 am CST

Phillip Oxmore joined his team to find Amy Weikert, Jim Neighbors and Alesha Deng hovering over a computer.

"Phil. You've got to come over and see this," Amy Weikert called out. Oxmore walked behind Amy and looked over her shoulder. He flared his nose. She was beautiful, but her deodorant had worn off. A second later he realized the smell was coming from himself. On the screen, a SWAT officer in full gear was conversing with Dr. Redmond.

"Who's that?" Oxmore was intrigued.

"His name is Christos Sokolov, one of Chunn's SWAT team snipers," Neighbors explained.

"What's he telling him?"

"I just spoke to Dr. Redmond. He says Officer Sokolov told him to ask Gudrun to fetch his watch from the call room," Tedder sneered.

"Now look at this," Neighbors redirected. The video changed to the emergency room. The footage was from the previous evening archiving Abdullah Burja's arrival to the hospital. Next to Burja's gurney, a SWAT team member in full regalia was walking by his side.

"So, Sokolov was with him in the ambulance?" Phil was getting the point.

"Yes, it looks that way. And now how about this?" The video switched to the front entrance of the physician call rooms. Two men were easily seen walking in. Neighbors anticipated Oxmore's next question, "Yes, that's Sokolov too. And when the nurse was found, it was he who stayed with the nurse."

"Where is Mr. Sokolov now?"

"Disappeared with McCammon and the rest of Chunn's team."

"Does anyone have any ideas?" once again it was Deng who had the quick answer: "He's CIA."

"How do you know that?" Jim Neighbors instantly challenged, but Oxmore internally agreed with Deng's assessment. He had just gotten off the phone with Taylor and had heard the truth directly, but he was still interested in her logic.

"I've listened to 10 minutes of his dialogue now at least a dozen times," Deng explained, "He's using a structured sentence delivery technique that was developed jointly by the DEA and CIA to conceal codes within common speech. I know about it because I helped invent it."

The blank stares told her no one had any idea what she was talking about, so she decided to help clarify it.

"Someone else is listening into his conversations."

9:50 am

Sokolov maneuvered his commandeered Hyundai beyond a row of cars lined up outside the expansive Federal Express Employee parking lot security gate and parked next to two flashing blue light MPD cruisers flanking the guard house.

It looks like he's in the FedEx complex. MPD is already here," Sokolov reported in to Tyler Center on his encrypted iPhone, his voice pressured and his mind on an adrenaline high the likes of which rivaled Colombian foo-foo dust.

"We need you inside. No air coverage," Michaels ordered. Sokolov hung up the phone. No word was spoken. None was necessary.

"You're kidding, right?" Branson was incredulous.

Avery elaborated, "There's no other explanation."

"There are always other explanations." Branson's cliche retort was comical, but no one was laughing.

"There's got to be another gun," Chunn offered.

Avery was not letting down, "You've seen the bank videos. He only had one gun. The Sig in his hand is the same one the boy was killed with."

"Unless he reloaded," the Commander offered.

"Then where are the spent shells?" Avery shot back and Chunn had no immediate response. "The FBI swept the mall thoroughly and CSI inspected the accident scenes. There was no other guns, no other ammunition, and no other opportunities to do anything else."

After a contemplative pause, Chunn added the obvious alternative, "The only other explanation is a cover-up."

"Cover-up?" Avery questioned in a high pitched breathy voice. Branson was speechless.

"As ridiculous as it sounds, it's possible." Chunn directed his explanation to his boss, "There are a number of inconsistencies. When you really start to think about it, it stretches credulity: the executed bank guards, the loaded gun that supposedly shot them, the suicide bomber who was anything but…." He slowed his phrasing for emphasis, "the power loss at the mall… the death of the clerk…"

Branson's temporal artery was about to pulsate through his skin, "You think the boy was snuffed?"

"No witnesses," the Commander continued.

"Maybe the bank guards were killed by someone else, and they tried to pin it on this guy," Avery added.

Chunn could tell the Major was unconvinced and elected not to press the matter when his boss changed the subject. "So, where we do we stand with the nurse homicide?"

Avery was ready for the change-up, "That's pretty cut and dry. One of the staff physicians is the clear suspect. We have him on video entering the call room where the murder occurred. A clear struggle took place and it looks like the woman was beaten and stabbed. We also have him fleeing the scene and his prints are all over the room."

"Where is he now?"

"On the run," Avery answered.

Chunn was half listening. He was as much preoccupied with the terrorist as he was with the nurse's murder. "There has got to be more going on here. It's too bizarre that an ER nurse is killed by a doctor just a few hours after treating an international terrorist in their Emergency Room."

The conference was suddenly interrupted by the day watch commander providing an urgent update: A 911 had just been received on a hit and run near the airport. The perpetrators description matched those of the doctor wanted in connection with the hospital murder. TSA, homeland, and airport security had already been notified and were rolling units. Officer's Sokolov and Reynolds were nearby and were already responding. Branson thanked the commander and then led the two out of his office. He wasn't buying it. There was no cover up. There were two cases here – not one. And with the first suspect in a body bag, he was going to focus on the second. No more conspiracy theories, he decided. They were going to catch themselves a nurse killer.

"So now what," Tedder asked. For once, he was not trying to be funny.

"Let's change gears," Oxmore offered, "So, what do we know about Gudrun? And don't tell me he's a doctor."

Neighbors had unofficially already taken this challenge on. Information, after all, was his forte. Despite his boss's plea, he began his report as he had memorized it. "He's a doctor," He ignored Oxmore's scowl, "Board certified and boring. His testimony," referring to his inquiry comments that he had given to Oxmore and Tedder in the wee hours of the morning, "was accurate. He grew up in the Memphis slums to a disabled janitor and a housemaid. Financial need grants and scholarships got him through college and medical school. He's an only child. Father is long dead. Mother lives in her ancestral home in rural Arkansas about an hour away. He's got no priors; no record."

"Friends and acquaintances?" Weikert wanted to know.

"Acquaintances? The entire hospital. Friends. Amber. Apparently he was a real loner otherwise. No one at his condo knows him. His mailbox only had bills and junk mail and he uses a local bank and no credit. He saves much of his money and his debit transactions are routine. He has no apparent hobbies; no gym memberships; no clubs; no apparent political affiliation. He holds some professional organization memberships but he's not active. And his online footprint is no bigger. He has no social networks – not even business ones. She has a Facebook page – he doesn't. His face is all over hers it but there are no comments or tags. And he has no blogs or websites. He doesn't tweet. The only email account I could find for him is through the hospital. He doesn't have an iTunes, Netflix or Amazon account either. In fact, there is no evidence that he has ever bought anything on-line: No airline flights, no porn sales, no gambling, nothing."

"So, we follow the only lead," Oxmore casted.

Tedder took the bait, "Let me guess. We're headed for the country."

9:58 am

Amber walked out of the ladies changing room. Even in a sweat-stained FedEx T-shirt Paul had stolen from a hamper, she was beautiful. She had pulled her natural golden locks back into a bun and washed her face. It was not much, but it was enough, and she smiled at Paul as he caught her eyes. A moment earlier she had been a half-angry, half-scared kitten not knowing whether to strike or scamper. Now she was a woman, the object of both his lust and affection, and she was suddenly calmed and confident. They both walked up to the clerk who swiped each of their badges without a word. The cashier was gussied in all manner of corporate paraphernalia, but her soul betrayed the truth. This place was just a job to her.

Paul spotted a black landline phone from behind the counter. "Do you mind if I make a phone call?" he asked, "I need to call my wife." The clerk looked at the two of them, especially at the way the blonde gazed lovingly in the man's eyes, then raised an eyebrow and motioned toward the phone.

Paul took the opportunity. She watched as he dialed the phone and then listened to the one-sided conversation, "Hey, Charles. It's Frank. I sent a priority request by email about an hour ago. Did you get it? ... Yep, right now. How quick? ... Good. That's terrific. I will be there in 10 minutes... Yep. I need this. I owe you...Thanks."

The clerk looked at him funny, "I thought your name was Paul."

He chuckled inside. She was smarter than she looked. "Frank's my nickname. I need my wife to print out another copy of my ex-boss' recommendation letter. Personnel wanted another one."

The clerk raised her eyebrow again – the what-a-looser eyebrow.

Gudrun and Amber walked back into the hallway and Paul was amazed at the transformation – not her appearance, but her demeanor. She was now actually excited, almost giddy. She almost giggled as she asked what was next. Instantly, Paul deduced the psychology. She believed this was all a put on. He struggled with telling her the truth but quickly chose to lead her on – better unwitting and alive than witting and dead.

XXXI

9:58 am

Phil Oxmore finished his update report call with Brent Taylor and hung up. He, Stone, Weikert and Deng were driving quickly out the main entrance of the hospital. Oxmore had left Jim Neighbors to tear down the makeshift command post. It was no longer needed. Gudrun was on the loose and out of the hospital, and so was Sokolov. Now there was evidence Gudrun might have taken a nurse, Amber Chase, possibly taken as a willing hostage. They had specific orders but no real leads. The only thing Phil could think of was to learn more about Gudrun and where better to start then with his mother.

The vehicle was strangely quiet. Amy and Alesha were both pounding their laptops in the back seat. Tedder was quiet as a mouse too. Phil noticed he kept taking glances in his rearview mirror.

"Are we being followed?" Phil asked.

"No, I don't think so. Why?"

The FBI SAIC quickly turned his head toward the back and instantly realized the source of Tedder's distraction. Amy's blouse had popped open again, and Tedder was admiring the cleavage he had missed earlier. Phil said nothing. He just repositioned the mirror.

10:12 am

Christos Sokolov was frustrated. How Gudrun had managed to get in so easily he had no idea. It had taken a torturous ten minutes to obtain security clearance to enter the facility, but he and his partner were finally waved through. The FedEx employee parking lot was expansive, but Sokolov drove instinctually to where Paul and Amber had parked their motorcycle. It was in the exact spot he would have left it had the tables been turned.

The two slammed their car doors closed in unison and ran up to meet the SuperHub security team waiting for them on the employee parking lot connector bridge. Sokolov introduced himself and his partner to the guard captain as MPD Special Investigations and the three talked as they briskly walked through the turnstiles and metal detectors and into the security office. Apparently two individuals matching the descriptions of the perpetrators had indeed managed to slip through with forged IDs.

Sokolov pressed on with a barrage of questions, sensing the officer was wondering how hit-and-run punks would just happen to have forged passes. Sokolov raised the stakes, calling Gudrun a dangerous fugitive wanted in both a hospital murder investigation as well as a thwarted terrorist attack. This seemed to get the guards' attention, and he used their trepidation to learn more about Gudrun's location. Instantly, he learned that badge tracking had localized them to the uniform shop 20 minutes earlier and then into the Primary Sort Room 8 minutes after that but there had been no activity on either badge since that time and video surveillance had failed to identify any unusual activities, disturbances, or violations of restricted areas.

They were considering a systematic search of the facility, when the phone rang. The guard captain answered as Sokolov stood tensely, hoping for good news. The guard listened with gravity and with a terse "yes, sir" hung up the phone.

"I've been ordered to take you to the bunker," the guard announced.

"The bunker?" Sokolov wondered out loud.

"FedEx's world command and control center."

Words did not have to be exchanged. The captain had worked for FedEx for almost a decade and imagined he had seen it all, but the order he had just received had been a first. There was no question these fugitives were not just a couple of thugs running over a bum. And something in the back of his mind told him the two men standing before him weren't just the police either.

Paul walked through the sixteen square mile complex as if he had worked there for years. The mail sort rooms were louder than an air force tarmac, and these were the calm hours – nothing like the graveyard shift when the real action started. Then, nearly 200 planes flying out every ninety seconds would transport upwards of a million and a half parcels. But even during the day, the cavernous 1.6 acre Primary Sort Room choreographed 50000 packages an hour through 125 miles of conveyor belts and laser-driven bar code tracking systems.

Amber trailed closely behind Paul, her hand no longer in his. The appearance would have been unprofessional and grossly inappropriate. The plan was to arouse no attention. In fact, she allowed herself to fall several paces behind trying to be an inconspicuous as possible. She watched and followed as he turned into the International Room and headed for the loading docks.

Paul wished it were later, but then again, maybe not. Management was not as obsessive-compulsive in the late morning; operations were not quite as mission critical during day shift. Paul looked around and spotted his prey. In front of him was a local truck, packed with packages and ready to depart. It was manna from heaven. He stopped to allow Amber time to catch up.

"Get in the truck." he ordered.

"What?"

"Get in the truck," he said again while boarding the driver's side himself. Per standard procedure, the key was in the rig. This was a secure environment and the risk of delivery delay was far greater than theft. Amber obeyed, and they pulled out of the slip and headed for the exit, not toward Democrat Road and the interstate, but toward Memphis International Airport.

The service road curved around, and the Memphis airport terminal and control tower were visible in the distance. Amber was about to ask a question when Paul slowed the truck and turned left into a smaller complex of white-washed buildings, covered awnings and small planes. They parked along the curb. Paul turned to his girlfriend, and his eyes said only one thing: follow me.

They each got out of the truck and walked toward the largest building. The marquis was brightly illuminated even during the day but the words invoked only questions:

Wilson Air Center.
Voted best FBO fourth year running.

Her bewilderment grew as she entered the building, welcomed by a steward who addressed her by name, "Welcome Dr. Gudrun. Welcome Amber. Nice to finally meet you."

"What is this place?" Amber muttered.

"We are a fixed-based operator," the steward explained, "we are kind of like a private airport within an airport. We provide refueling, maintenance, storage, and other services to private aircraft owners." The steward continued with his explanation as he escorted the two or them into a chic lounge with a full brunch spread complete with an assortment of delicacies from oysters Rockefeller and escargot, to Cornish hen, braided lamb, beluga caviar, king crab tail, and southern grits with biscuits and sausage gravy. Amber was overwhelmed.

She looked to Paul who only smiled a thought, "I promised you breakfast."

The lover's body language banter was truncated by the steward who whispered to Paul, "Ariel will be ready shortly."

"Are you sure? We are in a big hurry."

"I'm assured sir."

Amber was only half listening. She was already fixing herself a plate of Wisconsin cheese, filet mignon, saffron poached egg and mango.

XXXII

Marked Tree, Arkansas
United States

10:45 am

The drive to Marked Tree, a small town in northeastern Arkansas with a population just under 4000 and roughly 45 minutes outside of Memphis, was essentially uneventful. Passing through acres of cultivated farm land, sparse woodlands, and the occasional human settlement, Phillip Oxmore, Tedder Stone, Amy Weikert, and Alesha Deng occupied Phil's command vehicle and spent the first half of their time working independently. Amy focused on learning about Paul Gudrun's mother. She was a weaver for a window blind maker until she married and spent the rest of her life as a mother and housewife. Her husband, Paul's father, a janitor for the Shelby County School System, struggled with emphysema for years. He died of pneumonia in 2006 and she had been on her own ever since. She was a relative loner, rarely accepted guests, and lived in her parent's house in the country. Her FBI file was, in a nutshell, squeaky clean. And so, for that matter, was Paul's – at least up until now. Phil was thinking about the bizarre evolution of events over the previous 12 hours: the bank robbery that was really a thwarted terrorist act that turned into an assassination that had somehow transformed into a national security incident with a fugitive doctor as the chief suspect. How the CIA was involved he was not sure, but several people were dead, an interstate manhunt was on, and he was leading the investigation. Paul Gudrun was emerging as an antisocial and homicidal psychopath. Still, questions continued to nag at his soul: why did Abdulla Burja silence the boy at the mall and what, exactly, did he tell Paul Gudrun? Alesha, meanwhile, was glued to her laptop, frantically surfing the Internet for any clues to the meaning of the second poem: *The Temple*. She was sure it hid a deeper message.

Tedder pulled into the limestone gravel drive next to the mailbox matching the address on Anna Gudrun's dossier. The property was grassy and splattered with just a few oak trees, yet the drive wound into the distance with no house in sight. Tedder drove slowly, hoping to avoid a flat tire, and kept quiet. In fact, all of them were suddenly silent, almost reverent, like pilgrims visiting holy ground.

Although the property was impressive, the house at the end of the quarter mile-long driveway was modest. Designed in classic 1970's craftsman style, the home was a single story ranch that looked to have maybe three bedrooms. A lonely and rusted Chevy Malibu sat in a detached open carport.

Tedder parked and the four of them simultaneously opened their doors. The air was moist and uncharacteristically cool for a late December Arkansas day. The four walked slowly up to the solid oak door. He expected Mrs. Gudrun to be elderly, perhaps frail, and certainly frightened. He hated making house calls of this type but, at the same time had warned Weikert and Tedder to be ready. He doubted Gudrun would have fled to his mother's house, but nothing surprised him anymore. Or so he thought.

Phil took the point and knocked firmly but politely. On the second rap, the door creaked open to reveal a slightly plump but quite healthy appearing woman. Her hair was a beautiful silver, well groomed and worn longer than women of her age generally do, and her skin was fair but not pale and materially devoid of wrinkles. Alesha judged her to be in her late 60's, but Amy knew the truth. She was 82.

"Mrs. Gudrun?" Phil started.

With a broad smile, she greeted them but Phil was not about to take advantage of her. He made a proper, polite, and respectful introduction, and with twinkling eyes, she continued her welcome, "Yes, yes. Come on in. I've been wondering when you were going to come by."

Phil's heart sank. She was confusing them for someone else. His mind flashed back to memories of his own grandmother who had been afflicted with dementia in her later years. "I don't think you understand."

"Oh yes, I think I do. You're here to talk to me about Paul. Right?"

The look of surprise on the face of Phil and the others answered her question.

"Did someone call you to tell you that we were coming?" Tedder asked.

"No. Not at all." She ushered the four into her immaculately appointed living room and asked them politely to sit. The chair Alesha reclined into was made of mahogany, exquisitely hand-carved and upholstered in a plush, chocolate brown fabric that just seemed to swallow her in. Phil and Amy both chose the matching ball-and-claw sofa while Tedder took the opportunity to stand and admire the furnishings, accessories, and objects d'art that adorned the room. The walls were tastefully covered with beautiful paintings and a bronze sculpture of a nude male javelin thrower caught Tedder's eye, the sculptor's attention to detail and capacity to capture the athlete's effort overcoming the conspicuous male genitalia.

"Mrs. Gudrun," Philip continued, "you are correct. We are here on official business to ask you about your son."

Anna Gudrun was all smiles, "Would you like some tea. I was just about to make myself some."

The four responded in four different negative ways.

"Mrs. Gudrun," Phil continued, "We want to first assure you that to the best of our knowledge, your son is fine. Unfortunately, he is wanted for questioning in regards to a serious crime." Anna's affect remained unchanged; she continued to smile. "Do you know where we might find him?"

The elderly woman shook her head. "In Memphis, I suppose. Perhaps with his lovely girlfriend Amber. Did you try to call him?"

"Yes, ma'am. We have gone to great lengths to find him."

"If he doesn't want you to find him, then you won't." Her answer was pleasant and matter of fact.

"Mrs. Gudrun, it's important that we do find him." Phil placed emphasis on the word "do" and then proceeded carefully, "This may be upsetting to you, ma'am, but he is wanted for questioning in a murder investigation."

"Oh, he could not possibly have murdered anyone," Anna Gudrun rebuked. It was the first time her demeanor had changed at all. But she wasn't angry or insulted, just pleasantly defiant.

"Most parents, particularly mothers," Amy responded, "can't believe that their sons are capable of taking a life."

"I didn't say that Dearie," Mrs. Gudrun answered, "My son is quite talented and more than capable of taking a life."

Amy wasn't sure exactly what the old woman meant and was about to ask for elaboration when Phil interrupted, "Mrs. Gudrun, does your son have any other family or friends? Anyone that you can think of that he might be staying with?"

"I'm his only kin. Paul is adopted. We have no other family."

"We were aware of that" In truth, they weren't but it didn't matter much. Still, he did his best to conceal his deceit and moved on, "Does he have any friends that you know of?"

"Amber."

"Any others?"

"Well, Yusuf I guess."

"Who's Yusuf?"

Anna smiled as she recalled, "Yusuf was Paul's best friend when he was growing up. A Nigerian boy. Come to think about it, he was Paul's only friend." She was reminiscing now, "They were inseparable."

"Do you know where Yusuf lives now?" Phil continued his questioning.

"North Carolina. Charlotte, I think. Paul still visits him from time to time."

Throughout the conversation, Alesha's eyes were scanning the room. She was more interested in her surroundings than the chatter. The house was not large but was a showcase befitting Architectural Digest. Mrs. Gudrun's choice of art was exceptional. Alesha had taken note of the bronze nude as well, but it was the image above the fireplace that most intrigued her. It was a portrait of Anna Gudrun taken when she was perhaps ten to fifteen years younger. At first she assumed it was a photograph, but after closer inspection noticed a signature in the right lower corner. It took a moment for her mind to grasp the truth. It wasn't a photograph at all; it was a painting!

"Is that a painting of you?" Alesha interjected, feeling a pressing need to solve the mystery.

"Yes. Do you like it?" Mrs. Gudrun beamed as if anticipating the complement to come.

"It's stunning!"

Paul interrupted Alesha's interruption, "Do you know Yusuf's last name, ma'am"

The elderly lady did not seem offended but appeared pensive for a moment and then smiled broadly once again, "A name I could never pronounce."

Her words draped a pall of silence that suddenly shrouded the room, but it was Anna herself who quickly lifted it, "Are you sure no one would like a cup of tea?"

"Sure, I'll have some," Alesha conceded. At this point, it would have been impolite to refuse. Besides, she wanted an opportunity to discretely look at the art more closely. Mrs. Gudrun retreated to the kitchen, delighted at the opportunity to offer refreshment. Amy stood and followed her, insisting on lending a hand.

With Mrs. Gudrun occupied by Amy and Alesha engrossed with the artwork, Phillip and Tedder took the opportunity to conference. "What do you think?" Phil enquired of his trusted assistant.

"She seems genuine enough."

"What about Gudrun's friend?"

"A Nigerian best friend? That's way too much of a coincidence."

"Agreed. Contact Neighbors. Have him run a name search for Yusuf in the Charlotte surrounds. Have him do a cross agency check. Make sure it includes immigration, Harmony, the grey list, FinCen, everybody. Got it?"

Tedder nodded, pulled out his cell phone, and ducked into the hallway, "There are going to be lots of Yusufs. We're going to need some luck."

Phil left Tedder and returned his attention back to the living room. Anna Gudrun and Amy were still in the kitchen chuckling about something and Alesha was sedulously inspecting an ethereal impressionistic landscape.

"She has good taste in art," Phil observed intending to make only small talk with his interpreter.

Alesha looked up with a surprisingly serious look on her face, "Yes, they are. In fact, they're downright incredible. Come look at this," she beckoned to Phil, "Each one of these paintings was painted by the same artist."

Phil walked up to her. The painting was indeed beautiful, cast in vibrant colors and vivid yet surrealistic photorealistic imagery. But his eyes followed her finger to the point of interest: The signature. It wasn't what he expected. To Phil, it appeared to be in Chinese; a single symbol reproduced precisely on every painting in Anna Gudrun's home:

Phil looked quizzically at Alesha who knew his question but had no answer. Their contemplation was mercifully truncated by the traveling voices of Amy and Mrs. Gudrun as they returned from the kitchen with a smoking kettle of oolong tea, a plate of mugs, and a platter of scones and crumble cakes.

"Mrs. Gudrun, you shouldn't have," Phil's gratuity was genuine.

"Don't be silly. This was my pleasure. And I got the pleasure of getting to know Amy."

"Yes, and I learned that Paul visits here several times a year and still has his own room here," Amy stared straight at Phil Oxmore as she placed the platter of mugs down on the ornate coffee table.

Oxmore took a few sips of the tea and a couple bites of cake. The others followed Phil's lead. He had read the assistant SAIC's body language perfectly but respectfully took his time, "Mrs. Gudrun, you have been very cooperative and helpful. If it is not too much to ask, we would like to see your son's room."

"I've watched enough TV to know you need a warrant to search my house," Anna sternly replied.

Phil still was not about to be coercive to this woman, "Yes ma'am, we do."

"No matter. Sure you can see his room. It's not a traditional room; I warn you." Anna Gudrun grinned as she spoke and smiled a gracious, welcoming smile, beckoning the four of them down a separate hall toward the back of the house. They passed a study and a comfortable guest bedroom before coming to a room with a solid, unpainted oak door.

Anna slowly opened the door. The space was filled with a kaleidoscope of colors from sunlight passing through a simple stain glass window. The five of them solemnly entered the chamber and Anna gently closed the door. It was instantly apparent this was no ordinary bedroom. In fact, it had no bed. In the center of the small room, a thin, human-sized pad lay on the floor. It appeared to Tedder to be a simple blanket and in front of it was a small wooden bench. Alesha recognized it immediately as a Muslim sutrah, part of the Islamic prayer ritual. But that's not what caught Amy's eye. Against the far wall was a marble wall table. Resting on the buffet was a Jewish skull cap, a kippa, and next to it, folded properly, lay a bright blue prayer shawl, a tallit. In the center of the table, a tabernacular seven-lamp menorah forged out of solid gold stood proudly and on the opposite side of the table, a set of unusual black boxes with accompanying black leather bands were neatly arranged. Amy recognized them. She remembered her grandfather wearing them each time he prayed at synagogue. They were tefillin, and contained parchment inscribed with verses from the Torah used by orthodox Jews during weekday morning prayers. Phillip saw the menorah, but his eyes were enraptured by what he saw above the wall table. Hanging several feet above the makeshift Jewish alter, a framed fire-singed portrait of Osama bin Laden hung prominently looking downward.

He felt a bite of anger intermixed with a modicum of nausea but the feeling was quickly overcome by curiosity. On the room's left wall, sitting on the floor, sat a solid cedar hutch. Perched on it was a stone orb resting on a pewter pedestal. To the right of it, an unlit brass oil lamp sat, and to the left of it, a silver platter. High above the hutch, higher than anything else in the room, a second orb was carved into the wall with a mark Phil recognized immediately. It was the same symbol inscribed on all of Anna Gudrun's paintings:

"This is Paul's bedroom?" Amy wondered disbelievingly.

"It's his room honey, I never said he slept in it," the elderly woman spiritedly answered. "When he visits, he arrives pretty early and then leaves right after nightfall. But this is where he spends most of time when he's here."

"What does he do in here?" This time it was Alesha who was wondering.

"He meditates or prays, I think. The door is always closed when he's inside."

"Osama bin Laden?" Tedder wondered out loud.

Anna Gudrun shrugged and said nothing else.

Realizing that there was little else to be gleaned from the room, Phillip Oxmore thanked his hostess and made his salutation on behalf of the group. Tedder wasn't listening; he was thinking. He had seen a Muslim prayer mat before, the Jewish artifacts were obvious, and he was pretty sure that was a Hindu shrine along the side wall. The symbolism of bin Laden reigning above them all was clear. He had a gut feeling from the beginning about the so-called doctor; he was dangerous and a terrorist at the most and an Al-Qaeda sympathizer at the least. What he didn't understand was the conspicuous absence of any Christian symbolism. Then he turned around, and his silent question was satisfied. Hammered into the back of the door, two wooden planks were fastened with rusted nails in the shape of a matted cross.

Tedder's mind tumbled to the only logical explanation: He was standing in a church; the church of bin Laden, Lord over the religions of the earth.

And Gudrun was paying his allegiance to him…praying under him. Tedder shuddered as he reached the inescapable inference:

Al-Qaeda's ultimate ambition…

Four faiths ruled by evil. Four faiths governed by terror.

XXXIII

Memphis, Tennessee
United States

10:58 am CST

Paul stood across the dining room admiring Amber's form. Even in dirty clothes, a baggy Fed-Ex shirt, hair askew, and skin covered in road grime, she was beautiful. He had stolen three minutes away from her, just long enough to relieve himself and check the status of his plane. Wilson Air Center was well known for its customer service and had always been prompt. He had given them plenty of time, but today they were running behind.

    Amber caught Paul's eye and beckoned him over with a smile. She offered him a strawberry dipped in cream and a sip of a mango juice mimosa. He enjoyed the morsel but barely let the cocktail touch his lips. His fatigue was mounting, and they literally had miles to go before they slept. He watched her as she playfully snuck a miniature pastry into her mouth. Even through the muck, her eyes glowed and her radiant smile filled his heart. He was tired... and scared for the both of them...his enemies were close, he could sense them, but he could not help himself. He loved this woman.

Paul grabbed her by the waist and gently spun her into his embrace. She was still noshing the cream puff with her mouth in a half open grin. She giggled and was about to say something cute, but he didn't want to hear it. He pulled her close and stole a French kiss, driving his tongue into her sugar-filled mouth. She responded with a diaphragmatic chuckle that subtly transformed into a visceral moan. Unconsciously, she let herself fall into him, wrapping her arms around his shoulders for support. He inhaled her scent and continued his lingual exploration, caressing her scruff through the blonde locks, feeling the warmth of her body caressing his chest.

Amber took in a breath of her own and returned the favor, plunging herself back into his mouth. His musk was subtle but distinctive. This was her Paul. He loved her; she could tell. She gyrated her hips ever so gently and could feel his response. For a moment, Amber contemplated pulling him down onto the desert buffet but a polite cough interrupted her naughty plan.

Paul broke the embrace and turned to the harrumph. The attendant apologized, but Paul quickly recognized his intention. He took Amber by the hand and began to lead her to the door ignoring her coy attempt to hold back and pluck one more petit four from the table. It was clear she thought this was a game, and he kept up the pretense. He had hated frightening her earlier and now was enjoying delighting her. He looked into her twinkling eyes with a grin of his own as he offered up his surprise: a vivid red carpet that led from the VIP lounge, through a small lobby, onto a covered tarmac, and toward a bright white business jet with its engines producing air warping exhaust.

No longer buffered by the sound proof doors, the roar of the modified Learjet 45 was overwhelming. Amber's emotions progressed from cautious expectation and apprehension to schoolgirl bewilderment and excitement. He saw her smile grow as they walked toward the plane, hand in hand. It was easy to read her mind: this was just a big game, a "put-on", a prelude to a ring awaiting her at the end of the day. He felt a pang of deception in the pit of his stomach as he helped her climb the stairs into the cabin. Somehow, he would make it up to her.

Nodding to the groundsman operating the stair gantry, Paul secured the hatch while Amber ogled the inside of the plane. The cabin was like none she had ever seen. She was immediately reminded of the interior of an ultra-luxury limousine, one you didn't have to stoop to walk through. Along the left wall was a wide, plush, off-white Italian leather couch with a couple of taupe-colored suede throw pillows. Across from the couch, a 42 inch Panasonic flat screen hung above a console of cobalt blue-lit amplifiers and video equipment.

Knowing he had a few minutes before the ground crew cleared the plane, Paul indulged his girlfriend with a brief tour. Beside the television, a solid oak bar stood adorned with a variety of liquors and dangling glasses. Below it, an ice maker and a small refrigerator filled with a collection of wines and champagne were tucked away. She cooed as he popped a bottle of Perrier, poured her a glass, and then continued aft past a freshly stocked pantry filled with breads, chocolates, and assorted snacks. Behind the pantry, a pair of captain's chairs sat separated by a black marble table. In the back, a lavatory, larger than a commercial airliner "head" and sporting a small shower and a porcelain sink, completed the living space.

He returned her to the front of the plane quoting a few technical specifications and mumbling about some extra special modification features. Amber was half listening as he had her sit in the copilot's seat. The bright sunlight blanketed the tarmac, and the windows provided a panoramic view of the runways, hangers, and illuminated taxiway signs, but Amber was oblivious. She was lost in the enchantment of the moment. She watched Paul climb into his seat, don his microphone headset, and check-in with the tower. Paul had always excited her, but she more turned on now than ever. He took the headset off and kept talking, and she kept not listening, staring lovingly at his moving mouth and brilliant blue eyes. Only the sound of her man calling another woman's name was able to break her trance.

"Who is Ariel?" Amber wondered, her subconscious doing all of the asking.

"You are sitting in her." Amber's silence and quizzical look made it clear she was not amused.

"Ariel, I would like you to meet Amber," Paul announced.

"Hello, Amber. It's so nice to finally meet you." The voice of a polite, sophisticated young lady rolled off of the speakers.

Amber was still confused, "Hello? Who are you?"

"I'm your plane."

Paul decided it was time to elaborate, "Ariel is the pilot of the plane."

Amber figured it out. "A computer?"

"I'm sure you've heard of unmanned military drones, right? Well, Ariel is an advanced automated piloting system that's a next generation version."

"You mean like an automatic pilot?"

"You could say that. But she's more like a decorated navy combat ace with five thousand hours of flight experience. She's a much better pilot than I am."

"You're kidding, right? You're really the one who's going to be flying the plane."

"I'd like to think I'm the executive pilot."

Explaining this further was going to take more time than they had. Sometimes action is the best teacher. "Ariel, Complete the preflight check. We are going to Charlotte to see Yusuf."

"Very good. The weather is favorable. Preflight is complete. We are ready to taxi."

"Excellent. Initiate taxi protocol." With Paul's words, the engines increased in pitch, and the plane gently nudged forward. A groundsman with orange batons began waving them forward. Amanda was no pilot, but she could tell Paul was not doing a thing.

"Is she following him?" Amber was already calling Ariel by an anthropomorphic pronoun.

"She can do more than that." Paul addressed the plane, "Ariel, assume my identity and initiate ATC clearance."

Ariel emulated Paul's voice and spoke out, "Memphis Ground, LR 3674K, at Wilson Air, Request IFR Charlotte, ready to taxi."

The air traffic controller quickly responded, "LR 3674K, Memphis Ground, taxi runway 27 via C2, Contact departure control 124.0, Squawk 1867, Hold short runway 27, stand by."

Ariel confirmed the instruction and began maneuvering out of the Wilson Air area making a variety of turns, stops and starts along the way. As the plane entered the taxiways, Paul sat back and turned his head towards Amber's mouth-agape expression, clasped his hands behind his head, and smirked an impish grin.

XXXIV

Memphis, Tennessee
11:10 am

The walk to the bunker was surprisingly quick. Sokolov and company trekked past a series of unmarked and unassuming office buildings that housed FedEx upper management. One of them contained the modest office of Fred Smith, the company's visionary founder and chief executive officer. The jaunt continued toward a partially subterranean structure covered with vines. Barely saying a word, the group walked down a concrete staircase, past a series of security checkpoints and into an ice-cool, darkened, control room. At the door, a tall, thin gentleman wearing a white long sleeve button-down shirt introduced himself as Jimmy Anderson, Federal Express' chief operating officer, "Welcome to the Global Operations Center. Everything happens in the sorting rooms, airplanes, and delivery trucks. But here, this is where we watch everything happen."

Sokolov took a moment to gaze around the massive room studded with high-tech computer consoles as he listened to Anderson's brief explanation, "We are staffed here with teams of operations managers directing everything from ground transportation to domestic processes and from flight control to international operations, and we watch the weather closer than the national weather service. But you couldn't care less about all of that. Am I right?" Sokolov's face was expressionless. "I understand we have a couple of uninvited guests on campus. Let's find them."

◆

11:34 am

The plane stopped short of runway 27 as expected. Ariel requested takeoff clearance but had been kept on hold. The airport was busy, and Paul had expected a delay but the wait was nerve-racking. Making matters worse, Amber was wizening up and asking questions – good questions. Was this his plane? How rich was he? How come he never told her about it? How much did Ariel cost? Where were they going? Did she hear Charlotte? Who was Yusuf? Paul offered good answers, mostly semi-truths, but Amber was in no position to hear much more. For the most part, he believed she was buying it. She loved him and wanted desperately to trust his explanations. He decided to try some more levity, hoping a little awe might inspire her more.

"Okay, in a minute, I'm going to need your help. When I tell you, I need you to say 'Initiate takeoff protocol, authorization delta five'," Paul announced.

The two of them bantered back and forth, she wondering what he was asking her to do, he asking her to trust him, lightheartedly practicing the line, and sharing some cackles and jokes along the way. Amber was laughing again, and Paul was glad. They were in grave danger, and the longer they stayed on the ground, the more serious their situation was becoming. This was already taking much longer than he had planned. Could the delay be intentional? Perhaps his enemies were surrounding him this very minute. Contingency plans began swirling through his mind. He'd make a run for it if he had to. Ariel was very capable, but he had to admit, his options were limited. Still, he worked the permutations, keeping his calculations private, his face betraying nothing, his mouth telling his girlfriend a joke.

Marked Tree, Arkansas
11:34 am

The four of them climbed back into the specially equipped Explorer. Tedder started the vehicle and turned the heat up, but all of them were numb. The sensation was a mixture of bewilderment and awe. Phil felt drained, almost as if he had just walked out of a thirty minute deep muscle massage.

"Wow", Amy pierced the quiet, "That's got to be the most bizarre home visit ever."

Tedder put the gear into reverse, looked over his shoulder, and began backing up, "This guy is just a wacko. Who has a half Muslim, half Jewish, half Hindu, half Christian bedroom with Osama Bin Ladin watching down over him?"

"It was a prayer room Tedder," Amy retorted, a bit condescendingly.

The sound of Oxmore's cell phone ring interrupted the tension. It was Martin with an update.

Phil put his iPhone on speaker and Martin's booming voice echoed through the truck, "It looks like Gudrun and Chase have been racing across Memphis. MPD says they have a potential sighting of them at the FedEx SuperHub. We've checked out the girlfriend's apartment. There's not much there, and it looks like they left in a hurry."

Oxmore thanked him and hung up.

"So, Gudrun and his girlfriend are officially on the run," Stone concluded, "Do you think she is a willing accomplice or just a dupe?"

"I just hope she's not a hostage," Amy contributed.

A morose silence filled the truck. Alesha decided to change the subject, "Did you notice all of that stunning artwork Mrs. Gudrun had in her house? And that fabulous painting of her above the fireplace?"

"That was a painting?" Tedder questioned turning the wheel.

"Yes! Believe it her not! And hand painted, not brushed. And all of them were signed with a single Chinese character – the same symbol that was on that medallion in Gudrun's room!" Alesha gushed.

"That's because they were all painted by him," Amy revealed the mystery.

"What?" Alesha was almost speechless.

"Anna Gudrun told me that when I was in the kitchen with her."

Alesha's mind was working. She was not an artist but had worked as a docent at the Frist museum of Art in Nashville. "Those paintings were masterpieces – and originals!" she spoke incredulously and almost under her breath.

Phil had been quietly listening but finally entered the discussion, "She said he was talented."

Tedder shifted into drive and began making his way down the pitted gravel driveway toward the road, "He's a talented kook. Kook's sign their names in Chinese."

"So all Chinese are kooks. Is that what you're saying Tedder," Amy Weikert's sarcasm was biting now. Few people irritated her as much as Tedder Stone. But he had Phil Oxmore's confidence, and that was all that was important. Tedder tried to explain away his prejudice, and Phil felt like the tired father trying to keep the peace between his squabbling children. He couldn't wait for them to sleep together. Maybe that would calm the two of them down.

Oxmore's prayer was interrupted by his cell phone. Jim Neighbors was excited about something and could virtually contain himself. He established a secure connection with the vehicle's onboard computer all the while mumbling "I've hit the jackpot" and "you've got to see this". Oxmore had never seen him so animated.

A photograph of a group of men dressed in traditional Muslim attire filled the screen. A handsome adolescent young man wearing a scarf, smiling and pointing, filled the left hand of the image and was clearly the focus of the photograph. Behind him, a crowd of similarly dressed but stoic men holding rifles stood guard. Whoever the boy was, he appeared to be the center of attention.

"So, what am I looking at Jim?" Oxmore inquired.

"Look at the back row – second from the end – the white guy with the blue and white scarf standing next to the black man."

Tedder was the first to make the connection, "Well, that kind of looks like our doctor!"

"There's a resemblance, but that's about it," Alesha countered.

"This photo was taken 9 years ago," Neighbors explained.

"During the good doctor's mission work," Oxmore calculated.

"Correct. Age progression and facial recognition analysis place the probability of a match at 98%."

"Interesting, OK…" "Oxmore began, but Neighbors interrupted his boss. He wasn't done yet. "The black guy next to him is Yusuf Sandodele, a self-made, Nigerian import-export magnate. His father immigrated to the US when he was a boy. He grew up in the Memphis low rent district and went to the same high school as Gudrun. The guy is worth millions, and CIA thinks he's dirty."

Neighbors continued explaining Sandodele's position on the CIA's grey list, referring to individuals and entities whose loyalties remain under suspicion. "Apparently he communicates frequently with interests throughout northern Africa, the Middle East, and southwestern Asia; travels often to Africa and Asia; and uses a proprietary encryption standard that NSA had been unable to crack."

"Let me guess where he's based out of," Tedder interrupted.

"Well, his company's offices are in Newark, but he maintains a palatial residence in Charlotte, North Carolina."

"There you go!" Tedder responded to the news, slapping the steering wheel.

"Good work, Jim. I knew I could count on you," Oxmore congratulated.

"But that is not the pièce de résistance," Neighbor's added using his best French accent with a touch of dramatic flair, "Guess who the young dude the picture's being taken of is?" He paused for effect he knew the answer would bring, "That's none other than Hamza bin Osama bin Mohammed bin Awad bin Laden."

"You have got to be shitting me!" Tedder screamed out.

"The crown prince of terror," Amy blurted out, slightly stunned.

Alesha was confused, "Who?"

"Osama Bin Laden's son and surviving heir!"

XXXV

West Arkansas
United States

11:40 am CST

The revelation of Dr. Paul Gudrun's Al-Qaeda ties was startling but not altogether surprising given the doctor's flight and the findings at the Gudrun house. But none of it was incriminating per se. Paul Gudrun was peculiar and eccentric, but there was no law against that, and other than a photograph, there was no evidence that the doctor sanctioned or condoned anything – much less terrorism.

As Tedder Stone turned off the country service road and drove through the quaint old town of Marked Tree and on to SR63, Weikert was blabbering incredulously, Stone was waxing chauvinistically, and Deng was quiet. They were not getting anywhere, and Oxmore desperately needed his team to refocus. Besides, he was famished. He ordered Stone to pull into a Sonic Drive-in on the edge of civilization. After splurging on a round of hamburgers, onion rings and root beer slushies, Phil got down to business. He turned himself to partially face everyone and dove in, "Ok.

Let's start from the top." His statement silenced the chatter and set the stage for his impromptu inquiry, "What do we know? What do we think we know? And what do we think? You first, Alesha."

Deng was startled by the call-out, but she had already asked this question of herself several times and was ready to answer, "I think the key is Abdullah Burja."

"Really?" Oxmore was taken slightly aback but wanted to hear more, "Go on."

"What is a non-English speaking, Muslim terrorist with African Al-Qaeda ties doing inside of a maximum security United States Federal Reserve Bank?"

"He was trying to refinance his camel?" Tedder quipped chomping on his burger. Oxmore tried to stifle a laugh, but a blurt escaped. Amy was less amused.

"You are such an ass," Weikert reprimanded and Oxmore was having trouble deciding who was funnier. The day had been remarkably long, and everyone was sleep deprived, most of all him. He secretly appreciated the little bit of levity.

Dr. Deng felt it too, but she had a point to make, "He was invited there. He had to have been." The comment was met by silence and empty stares. Not waiting for feedback, she elaborated, "He's a mole – a double agent! It's the only thing that makes any sense."

Deng paused briefly waiting to see if her theory met with any traction. Sensing tacit agreement and hearing nothing to the contrary, she continued, "And I think that, while he was there, he was made gaining access to some highly sensitive information – so sensitive that his local handlers wanted him dead."

"So you're saying he smelled it out and bolted," Tedder stone reacted.

"Yes. And whatever it was he learned, he felt it important enough to tell someone back home."

"That's why he wanted the international cell phone," Weikert pondered.

"That's why he didn't blow himself up," Deng finished.

"Interesting!" Oxmore was impressed. It had been a while since his team had worked this well together, "I like where this is going, Dr. Deng. Keep going."

Alesha's demeanor changed for the sadder, "I think Burja must have told the store clerk."

"So… you think Burja didn't kill him, we did?" Amy incredulously completed Alesha's theory.

There was an unintentional, brief moment of silence.

"I don't buy it. We don't kill innocent civilians," Stone countered.

"Come off it, Tedder," Weikert echoed Tedder's earlier jab, "You know better than that."

Oxmore appreciated both Amy's sarcastic joke and Tedder's loyal patriotism but knew Amy was right, "It's possible." Taylor had all but confirmed covert ops involvement. "They could have assets imbedded in Memphis SWAT."

"That guy, Sokolov, you think?" Weikert wondered.

"Yes. But he had to have had help," Oxmore clarified. "There were too many times when he was in the right place at the right time – at the mall, in the ambulance, in the ER, in the call room. Somebody had to orchestrate that."

"Chunn?" This time it was Deng doing the supposing.

"Or McCammon."

"So, where does Gudrun fit in?" Weikert directed the question to Oxmore, but Deng had the answer to that too. "We know Burja passed at least two pieces of information on to him: The IP address to the International Poetry Society webpage and a poem. The webpage prominently features two poems, *The Quest* and *The Temple*. Burja recited one of them shortly before he died."

"So Burja must have been offed too," Stone finally entered the conversation, resigning himself to the truth.

"I think so. And a couple of hours later, somebody tried to kill Gudrun."

"Whoa! Are you talking about the nurse? She's the one that's dead, remember? I thought we had said that she was the one who confronted him and then he killed her!" This time it was Amy who was confused.

"I'm not sure about that either Alesha," Oxmore added, "The nurse had worked at the hospital for years and was well known and highly respected."

"Yes, but look at the data. How did that nurse get in the call room?" Deng asked.

"Something tells me she wasn't the only nurse that had ever gotten in there." Stone's attempted humor seemed forced.

Alesha ignored the remark and directed her pleas directly to Phil, "You said yourself that someone outside the hospital hacked in and erased any evidence of her entry. And it was Sokolov that directed Gudrun to the call room."

"It still could have been a planned rondeveoux," Weikert countered.

"It could have been a number of things," Oxmore agreed, "extortion... accident....drug deal gone bad..."

Alesha was silent. Oxmore had a point, but her gut told her something different. "I don't know. I just have a feeling the doctor's an innocent bystander."

"Innocent?" Tedder exclaimed. "You can't tell me he's just some poor ole bloke that just got caught up in all this. He didn't look too innocent holding that AK45 in that photo of little Bin Ladin. And that woman was down when she was found. We watched it in real time." His last statement was directed to Phil. "And he hacked a security system, stole a car, cyclejacked a dude, and God knows what else! And I don't care what you say Amy, that room we just saw...that was whacked!"

There was silence after Tedder's outburst. Tedder may have been tactless and sophomoric, but his points were well taken.

"Okay," Phil sighed. "One thing's for sure Tedder, we know where you stand." This time it was the women doing the chuckling. Oxmore redirected, "Why on earth would anyone kill for a couple of poems?"

"Because they aren't poems. They're clues," Deng was quick to answer.

"Clues to what?"

"I'm not sure, but the poems both have spiritual or religious themes. One is describing great works of literature, and the other is describing a shrine or a testimony to an author. It's unstated but the coupling of the poems suggests the author in the second poem is the writer of the works of the first."

"What the hell are you talking about?" Tedder bellowed out.

Oxmore tuned out his agent, "Ignore him, Dr. Deng." Tedder kept mumbling nonsense about hidden launch codes and coca cola recipes while Phil focused his eyes on Alesha, "So, you think these poems are directing us to something or to somewhere?"

"Yes."

"Do you think you can make sense of these 'clues' Doctor?"

"I can try."

In seconds, the truck was quiet again. Stone pulled out of the Sonic parking lot, and the truck resumed its trek back to Memphis. With full stomachs, Alesha and Amy both got to work immediately, each taking a poem and diving in. Tedder broke the subdued clatter of keyboard clicks with a whisper to Phil, "I've been doing this shit for a while, and in all my years, I've never seen anything so damn crazy!"

"Yea. This case is giving me a magnificent headache."

Alesha was listening, and the irony of Phil's unintentional play on words was not lost on her, "Magnificent and True."

"I think we found something!"

Word had circulated that two persons of interest had penetrated FedEx security. Whether this was for real or just a drill, it was no joke. The Feds had both Customs as well as a TSA branch on the premises. Any breach of security was a major deal. Anderson was enthusiastic, but Sokolov was muted. He was done getting his hopes up prematurely.

The security technician continued his report, "A ground transport is not at its loading bay where it's supposed to be."

"Which one is it?" Anderson was doing the talking.

"Not sure yet, but we're figuring it out by process of elimination."

A second later, Sokolov's cell phone rang the distinctive chime of his Texas handler. As expected, it was Tyler Center requesting an update. Stepping away from the group for privacy, he filled Michaels in, "We're closing. He's crafty, but he's making mistakes. We're tracing a phone call he made, and now it looks like he stole a truck that we should be able to track too."

Michael's friendly voice was replaced by one gruffer and about a half octave lower. "Son, do you know who this is."

"Yes sir." Christos recognized Coombs' voice immediately.

"I've greased the rails for you."

"I can tell sir."

"Then find this mother fucker and his bitch."

Sokolov didn't have to answer. The message boomed. The call dropped, and he swallowed hard but then a melodious sound from the security technician filled the air, "The missing truck is Oklahoma City. But it's still nearby. It's at Wilson Air!"

"Wilson Air?" This time it was Sokolov's partner doing the asking.

"It's a private aviation support center. It's literally right around the corner."

"Why would he drive there?" Reynolds wondered out loud.

Anderson offered a possible answer, "There's a large parking lot there. Maybe he's looking to trade to another vehicle."

Sokolov deduced the answer. Gudrun was looking to trade up, but not to another car. The security technician gave him all the confirmation he needed, "The cell phone he called has been deactivated, but it's a business phone registered to the Wilson Air Center Concierge."

"Contact airport police!" Sokolov screamed out, "Have them roll all units to Wilson Air! And get me Air Traffic Control. We need to shut down this airspace now!"

The silence Paul had been waiting for had finally broken, "LR 3674K, this is Memphis Tower; you are cleared for takeoff runway 27."

Paul wasted no time. "Ariel, authorize command Amber and initiate ATC takeoff verification."

Ariel immediately radioed in verification and waited. Paul turned to Amber and with a smile hiding his adrenaline driven pulse, he offered his open palm and nudged, "Ok, my love, you're on."

With a giggle, Amber complied with her well-rehearsed line, "Initiate takeoff protocol – authorization delta five."

In time, the engines began to whir loudly again, this time reaching a crescendo pitch just before the plane began to accelerate.

XXXVI

Tennessee Airspace
United States

12:00 pm CST; 1:00 pm EST

It took less than 20 minutes for Ariel to ascend to her 32000 foot cruising altitude. Amber took the opportunity to gaze quietly out of her starboard window. She watched as the houses, traffic laden roads, and downtown skyscrapers shrank from view until nothing was left to see but indistinct parcels of land in various shades of green and brown shielded by wafts of grey stratocumulus clouds. Throughout the assent, she remained quiet, deeply entranced in the beauty and majesty of nature. She felt warmth pass through her body, something she almost couldn't describe. It was like a comforting hug, or a warm fire on a snowy winter day. Then something broke her trance.

Amber turned to see Paul staring at her. "What are you looking at?"
"Something beautiful," her boyfriend replied.
"Yeah, right." This time it was Amber reading Paul's mind. "I've got rocks in my hair, I'm covered head to toe in road grime, I'm wearing a used FedEx uniform, and I smell like fried cigarettes."

Paul burst into laughter, "You know you can freshen up back there."

"Don't I have to stay buckled up in this thing?" She asked reaching for the clasp as if she had jumped back from the future already having heard his answer, "Has the pilot turned off the fasten seatbelt sign? Oh, wait a second. Let me ask? Ariel. Is it safe for me to walk around the cabin?"

"Yes. Anticipated turbulence for the next forty five minutes is expected to be low. Please exercise caution," Ariel informed.

"Thank you."

Paul just smiled silently, allowing himself to be the brunt of her playful sarcasm. Pity the fool that would dare underestimate her blonde locks, blue eyes, and perfect smile. She clearly had become comfortable with the situation. She was no longer frightened. Now she was playing along.

Amber pulled herself out of the chair, "I'm still thirsty too?"

"Well there's more Perrier if you want," Paul offered as he rubbernecked, following Amber as she walked to the cabin galley.

"That's not want I was thinking." She was being playfully feisty, opening the refrigerator and checking the stock. Paul was having just as much fun watching her. "You made me leave my mango mimosa behind," she whined.

"I doubt there's mango juice on board but I'm sure there's champagne."

"I see it. But maybe later. What I would really love is a shower."

"Go for it," Paul offered, "There are some towels in the closet and I keep some scrubs in there."

Amber grinned silently, flicked her hair, and walked to the rear of the plane. Paul watched her as she sauntered into the lavatory, took one last sultry peek at him and closed the door.

The latch clicked, and Paul turned his attention once again to his plane. Amber was wonderful, beautiful, and exciting, but she was a distraction. A quick glance at his instrument panel reassured him that all was well, and a look out the window at the darkening blue sky relaxed his mind and focused his concentration.

The last fourteen hours had been the craziest of his life, but he was sure his day was far from over. His pursuers were relentless and had shown brilliant resourcefulness. They had underestimated him at the hospital, and he had surprised them at the park, but those were errors they were unlikely to repeat. A cat and mouse strategy never worked out well for the mouse in the long run; if he and Amber were to survive, they would need another solution.

He contemplated the permutations. Yusuf was the ready answer. The home had been a sanctuary to Paul for years; it was going to have to be one again. Paul made a point to visit his old friend at least once a quarter. In fact, it was where he regularly took vacations. It was a place where he could be himself, free from judgment and curious eyes. He just hoped he hadn't miscalculated, tipped his hand, and endangered his friend. But then again, where else could he go? His mother was too frail to help, and others at the hospital were kind but had proven to be untrustworthy.

His ramblings rekindled memories of the hospital. He still was stupefied by Ophelia's actions. Who was she? He thought he knew but clearly not! She called the terrorist by name! Burja she called him. How did she know that? And what did she want? To find out what the terrorist had said. Why? To hide some secret Facebook for superspies? That all seemed so trivial. Then he recalled a question that he had considered before but had eluded him: Why did Burja recite the poem? The poem wasn't necessary to access the database. Was it just to legitimize the trail of breadcrumbs and encourage continued probing? Possibly, but Burja recited the poem not once but multiple times. Why?

The poem clearly had a hidden meaning, but he had already minced the riddle for hours and had made no headway. There were simply too many possibilities to factor. Then something struck him. Maybe he needed the second poem, *The Temple*, to make sense of the first.

Designed by a pope
Like one in rome,
Dedicated to an author
Who never won a pulitzer,
For his writing
That changed the course of history,
Commissioned by a man
Who did the very same thing,
Surrounded by gifts

STRONG EMERGENCE

> From a future mortal enemy,
> It is the southernmost point
> Of a recumbent cross,
> Whose center is a tribute
> To the father of us all.

The imagery of the poem's title and the first lines of text were clearly meant to suggest a religious structure or artifact, but Paul saw through the smokescreen – it was too obvious. He deduced an alternative interpretation: something people or society worship instead, perhaps in the secular world, like the Rose Bowl, Buckingham Palace, Time Square or Wall Street or to a structure of major secular significance like the Eiffel Tower or the Empire State Building.

His mind kept racing: Maybe it referred to a building or monument or work of art. The next lines told of it being commissioned by a famous man to honor another famous man – both who changed the course of history. But were other explanations possible? Works of art were not the only things commissioned. So were experimental studies, Legislative action, naval vessels and even people.

Perhaps that was it. The word 'Temple' is often used as a metaphor for the human body and suppose in this case, the poem was referring to a man, a man who was given a commission by another great man. Could the poem be describing the eleven disciples receiving the Great Commission from Christ? Maybe. But it could have been just as easily a reference to Christopher Columbus receiving his commission from Queen Isabella and Ferdinand in the court of Spain.

One thing was fairly clear, though. Whoever *The Temple* celebrated, it was someone who authored something famous, something that "changed the course of history". That was the link between the poems he was looking for! Something magnificent – something true!

The words kept pulling Paul to Christian theology, to the apostle Paul, his namesake. The apostle was certainly an author who changed history by writing at least seven of the New Testament epistles. There it was – the word epistle – another connection. Was that a coincidence? It couldn't be. But then again, something was gnawing at his soul.

He looked out over the horizon into the vast blue expanse and sighed. He couldn't put a finger on it, but a feeling told him he was on the wrong track; he was still missing something.

12:14 pm CST

Traffic on I-55 south heading towards West Memphis was quite light, but Phil was oblivious. His mind was churning: Burja really did appear to communicate apparently valuable intelligence to Dr. Gudrun. So valuable, in fact, that the doctor was being targeted. CIA was involved, and there was good evidence that Burja, the store clerk and most likely the nurse were all assassinated. He needed more information. What he really needed was to find Gudrun.

As if suddenly hit by an epiphany, he broke from his muddling apprehension and started clicking on the truck's onboard computer keyboard. Within a few seconds, Oxmore was linked to the Memphis RTCC. Phil quickly donned his headset and opened a line, "MPD Center this is Agent Phillip Oxmore, MFBI Special Agent in Charge. I need to speak with the Watch Commander."

An officer briefly put the agent on hold but within a minute the silence was replaced with a familiar voice, "This is Lieutenant Avery. Can I help you sir?"

"Avery? Weren't you on last night?"

"Yes, sir."

"Don't you sleep?" Oxmore quipped.

"Don't you, sir?"

Oxmore howled, and Avery followed suit. The two quickly shared intelligence. Oxmore discovered that Gudrun was still on the loose. They had tracked him to the FedEx SuperHub and then to a private aviation center at the airport but had lost him. Oxmore learned MPD had closed the airspace, concerned that Gudrun might try to escape by air, and were conducting a systematic search of the airport, the SuperHub and the surrounding grounds and were interviewing ground personnel. So far, the investigation had been fruitless.

Oxmore listened quietly. The mysterious actions of the nonsuicidal suicide bomber and the violent healer were still rollicking through his sleep deprived mind. Then, in the chaos, a couple of synapses made a connection. "Who closed the airspace?" Oxmore uttered, almost unintelligibly.

"We did." Avery was confused. He though he had just said that.

"I mean who specifically?" Phillip clarified.

"I believe Officer Christos Sokolov is commanding at the scene."

Sirens and alarm bells began clanging in Philip's head, and he felt the pit of his stomach drop. "Did any planes take off before you closed the airport?"

"Yes, we've thought of that," Avery quickly answered, "Four commercial flights and two from the private air center, a Cessna 152 and a private jet. Neither filed flight plans."

"Where's the Cessna going?"

"It's on course for New Orleans but if it keeps going to sea it might end up in Mexico. We have already notified the coast guard."

Phil heard the words. It was a logical deduction. If he were Gudrun, he would escape to Mexico if he could. But something didn't sit well with the Special Agent. He had only met the man twelve hours earlier in a midnight debriefing, but neither his impression then nor now, after spending an hour with his enigmatic mother and visiting the doctor's mysterious prayer room, was one of a fool. A race for the border was too obvious.

"Where is the corporate jet going?"

"It's flying east. Possible destinations are Asheville, Charlotte, Wilmington, or it might go out to sea too."

The lieutenant kept talking, naming the commercial flights and listing other possibilities but Oxmore wasn't listening. He had already fixated on one word: Charlotte.

Phillip abruptly interrupted the police officer, stopping him in midsentence, "Has anything else happened? Anything unusual?"

Avery was taken aback but quickly recovered, "In Memphis, everything is unusual. You know that, Sir."

"Come off it. You know what I mean?" Oxmore was tired and in no mood.

"There was a call about a hit-and-run outside of the FedEx that sounded like our man, but emergency personnel were never able to find the victim or the man who called it in..."

Oxmore was listening now, "Anything else..."

"Well, there was a crazy report of somebody shooting a rifle from a news helicopter in Shelby Park. But I guess you know about that."

"What do you mean?"

"Your office called us off. I took the phone call myself from Agent Taylor."

Suddenly, Phillip Oxmore saw with the sparkling clarity of a precision telephoto lens. And then he felt his stomach fall another couple of feet.

XXXVII

Tennessee Airspace
United States

12:20 pm CST

Amber stepped quietly out of the lavatory half expecting Paul to be standing there with a glass of Dom Perignon in his hand. He had really outdone himself, and she was both excited and curious to see what else he had in mind. The shower was small, and the turbulent bumps were initially unnerving but the warm, refreshing water and the luxurious Sabon bath soaps almost made her forget where she was. As the filth washed away, she felt progressively energized and almost giddy. After all, how many people get to fly in a private jet and bathe in a luxury shower at twenty thousand feet! The musing made her feel special and furiously sexy. She closed her eyes and allowed her hand to rub down across her pubis, feeling that pleasurable tingle begin to stir in her pelvis. But then she stopped herself. She had a better idea.

She turned off the water, opened the door, and spied a too-short white terrycloth towel in the closet. She carefully wrapped it under her arms so that it rode a couple inches high, just enough to provide her man a peek-a-boo tease. To complete the look, she left her hair intentionally water-logged. The effect made her hair straighter and morphed it three shades darker, a look she knew drove Paul mad with desire. But Paul wasn't looking. She wasn't sure exactly what he was doing, but he wasn't paying attention to her. That would have to change.

Looking out the dinette table porthole, Amber unwrapped herself, exposing her firm, athletic, lightly tanned body. She took the cloth and dried each if her smooth legs then patted her firm abdomen and ample breasts. She hoped that her motions would attract his attention, but her effort was for naught. He was still sitting in his pilot's chair staring straight ahead. Frustrated and a bit disappointed she bent over again allowing her long hair to hang forward. She wrapped her hair in the cloth, twisted the towel tightly and threw her head back flipping the towel back over her head. She tucked in the edge as she hatched another scheme.

She walked to the bar, opened the wine refrigerator, and bent over to look inside allowing her breasts to dangle alluringly, hoping that would catch Paul's eye. There was no Dom Perignon, but she did find a bottle of 2004 Crystal Champagne. She pulled out the bottle, unwrapped the foil, removed the wire cage, and popped the cork. Unfortunately, she had not considered the combined effects of air flight jostling and a change in cabin pressure. She tried to control the fizzling wine, but the liquid escaped the bottle and began spilling onto the floor. She let out a squeal and jumped back, trying to dodge the spew.

The commotion finally broke Paul's trance, and he turned his head back just in time to catch the comedy. His spectacularly beautiful and hourglass proportioned girlfriend was giggling and dancing nude as a garden nymph trying to avoid the oozing bubbles of two hundred dollar champagne from dripping all over her. He should have been angry but, instead, was mesmerized. A smile of joy erupted on his face, not of amusement but of utter delight at the witness of the vision. She was perfection personified, and she was his.

Amber regained her composure, her tan a shade pinker, and poured two glasses of the Crystal. Paul was laughing out loud now, and so was she. But his laughter turned to butterflies when she turned toward him, glasses in hand, brandishing a haunting smile that telegraphed her desires.

Paul felt his mouth go dry. Amber spent hours at the gym and even longer at the spa. She kept her body toned and well-manicured in the Brazilian fashion, and he was having trouble keeping his eyes focused on her face. She spared him by kneeling down and offering the wine, "Want some?"

"Of course I do," he drooled.

"Of the wine, silly," she playfully retorted thrusting the flute toward him.

He took the wine from her returning the grin, trying to be clever, "I probably shouldn't. It's not a good idea to drink and fly."

Amber could sense his unease. They had been dating for over a year and were deeply intimate, but he was nervous, and she loved keeping him on his toes, "I thought we already established that. You're not flying, remember? Ariel is."

Paul took the glass. It was less than half-filled, a mere couple gulpfuls he reasoned. "Oh, what the hell," he conceded and downed the whole glass. Amber grinned as she sipped hers slowly, watching him with a wicked gleam as she set the glass down and removed the towel wrap. The terrycloth had done its job. Her blonde curls were back, and she shook out the tangles fluffing her hair with her hands. Then erotically, she leaned forward pressing her torso into his face. He nuzzled his nose into her belly tickling her with it, and she chuckled as she slid her hand forward over his thigh and toward his manhood.

Paul's trousers suddenly became uncomfortably constraining and he tried to regain control, "Still, I don't think…"

This time it was Amber who was reading Paul's mind. "Shh. Don't think," she interrupted then spoke louder, directing her words to the ceiling, "Ariel, do you mind if I take Paul away from you for a little bit?"

"Of course not," the plane answered and then added, "All flight operations are nominal, and there are no nearby radar contacts. Weather is expected to be favorable for at least 40 minutes. You will be notified as conditions change."

"You see," she whispered, "The women have it all under control." She bent over him allowing her feminine rondure to hover tauntingly close to his lips and then swept down like a bird of prey plucking a deep, suckling kiss as she unbuckled his seatbelt and pulled him out of the chair.

Paul allowed her to lead him this time, pushing himself up by his arms and kicking his feet like a scuba diver trying to reach the surface. He stumbled out of his seat, laughing and choking, heaving awkwardly until he was fully standing and in her embrace. Her heat radiated through his body, and he held her tight, allowing his hands to enjoy the bliss of her soft skin. He stroked her back twice before settling his palms onto the globes of her smooth bottom. Her hands were busy too, unbuckling his belt and unbuttoning his shirt, "Dance with me," she murmured into his ear.

Paul pulled back slightly. This time he was the one looking up. "Ariel, something appropriate please."

The lights gently dimmed and the hum of the engines was replaced with a soft rhythm and the sound of a saxophone. Paul chuckled internally at Ariel's wit. The computer had chosen 'Songbirds' by Kenny G.

Amber recognized the tune too, in a different way, as she swayed to the music, "This is the song in Pretty Woman where Julia Roberts greets Richard Gere wearing only a tie."

"Yes, but unlike you, she was overdressed."

Paul was being crass, but she was too horny to care. She dropped to her knees pulling his trousers down as she descended. She teased him with the tip of her tongue but did not linger, standing back up in a controlled climb, planting a train of kisses on his abdomen and chest as she arose. "Do you think I'm a pretty woman?" Amber coyly asked.

Paul could not lie, "You are absolutely beautiful."

Amber responded to the complement by taking Paul by the hand and leading him to the leather couch. She pulled him down on top of her, wrapping her legs around her back in a frenetic embrace, filling his mouth with her tongue. In rhythm with the music, she gyrated her pelvis with his. She waited until the second refrain to release her kiss and pull his head to her breast. Then as he suckled, her free hand grabbed his firmness and stroked it gently while she positioned her hips and slowly guided him into her.

Tedder Stone had the Explorer screaming down Interstate 40 heading straight for the river. This was not the same contemplative, industrious ride that left the quaint village of Marked Tree. Instead, Stone was weaving through traffic, the Special Agent in Charge was barking on the phone, and Weikert and Deng were in the back seat holding on for dear life.

"Marquis, is that jet ready? We are going to need to be wheel's up when we get there!" Oxmore was yelling.

"Plane's warming up as we speak, Boss. Where are we going?"

Oxmore was running on adrenaline, "Charlotte, North Carolina. Round up Neighbors. We are going to need his expertise. And we are going to need Jones, Martin or both of them. Have them load for bear. Do it now! Then contact CIRG and have them mobilize the hostage rescue team. Tell them we have a probable location on a high value target with a likely hostage!"

"You really think Gudrun has taken Amber Chase as a hostage?" Weikert leaned forward and asked as Oxmore ended the call.

"Not any more that I think he's American Al-Qaeda leadership. But we have our orders and he's still the primary suspect for the nurse homicide. And I know good and well what the CIA's intentions are here. For whatever reason, they want him dead. We're the best chance to save this man's life – not to mention his girlfriend's."

PART 4

> "Although strong emergence is logically possible, it is uncomfortably like magic..."
>
> Mark A. Bedau

XXXVIII

Untereigerbasis
Mont Eiger, Jungfrau Region
Switzerland

7:50 pm CET

Alexander Nef's office was large by most executive standards but was completely windowless. Although his boss' luxurious office dwarfed his and was lit by expansive windows that brought in abundant sunlight, he preferred his surrounds. Buried into solid granite two hundred feet below the Administrator's office, Nef's workplace was a good fifteen degrees warmer too. A knock on the door disturbed his work. Once again, he peered up over his wireframe bifocals to see his Bavarian assistant, Dolf, poking his head through.

"What is it?"

"Sir, a moment, please," the young, brown-headed German carefully requested. He knew the Director hated to be interrupted.

Nef waved his assistant in, "Is this about our American projects again?"

"It is. You wanted something more. It seems we have it." Dolf always seemed to have the gift of the dramatic. "Subject Two has eluded capture."

Nef raised his eyebrow. For once, the drama was deserved, "Escaped?"

Dolf nodded in the affirmative.

"Amazing! How?"

"He stole a plane!"

"Interesting. And the status of his Predicate?"

"Dead."

"Dead?! By his hand?"

"It might as well have been." There was a pause. "She was activated by the American Quest unit with orders to kill him. From her perspective, the command was coming from us. She tried to quiet him, and he turned the tables. The CIA put her down appropriately to secure her cover but unfortunately now we don't have anyone directly observing him." Dolf paused again, "Should we bring this to the Administrator?"

Nef contemplated the request for a nanosecond. "No," he huffed, "This is a complication he will not be interested in."

"But what about everything else?" Dolf reacted incredulously.

"There is not close to enough evidence yet. The experiment needs to run much longer."

Dolf disagreed, "Sir, the experiment is complete! Subject Two… his name is Paul Gudrun. He received intelligence from the first subject, Abdullah Burja, and acted on it independent of direction. He has eluded the CIA, FBI, the local police, even another subject. He hacked into the Mediator, a hospital network, FedEx, and he escaped from the FBI and the CIA. And now it looks like he commandeered a plane. He never took so much as a single computer class in college and has never flown a plane – at least not according to any evidence that we have amassed on him to date. This is clear emergent behavior! It is everything we have been looking for! The signature is unmistakable! What more do we need to see?"

"I am not convinced, and *he* will not be impressed. Trust me; you do not want to bring this to him yet. Keep watching, and we will see where this goes." Dolf was visibly disappointed. "I will give you this much. He is our first Observation Status B. Are you still tracking him?" Alexander asked, trying to be sensitive.

Disgruntled but still humble, the assistant politely answered, "The CIA has directed Subject Three to apprehend him. Subject Three's predicate has been ordered to observe both of them," but then Dolf hastily interjected, "But, sir, you must admit that he has clearly transcend..."

The Director silenced the young man with an upwardly pointed index finger, "Be careful, Dolf," Nef spoke firmly and directly, "The technology may be working, but transcension occurs if and only if *he* declares it so." After a subtle pause for dramatic emphasis, he punctuated, "Understood?"

There was a brief awkward silence as if the young man wanted to plead his case just one more time, but Nef detected his body language and pre-empted the request, "That will be all."

With a curt nod, Dolf kept quiet, turned, and left the room.

XXXIX

North Carolina Airspace
United States

1:55 pm EST

What a difference 531 miles makes. In Memphis, the temperature hovered in the mid 30's, the skies were bright blue, the winter rye grass was leaf-littered, and the air was dry and crisp. In Charlotte, the temperature was ten degrees cooler, the sky was murky gray, an inch of day old snow covered the rooftops, and the air was damp and raw. Anticipating the weather change, the plane's highly advanced artificial intelligence digital pilot carefully accommodated, communicated with Charlotte Approach and planned the optimal landing strategy. Their ultimate destination was not the city, but a grand estate on the banks of Lake Norman, a 50 square mile manmade lake north of town lined with expansive retreats and beautiful villas. There, Paul's friend, Yusuf Sandodele, named the manor CountryView, in honor of their childhood home, and had lived there since it was built. Just twenty years had passed since their days playing soccer in the crabgrass outside of their parent's rusted trailers. In that time, the two boys lives had grown intimately intertwined. Yet to the outside world, they could not be more different. One was a quiet, almost reclusive, city doctor — the other, a lavishly rich mogul living the American dream. Appearances could not have been more misleading.

Paul and Amber were awoken by the gentle tussle of turbulence as Ariel began her decent, and the jet dropped below the tropopause. Paul had just enough time for a power-shower before the plane entered the clouds and the rocking intensified. As she was expected to, Ariel expertly guided the plane to the single airstrip at the Concord Municipal Airport, fifteen miles northeast of downtown Charlotte, free from human assistance, without a hiccup, and right on time.

Paul favored the airport over the larger Douglas-Charlotte International Airport. It was no closer to the house, but it offered an incomparable level of anonymity. The airport's FBO was competent, courteous, and — most importantly — discreet. They never asked questions — ever. It was a trait not even Wilson Air could match. The facility itself was small, but the 24 hour service, on-campus fire and safety, and ample hanger space were sufficient for Paul's infrequent needs.

On the ground, the plane was met by a stretch limousine and a black-capped, statuesque chauffeur who properly took Amber by the hand and gallantly sat her inside. Paul eased in beside her, comfortable that the ground crew would take good care of his plane. He gave the driver a knowing glance just before the gentleman closed the door behind the two paramours, each wearing blue-grey scrubs and looking to casual onlookers like two transplant surgeons on a mission to harvest an organ.

But inside the limo, Amber was doing all of the operating. She was giddy and playful and perhaps the happiest Paul had ever seen her. They had never discussed marriage. In fact, he had always believed it was the furthest thing from her mind. For months, she had talked about traveling and parties, girl trips and shopping sprees, and concerts and cocktails. But there had never been any mention of children, country living, or buying a home. Now everything had somehow changed. Amber had always been affectionate and sensuous but now she was bathed in a loving calm combined with a lighthearted excitement. If there had ever been a doubt as to her answer to a proposal of marriage, her coziness in the limo would have washed it all away. The realization made his job all the harder and within a minute of her nuzzling into his chest, he convicted himself to tell Amber the truth – the whole truth – when the time was ripe.

The driver took his time meandering through the forests of suburban Charlotte. It was standard protocol. The winding roads obfuscated ground followers and the canopy of trees made tracking by air and satellite difficult if not impossible. The first few minutes of gleeful banter gave way to relaxed silence. The quiet gave Paul the time to think. He played out the next few hours in his mind: Yusuf's introduction, the tour of CountryView Manor, and what would amount to the 'Great Reveal'.

The introduction of his friend would be the easy part. Yusuf Sandodele was charming and the consummate host. His ability to make people feel at ease was his forte. The plan was to introduce the mansion as an elite Bed and Breakfast retreat and his friend as the property's innkeeper. The two of them conspired on the plane during Amber's bath, and Paul felt the cover perfectly matched Yusuf's personality. So much so that perhaps in another life, it could have been his chosen vocation.

The house posed a more difficult challenge. Perched on 5 acres of prime Lake Norman real estate, it was stately and massive but not inappropriately so for an inn – at least on first glance. The first two floors integrated well to maximize space and the wrap around front porch, and the English vines softened the home's exterior. But the mansion hid a full, finished basement, a cavernous subbasement and the attic squeezed in another 3500 square feet of unfinished storage. Altogether, Country View Manor sported an impressive 33000 square feet –

and most of it was full, not with guest space, but with storage for an eclectic collection of original creations. The distinction prompted Natote, Yusuf's housekeeper, to joke that the house resembled a fine furniture store or museum more than a home. Paul knew Amber would sense the same thing and demand an explanation. He needed to ward off her curiosity – at least until he had the opportunity to explain himself.

That would be the real challenge.

STRONG EMERGENCE

Tennessee Airspace
United States

1:05 pm CST

Despite an explosive temper and his best sarcastic cajoling, it took nearly forty-five minutes for Phil to get his plane off the ground. He had expected the assault team to be the rate limiting step, but SWAT was on standby staking out Doctor Gudrun's condo just where Weikert had left them. It had only taken Martin the travel time necessary to mobilize his unit from Germantown to the airport. Charles Marquit, on the other hand, was a different story. He had been able to find a plane but had trouble finding a flight crew. For a moment, Oxmore contemplated buying a dozen airline tickets but Marquit came through at the last minute, and the plane was finally off the ground.

Martin and Jones along with four other SWAT team members cross-trained in hostage rescue were in the back of the Cessna Citation discussing strategy and getting some sleep while, in the front of the plane, Tedder, Amy, Alesha, Jim and Phil were reunited once again. Alesha and Amy were sitting on the plane's starboard side in a bench seat facing forward across from Phil. Opposite the three of them, Tedder and Jim were sitting in their own seats.

At takeoff, a buzz of nervous excitement engulfed Phil's team but it did not take long for the plane's soft drone and gentle rocking to unleash its hypnotic effect. Phil watched as Tedder and Amy nodded off to sleep. With their tacit suggestion, he finally allowed himself a moment of rest and within seconds of his mind's permission, the utter bliss of sleep began to wash over him. The stress of the terrorist scare, the Memphis murders, the mystery poems, and the Gudrun manhunt began to melt away as he began to gently drift, feeling comfortable, warm and relaxed.

But then the sensations changed. Without warning, a wave of helplessness crashed upon him. He saw a ménage of faces with confused expressions. He tried to speak but the faces did not understand him; he reached out to them, but arms held him down. He had something important to say, a message that could save lives, a revelation that could change the world, but his words were unintelligible. He waved to them, pleading for understanding, but the faces became angry – then professional – then detached. He tried again, but every word seemed to push them further away, to make him appear plainly irrelevant, utterly disturbed, and clinically psychotic. The louder he screamed, the softer his voice became. He felt frantic, obsessed, and frustrated and then a new emotion emerged: panic. He could see him: someone dark and foreboding. He flailed his arms, kicking out, trying to make them see. Then he cried in wild desperation as the faceless face began to draw a hood over his eyes.

Lake Norman, North Carolina
United States

2:58 pm EST

The 8 passenger modified Lincoln Town Car limousine pulled into the property through the wrought iron gate just as the sky finally made good on its threat and began dropping sheets of shimmering snow. The drive wondered through a collection of white oak trees to the grand estate nested on the land's highest point. The house was barely visible from the road but hid a panoramic view of the lake behind it.

The car pulled into the expansive motor courtyard and parked. Paul reached over Amber's lap and lowered the power window letting flakes of snow cascade inside. He wanted to see the manor just as much as he wanted to show it to her.

Yusuf had outdone himself. The house was classically decorated in traditional Yuletide adornments. Although still mid-afternoon, colored lights decorated the trees, large wreaths hung in each of the windows, and every light in the house was on. The chauffeur opened the door and helped each of them out. Amber wore a persistent smile as she took in the Rockwell-esque scene. She twisted her body about in dizzying circles as she staggered up the porch stairs, trying to take it all in. A moment later, a thin but muscular black man with high cheekbones and sharp features opened the door.

"Hello, my friends! Welcome. Welcome to my home!" Yusuf Sandodele bellowed.

Paul could not keep his smile contained and grinned broadly as he embraced his friend, "It's good to see you!"

"It's good to see you too my friend." The stately, well-dressed African turned to the beaming woman, "And this must be the beautiful Amber. I have heard so much about you. You are even more gorgeous than I imagined!"

Amber could not suppress her blush even though she knew his compliment was cliché and his platitudes mere etiquette. Yusuf ushered the couple into the grand foyer. With her eyes, Amber followed the beautifully decorated spiral staircase adorned with real holly and illuminated with hundreds of tiny white lights. From there they walked past the ornate formal dining room with Yusuf continuing his informal introductions, "Tonight we will dine here. Pablo is preparing braised lamb with mint sauce, and for dessert, I think he is making a rhubarb souffle." The host directed his glance to a Hispanic petite man wearing a chef's smock busily setting the table with Christmas finery. Pablo took the moment to nod to the couple doing his best to remain nonchalant and feign unfamiliarity. Paul's instructions were explicit. He wanted to be the one to explain all of this, to explain that this was not Yusuf's house, and Pablo was not Yusuf's chef. That would be confusing enough but would only be the start. Paul wanted – needed – to gently introduce Amber to the truth, slowly, in bits and pieces. It would begin with the house, its furnishings and its attendants. And then, as she absorbed it, he would tell her more.

Amber felt her mouth water. She had been eating like a queen all day, but it had all been a smorgasbord of gourmet appetizers, and none of it had satisfied her apatite. She was hungry and the idea of a proper meal sounded scrumptious but then actuality set in: dinner was hours away.

The group continued their quick tour into the rustic den adorned with a stone fireplace and a cathedral ceiling crowned with thick cherry wood crossbeams. The entire room was in common with the oversized gourmet kitchen.

"Unfortunately, your bedroom is not quite ready. My apologies but my team is working as fast as possible," Yusuf continued. Amber's heart sank but sensing her consternation, he quickly added, "But you must be hungry from your trip. Come. I want to show you what I prepared for you."

"What? I didn't know you cooked," Paul joked but Yusuf was prepared with a retort that was lost on the girl.

"I have secrets too my friend."

"I figured it out!" Phil awoke to Alesha's exclamation, palpitating, and with the unusual sensation of bees swarming within his abdomen, down his back, and out his toes.

"It's not a Chinese symbol at all!" Alesha almost screamed out, waking everyone except Jim, who was already awake and busily clicking his laptop mouse and Tedder, whose chin was still on his chest.

"I thought you were working on the poem?" Amy wondered through a stretch and a yawn.

"I was. I wasn't getting anywhere."

Phil saw Jim smirk. He was about to say something, but Alesha's words interrupted him. "... so I started thinking of Mrs. Gudrun's house and about all of Paul Gudrun's amazing paintings and the funny mark that he signed all of his artwork with. And then I started thinking about the prayer room and the poem's religious themes. And when I remembered the symbol was also on that Hindu shrine, I thought, well maybe, there's a connection, so I googled Hindu images."

"And I hope you have a point," Tedder muttered. He wasn't sleeping after all.

"The symbol is all over the Internet. It's not Chinese! It's Sanskrit!"

"I'm not getting you," Amy prodded.

"It's the symbol of the Hindu religion!"

Everyone's face betrayed their confusion. They still didn't understand.

"It's the Hindu equivalent of the Christian cross!" Alesha explained triumphantly.

"So, he's Hindu now?" Amy stared incredulously at Alesha and then turned to Phil, "I thought he was Muslim."

"That's one confused motherfucker," Agent Stone critiqued, his head pointed down like he still was sleeping but, in reality, he was hearing every word. His remark momentarily stunned everyone. Once again Tedder had a knack for crassly saying out loud what everyone was secretly thinking.

The solace was broken by the sound of mouse clicks. Jim was still typing and clicking like a madman. He had arrived moments before the crewman closed the doors mumbling about *The Temple* poem but, at the moment, Phil had been uninterested in hearing it and scurried him into his seat. But now his curiosity had peaked, "So Jim, what are you doing over there?"

Neighbors was still dialed in to his laptop plucking away, but he stopped and looked up at the sound of his name, formed a cheesy self-congratulatory grin, and almost gloated, "I think I solved *The Temple* poem!"

XL

3:10 pm EST

Amber and Paul each took seats at the eat-in bar with Yusuf taking the bar stool next to Amber. Pablo promptly set out three glasses and poured a tangy, medium-bodied Pinot Noir. Behind him, Natote served a platter of hors d'oeuvres on an ornate, bronze platter. "These are family specialties that I cooked up for you,"

"You cooked these?" Amber chuckled.

"You doubt me?" Yusuf smiled spritely offering a brief glance to Pablo, "Hausan cuisine is the best in Africa. I learned all of this from my mother. And my mother... Well, she was one of the best cooks in the village."

Amber sampled the croquet, "This is delicious!" Yusuf absorbed the compliment with a sincere grin. As the warm morsel touched her stomach and began to quench her hunger, something else dawned on her, "I just remembered something." She turned to her boyfriend with her blue eyes wide open, a touch of panic on her cheeks, and her hands grabbing her threadbare scrubs, "I don't have anything to wear for dinner tonight!"

Paul tried to quiet her concern with levity, "Neither do I."

Pablo interrupted the conversation, "Perhaps the dress shop?"

STRONG EMERGENCE

"Excellent idea!" Yusuf clapped his hands and called for Natote and William, the chauffeur and florist. William was metrosexual and had interests that spanned from cars to interior design to fashion. His favorite was feminine couture and the fine arts. From Paul's perspective, he had been a fabulous and important addition to the CountryView staff. William escorted Amber from the bar with a bit of fanfare and Paul watched with affection as his beauty turned down the hallway and out of sight.

"So don't keep us in suspense!"

Alesha Deng regretted making that plea. She had made it 10 minutes ago and since then, Jim neighbors hadn't stopped talking. He was giving a master class in poetry riddle cryptology. He started by turning his laptop around and showing Oxmore and his team a picture. It was the image of a floor plan – a floor plan in the form or a cross – a cross that appeared to be lying on its side.

"This is a sketch of the floor plan of London's Old St. Paul Cathedral that stood on Ludgate Hill," Neighbors began, "in the tallest point of the city until 1666 when it burned in the Great Fire of London." That sentence began it all, and he had barely taken a breath since. "Sir Christopher Wren, the nation's premier architect at the time, was commissioned to design and build a new cathedral. Essentially, he created a cathedral in the shape of a cross like the recumbent cross of its predecessor." He tapped a key on his laptop, and the floor plan of the new cathedral popped up, less obviously a sideways Latin cross but still meeting the criteria nonetheless.

"He entertained several design options but his final, constructed version, featured the now famous, 3 layered crossing dome inspired by St. Peter's Basilica - like one in Rome. Wren's dome happens to be one of the largest in the world, even to this day, and has inspired many other dome styles throughout the world including our very own United States Capital building!"

There was more. He barely inhaled before continuing, "The center of the dome is centered on the central crossing of the cathedral. And the center of the dome is marked by a seven ton lantern resting on the top of the dome, itself topped by a golden cross. I would say that is a magnificent tribute to the Father of us all."

He kept going – like a tsunami wave overcoming a coastline village, "And on the exterior of the southern transept of the church, the southernmost point of the recumbent cross, high above the south door, is a sculpted tympanum of a phoenix that symbolizes the rising of the new St. Paul from the ashes of the old. Carved into the stone below the phoenix is the word 'Resurgum'. Tradition has it that Wren himself picked up a stone from the old church that had this word inscribed on it, and it became his motto for the reconstruction of the new cathedral. The word is Latin. It means 'I shall rise again'".

Jim had been rambling nonstop, excited about his discovery, and eager to reveal it. He finally paused to catch his breath, a smile of pride and satisfaction filling his face and a sense of calm relief filling his heart from the silence that filled the cabin.

Tedder shredded the quiet, "Isn't that the name of an Al Greene album?"

Phil couldn't help himself, "You're thinking of 'I'll rise again'. My sister had that LP."

Tedder turned to Jim, who looked a little befuddled and jabbed again, "You've been reading way too much Dan Brown. Everyone wants to bash the damn Catholics."

Oxmore sensed that Jim's feelings were hurt and quickly tacked in support of his agent. Jim's interpretation of the poem did seem a little stretched, but it was definitely better than anyone else had done. He opened his mouth intending to offer a complement but before he could say a word, Amy and Alesha countered with a knockout combination of their own.

"Where are the gifts from future mortal enemies that surround the church?" Amy asked.

"I'm not sure," Neighbors stuttered.

"And was there one person who dedicated it? And did that somebody change the world?"

"Uh, I don't think so," Jim was beginning to see the cracks in his case, but it was Alesha who shattered it completely.

"Jim, I thought of that recumbent cross floor plan already. The problem is that most churches, cathedrals, basilicas, abbeys, and even some mausoleums built from the fourth century on were built in a cross shape. Most had a dome, spire, or tower of some sort over the transept crossing. You could say those were all tributes to God. And the recumbent cross is not limited to church designs. It's not even limited to Christianity. The earliest known crosses are the Celtic recumbent cross slabs of Ireland. And the southernmost point does not necessarily mean a compass direction, either. It could be a metaphor for the bottom or the base of the cross or even for something more abstract..."

"Like hell," Tedder added with his eyes still closed.

Amy piled on, "I think I have to agree, Jim. What you have described so far is very general and could apply to many different places. I think the surrounded by gifts line might be the real clue."

Suddenly there was silence, and Phil could viscerally feel Jim's dejection, "Good work, Jim. We shouldn't have laughed." He took a moment and then finished his statement, focusing on his agent's eyes, "This day has been full of deception, and this poem is just another part of it. For all we know, we're on a wild goose chase and those poems are just that – poems! I must say, Jim, that at least you have proposed a theory. That's more than the rest of us can say, but Amy is right. If these poems really are puzzles then any solution has to fit them perfectly – like a key." Phil then looked away from Jim and directed his comments to the rest of the team, "That's true for everything that has happened tonight. There are a whole bunch of inconsistencies here, and that means a whole bunch of lies. The truth is out there and it has to fit the facts – like a key. I want us all working on this – you too Tedder. I want us all thinking about everything that has happened. Don't be afraid to hash things up, question assumptions. I am challenging all of us; including me; to think outside the box!"

Oxmore paused to allow his words to sink in. It was only a fraction of a second but long enough for Alesha. "Agent Oxmore," she began, "Jim was right to focus on the poems. I can't explain it, but I have a gut feeling that wherever they lead us – that's where the truth is."

3:18 pm EST

Natote escorted Amber upstairs to a gorgeously appointed room that appeared more like an oversized walk-in closet than a garment store. On each of the rungs held dozens of beautiful gowns, dresses, tops, and slacks suspended from scented padded hangers. On the opposite side, a cascade of designer shoes in various styles adorned the wall. "We call this *The Closet*," William explained, "Your boyfriend called ahead and told us your sizes. Everything here hopefully fits you. Choose anything you like."

Amber wandered around the room with glitter in her bright blue eyes and with her mouth partially agape like a preschool girl in a Christmas toy store. Natote guided her to a wardrobe filled with fine lingerie, some pieces more functional, others plain sexy. William helped pull some style offerings from the drawers and off the rack. At first, Amber was put off but then quickly caught on; William was more of a girl than the housekeeper.

The tall, slender café au lait-skin blonde choose three dresses: a white, diaphanous, lacy sundress; a sparkling silver-grey sequenced form-fitting dress that chased her curves like a precision sports car; and a bright yellow plunging neckline sweater that ended teasingly high on her legs. For the dress, she chose black, patent leather pumps; for the sequenced outfit, a pair of silver, open toed stilettos; and for the sweater, black tights and tall charcoal boots. With each outfit, she chose a variety of undergarments, leaning toward the romantic, and chose a special negligee for later on. Natote led her from the shop into an ultra-feminine boudoir with a changing room and a large vanity covered with a broad selection of fine perfumes and an assortment of accessories and makeup.

The young woman was overtaken with gratitude. William offered to help with her styling but Amber graciously declined. She had always preferred to groom herself and her attendants graciously let her be.

"When you're done, please ring the bell," Natote instructed just before she left, motioning to the small signaling bell on a mirrored platter sitting next to the eyeliners. Amber nodded, excitedly and almost imperceptibly as she took the clothes into the changing area, absent-mindedly disrobing before William and Natote had fully left the room.

Paul kept his back turned away from Yusuf and the cook as he watched Amber leave seemingly fixed in a daydream trance. He was so angry with himself. How could he have drawn her into this? He had been so selfish and careless. He knew in the back of his mind and deep within his heart this day would come. Sooner or later, others would learn of his capabilities and seek him out: Some for good – others for evil. The truth was he had cast Amber's lot the very first day they met. He remembered it vividly. He almost missed his friend's masquerade party. He had originally planned to go to the movies instead. He used to think what a mistake that would have been. After all, she was stunning, fun and molten hot! So, he let her curves woo him and her infectious laugh penetrate his heart, and now her life was at stake, and her world was about to shatter. What a selfish bastard he was! He closed his eyes in prayer. He asked for forgiveness and vision. And then he asked for guidance.

The Nigerian quietly opened another bottle of red wine, this time a Chilean merlot, before uttering his next words, "Magnificent. I know you could have any woman, but you have certainly chosen well. She is absolutely stunning."

Yusuf's compliments were genuine, and Paul knew it. His words interrupted Paul's prayer, but the doctor was secretly relieved and turned to his friend with a specious smile, "Thank you."

Yusuf raised his goblet of wine in a toast and took a sip, "Her pictures are nothing but a scurrilous likeness," he gregariously pronounced with a jovial swagger.

Paul nodded in appreciation, almost imperceptibly.

"What does she know?" Yusuf was dying to learn.

"She thinks I'm going to propose to her tonight."

Yusuf barked, "And this is all some sort of rouse?" Paul's friend gesticulated incredulously – almost humorously, "Some sort of adventurous prelude?"

Paul nodded again trying hard to hide his remorse.

"Well, you had better tell her before she turns on the television!"

"What do you mean?" Paul asked suddenly concerned.

"You are the talk of CNN – you and Miss Chase, my boy – are the subject of a nationwide manhunt. They say you are the leader of an American Al-Qaeda sleeper cell – the mastermind behind a terrorist attack on a Federal Reserve bank and an attempted suicide bombing of a shopping mall..."

"And you killed a nurse too – or so they claim," Pablo added while wiping down the counter.

Paul sat back in his barstool trying to absorb it all, "She tried to kill me." A hushed silence engulfed the room, "Her injuries were not severe enough."

"They are cutting loose ends, my friend," Yusuf explained, trying to be comforting yet serious, "They are eliminating everyone who has come in contact with you. What you have stumbled across is frightening them greatly."

"It sure seems that way, doesn't it," Paul muttered then paused again, "I shouldn't have come here."

"Don't be silly. This is your house, Paul. Of course, you should have come. We knew the danger as soon as you called. We are prepared."

Paul's expression betrayed his emotions. No precautions were adequate enough. The house's best defense was her seclusion and stealth. If that were compromised, the options for everyone were limited.

"Right." Yusuf matter-of-factly turned to his cook, "Pablo, go find the others. Have them be at the ready."

"Yes sir," the chef responded instantly and, without hesitation, interrupted his work, and left the room.

"So, what are we dealing with?" Yusuf asked. Subconsciously he knew the answer but did not want to admit it.

"Black ops. The best. Highly organized and well equipped. They almost had me three times."

"American?"

Paul was silent, and Yusuf took the hint. They were American for sure. "So then, we better get on with it."

3:25 pm EST

The FBI private charter landed at the Charlotte International Airport and was met by the Charlotte district FBI SAIC Melissa Brown and her team in the middle of the plane's jetway. Phil had met her several times before, but they were only professional acquaintances. Melissa was stocky, kept her hair short and undyed, and rarely wore makeup. Tedder and most others had pigeon-holed her a lesbian, but Phil had met Melissa's husband, an earthy Appalachian-reared huntsman who had no use for girly-girls. The real bigot was Melissa. She instantly cringed at the sight of Amy Weikert. There was no way she had ascended to her rank by merit alone, she reasoned. Her beauty and body had gotten her there, and it didn't matter if Phil Oxmore was bedding her every night or not, he was guilty just for keeping her on his payroll.

Agent Brown extended her hand first to welcome Agent Oxmore and his team. She even welcomed Agent Weikert – officially – but Amy and everyone else knew what Melissa was thinking. Tedder told himself a private joke, "Oh, how he wished Melissa Brown played poker."

"Welcome to Charlotte," Agent Brown offered.

Oxmore responded in kind and quickly introduced his team. Brown knew Weikert, of course, and had worked with Tedder Stone back in the 90's in Denver when they were both starting out, but she had never met Jim Neighbors or Alesha Deng. In kind, Special Agent Brown introduced her staff, including Rob Simon, her Assistant SAIC. A retired Army Captain, he was full headed, curly-black haired, physically buff, and highly energetic in a controlled way. Rob immediately made a connection with Phil's team. Tedder liked his sense of humor, Phil liked his enthusiasm, and Amy and Alesha liked his topical attributes. Not to be outdone, Agent Brown's administrative assistant, Brad Nockapoa, was a chiseled, golden-skinned Hawaiian Tiki God, who had a knack for rubberizing women's knees with his warm baritone voice. Tedder noticed his effect on Amy immediately.

After the brief exchange of pleasantries, Phil jumped right to the point, "So, where do we stand?"

"Yusuf Sandodele does indeed have a residence nearby," Brown revealed, "He maintains a multimillion dollar estate on the north shore of Lake Morgan, about a half hour from here. He has no official criminal record, but as you know, NSA has been keeping close tab on him for years. The house is secluded and is accessed by a single road. There is also a dock and a small beach on the lake." Melissa extended her hand and Brad filled it with her iPad displaying a bird's eye view of the property, "We have no way of knowing if your suspect is there or not, but a private plane from Memphis did land at a small regional airport nearby about an hour ago."

"What do you suggest?" Phil was all business.

"I will explain as we walk, I have trucks waiting for us right beneath us and our SWAT team has been mobilized as you requested. HRT has been notified as well." Agent Simon led the group through an access door and down a set of metal gangway stairs to a triplet of waiting hummers. Light snow was swirling on the tarmac and was just beginning to accumulate. At Oxmore and Brown's co-direction, Nockapoa drove the lead car with Oxmore, Weikert, Simon and Brown. Chris Martin and his assault team took the second vehicle. And Tedder Stone piled into the trailing vehicle with Deng, Neighbors, and a couple of Martin's men. Tedder was not happy about it.

Nockapoa had barely warmed up the engine when Brown spoke again, "Is this really a hostage situation or more like a Bonnie and Clyde?"

"I'm not sure yet. My gestalt is that she is unwitting. Or at least she was initially. We actually know remarkably little about the suspect. CIA is chasing him making me think he's a deep asset gone rogue. But he seems to be going out of his way to protect this woman."

"Or use her as a bargaining chip."

"I guess," Phillip sighed. He hoped the doctor had a more noble reason for his actions but had to concede Melissa's point.

Paul and Yusuf quickly compared notes, took one last gulp, stood from their barstools and started toward a dimly lit hallway walking past dry pantries and storage closets. Near the end of the hall, before the laundry, a set of stairs led downward. Paul followed his friend down the carpeted steps to a large room paneled with thick crown molding. The walls were lined with a curious combination of rare book-stocked mahogany shelves, built-in curio cabinets displaying a collection of artifacts, and a back wall floor-to-ceiling salt water aquarium filled with a variety of colorful fish. Dwarfed in the center of the room, a small oak desk and its accompanying tattered leather chair sat alone. Paul had rescued the desk from a garbage heap the year their old high school principal was promoted to assistant superintendent. Yusuf assumed the desk was antique but never asked. He simply had it shipped to CountryView, and it had been in Paul's office ever since.

On top of the desk, three transparent rectangular plates were perched on small silver stands arranged in a viewing triangle. As the two walked around the desk to face it, the gel monitors changed from translucent to opaque, and all three presented different information in ultra-high resolution. On the center monitor, a snapshot of the International Poetry Society web page with the two poems, *The Quest* and *The Temple*, was displayed.

"So I see you got it."

"Sort of. They began tracing me and soon as I logged on. I took your advice and ran the connection through two proxy servers and an onion router, but they were still on me in less than three minutes."

Paul was noticeably concerned, "Were you able to log into the database safely?"

The Nigerian laughed, "Who do you think you're talking to? Of course, I did! I used Alaska." Paul did not seem eased, so he doubled-downed his quip, "It's winter. It'll take days for them to get dog sleds out to Nome." Rarely did he have the opportunity to scoop Paul and he was making the most of it, "You won't believe it. It's a database alright." Yusuf was dragging things out, and Paul was becoming impatient, "It's the world's largest money-laundering protection racket ever! The developed economies are paying off Tehran in precious stones and metals for protection from something big. They are using this website as a means of coordinating and managing it all, and some administrative entity is taking a whopping percentage. That's what set Burja off. This isn't about Allah or Jihad. It's all about money and power and some fat cat in Europe taking a handsome cut. Burja figured that out. I guess he thought that if others knew what was going on, it would put a stop to it."

"You have got to be kidding!"

Yusuf was still smiling and nodding his head as if telling some cruel practical joke. Unfortunately, it wasn't, ""And it goes to the highest levels of power, not just in the United States and Europe, but in Russia, China, Japan, Brazil, India, Australia...."

Paul was starting to look worried, but Yusuf had to finish, "I think it must be nuclear terrorism. Whatever it is, it's big. Transferred funds are in the order of tens of millions of U.S. dollars, and the drops are happening several times a year. That's what Burja was doing: picking up diamonds!"

Yusuf gloated with a self-indulgent grin like he had just delivered the punchline of a dirty joke but Paul began to see the deeper truth with suddenly newfound clarity, "Now I understand the American government's motivations."

Yusuf's smile faded a shade, "What do you mean?"

"Why the Americans would so want to keep this a secret."

"Because they would look like pussies! Imagine the humiliation!" Yusuf chortled.

But Paul did not smile back, "Yusuf, you do not understand. If word of this leaked out, there would be riots in the streets – markets would tumble – governments would fall. The life of every Muslim in the non-Muslim world would be in danger and vice-versa. Armies would be mobilized – missiles fired – bombs dropped. There would be retaliation and retaliation against retaliation..." He paused for a moment to collect himself, "A lot of people would die."

Yusuf's smile was gone, "Sounds like World War III, my friend."

"But not a nuclear war…"

And the Nigerian finally understood, "A Holy war."

Paul shuffled and altered his demeanor in an attempt to refocus their energy on more profitable pursuits, "Let's hope it doesn't come to that. So, tell me about these poems."

XLI

3:42 pm EST

Amber chose the white dress. It fit her perfectly and flowed across her form in a subtly alluring way. She would have preferred to wet down her hair again but chose instead to embrace her curls, pulling up the right side with a fancy clip. Her hair draped beautifully over her shoulders, and she was pleased. She took her time with her makeup, carefully manicuring her lashes and lining her eyes, and then added just a hint of blush over her foundation followed by a few dabs of L'Air de Temps on her neck. Pleased with her look, she rang the bell but there was no response. She walked back into the boutique, but the room was empty, and there was no one in sight.

She rang the bell again and called out first to Natote, and then William, but neither answered. She was disappointed. She was looking forward to some positive feedback. She reentered the boudoir, walked through to the opposite side and opened the door she had noticed earlier, hoping her two attendants were nearby. But the door led to an unexpected place.

Once again she felt a sensation of blissful wonder as she carefully stepped into the brightly lit space. It was a music conservatory. An assortment of musical instruments covered the floor and hung on the walls: brasses, woodwinds, strings, and a variety of drums, bells, and chimes. In the corner, a full grand piano sat with a composition on the music holder. She sat on the bench and lightly caressed the keys. She had always wanted to learn the piano, but her parents could never have afforded one much less have paid for the private lessons. The child in her wanted to plunk on the ivory, but she refrained. Instead, her curiosity directed her attention to the musical piece in front of her. Although she didn't play an instrument, she had sung in her high school choir and had passing knowledge of musical notation. The piece was highly complex and completely hand written. Page after page were the same, all except for the last. At the end of the score, she noticed an unusual notation, one she had never seen before. It looked peculiarly like Chinese.

She picked up the music to have a better look, but something else caught her eye. Carved on the piano, where ordinarily a brass plate would identify a Steinway or a Yamaha, was the same Chinese-like character. It stared at her like an all-knowing eye. Curiosity began to overwhelm the nurse, and she stood up from the bench and raised the seat. Reams of sheet music were stuffed inside – all hand written and all stamped with the same mysterious symbol. She closed the seat and walked around the room inspecting the violins, clarinets and saxophones. The symbol was engraved, etched, or carved into each and every one.

The mansion was awe inspiring and The Closet was amazing, but the music room was mysterious in a wonderful way. She decided to leave her peculiar finding and continue her search. It would have been nice to have the maid's opinion, but it was Paul's that really mattered. Impulsively, she decided to seek him out. She recalled her steps and found the grand staircase. She glided down the stairs, enjoying the feeling of the soft fabric gently caressing her skin and pleased that she was finding the way.

Amber walked into the living room hoping to surprise her lover but again no one was there and a holiday movie, *Elf*, was showing silently on the flat screen above the warm fireplace. Amber suspended her search and watched for a minute, reliving her youth, and smiling during Elf's outing of the fake mall Santa. The movie broke to a commercial for the evening news, and Amber was about to turn away and continue looking for the others when a vision on the screen stopped her in her tracks. It was a picture of her and Paul and the smile on her face disappeared. The reporter was profiling them. On the bottom of the screen a banner read 'Doctor wanted for Murder'. Even without the sound she absorbed the gist. He was a suspect in a murder investigation, and both of them were wanted for questioning. He was considered highly dangerous, and she was a possible hostage.

Amber's head began to spin. Was this some kind of practical joke? Her mind was in full denial but suddenly, the beautiful house gave Amber dread. What was a moment ago grand now seemed monstrous. Where was Paul? She needed an explanation – some reassurance – some love. She loudly called out his name, but there was no answer. Where was he? And where were Natote and William? Disquiet struck, and she rushed into the kitchen hoping to find the cook but he was not there either. The salon was deserted too and immediately she felt panic begin to seethe. She considered crying out but hastily decided to make a phone call instead. She ran back to the kitchen, picked up the wall phone and was about to dial when a sound startled her. She turned and gasped.

Pablo looked quizzically at the beautiful and clearly frightened girl, "What's wrong Miss?"

"Where is Paul?"

"He is downstairs with Yusuf."

"Take me to him!"

Pablo momentarily considered her request but then thought better of it, "Maybe I should go get him."

"No!" Amber's fear was now obvious.

Pablo tried to be as reassuring as possible, "I insist. I will be right back."

Amber watched the cook scamper, disappearing down a darkened corridor. As soon as he was out of sight, she picked up the phone again. Instinctually, her trembling fingers began to punch in Paul's cell phone number. Could this be true? She believed this had all been an elaborate ruse for a proposal but now she didn't know what to think. As she depressed the third number, her concentration was disturbed once more. She heard another noise. This time her heart leaped, hoping that her lover was behind her, wishing desperately to see his comforting face. But the sound was not Paul. Amber turned just in time to see a flash of smoke as the almost silent bullet drove through her skull.

"They are riddles – not poems," Yusuf took Paul's request for analysis seriously; "They don't have the appropriate meter. I think they are meant to be taken as a set. Look, Not only are they side by side but the font is the same. And they both have similar religious imagery, but at the same time, I think that may be a bit of misdirection. What do you think?"

"I agree." Paul was already impressed. His friend was brilliant.

"One thing I noticed immediately was the capital letters. There are none in *The Temple*. Look. Not even Pulitzer is capitalized. And Creator and Father – assuming those words are meant to refer to God."

"Interesting. There is a conspicuous lack of capitalization, isn't there. Rome isn't capitalized either."

"I was convinced that was a clue – perhaps a hidden word. But I couldn't make out anything. Then again, perhaps the clue there is that creator and father don't mean God."

"Something more secular," Paul edited, "I considered that possibility too but there are too many permutations. We are still missing something – something obvious. But I agree with you. The lack of capitalization is significant…"

Then Paul saw it.

"Maybe that's it! What if there are words here that should be capitalized but aren't?"

"I don't understand," Yusuf scowled, clearly confused, "I thought we just said that. Like Rome and Father."

"Maybe there's another one…"

Yusuf looked at the poem again and read each word one by one and each phrase line by line until he got to the last stanza:

the father of us all

"Of course! It's not the word father that should be capitalized! It's the word US! U-S! United States!"

the father of US all!

"George Washington!" Yusuf exclaimed.

"If that's true, then the center of the recumbent cross is a tribute to George Washington," Paul concluded.

"The Washington Monument?" Yusuf was really excited like a school boy about to score a game winning touchdown. Paul had emphasized the importance of all of this. He allowed himself a second to be humbled by his friend's enthusiasm. Yusuf had dropped everything for this.

"Perhaps," Paul's calm mood dampened Yusuf's enthusiasm, "But there other possibilities. The George Washington Bridge…Mount Vernon… Mount Rushmore…"

Yusuf was unfazed and rudely interrupted Paul's recitation, "Isn't the Washington Monument the center of a geographic cross?"

The sentence stopped Paul in his tracks. He suddenly recalled the history. The City of Washington was a planned city, whose initial design by Pierre Charles L'Enfant, was cast aside for over a hundred years as the city fell into disrepair during the reconstruction. It wasn't until 1901 that L'Enfant's vision was largely restored by the McMillan plan. The legislation reestablished the grandeur of the National Mall and the capital grounds and called for additional monuments to be built including one at the end of the Mall, opposite the capital. In 1914, the first stage was fulfilled by the construction of the Lincoln Memorial.

Paul waved his hand over the table in front of the left monitor, and the screen came to life. A web browser opened, and an old fashioned microphone icon flashed in the upper right corner, "Show me a map of Washington D.C. Zoom in on the Washington monument." The computer complied and within seconds, Google Earth focused on the monument with a slight angular projection. The monument, capital building and Lincoln memorial were clearly visible on an east-west axis. Slightly northwest of the monument, the impressive White House with her expansive north and south lawns connected to the National Mall by the 52 acre Ellipse Park was also obvious.

Yusuf saw the cross immediately – two virtual lines – an east-west line connecting the Capital and the Lincoln Memorial and a north-south line connecting the White House with...

"The Jefferson Memorial! It makes a cross! The southern-most point!"

With his fingertips, Yusuf drew on the screen. The north-south axis of the shape was shorter than the east west axis. He was drawing a cross lying on its side – a recumbent cross.

Paul began to explain. "It's called a Latin cross..."

But once again Paul was rudely interrupted. This time by gunshots.

XLII

4:02 pm

Pablo heard her fall and rushed back calling out Amber's name. He saw the red laser light and jumped back just in time to avoid the bullet rushing past his ear as the CIA's black-dressed, SAG/SOG paramilitary assault force, less well-known than the famed SEAL Team 6 but just as deadly, began making its way carefully toward the cook's position.

Alpha, the first floor team, was built from the ground up by America's best and brightest. Samuel "Sammy" Pendleton hailed from south Detroit and was recruited into Marine Special Operations straight off of Paris Island. Lee Tolley, Sammy's wingman, was ex-army with special training in breaching and explosives and Fernando Gomez was a delta force crossover from West Tampa. The helicopter pilot from the park was there too. Brent Stokes, like Caryn Lund, the Alpha team leader, were both born not of the military, but of the intelligence community, recruited out of high school, and trained from the beginning in all manner of tradecraft including operations of high technical expertise – like sharpshooting and piloting a helicopter. They were all part of the Special Operations Group, a CIA ultra-elite team of civilian special operations personnel authorized by the President to function anywhere in the world, even within national borders, in the clandestine paramilitary interest of the United States – and this was certainly one of those instances.

Team Two, call sign Bravo, had entered top down from the roof and had second floor responsibility. All four of them were part of the 407th Special Operations Squadron out of Pope Air Base near Fayetteville. They, like Alpha, were SOG and were led by Agent Hector Malgieri, an ex-ranger and a veteran of Desert Storm and Iraqi Freedom. Both Christos and Caryn had worked with Hector both stateside and in Afghanistan.

From the lake, Team Three, call sign Charlie, crept in. Their responsibility was the boat house and subbasement entrance. Led by Lieutenant Jorge Ivey, they were the only members of the assault group not SOG. The team was composed of a small contingent of the 5th Special Forces Group SEALs that happened to be maneuvering at Fort Bragg when the call came in. The plan was to clear the house systematically and expeditiously in a pincer movement, joining up with the second floor and ground teams. The entire strike force was led by Christos Sokolov.

Outside, McCammon was commanding from one of a pair of the 407th's Sikorski UH-60 stealth Black Hawks circling overhead and two additional team members, each an ex-green beret, were securing the front edge. Three more spotter-sniper pairs were covering the sides and back.

McCammon was sure Gudrun and Chase were on site and was taking every precaution to prevent their escape. He had watched them land and take a leisurely drive to a beautiful lake estate from the comfort of his iPad linked to the video feed from the unmanned MQ-9 Reaper aerial drone he had scrambled to track their plane. It had not taken long to deduce where Gudrun and his girlfriend had gone. The Reaper was flying 7 miles overhead and had archived everything, from Paul Gudrun's first steps off his jet to Amber Chase's expression when she arrived at the house. But the UAV had its limitations; it could not see inside the building. In fact, interior recon was virtually nonexistent. No floor plans were available, and the home's walls and windows were thermal imaging opaque and resistant to electronic eavesdropping. To compensate, McCammon chose to attach Sokolov to Alpha forming a six man team of two three man sections with the goal of clearing the cavernous first floor as quickly as possible.

The chef's heart was racing. He reached back into his pocket and pulled out his cell phone. The signal was jammed, and it was at that moment he realized he was about to die. Several shots rang out, and the concussion wave rocked the kitchen. Pablo immediately knew he was dead, but his palpitating chest told him differently. The sound was from the housekeeper's AK. Natote had waited in ambush and after speaking a silent prayer, opened fire. Tolley took two slugs to the head, and Sokolov crashed to the ground from the force of a bullet that impacted his back. In the confusion and Natote's brief triumph, Agent Lund took the open shot shooting the maid twice: once in the chest and again in her neck.

In the confusion, Pablo ran for the kitchen plucking a butcher's hatchet from the countertop knife block. Stokes chased him with Pendleton taking the covering position. The pilot fired several shots hoping to keep his man pinned. Pablo waited for the pause and listened closely for the magazine switch signaling the shooter was reloading. He heard the faint click and took his chance. In a swift move, he barrel rolled out from the safety of the cabinet and flung the knife. Like an adult game of mumblety-peg, the blade spun through the air and sunk in Brent Stokes' head bisecting his nose and lodging deep into his frontal lobe. Pablo leaped back and turned to the counter to fetch another knife hoping to repeat his success with the other shooter but Sammy was a professional. Unfazed, the Marine settled back and unloaded his M4 into Pablo's back.

Yusuf and Paul both heard the gun shots and carefully rushed to the head of the basement stair, hugging the wall and keeping quiet, carefully listening to the scuffle upstairs. Paul hand-signaled to Yusuf to retreat back to the desk.

"They found us," Paul whispered.
"How? So fast!"
"I don't know."

Yusuf felt unnerved, anguished that he had somehow erred but knew that he hadn't. Paul had no time to set his friend at ease. With a few swipes of his hand, video from a variety of hidden interior cameras filled the computer screens. Instantly, their predicament was obvious. Intruders were in the house and the subbasement.

A couple more table taps and the cameras moved outside. The snow was obscuring the thermal imaging, but he could still discern the characteristic signatures of eight human forms, two on each side of the house.

"We're surrounded. And the ones downstairs are near the computer," Yusuf's voice was pressured and a half-octave higher. In all their exploits, he had never felt so much fear, "And they are heading for Ariel!"

Paul began furiously typing on the computers virtual keyboard. Once again, a dizzying spectacle of windows and dialogs bounced off the screen in a symphony of symbols and strange words.

Minutes were passing, and the sweat was dripping into Yusuf's eyes, "They're 82 kVolts running through that bus and the circuits are open air!" He felt his heart rate soar dangerously fast.

"Yes. And they are carrying M4 semiautomatic lightning rods. Let's hope they can read," Paul joked trying to ease his friend's concern.

The look on Yusuf's face was not one of amusement.

"Do you have any weapons down here?" Paul asked not taking his eyes off the screens or slowing his hands.

"Of course." Yusuf inched to a built-in cupboard along the back wall of the office. The furniture had an ornate centerpiece that doubled as a knob. He rotated the structure counterclockwise and unlatched the door. The cabinet hid a small safe with an electronic keypad. Yusuf entered the code and opened the heavy door. Inside laid a pistol and an intimidating assault gun. He loaded ammunition clips into both of them and set them back on the desk.

"What are you doing?" Yusuf's curiosity was suddenly piqued. Paul was still typing madly.

"Using their technology to our advantage." He paused briefly, inspected the weapons, took hold of the larger gun, and handed the pistol to Yusuf.

"What the hell do you expect me to do with this? Do you think I'm you?"

"I want you to take it," Paul whispered with authority, "Then I want you to use the tunnel and get the hell out of here."

Yusuf reminded Paul that the passage he was referring to had not been used in years. The tunnel ended at a replica of an old mill and exited in the middle of a dry well. From there, it was possible to climb out – but not gracefully. It was an emergency escape route Paul had designed into the house for just such a contingency. For years, the mill had been used as a garden storage shed and a storehouse for mountain bikes and hiking gear. But that was long ago. "I cleaned it out a few summers ago," Yusuf announced, "It was infested with red ants and termites. There is nothing in it now."

"You don't have much choice. We're surrounded. It's your only chance to get out of here."

"What are you going to do?"

"Draw their attention."

"Paul, you can't do that!"

"Look at me Yusuf," Paul's eyes bore through the Nigerian down to his soul, "They are looking for me and won't stop till I'm dead. There is no way this is going to turn out good for me. Do you understand? Besides, Amber's up there."

Yusuf finally made the sad mental connection, "Oh, my goodness, Paul. I am so sorry. Maybe she's alright."

"With any luck, she's in custody. Don't worry. I'll find her, but first I need you to get out of here. Get safe. Besides, I need you to finish deciphering those poems. There is special significance to them; I know it! Why the Jefferson Memorial? What's there? Promise me you will do this Yusuf!" Paul could tell his friend was more scared for Paul's well-being than his own, "I will be alright. I have a few tricks up my sleeve."

Yusuf finally nodded a yes and hugged the wall while Paul made his way to the staircase. Paul took one last glance at his childhood friend, casted a reassuring grin, raised his weapon, and entered the stairwell. He began slowly climbing step by step remaining vigilant for any hostiles. He saw no one.

As he watched, the Nigerian businessman felt a sense of dread – a sense that it might be the last time he would ever see his friend and mentor alive again. He took a deep breath and began inching his way to the wine cellar. From there he would do as he was told; he would leave their beloved CountryView estate and escape through the tunnel.

Agent Caryn Lund rushed to Sokolov's aid. He only had the wind knocked out of him. Natote's shot was off mark and had struck him in his armor-protected back. Pendleton was standing next to him, sweating profusely, weapon drawn and hyperventilating.

"Are you OK?" Lund asked with honest sympathy, helping him to his feet. It was no secret she believed Christos was attractive.

"My back hurts like hell," Sokolov groaned, wincing in pain.

"It looks like she got you right under the scapula."

"Bitch!"

"Don't worry. She's in hell now," Caryn gloated, hoping Christos would find her strength sexy.

Sokolov grinned appreciating the sarcastic jeer, "What's our status?"

Agent Lund collected herself, "Stokes and Tolly are down. We got the girl, the cook and the maid." Before she could finish, additional gunshots rang out from above.

Agent Gomez peeked around the corner adjusting his earphone and completed the report, "Bravo took fire with no casualties. They aced the driver in the north wing and are continuing. Charlie is slowly clearing the subbasement. So far, they report no encounters."

"That only leaves Sandodele and Gudrun still unaccounted for," Lund finished.

Sokolov nodded and opened his com mike, "Press Box. This is Quarterback. SITREP." He needed to update McCammon on the situation.

McCammon acknowledged by keying his microphone switch twice.

"Alpha contact in 1 Mike. Bravo contact in 2 November. Three Lineman tackled. Extra Point scored. Two Heroes are deep down. No status on Field Goal or Touchdown. Weapons green. Surprise is lost. Alpha combat effectiveness compromised. Request charges or recommend Alpha reorganize into single element."

McCammon answered but it was not what Sokolov wanted to hear, "Understood Quarterback, but unable to endorse. No charges available and optimum speed now more critical than ever. Keep original mission parameters and continue."

Sokolov double clicked back and growled. He saw the worry in his team's eyes and reacted by shouting out orders, first to Lund, "We need to continue two by two. Take Pendleton and sweep the north wing. Gomez and I will take the south."

"We can't leave them! Should we pull them out?" Pendleton was CIA SOG now, but the Marine in him was ingrained to the core.

"No time. We will come back for them later," Sokolov lied. They were food for the rats now.

Sokolov dispersed Alpha and watched as Agent Gomez joined his side and Lund and Pendleton took their assignment. A sharp pain filled his shoulder, and he winced again. The stab reminded him of his bumbling ineffectiveness and how it had cost him two strike force members. Humiliation was not an emotion he was accustomed to and it seeded an anger that was slowly boiling to a homicidal rage. Venomously, he pulled out his pistol, cocked the action, and began the search.

The four separated and Sokolov and Gomez headed to the salon. The room was filled with fine artwork and furnishings, and a Waterford-crystal trimmed Christmas tree adorned the corner. They kept their weapons high, protected their flank, and slowly advanced through the elegantly decorated space. From there, they explored through a closed door and into an adjacent parlor.

The room was bursting with tapestries in various states of creation. The space was vacant, but the two could not help but pause a moment to admire the dozens of fine fabrics in various styles that lined the walls. In the corner, a loom was loaded with a half made fabric. Gomez picked it up and admired the incredible detail and symbolism: an intricate snowflake design with an unusual stitching in the right lower corner. How strange, he wondered. Maybe the character was Chinese for snow.

He dropped the cloth, and the two continued their systematic search, passing through an arch and into a short hall with two closed doors. The first hid a small lavatory, but the second hid something bigger. Sokolov entered with Gomez providing cover. The medium sized space was two stories tall and filled from floor to ceiling with dusty, hard-bound books. The library was gorgeously finished in dark mahogany shelving and was illuminated by a single table lamp. Late afternoon twilight flowed through two massive windows flanking an unlit fireplace. Unlike the rest of the house, the room was modestly decorated with green holly above the archways and little else. Sokolov's eyes were immediately drawn to the back of the library. There, a heavy wooden door protected the entrance to what he perceived as the last room of the south wing.

Sokolov and Gomez stacked up behind the door. Gomez tested the knob. It was unlocked. Sokolov gestured, and in a coordinated movement, Gomez turned the knob and opened the door as the strike force commander spun around with rifle drawn and entered the room.

XLIII

4:22 PM EST

Charlie slowly made their way through the aisles of crates and artifacts within the cavernous subbasement. Save for the boat garage, the remainder of the level was subterranean, dark, and unfinished. It looked more like an industrial warehouse than part of a sprawling, luxurious estate. The floor was poured concrete, and the ceiling was clothed in a maze of pipes, conduit, and circuit boxes with the only light coming from a few dim LED service lamps. The largest ceiling tubes all were directed to the north side of the building. The SEAL team slowly followed the breadcrumbs into the darkness, methodically searching the corridors of stacked boxes, vigilantly watching for an ambush.

The war in Iraq had exposed a major flaw in American military might. Despite overwhelming firepower, integrated communication, and superior tactics, the capture of the city of Fallujah west of Baghdad took considerable effort, treasure, and life to secure. The accomplishment was easily the bloodiest battle of the entire war. During the nearly 20 month campaign, urban combat strategies were refined and tactics honed. Phantom Fury, the US marine-led second and final attempt to rid Iraqi insurgents and Al-Qaeda terrorists from the city, succeeded at the cost of 613 allied casualties, the loss of at least as many innocent civilians, and the destruction of nearly 20 percent of the city's buildings. Team leader Lieutenant Jorge Ivey and Special Officer Leon Gold, Ivey's newest team member, were both veterans of Fury and were well aware of dangers of MOUT – military operations in urban terrain. They moved swiftly through the near darkness illuminated by their AN/PVS-7 night vision goggles and armed with their infrared-sited M4 carbines.

Ivey noticed an interesting alcove protected by layers of Visqueen and directed the team to maneuver behind the polyethylene plastic. Special Officer Gold bathed the room with infrared from his M249 machine gun rail mounted light.

"What the hell?" Gold vocalized his bewilderment.

"It looks like a clean room for building integrated circuits." The words were spoken by Bill Munson, Ivey's CSO – his Chief Special Operative. He had special competencies in chemical weapons and munitions, but he was no engineer. Still, Ivey agreed with his assessment.

When he was at the academy, Ivey had visited an Intel manufacturing facility. The equipment he was looking at was the same kind of high precision laser chip-crafting technology he had seen then. What the hell was this doing here? Charley team swept the area. Several small storage rooms were adjacent to the lab. All were filled with sensitive equipment, complex integrated memory modules, and technological components that looked straight off a Star Trek hot set, but there was no sign of life: No Touchdown; no Field Goal; and no one else for that matter. Ivey watched as his men cleared the rest of the closets and took a moment to absorb it all. This was clearly foreboding. He had very little prep time or briefing on the high value individual they were ordered to apprehend. All that his team was told was that the apprehension of the HVI was in the highest national security interest. He was beginning to understand why.

Sammy Pendleton made his way through the den and kitchen and began to head down the back hall. The corridor was dark, but he could see a glow ahead emanating from a threshold to a stairway leading downward. Caryn Lund kept back and stayed in the light with a clear view down the hall while Sammy pulled out a mirror from his utility pocket and angled it like a periscope. He could see faint lamplight from the lower floor, but the stair was empty. Taking advantage of his rifle's night vision laser sight, he raised his weapon and started down the stair. Timed carefully to the moment Sammy's right foot just touched the second step, Paul pivoted from the shadows landing the butt of his gun into Pendleton's occiput sending him simultaneously into unconsciousness and careening down the stair.

In less than a second, Paul saw the red dot of a laser-sighted M4 CQBR dash in his eyes. He instantly dropped his weapon and raised his hands above his head.

"Dr. Paul Gudrun?" Caryn called out.

"Yes."

"Keep your hands above your head!"

She wondered for a moment why he hadn't shot her. He was hidden in the shadows, and she was exposed, but perhaps he wasn't as dangerous as she was led to believe. She had an epiphany as she painted his face with the laser: She could finish this now. He had surrendered but killing him would be much easier. One shot and it would all be over. Unfortunately, Sokolov's orders were quite clear: Capture Gudrun if possible, kill only if necessary. Casting the notion aside, and keeping her weapon trained, she continued her commands, "Kick the gun to me – carefully."

Almost before she could finish her sentence, a high-pitched hiss filled the air. It was the sound of Gudrun's gun sliding across the floor. It came to rest a few inches away from her feet. She glanced at the weapon and almost could not believe her eyes. It was an HK MP-7, a German made Personal Defense Weapon only available to the military elite and capable of piercing body armor. She knew the weapon well; she had one at home. Now she was completely confused. He was clearly an operative; no civilian could get his hands on one. So why didn't he kill her... or kill Pendleton for that matter?

Keeping her eyes focused and her head upright, she extended her right foot up and over the MP-7 and with one movement, swept the gun back, pushing it several feet behind her. She heard it slide to a stop and then continued per protocol. Adjusting her headphone, she called in, "Quarterback. This is Call Sign Alpha, Copy."

Her hail was met by silence. She repeated the call with no luck. She tried Bravo, then Charlie, and then with some exasperation, went straight to the top, "Press Box. This is Call Sign Alpha. I have the subject. Request orders!" Again, only dead air filled her ears.

Paul finally spoke, "You are not the only ones with the ability to jam communications."

She considered screaming out, but Sandodele was still at large.

"Do not move your hands and walk slowly toward me. Make no sudden movements."

Paul complied obediently and emerged from the shadow of the hall into the brightly lit country kitchen still smelling of the samosa's Pablo had cooked up earlier. But now there were different intermingled odors: the smell of gunpowder and the smell of blood.

"Stop!" Agent Lund barked and again Paul complied. He appeared relaxed and resigned to his fate. Still, the lack of support was unnerving. Was she going to have to march him out the front door? Maybe she could restrain him somehow. Where was everyone? Anxiety was beginning to set in. What if someone was behind her now? For a second, she took her eyes off of her captive, just enough time to look around the room. Paul kept still. The brief respite gave her a modicum of short-lived comfort. But within moments, the solicitude began to overwhelm her again, and she called out for help.

"Screams don't travel far in this house. The walls are designed to dampen human voice," Paul's voice was deep and smooth but her apprehension was back with a vengeance. Sweat was starting to pour, but she remained professional, focusing on controlling her ventilation and keeping aim.

And then he felt it. It had been a long time since his mind was suddenly filled with thoughts and emotions that had no sense being there. It had been a long time indeed, not since poor Miss Kirby, almost twenty years since he allowed his mind the liberty to see into the hearts of others, "You know, Caryn, you don't have to do this."

The sound of her name drove a tingle down her spine. "How do you know my name?"

"Caryn Lund, Special Operations Group," Paul began. After a short pause, he methodically continued, "You are twenty four and grew up in Long Beach. Your mother raised you in public housing. You went to Woodrow Wilson High and had friends, but not many. You were a good student and had your sights set on Stanford or UCLA until a visit to a guidance counselor changed your mind."

Lund swallowed. It didn't help the lump in her throat. "How do you know all this?"

Paul began to drop his hands, sliding them off of his head but keeping his palms up.

"Keep your hands up!"

"I am not armed Caryn." Paul slowly spun around, "See what I am wearing. There is nowhere I can conceal anything." Paul was still wearing his scrubs. They were unforgiving. Still, Caryn retreated ever so carefully, quickly jerking her head around the room, looking for anyone friend or foe. Suddenly, she felt very vulnerable. She felt her foot rub up against Gudrun's gun. She wanted it close.

He turned back around to face the agent. "Caryn, this is not your destiny. You are not a slave to the Agency. Your handlers do not own you. McCammon does not own you."

"Shut up! Keep your hands up. How the hell?..."

"I am not here to hurt you. I know you can't fathom this. But I want to help you." He saw her eyes briefly look down to his MP-7 lying by her foot.

"Your rifle must be very heavy. Go ahead. Pick up mine. It's much lighter."

"You must think I'm an idiot? That's why you didn't shoot me, isn't it? It's loaded with blanks, right. Or is it just a fake?"

Paul was silent. Keeping her aim true, she slowly squatted and, with her left hand, picked up Gundrun's HK. It felt authentic. It was loaded with a twenty round cartridge and set in semiautomatic mode with the safety off. As she glanced up poised for her next retort, Gudrun's face had turned away from hers. He had found the cook and his expression was a mixture of solemn and pain.

"His name was Pablo. He was a talented chef and a good friend." Paul turned to his arrester, "He has two boys and a girl; the oldest is in middle school."

She wasn't sure where it came from, but she felt a brief pang of guilt, "He killed my partner." Her vindication was hollow, and the crack in her voice exposed it but Paul respected her defense.

"He was trying to protect me."

"Protect you? Why?"

"Because I was his teacher," Paul answered.

"Teacher? Are you some kind of Paula Dean?" Her attempt at sarcasm was forced. There was something about this man that was affecting her.

"That coat of hatred that you are wearing does not become you. You don't have to wear it." He paused a second and stared into Caryn's eyes – straight into her soul, and then gently continued, "Your father was sick."

The words ricocheted through Agent Lund's mind. A wave of tumultuous emotion erupted from deep within her being, "How the fuck?"

"The terrible things he did to you, his uncle did to him. That doesn't justify his actions, but neither does it condemn you." Caryn was beyond knowing how this man knew all of these personal details of her life. She was focused on trying to keep the muscles above her eyes from contracting.

"You think the counselor offered you a way out but she didn't." Paul continued slowly walking toward the woman whose eyes were now misty.

"Yes, she did. I just disappeared," Caryn muttered feeling a teardrop slide down her cheek.

"You ran away from him but you didn't run away from the shame and the guilt. You channeled your pain, and it has made you a stand out agent. But all of this cloak and dagger stuff and allegiance to flag and country is just a closet to hide inside. It's not you."

Paul stared at the flushed woman with her hair pulled back in a masculine bun. Her face was covered in grime, sweat and tears, but Paul saw the smooth and warm skin underneath, "You're a beautiful woman."

Caryn's eyes cramped harder as her lips twitched a subconscious facetious grin. She was distrustful of the complement but simultaneously flattered. Her mother called her pretty, but she never believed it. Cunt, slut, bitch, whore, slave, cocksucker – those were the names her father and his friends called her but no man had ever called her beautiful. For a while, she had even turned to women but they treated her no better and she spent most of her life numb: pleasuring some, pleasing others, depriving herself. Suddenly her arms felt weak. Pointing her weapon at this man suddenly felt very wrong but her orders were explicit. She trembled to maintain her composure; she had honor and a duty; she would walk him out the front door; this was wrong and she knew it; O Lord, please help me.

XLIV

4:30 EST

McCammon recognized the problem immediately.

"Tyler. We have lost audio with Home Team!" he reported in.

Michaels knew the answer but stood true to protocol, "Do you have technical issues?"

"Negative. Sierra is in touch. They report no contacts."

Michaels double-clicked in the affirmative and took no time to toss in his two cents worth, "They're being jammed."

"No shit, Sherlock." Wade added his own worthless penny.

Victor Coombs stood motionlessly and quietly behind the three men. He had personally authorized this mission. With less than three hours' notice, he had received authorization to call up a SEAL team and another SOG unit and assembled a strike force to capture this Paul Gudrun.

With time short, he modeled the assault loosely after Neptune Spear, the operation that killed Osama Bin Laden. They had a similar setup and similar surprise. It was a bigger house, but they also had the advantage of information. NSA had a dedicated watch team on the house and over two years' worth of intelligence on the whereabouts and movements of Sandodele and his house staff. There were six and only six people in the house: Gudrun, Chase, Sandodele, a housekeeper, a chauffeur and a cook. They had overwhelming numbers and firepower, and they had the perimeter and the sky. Even if Gudrun managed to retreat into a safe room, it would take little time to find him and smoke him out.

Then why did McCammon's report drive a vibration of doom down his back? Active jamming meant several things: Surprise was lost, his strike force capability was degraded, and the enemy was robust. Most importantly, it confirmed what deep in his heart he already knew: This estate was much more than just a pretty house on the lake and Paul Gudrun was much more than a trauma doctor who liked to play soldier on the weekends. What he had learned about this enigmatic man was frighteningly Spartan, but he knew a few things: His actions and behaviors suggested excellent training and sophistication. He had to be Special Forces for somebody; he just didn't know who.

Victor's musings were interrupted yet again. This time by Gonzalez who managed to re-strum the vibration of doom, "We've been hacked!"

"What?" Michaels was incredulous, but Coombs wasn't.

"Nature and threat?" Coombs bellowed.

"I can't believe it! It's a binary attack. They piggybacked on to the UAV pipe! That's impossible!"

"English please!" This time it was Michaels who was channeling Wade's personality.

"The hacker has accessed the Reapers navigation logic," Gonzales clarified, "That's super-encrypted!"

"Is it still under our control?" Coombs asked rubbing his forehead. His tension headache was returning with gusto.

"Right now it appears to be. I think I know what they did. I might be able to patch it."

"Run it through its paces," Coombs ordered, "then bring it in and decommission it."

"Maybe that's what they wanted us to do. Have us question an asset in order to weaken us," Michaels offered his unsolicited assessment.

Maybe, Coombs deliberated. But until contact with Home Team was restored, he was going to take every precaution.

Paul imperceptibly inched forward as Caryn contemplated his remarks. He watched as her QCBR was growing exponentially heavier, and her tremor was becoming harder to control. Then he saw her. Without asking, Paul ignored the rifle's muzzle and walked into the kitchen, bellowing a primordial moan at the sight of his Amber crumpled on the floor, lying face down in a pool of blood. He dropped to his knees by her side, rolled her onto her back and cringed. The lethal bullet entered her face just below the right eye with such force that the orbit shattered. What was once a fair haired blue eyed beauty was now a ruined masterpiece, a priceless Monet defaced with grey soot and splattered with a crimson patina. He lowered his head and sobbed silently feeling an ache in his throat. Tears dripped from his face as he bent down and gave her a kiss on the lips, running his hands through her bloody hair and coating himself in the process. Paul looked up at Caryn. She had lowered her gun and was quietly sobbing, her expression betrayed the anguish she was feeling. Something had come over her. She suddenly felt so guilty and ashamed. The wall, the shield that she had always been taught to keep between her actions and her emotions, crumbled before her eyes. For a moment, she even contemplating turning the rifle against herself but something about Paul quieted her. He extended his hand to her – this time palm down. Perhaps she should have known better, but she could not help herself and extended her free hand to his. She trembled, and her lip quivered an "I'm Sorry". There was something special in that moment. Everything had somehow changed. She couldn't explain it. No one would believe it. She wasn't even sure she believed it herself.

Paul withdrew his hand and looked back down at the fallen girl. With resolve, he sat up on his haunches and dipped his finger into her blood once more. Amber's head was lying inches from an enamel white cabinet door. With care, he positioned her head just so, and with his bloody fingertips, he drew a large symbol on the door.

Agent Malgheri lead Bravo quickly and methodically through the upstairs rooms. His team cleared the boutique and then progressed through the large dressing room Amber had changed in earlier, through the music room, the hall, and into a huge vaulted room filled with art. The hall was breathtaking. Every square inch of wall above waist high was adorned with fabulous artwork in a variety of styles: Realistic, Abstract, Impressionistic, Expressionistic, and Surrealistic. The team wandered around the room. Even the ceiling was painted. One of Hector's men recognized it immediately. It was a recreation of a portion of the Sistine Chapel. Along the walls, dozens of additional paintings were stacked in piles like one might find in a home decor store. At the end of the room two easels, each with half-finished paintings, sat waiting for their creator to return and finish them.

Malgheri's curiosity was peaked, and he began flipping through the paintings leaning against the wall. All were stunning, different, and worthy of a museum. He looked for a signature but couldn't find one. Instead, each piece had a curious symbol in the right lower corner. He laid the paintings back against the wall, regained his composure, and checked-in with Sokolov.

"Quarterback, this is Call Sign Bravo."

His earpiece was filled with silence. He repeated the broadcast, but again his invitation was met with dead air. He changed again, "Alpha, this is Bravo." Again, there was no response.

Malgheri's entire team was in the room but naturally distracted. He quickly refocused their attention, "Bravo, form up."

Bravo quickly coalesced.

"We've lost com. Stack up and clear back to the main staircase. Regroup at the landing. Fire condition Orange. We may encounter friendlies."

Bravo took position aside the exit door to the hallway. Malgheri verified each man's readiness and took a deep breath himself.

"Go!"

The tall Nigerian was startled at the sound of a rolling knocking thud and was drawn back to his office with his handgun at the ready, his heart pounding with the vigor of a woodpecker. He raised his gun but could not pull the trigger. Fortunately for the businessman, his fear erupted into relief at the sight of the man plopped at the foot of the stairwell: a mass of flesh, blood oozing from his nose, his left knee twisted back in an unnatural contortion, and his rifle slung harmlessly across the room. Yusuf took a deep breath knowing the man was either dead or, at the very least of no threat, and headed back down the hall.

The file room turned wine cellar sported a false wine shelf, and he pulled it open. His adrenaline had forged a plan in mind. One of his snobbish neighbors was an antique car aficionado and kept his barn filled with cars in various states of repair. Just last week, his neighbor had invited Yusuf and another of his golf buddies on a joy ride in a street legal 1987 Buick Grand National GNX. The car drove beautifully and had the mass and tires to handle the snow. He knew this because the blow-hard liked to boast the fact. Yusuf felt excited. The Buick would make a great get-a-way car, and he even knew where the keys were.

The shelf hid a thick steel door. At first glance, the structure was another safe but the door wasn't to keep people out; it was to keep people from coming in. The hatch led to a 100 yard tunnel underneath the home and gardens that hadn't been opened in years. Yusuf removed the crossbar, unlatched the deadbolts, and opened the door. A musty, wet, cold draft filled the room, and he covered his nose. He reached for a flashlight on a nearby rack and turned it on. As far as he could see, the shaft was empty save for mud and puddles in the distance. Then a sudden realization hit him. He was not dressed for this. It was freezing outside already, the temperature was only going to plunge after nightfall, and he was going to have to walk at least a couple miles in the snow. At the very least, he was going to need better shoes and a jacket.

4:39 pm

Sokolov felt a cool tingle of awe rush through his veins. The room was long and narrow and completely illuminated with natural light from a large picture window. The afternoon was getting late and with the sky darkened by the clouds, the room was cast in dim shadows. Still, there was sufficient light to illuminate the single artifact in the room. Along the right side, standing upright and slightly lean-to, a life size crucifix sat against the wall. Christos was drawn to the petrified wood. His left hand was drawn almost uncontrollably to it. He could barely see in the fading light, but there were nails hammered into both ends of the crossbeam. The wood was rotted and charcoal-like but seemed darker around the nails – black – like denatured blood. He was just about to inspect the cross more closely when a gunshot soured his curiosity. He drew his weapon and headed to the door. A second gunshot rang out, and the problem became instantly apparent. Everyone on his team was caring sound suppressor equipped rifles. The gunshot possessed the characteristic report of a semiautomatic submachine gun. His team was taking fire. Sokolov began calling out to his team members over his headset but quickly realized communications were jammed. He hand-signaled to Gomez. They moved from room to room, clearing each one in turn, moving through the library, past the tapestry room, and into the hall. They stopped and hugged the wall in response to another gunshot, this one coming from the kitchen. Sokolov slowly inched forward. As he turned the corner into the grand foyer, he could make out a form crumpled on the floor. He slowly advanced, remaining vigilant and protecting his flank until he was close enough to positively identify the body. Lying on his back, Malgheri stared straight at the ceiling posed with a curious expression of bewilderment. He was sporting a bullet hole right between the eyes. Two more Bravo were dead on the stairs.

Sokolov listened. There was no sound and no movement. He signaled to Gomez to follow him toward the dining room. There another agent laid prostrate on the floor. Sokolov recognized his forearm tattoo. It was Bravo-2, and there was no doubt of his status either. This was not good. Someone was taking out his strike force one-by-one and he had no doubt who that was. Gudrun might have been resourceful at the hospital and lucky at the apartment, but his escape of Memphis was the work of a high level professional. He needed backup but had no communication.

Sokolov and Gomez carefully entered the den. There was still nothing but dead silence surrounding them. The television was still on but barely hummed. Sokolov contemplated his next move and then saw the body, crumpled in the north wing hall. Bravo-4 was the victim of a single bullet expertly placed with great precision – just above the bridge of the nose and between the nasal canthi – literally right between the eyes. He felt his anger reaching a rolling boil, but his wrath was interrupted by a soft groan. It was coming from the hall. Sokolov followed the voice to the top of the basement staircase leading down to Yusuf's office and could see Pendleton contorted at the base. Gomez kept back in the great room, providing cover and protecting the rear.

"What happened?" Sokolov called down the stair.

"I was coming down and got hit from behind, I think," Agent Pendleton reported, clearly in agony.

"What's down there?"

"Some kind of office," Sammy answered and then pleaded, "I need help!"

"Anybody down there?"

"Not that I can see," Sammy moaned.

"Where's Lund?"

"Not sure. She must be down." Sammy winced again and then groaned for help.

"How bad are you hurt?"

"My leg is broken, I think."

"Can you walk?" Sokolov feigned concern. He had none.

"Hell no," the injured agent chuckled, "My leg is broken!"

"That's the best you can hope for..."

"What's that?" Sammy wondered still giggling.

Dispassionately, Sokolov raised his pistol and coldly shot the agent, "To die laughing." His first bullet was fully effective, but he fired a second shot – for grins. Sokolov's orders were explicit and directly from the top: Capture Gudrun if possible, kill if necessary, acquire at all cost. Eliminate all hostiles including non-viable team members that posed a capture threat. Coombs also made it very clear; clandestine operation was paramount. Everyone was expendable. The decision to kill Sammy was an easy one. Although his assault force was no longer combat effective, his mission remained.

Sokolov contemplated firing a third round, but another sound distracted him. It was Gomez. The sound of a gasp-preceded explicative caught his attention. He turned his head just in time to see the blood splatter from the back of Gomez's head from a single bullet driving through his skull. Sokolov moved quickly against the wall and crouched low. He was exposed and knew it. He double tapped his rifle and dropped to the floor. He quickly shimmied forward expecting return fire, but none came. He reached his partner before scrambling back to his knees. The agent was definitely dead. Charley's status was unknown, but he was all that was left topside. He crept into the kitchen passing Amber's body, ignoring the crimson sign Paul had left behind. He made his way through the bloody dining room, skirting Malgheri's corpse and out the front door. Gudrun was gone, and there were two sets of footprints in the snow. Christos was livid! Then something else caught his eye; another of his agents was dead in the snow-laden grass. Sierra-2 had a single bullet in his skull, and Gudrun's signature was unmistakable. Blood streamed down the man's face, along the crease of his nose, over his lip and into his agape mouth. Sierra-1 was dead in the trees too. Exasperated, He picked up the fallen agent's weapon and called McCammon hoping he was no longer jammed. He wasn't.

"Press Box! This is Quarterback. Status Black! Touchdown and Field Goal are in the open!" Sokolov reported, "Assistance needed to neutralize. Targets are highly dangerous. I am going to need major cleanup."

"Negative Quarterback," McCammon responded, "Orders are to contain and capture. Additional units are in route. Extract all of your personnel."

"All of my personnel are deep down! Like I said, I am going to need major cleanup!"

XLV

4:46 pm

Yusuf stood in the shadows, paralyzed and palpitating. Swarms of butterflies filled his belly and his heart felt like it was moments from popping out of his mouth. He had heard the conversation, the gunshots, and the voice of evil reverberating through the basement, "That's the best you can hope for... To die laughing." He shuddered. The cruel derision echoed through his mind. What kind of evil kills one of his own – in cold blood. He tried to put the words behind him. He needed to make a decision: return to the relative safety of the hidden passage or press forward into the office, past the man he knew must now be dead, and into the storage closet to get his gear. He weighed the options. His pistol was no match for a high-powered semi-automatic. And what if the shooter was headed downstairs? He kept still and listened. At first he heard gun shots, commotion, footsteps and doors slamming but now there was nothing but clear silence.

Yusuf took a chance and pressed forward. The man at the foot of the stairs was grey. The force of one gunshot had ripped open the top of his cranium and another large bore hole had left a gaping cavity in his upper leg. He crept forward and cautioned a peek up the stairwell. There was nothing there but still air.

He was less than fifteen feet from the closet but suddenly a rush of realization washed upon him. There were people up there: friends and colleagues of his that he knew, loved, cherished and respected. He was not a fool and knew the realities and poor odds, but the crashing feelings overwhelmed him. What if just one had survived? In a brief second, he decided the risk was too great not to exclude the possibility, and he changed course and headed upstairs.

Sokolov stood in the snow and looked out over the tree-lined drive and rolling meadow that led from the house to the road. The pastoral scene was lost on the agent. Anger and frustration mixed with the fear of failure consumed him and with good reason. His instructions had been made clear from the onset as had been the price of failure. He had no intention of sitting and patiently waiting for *his* bullet to arrive.

He panned his surroundings. To the right of the house, beyond an auto courtyard, Sokolov spotted a six car free standing garage. He ran to the out building. The garage doors were made of thick wood and electronically driven. He ran to the side of the structure and spotted a service door with glass panes. He peered inside. Closest to the door, in the dim light, Christos could just make out a jet black Lincoln Town car. He tried the door, found it locked, turned his torso, and drove his elbow hard and swiftly through the glass pane, shattering it completely. He reached inside with his left hand and opened the door.

He took a quick inventory of the garage. He was right. The car nearest the door was a town car limousine. He opened the door and quickly searched for keys in the glove box, under the seat, over the visor, and in the console but came up empty. He considered performing a hot-wire but decided to check out the other vehicles first. Parked next to the Lincoln was a small rear wheel drive Jetta sedan Sokolov immediately excluded. As he was about to check out an ancient Ford flatbed, he sensed movement in his peripheral vision. He looked up to see two faces in the door window. For the second time, he couldn't believe his eyes. Sokolov drew his gun and shot twice, but the faces were gone.

Were his eyes deceiving him? Was that Gudrun with Lund? What the hell? He was next to certain he heard Caryn say shit. Was she a hostage? Could Gudrun somehow have turned her? His mind was tumbling with adrenaline driven possibilities. He took a defensive posture behind the Jetta, not sure exactly of their intentions and radioed in a pressured voice slightly louder than a whisper, "Press Box. Quarterback. SITREP. Touchdown sited with complication. HVI seen with friendly. Possible hostage. Possible complicit. Combat ineffective. Defensive position taken. Need charges ASAP."

McCammon answered, "Understood. Sierra Alpha not responding."

"Yes. Sierra Alpha is down!"

"Moving Sierra Bravo and Sierra Delta to support. May take minutes to reposition."

"No minutes available!" McCammon was an idiot! He wasn't getting the gravity of this. Maybe somebody else would, "Touchdown is in the open! Mission is Black! Black on Black! If there is a Plan B, need it now!"

Somebody was listening – to every word. Coombs stood right between Michaels and Gonzalez. Secretly, he had already come to his decision the moment communication was lost with Home Team. James Bond was a fictional character, perhaps modeled after the great super-spy Sidney Reilly. But Gudrun was for real. And the probability of taking him alive was low. He placed his hand on Michaels' shoulder and gave the clear order, "Have Press Box take the entire sector out from the air. Burn the place down if he has to. They can use the Reaper if it's available."

Coombs looked at Gonzalez who hadn't stopped typing. "The Reaper is coming in."

"Good."

"Maybe," Gonzalez hedged, "the UAV is not accepting some codes. I've managed to disarm it, but it won't run a diagnostic."

Yusuf crept up the stair listening carefully for any sound. There wasn't any. He reached the landing and slowly inched toward the den, keeping his weapon high. Something directed him toward the kitchen. He found his friend Pablo first, and he closed his eyes tightly stifling the desire to yell out in anguish. He felt his neck, hoping unrealistically to find a pulse, but his skin was mottled and already cooling on the cold tile floor. Then he looked up and saw the feet of someone else – someone with manicured toes in designer flats – and he instantly knew who it was.

He stood and walked to the body suddenly unconcerned with his safety. He quickly looked around, expecting Paul to be lying next to her, but the only two other corpses nearby were wearing black tactical gear. He stooped to Amber's side to pay his respects. There was no need to check her pulse, he could see her brain. He was about to pray when he looked up and saw a blood drawn X finger-painted on the cupboard door – a recumbent cross. His right brain dwelt on the irony for only a split second before his left brain kicked in to drive home the true intention of the symbol. He bolted upright and quickly ran back down into the office and to Paul's desk.

Yusuf logged in to the computer and quickly navigated to a private directory and started a program he never imagined he would ever run: Extirpate Professional. He entered the username and password. The program started and began a system check. He took the time to run to the closet. He quickly picked out a pair of galoshes and slipped them over his shoes and then grabbed a thick winter coat before heading back to the desk. A dialog box on his computer screen asked for the arming code. He entered it. Paul had programmed the delay for 1000 seconds – 16 minutes and 40 seconds – ample time to reach minimum safe distance. The drab screen with a large white X was replaced with a multicolored circle that began spinning as the large number in the center began to decrement: 999...998...997...

As fascinating as the laboratory was, Ivey redirected his team and continued their systematic search clearing aisles of crates and following the trail of ceiling tubes to a portal reminiscent of a submarine hatch. The steel door was guarded by high voltage warning signs.

The team stacked up. Ignoring the danger, the Lieutenant carefully opened the door and tossed in a flashbang. The stun grenade exploded, and Gold entered first behind the deafening sound and flash of light. The remainder of Ivey's team filed in behind SO Gold, clearing the room in a typical four man approach, beginning with two men on each side of the doorway, alternately entering the room and quickly crossing to the opposite side. Ivey entered last covering the rear center and each man swept the room looking for any motion or hostile targets. There were none. Instead, they found a room filled with industrial electrical equipment and stacks of thin black boxes connected with strands of fiber optic cable and all illuminated with motion-activated fluorescent lights. Ivey gave the signal to crouch downward, and each corpsman scanned the room with their rifle.

"What do you make of this, Bill?" Ivey called out to his SOC.

"It looks like a cross between a transformer substation and a server farm but I don't hear any electricity," Munson answered. Ivey understood; the room lacked the typical hum of high voltage transformers.

His words were interrupted by the voice of a woman. "Stop! Do not advance any further. This is a dangerous area. There is exposed high voltage present."

Startled by the sound, the lieutenant gave a hand signal to hold and quickly improvised. "This is the police," Ivey lied only partially. They were law enforcement, sort-of, "Come forward and identify yourself."

"I am Ariel. I cannot come forward. You are in a dangerous area. I am unable to deenergize these circuits. I suggest you drop any metallic objects and carefully step back."

Munson signaled for two men to flank the voice from the left. Ivey and Gold took the right flank. The voice seemed to come from the back of the room, but Ivey could see nothing but a glow of white light, "Ariel, please come out unarmed where we can see you. We have no reason to hurt you."

Ivey watched the horrific site. Munson stood ever so slightly to move toward his teammate and, in an instant, a burst of light arced through the air followed by a deafening bull whip snap. The force of the bolt threw the warrant officer into the bodies of his comrades propelling the three of them into an unprotected capacitor bank. One of the men, Ivey could not be sure who, burst into fire as he fell dead to the floor. The others convulsed in a light show of sparks and flames until the three of them lay motionlessly in a crackling mass smoldering like the morning remnants of a campfire.

Ivey and Gold both instantly dropped their weapons and kept perfectly still. The putrid smell of burning flesh wafted through the room intermixed with the snaps and crackles of flowing electricity. Only utter fear kept the two of them from vomiting. In a split second, Sam Ivey's elite SEAL team had been reduced to two.

"Holy fuck! What the hell do we do now!" Leon was terrified.

"Keep low," Ivey whispered trying to calm his man.

"Do not move. The circuit breakers have just reset," Ariel announced trying to protect the two remaining men, "I am detecting a significant step voltage."

It was the last sentence that gave it away, "Ariel, are you a computer?" The lieutenant asked.

"Yes, I am."

"Then can you help us get out of here?"

"Unfortunately, there is a high voltage ground fault that is producing a hazardous step voltage." Ariel was talking about Munson who was still sizzling with current drawn from the capacitors and grounded through the floor." "It is expected that an impedance control relay should shortly deenergize this station. Unfortunately, extirpation protocol has been enabled."

"Extirpation protocol? What's that?" Ivey wondered.

Ariel did not answer.

"I play word power," Leon was sweating profusely and whispering frenetically, "The word *extirpate* means to totally destroy and leave no trace."

"You mean like vaporize?"

Gold nodded emphatically in the affirmative, "I think this place is going to blow!"

"By extirpation, do you mean self-destruction?" Ivey called out the question to the computer.

"Yes," Ariel answered but would not elaborate further. Ivey tried to obtain additional information but to no avail.

Hoping a less direct question would be more fruitful, Jorge Ivey asked one last query, "Ariel. How long until extirpation?"

"14 minutes 9 seconds," Ariel answered truthfully.

"When can we move?"

"Not yet!" Her answer was just as truthful.

XLVI

4:54 pm

McCammon had instructed Sokolov to hold and wait for support, but Christos Sokolov wasn't stupid. Unlike McCammon, he knew the score. Whoever the hell Gudrun was, powers way higher than even Coombs were calling the shots and probably wanted him dead. Everyone was expendable, and nobody even knew who he was. The best he could hope for was ink enough to write his name in a tomb buried under glass at Langley – a name in a book of fallen spies that no one would ever read. If he was going out, it wasn't going to be this way.

Sokolov crouched forward. The garage was empty. He rechecked his ammo and advanced to the door. The deck was clear. There was no one in the grass. With almost reckless abandon, he stormed forward. There, at the edge of the pavement he saw Gudrun crouched near the body of one of his snipers. He watched in utter disbelief as Caryn Lund was shooting, but not at Gudrun or Sandodele, but at one of her own. The man was wearing camo and a black balaclava. Sokolov watched as Caryn put a bullet right in Sierra's head, nearly blowing it off the shoulders.

As hard as he found it, his arm instinctually rose to shoulder level, and he pulled the trigger of his rifle blowing a hole through Caryn's humerus, sending the M-7 flying through the air. His second bullet went into her back with just enough force that it pierced the back plate of her armor, ricocheted off a rib, and lacerated her lung. Fortunately, the round missed her vital circulation, but the effect was no less incapacitating. She was prone on the ground facing Paul, gasping for breath, tears still flowing from her eyes.

Sokolov took no time in calling it in, "Touchdown! Touchdown!"

Without looking, Gudrun slowly rose with his hands straight up. He rotated deliberately making, for the first time, real eye contact with his pursuer. Sokolov had a realization as he pointed his CQBR straight at Paul Gudrun's face: He could finish this now. Gudrun had surrendered but killing him would be much easier. One shot and it would all be over. Unfortunately, his orders were quite clear: Capture Gudrun if possible, kill only if necessary. Casting the thought, he tightened his grip and began to slowly squeeze the trigger.

"FBI! Drop the weapon!"

The surprise threw Sokolov's aim and instinctively kept his flexor digitorum musculature from contracting. But oh, how sweet it would be! He could taste the kill on the back of his tongue.

"Drop it agent! Do not shoot! That's an order!" Oxmore bellowed through his megaphone.

Sokolov had almost decided to enjoy the moment but the FBI policeman made him pause again with his funny. Who the hell did he think he was giving orders too? No one was going to give his forearm muscles instruction but him. The tantrum he was having in his mind gave way to the sound of helicopters. Stealth as they were, the Sikorski's were still audible, and Christos knew exactly what they sounded like. He could just make out the roar of the Reaper closing too. With his eyes, Sokolov panned the environment in the dimming twilight. Men dressed in dark blue jackets sporting the letters FBI in bright fluorescent white were surrounding the two of them. All the while, Gudrun was staring right into his executioner's eyes.

His bloodlust subsided, and his rational mind resurfaced. Gudrun wasn't going anywhere. Mission accomplished. The FBI would have him first, but we would take it from there. Why call with a losing hand? Sokolov sighed as he reluctantly made the only decision that he could have. He lowered his rifle and then cast it aside.

"Hands in the air!" Tedder Stone screamed.

Sokolov complied and rested his hands on his scalp with his fingers intertwined. The choppers were getting closer.... And so was the reaper.

"We have a problem," Gonzalez yelled out to no one in particular.

Gonzalez looked nervous. That made Coombs nervous. Gonzales always looked meek, geeky, and sometimes arrogant, but never nervous.

"The reaper is not responding again."

"But it is coming in?" Coombs asked, trying to understand his officer's apprehension.

"Yes. But that's the problem. It's coming in hot!"

"Is this related to the hack?"

"Must be!" Gonzales kept typing.

"Can you redirect it? Or self-destruct?" Michaels asked.

Gonzalez turned his head to his boss, "I've been trying! It's autonomous!"

"7 minutes," Ariel counted down.

"We can't wait any longer. If we do, we'll barely have enough time to get out of the building," Leon pleaded.

"Ariel, is it safe to leave?" He knew the answer. Munson was still cooking. The stench of burning flesh was nearly overwhelming, and the smoke was getting thicker.

"That is not recommended," Ariel politely informed.

"We need to go for it," the SO's impatience was unmistakable.

"Hold fast. We still have time," Ivey ordered emphatically but he could tell his man was about to disobey orders.

"I can't sir. I can't just sit here and die!"

"Get a grip soldier!" Jorge belted. The officer was about to change tactics and plead for calm, but Leon could not help himself. Like a cat leaping from a crouch to capture prey, Special Officer Gold mustered all of his energy and surged forward. He was fast but not quite as fast as the speed of light. The moment his second foot hit the ground, the circuit between his feet was completed. The jolt enhanced by the momentum of his movement propelled him through the air. As crazy as it was, Munson's electrocution had not been enough to impress the control relay but apparently the added impedance change of Leon's sacrifice was enough and the circuit breaker threw driving the computer room into auxiliary power.

Half of Jorge's brain was in emotional shock watching the physical kind, but the other half remembered Ariel's words: breakers would automatically reset quickly. Moving was risky, but he had little choice. Time was running out. He made a leap for it as well and jetted for the door. Subconsciously he expected to die but there was no bolt of electricity as his second foot hit the ground. Relieved but without the luxury to enjoy it, he knew he had only a couple more seconds and practiced economy of stride lunging for the door and sailing through it just as the power returned. He crashed onto the cold concrete floor, hyperextending his knee, but he barely felt it. Without delay, Ivey stumbled to his feet and began weaving through the corridors of boxes, staggering like a drunken frat boy, following the trail of conduits in reverse, running past the Visqueen drapes and toward the boat storehouse, finally seeing the waning afternoon light peeking through the mouse hole they blew to get into the building.

Ivey took no time scanning the coast. Sierra Bravo was nowhere to be found, but he heard the sound of Press Box and Locker Room behind him. They were low to the ground below his angle of sight. He also heard something else. He recognized it immediately. It was the sound of a UAV approaching. Perhaps they had Touchdown or Field Goal but it wouldn't matter if there were a bomb. He checked his watch. A little over five minutes. The adrenaline obliviated the pain in his knee, and he raced around the perimeter of the house. People were probably still inside. He needed to warn them! Little did he know; extirpation was only half of the problem.

Christos Sokolov knew the drill. He was three meters from Paul Gudrun but neither was looking at the other. Both had their eyes on the cadre of uniformed FBI agents that surrounded them. At almost the same time, they both dropped to their knees.

Oxmore looked up at the descending helicopters and screamed through his bullhorn. "Stand to! FBI has jurisdiction." With Tedder Stone in tow, he walked up to Paul Gudrun first, screaming over the quieter but no less noisy helicopters, "You gave us a run Dr. Gudrun. But something tells me you're not just some city-slicker trauma doc are you? Where's your girlfriend?"

Gudrun said nothing. He kept his eyes straight ahead. "No matter, we'll find her." Phil knew he sounded a bit smug but 'spoils go to the victor' he reasoned.

Then the SAIC turned to Sokolov. "Aren't you a Memphis police officer?" Oxmore's sarcasm was viscous. He was incensed, "You were at the hospital last night. A rational question might be to ask what the hell you're doing here, and why on earth did you shoot this woman? But the fact you're both wearing black and carrying CIA gear and there are not one but two fucking Black Hawk stealth god damn helicopters flying over me makes me think those would be stupid questions!"

Sokolov, like Gudrun, said nothing.

He was about to scream some more but was interrupted by Tedder who handed him a cell phone. It was Brent Taylor.

"Yes sir. We have Dr. Gudrun," Phil almost screamed into the phone. But it was a happy scream, "And we have taken a suspect into custody who was witnessed shooting a woman. I have a team searching the house."

Martin and Simon had each led in a team. Melissa Brown had insisted on joining Simon and Amy Weikert was perfectly happy to keep behind the muscle of Martin and Jones. Charlotte took the first floor while the Memphis team took the second, sidestepping bodies on the staircase and landing. Amy had barely been able to keep up with Alesha as she almost raced down the hall, seemingly pulled in a singular direction by an unknown force. Alesha walked into the art conservatory, and they both stopped dead in their tracks.

Back outside, Lieutenant Jorge Ivey was almost shot as he turned the corner running, puffing, and limping. It was only his lack of a weapon that saved his life.

"There's a bomb!" Ivey screamed.

No less than five guns were instantly trained on him. He raised his arms in surrender, but his voice was unfazed, "The house is rigged to blow!"

He could tell the FBI agents were not impressed. At Tedder's instruction, Ivey dropped to his knees.

"Lieutenant Jorge Ivey, United States Navy, 5th Special Forces Group, 452485609. This house is going to explode in less than three minutes!" Ivey lied again. The truth was he didn't really know exactly what Ariel meant by extirpation, but it didn't sound good. His bravado and credential recitation did the trick. Tedder looked into the SEAL's eyes and knew he was serious.

Without orders, Tedder ran into the house screaming "bomb!". Fortunately, one of Brown's agents was in the dining room and had eye contact with the rest of the downstairs team. They had found Amber Chase shot in the head along with a number of others. Tedder knew his team was upstairs and ran up the grand staircase two and three at a time, stepping on corpses when he had to.

Tedder rounded up Marin and Jones immediately who directed him to the gallery at the end of the hall. There, Amy and Alesha were still standing, mesmerized by the sights.

Amy saw Tedder and smiled, "The symbol is Paul Gudrun's!"

Amy elaborated, "He's a polymath genius! He painted all of this, and the ceiling too!"

Tedder instinctively looked up as Amy kept talking.

"Everything here and at his mother's house was done by him. The art, the furniture, everything!" Alesha added. "And you need to check out the next room. There's a whole hall full of music that's got his symbol all over it!"

Tedder interrupted them. "That's all fine and dandy but this house and everything in it is going to blow up in less than ninety seconds."

XLVII

5:04 pm EST

"The Reaper is accelerating and heading straight for the lake! Thirty seconds out!" Agent Wade yelled.

"Twenty million dollars in the drink," Coombs muttered.

"I think I have isolated the code fragment. It's imbedded deep. Whoever did this knew exactly what they were doing!" Gonzalez yelled back.

"Can you fix it?" Michaels asked. Gonzales should have been amused at his remarkably pedestrian question but was too focused to care.

Suddenly, the Reaper altered course and turned toward the house.

Wade whooped, Michaels smiled, and Coombs felt a sense of relief. This was going to work out after all – a kamikaze drone would do the job just nicely. So what if there were a few extra casualties. He turned to congratulate his technical officer but found Gonzales still typing madly, "That's not me!"

The Reaper turned again. Wade watched for a second, quickly recalculated the course in his mind, and came to the devastating conclusion, "Ah, sir…It's changed course again." Then he paused and looked directly at his boss. This time it was Agent Wade that looked worried – deathly so, "it's not going for the house… it's angling for a better shot."

Coombs instantly understood, and his mind was reaffirmed by Gonzalez who simultaneously crashed his hands on the keyboard in furious aggravation.

Victor reached over Michaels' shoulders and grabbed the microphone, "Press Box. This is Head Coach. Black! Black! Take immediate evasive action! You've got incoming!"

McCammon heard the orders but had virtually no time to process the instruction. He looked around and caught a glimpse – just enough glimmer of steel to know the executioner was wielding his cast titanium blade and swinging the sword for his neck.

The Reaper drove its nose into McCammon's helicopter driving the frame into the second UH-60 hovering nearby. Both exploded into a massive fireball of ignited airplane fuel and jagged metal aircraft parts. Glass and twisted metal flung through the air. Most on the ground were spared, but a plate of metal struck Nockapoa in the shoulder, cracking his clavicle and knocking him out, and a chunk of windshield lodged in Sokolov's left hip, dropping him to the ground in excruciating pain.

Amy, Alesha, Tedder, Martin and Jones all witnessed the spectacle as they emerged from the mansion. Charlotte team was in front heading for cover. Martin and Jones took the Memphis lead dodging the falling debris and fireballs while still helping to get everyone out. Through the mêlée, Oxmore pulled away from Sokolov and ran to join his team with Ivey right behind him. Jorge put his arms over Alesha and Tedder over Amy, directing them toward the woods and away from the house and the falling wreckage while Lieutenant Ivey kept everyone focused. As catastrophic as all this was, there was still a bomb.

In the chaos, Paul slowly stood up and turned to view his magnificent CountryView Manor. He remembered the last time he walked into the house watching his beloved Amber twinkle and twirl in the new fallen snow. The house was still lit with her Christmas finery but now things were different. Everything had changed. Amber was gone. And soon so would he.

Paul slowly walked forward, up the steps and into the house. Christos watched and tried to follow, but the chard in his hip slowed him down. He forged his resolve, picked up his rifle, and lumbered after his prize.

Jorge watched as his commander limped inside. He screamed for Christos but to no avail. He handed Alesha off to Agent Martin. He ran for the porch, dodging puddles of burning debris and ignoring the pleas of Agent's Stone and Weikert and the direct orders of Phillip Oxmore.

The SEAL ran into the foyer and immediately saw two forms. One was Malgheri, lying on his back face up. He remembered him from the briefings. The other was Commander Sokolov on the ground, clutching his hip, writhing in pain. Gudrun was nowhere in sight. Ivey contemplated searching for the doctor but knew he was out of time. He wanted to leave no one behind but had to make a choice. He grabbed Sokolov and with seemingly new found strength, threw him over his shoulder in a modified fireman's carry and staggered through the entry door and down the front step.

Halfway down, Jorge felt warmth on his back. The heat steadily rose, and he recognized it immediately. His warning scream burst instinctively from the pit of his chest, "Incendiary!"

Ivey picked up his pace, balancing Sokolov on his back, and trudged down the drive, working hard to maintain his footing in the melting show. Simon, seeing Ivey's example, picked up Nockapoa the same way. The four ex-soldiers recognized the nature of the rising heat. All had either trained with Thermite or one of its militarized variants and had used it in combat themselves. In cacophonous unison, the word "Incendiary" filled the air. Paul Gudrun had designed the house with Thermite encrusted rafters and studs. When ignited, the combination of lead oxide and aluminum hydrate were designed to create an extremely hot, exothermic reaction, generating temperatures in excess of 1800 degrees. The reaction was oxygen independent and impervious to traditional fire extinguishing schemes, even capable of burning under water.

Everyone pulled back except Alesha. She was bound by the vision. Paul had gone back to be with Amber. She never really knew either of them, but sudden emotion racked through her being. He was greatly misunderstood and now our ignorance and fear had destroyed him. A tear fell as she watched the bright white light engulf the roof of the mansion and stream downward. The curtain of fire generated by the extraordinary heat and the molten elemental lead formed as the product of the reaction burned through all that was CountryView. It took with it all the art, the music, the sculptures, the jewelry, the furniture, the writings, the architecture, the textiles, the technology, and the memories of Paul Gudrun. In less than a minute, the house glowed with nearly the heat of lightening, becoming a crematorium for Amber and a shrine for Paul. Extirpation Complete.

Alesha felt a hand on her shoulder. It was someone she did not immediately recognize, an FBI agent of Indian descent, who pulled her away from the flames and toward safety. He sat her down on a stump. Clenched in her right hand, a fragment of canvas was crumpled into a ball. She had grabbed it from a gallery easel during her run from the house. It was her attempt to salvage any treasure from the home.

The gentle agent opened the interpreter's hand and recovered the fragment. He carefully opened it, spreading out the wrinkles as best as possible. It was a small 8x10 oil painting of a shoreline at sunset and in the corner was Gudrun's unmistakable symbol.

"It's his," she heard herself say, almost as if in a dream.

"That's Om," she heard him say back.

"Yes, the symbol of Hinduism. It's what he used to sign all of his works with."

"It's not just the symbol of Hinduism. It's Om, the visual representation of the fundamental vibration of the universe; the force from which all creation arises; the elemental from whom all else were born."

"That sounds like God." The blasphemous words rumbled unintelligibly in Alesha Deng's head and then another firm grip grabbed her by the hand and drug her to her feet.

"Come on. We can't stay here. The trees are catching fire." Alesha looked up. Phillip was holding her and behind him, Amy, Tedder and Jim stood with a combination of fear and concern in their eyes. Behind her, the house had become a brilliant white light impossible to directly look at. Alesha stood up and stumbled forward, following her compatriots up the drive in what felt like slow motion toward the safety of the road. Half way up she turned her head to find the Indian agent who had helped her, but he was gone. And so was Gudrun's painting. She wanted to go back and get it but knew that was impossible. The heat behind her was growing closer, and Phillip was in front, screaming and pleading for everyone to move faster. She resigned herself to Oxmore's direction but felt remorse at the same time. There was something so sad and unjust about all of this. Maybe Doctor Gudrun was an enemy agent or American Al-Qaeda. Maybe he did kill the nurse. Maybe he did kill the Hausan speaking terrorist. But what if he didn't? And what if he did? Did he really deserve all of this? And what about everyone else in the house? They all were dead. Did they deserve that? Was this justice?

As she reached the road she looked up at the sky and as night fell she shot up a prayer: a prayer of thanksgiving for her safety, a prayer of consolation to the families of the lost, a prayer of justice and tolerance for all humanity, and a prayer of petition for the souls of Amber Chase and Paul Gudrun: May you have mercy on them, oh Lord. And may you welcome them with all your compassion and grace into your house – your mansion with many rooms.

EPILOGUES

XLVIII

Undereigerbasis
Mont Eiger
Jungfrau Region, Switzerland

9:21 am, CET

Regis Lévesque sat at his mahogany desk surrounded by display cases holding rare manuscripts and yellowing parchments and illuminated from behind by crystalline floor to ceiling windows revealing the dramatic landscape of the Bernese Alps behind him. He enjoyed relaxing to the beauty of the scene. To the left, Mont Monch stood as a sentinel to the snows. Not to be outdone, Jungfrau mountain towered to the right and between the two, in the distance, strangely reminiscent of an ancient Tibetan monastery and reachable only by the Jungfraujoch railway, Sphinx observatory sat perched in the razor thin air, each day enduring the brutal elements, each evening daring a peak of heaven.

Even in the modern age, he preferred the pen to the keyboard, explaining the room's notable lack of overt technology. But the technology was there, hidden in unsuspecting places, like the microchip in his hand creating a noticeable tremor, or the nanoparticles in his hair coloring it a natural grey, or the carbon micromatrices that created the wrinkles above his brow. His discoveries had many implications and cellular degeneration inhibition was only one of many. But age implied wisdom, an important attribute a President of the largest bank in Switzerland should have. He meant to create whatever illusion met his needs even on a day when there was no need for masks and magic tricks; he wasn't presiding at the bank.

His sage, Alexander Nef, had full authority to enter the Administrator's office, but not to interrupt. He stood quietly, waiting for Lévesque to raise his head and acknowledge his presence. It took about thirty seconds, but Nef's boss finally spoke.

"I was wondering when you were going to come and tell me the good news yourself."

"I didn't want to bore you with idle speculation."

"One of my subjects makes the headline news, runs from the authorities, embarrasses the FBI and humiliates the CIA. That's pretty noteworthy."

"That any thief could do."

"And he penetrates the Mediator, kills his Predicate, and eludes a death order."

"Notable yes, but he didn't technically kill his Predicate."

Lévesque paused. He enjoyed the verbal spar with his trusted advisor and friend but this time he sensed something more, "So, what has changed your mind?"

"He deciphered a 256 bit encryption package, hacked into the logic of a UAV and gave it self-governance and the will to sacrifice itself!"

"Impressive." Clearly the Administrator did not understand where his adviser was headed.

Nef tried to remain calm. He tried to keep his Montreal-French composure, but he couldn't help it. His Toronto-American English accent came barreling through, "Doing that is impossible with technology rooted in the standard model, Sir. Almost certainly he has a deep understanding of T Theory. And not just abstract musing mind you, but real world application. And he did it by himself in a matter of minutes! Frankly, that's extraordinary!" Nef's visceral excitement and preeminent impatience was getting the best of him, "He had to have used a massive quasi-analog quantum computer at least two orders of magnitude more powerful than ours! – 30,000 cubits minimum!"

Regis put down his pen and looked at Alexander square in the eye. T-theory. Was that the official name now for what he took from his lover over 80 years ago? – The radical twist in Quantum Mechanics that had allowed all of this. To the world, Alan Turing was a brilliant mathematician, code-breaker, and artificial intelligence pioneer but to him he was just *Alaine*, his sweet, loving, beautiful and brilliant amour – his precious lamb.

Lévesque's anger boiled at the thought of his lonely and private friend, condemned for being different, banished from everything he held dear and forced to endure humiliating "treatments" that were more social commentary than scientific therapy. He was the same Alan Turing who discovered the fundamental mathematics of algorithm theory, the so-called *Turing Machine*, which underpins all modern computer software and helped the Allies decipher the infamous German Enigma code. In death he would become known as the "Father of Computer Science", but in life he was dismissed as a depressed fag who took his own life. Regis benefited from their incompetence and prejudice, but this did not lessen his venomous contempt. The authorities never seriously considered murder nor did they mount an investigation. They had not even bothered to test the apple that had supposedly put his sleeping beauty to rest! No one came looking for a box of formulas or a scientific manuscript. No one came knocking on Regis' door. Alan Turing was the 'Father of Computer Science'. Ha! If only the world really knew.

Brilliant minds throughout the subsequent near century would nibble at the edges of Turing's elegant discovery, but no one would make the quantum paradigm leap that permitted Levesque and his team of well-financed engineers to construct a computer in the mid 1960's capable of outperforming even modern supercomputers while the rest of the world was just discovering the silicon chip. Over the following decades, Levesque secretly manipulated markets, broke every encrypted code, installed presidents and toppled kings. All the while, his engineers and scientists further augmented the power of his innovations.

STRONG EMERGENCE

Long before scientists coined the words nanotechnology and quantum computing, Levesque had constructed ultrafast cubit logic quantum computers and molecule sized machines to augment the speed and accuracy of his creations. He preferred the term *atomic engineering* to describe his technologies, the same ones he would later use to develop biologic-process enhancing inventions – machines to accelerate synaptic conduction, muscle fiber twitch speed, energy metabolism efficiency, and coordination performance – all technologies that had been grafted into a cohort of forty boys and girls thirty three years ago – subjects in a grand experiment – Quest – the quest for the next step in human evolution – the quest for 'transcendent man'.

He tested the prototypes on himself and the results were promising but the larger experiment had proved to be a dismal disappointment. But that was gloomy yesterday. Oh, how Alan would have longed to see this bright morning – to see his dream becoming reality – to see his child being born from his beautiful womb.

But Nef was not done ranting, "He didn't transform yesterday," and then enlightenment struck, "He transformed years ago… He fooled all of his predicates: his adopted father, his principal, his college mentor … his nurse…even us!"

"His high school principal knew it but could not put the pieces together."

Alexander smiled. He was almost incredulous yet in awe at the same time. He couldn't believe it. He never really believed; he never imagined his employer's obsession was real; he had always been a skeptic – but now… He could not find the words.

Regis watched as the chest of his trusted friend heaved two and fro. The excitement and energy multiplied within his mind toward the utterance of the only question that mattered. Had he found what had eluded him for decades? Had he found the answer to the riddle? Regis sucked in a deep breath and asked the question, "Is he our son? – Alaine and I's gorgeous son?"

Alexander Nef weighed his answer. Should he be forthcoming? What if he were wrong? Perhaps a hedged or measured response was appropriate? His pause, however brief, was noticed, but Lévesque was not angry.

Instead, the Administrator repeated the question, with greater sincerity and without his air and routine pretentiousness. This time the question was more of a plea, truly like the yearning of a father longing for news of his missing boy.

This time Nef responded quickly, choosing forthrightness and honesty over propriety and self-protective caution.

"Yes sir. Yes, I believe he is."

XLIX

Washington, D.C.
Sunday

4:55 am

The drive to Washington took about as long as Yusuf had expected, given the fog in the Roanoke Valley and the snow outside of Richmond. Traffic at four in the morning was just not the same as four in the afternoon, particularly on the Sunday before Christmas. He pulled up along East Basin Drive cruising slowly past the brightly lit Jefferson Memorial. The first hint of the winter sunrise was casting shadows on the snow covered structure. The view was worthy of a postcard, but he was in no mood to admire it. He could hear the traffic on Highway One and Interstate 395 just over the embankment, but the street itself was sleepy, and the visitor parking lot was vacant. Yusuf chose to park on the street, halfway between the monument and the lesser known George Mason Memorial, a testament to the Virginia statesman who, along with James Madison, helped cofound the American Bill of Rights.

    Yusuf locked the car and began walking toward the memorial. The sound of his crunchy steps in the day old ice reminded him to periodically glance over his shoulder. While the FBI, CIA, or some other malicious organization could have tracked him, he was more concerned about the possibility of a random mugging. Black on black crime was still the dominant threat in the nation's capital.

Assured no one was following him, he walked along the side of the majestic structure surrounded by hundreds of leafless cherry blossoms originally gifted to America in 1912 from Mayor Ozaki of Tokyo, Japan. The offering, presented in peace to foster and encourage friendship was, ironically, a gift from a future mortal enemy to the United States. Thirty years later, Ozaki's emperor Hirohito would order the attack on Pearl Harbor that would ultimately usher America into World War II.

Yusuf admired the architecture as he approached the rotunda from the west side. He had unknowingly been on the right track when he had suggested that 'the creator like one in Rome' might somehow be a reference to a proper name. Indeed, the monument's architect was a Pope, John Russell Pope, who modeled the structure after the Pantheon, a temple erected by pre-Christian Romans to worship their many gods, "like one in Rome".

Yusuf slowly walked up the steps. Although the building was open to the elements, and there were no tickets to be bought, the hour was still unquestionably early, and he feared police or guards might be present. But he saw no one: no police, no homeless, no mischievous youth, and no malcontents. He was alone.

In the darkness and solitude, eeriness surrounded him as he walked into the monument more reminiscent of an ancient Greek ruin than a salute to the nation's third president and founding father. Only the bronze statue of an American patriot standing tall at its center realigned his mind to the location.

And then the rush of reality flooded in. Why was he here? O yes, the X. The vivid image of the girl's eggplant colored blood smeared on the white oak cabinet in a giant X flashed across his brain. He had immediately deduced the double meaning of Paul's message. The symbol was both an action order as well as a rendezvous suggestion: Extirpate and then meet up where X marks the spot; meet up where the poem directed; meet up at the Jefferson Memorial.

But why here? What was the significance of this place? Maybe it was just the answer to a poem riddle. For all he knew, it was a radio station publicity stunt or some kid's idea of a game. Something told him there was more here. Paul, after all, thought there was too. A sudden sadness rolled across him. The last vision he saw of his friend was the smile across his face just before he climbed the stairs to join his gorgeous lover. His vision was cruelly replaced by a flurry of gunfire, the racket of circling military helicopters, a blast louder than any thunder he had ever heard, and the brilliant flash in the night sky followed by such heat that Yusuf felt the sun must have dropped from the sky. Paul was surely dead. There would be no rendezvous.

Yusuf offered a quick prayer for his childhood friend and his tragic and beautiful Amber. He wiped a tear and then resigned himself, continuing his lonely self-guided tour, reading the inscription on the statue nameplate and the quotations carved unto the wall in the emerging predawn light. Each panel honored Thomas Jefferson's contribution to the cause of freedom and independence, selected and edited by the ideals and politics of the early twentieth century. The words on the northeast wall summarized Jefferson's views on freedom of religion:

"Almighty God hath created the mind free...All attempts to influence it by temporal punishments or burdens...are a departure from the plan of the Holy Author of our religion...No man shall be compelled to frequent or support any religious worship or ministry or shall otherwise suffer on account of his religious opinions or belief, but all men shall be free to profess and by argument to maintain, their opinions in matters of religion. I know but one code of morality for men whether acting singly or collectively."

He continued walking and reading, this time stumbling across excerpts from Jefferson's most famous writing, the Declaration of Independence:

"We hold these truths to be self-evident: that all men are created equal, that they are endowed by their Creator with certain inalienable rights, among these are life, liberty, and the pursuit of happiness, that to secure these rights governments are instituted among men. We...solemnly publish and declare, that these colonies are and of right ought to be free and independent states...And for the

support of this declaration, with a firm reliance on the protection of divine providence, we mutually pledge our lives, our fortunes, and our sacred honour."

Then suddenly it dawned on him. Of course! The Declaration of Independence. It was Jefferson's most famous writing, the writing that, obviously, never won him a Pulitzer because it was written over 70 years before Joseph Pulitzer, the Hungarian-American publisher and founder of the prize of literary achievement that bears his name, was even born! And more importantly the Declaration was...

"An epistle to a king!" The words echoed throughout the empty temple. Yusuf turned to the sound, half expecting to see a ghost but there, in the early morning sunlight, stood his beloved friend. He stood transfixed, almost believing he was seeing some transfigured being, but it was Paul.

Paul continued his sentence as he walked toward Yusuf and Jefferson's statue. "King George III, reigning monarch of the Kingdom of Great Britain and Wales. You know, the letter was never addressed nor personally delivered to the king. It was really written for the American colonists as a rallying cry and a formal rationale for war. The closest it actually got to the royal hand was a publishing in an Irish newspaper. But that's neither here nor there."

Yusuf couldn't help himself. He ran up to his friend in an open embrace. "I thought you were dead!" His elation was short-lived and remorse, once again, washed over him, "I am so sorry for Amber." Paul swallowed, but Yusuf did not see fear or grief. Instead, he saw resolve with a touch of indignation. He decided to avoid the obvious questions and asked the burning one, "And the note to the doctor?"

"Don't look up. There is a camera looking down at us to your left." Yusuf nervously complied, partially covering his face with his hand as he did so.

"Around the top of the rotunda and surrounding the statue are the words,

"I have sworn upon the altar of God eternal hostility against every form of tyranny over the mind of man."

"He was arguing against a state religion," Paul explained, "the words were from a letter Jefferson wrote to Dr. Benjamin Rush, a 'note to a doctor'."

"Ok. I think I get it, but what does it mean? Why bring us here? Are these words special? Is there another meaning? Is there a treasure buried under the statue?" Yusuf was exasperated and ranting. Paul let him burn himself out.

"The words are special, and there is a treasure here, but it's not buried. I swear my friend; Amber didn't die for nothing."

"What?"

"This is not the end. It's an illusion to trap the ignorant and the naive."

"I don't follow."

"Yes. But now I'm asking you to."

Then, almost without thinking, Paul looked up and stared at the camera. His physical eyes focused on the lens, but his mind bore through the glass, past the sensitive optics, and made its way down the copper wires, back in time to a simpler era when adversity could be avoided by hiding and where fear of persecution – or exclusion – could be sidestepped by secrecy. In the last hours of CountryView, Paul was transfigured, called for something more: more than Memphis, more than Charlotte, more than Washington. His mind spun back to his youth, to a vision in his high school courtyard, and the truth began to bubble: memories of his birth in a cold Swiss mountain home, of nanoscopic implants torturously infused into veins in his arms and legs, of foster parents testing a grand experiment: could a human child, enhanced with technological implants, use them in ways that were unexpected? Could new properties and capabilities *emerge*? Could the man become more than the sum of his parts? The answer was: Yes. But Paul was much more than even his designers could imagine.

Paul could not blink. Epiphanies splashed across his brain one after another. He was being observed – watched. He had always been watched. And somehow, deeply, he had always known: Mr. Burns and poor Ophelia. The vision continued searing through his retina and deep into his soul. He could have been spiteful but bore no anger. His enigmatic childhood memories resurfaced and suddenly their meaning became clear. He could hear

STRONG EMERGENCE

the calling, and he answered. He was a transcendent man – the ultimate expression of the man-machine interface – and now his time had come. No longer could he remain in waiting, snorting as if in some drunken slumber, protecting humanity from the knowledge of their imminent future. He had taught before; now it was time to teach again. But he was not naïve. He was sure powers, both foreign and domestic, would pursue him but it did not matter anymore. There were some who were afraid of him, some who hoped to exploit him, and some who believed they should destroy him.

Little did they know...

He was more than a transcendent man...

He had emerged... and He was strong...

He was reborn... and He had returned...

Truth.

Allah.

And the evening and the morning were the third day...

And it was good.

...But where there are prophecies, they will cease; where there are tongues, they will be stilled; where there is knowledge, it will pass away. For we know in part and we prophesy in part, but when completeness comes, what is in part disappears. When I was a child, I talked like a child; I thought like a child; I reasoned like a child. When I became a man, I put the ways of childhood behind me. For now we see only a reflection as in a mirror; then we shall see face to face. Now I know in part; then I shall know fully, even as I am fully known.

Paul
1 Corinthians 13:8-12
Holy Bible, TNIV

STRONG EMERGENCE

We may be just a complex, programmable technology:
A collection of functional brain states
and neurochemical networks;
Made of a soup of interacting molecules:
proteins, enzymes, DNA and carbohydrates;
Composed of a zoo of elementary particles:
protons, electrons, bosons and quarks;
Described by quantum equations and supersymmetry
existing in a multidimensional space-time multiverse.

And then again, maybe we're not.

Nelson Mangione

Disclaimers and acknowledgements:

First and foremost, this is a work of fiction. Any resemblance to any persons or recent events is entirely coincidental with a few notable exceptions.

The facts surrounding the events of Alan Turing's death are materially accurate. He was the Father of Computer Science as well as Artificial Intelligence. He was also gay. For the transgression of his homosexuality, he was decommissioned, fired from his academic post, and court ordered to receive estrogen injections. He died in his home from cyanide poisoning presumably from a laced apple sitting on his bedside. But the apple was never tested. When the authorities arrived they smelled burnt almonds (the odor of cyanide), and he was lying comfortably in bed just as described. In the back of the house, a percolating experiment was still running.

Although his death was attributed to suicide, ingested cyanide does not kill quickly as is commonly believed. It kills slowly and with usually violent abdominal pangs, nausea and seizures. It's the inhaled cyanide, released from the sudden biting of a cyanide capsule or exposure to cyanide gas which kills quickly. Ingestion of cyanide from a contaminated fruit would not be expected to have caused the peaceful death Turing experienced. Maybe the apple did kill Turing suddenly as the local authorities concluded, but the vignette, as presented, is also entirely consistent with the known facts of the case.

Alan Turing was fascinated with quantum mechanics and met frequently with colleagues working on the mathematics of quantum theory. Although his "discovery" is entirely fictitious, it would not have been surprising for him to have made such an innovation. In fact, had he lived, Turing biographer Andrew Hodges concluded that it was highly likely he would have contributed significantly to quantum theory, quantum computing, machine intelligence and artificial life.

Memphis does have a Real Time Crime Center, and its capabilities were faithfully represented. Unfortunately, there is also a real Frayser High School, and the school's demographics were also accurate as were the FedEx SuperHub statistics, general layout, and the features of the subterranean FedEx "bunker". Finally, every attempt was made to depict the capabilities of the FBI and CIA as realistic as possible within the context of a fantastical premise.

However, artistic license was exercised often. Memphis does have a very capable and highly respected Baptist Hospital on the east side of town, but the hospital's internal layout is fictitious, and while the Wilson Air FBO does do business on the grounds of Memphis International Airport, their capabilities are also completely fictional. And, there is no Ariel self-flying personal jet – at least not yet. My apologies for any clarifications I have missed and for any inaccuracies or portrayals included in this work, and no endorsement by any entity or business should be assumed. Also, there is no Tyler Center, no CountryView estate, no J.D. Auto Parts, and there is no Cadillac Cafe (though the characteristics of the bar parallel many found throughout the south). LSX is fictitious as well. Lastly, please don't go looking for the Untereigerbasis. To my knowledge, there is nothing beneath the Eiger but rock.

Finally, I would like to thank everyone who participated in the editing and research of this work most notably Angela Eward-Mangione, Sylvia Mangione, and Noreen Rodriguez-Fife, and my friend "the scorpion" who assisted with the back story. Above all, I would like to thank my son Christopher. Chris provided significant plot and character development advice and without his inspiration, this book would never have been written. Finally, much thanks to my wife, Karol, who put up with me through this process providing me support, love and guidance. I love you sweetheart.

Strong Emergence

Made in the USA
Charleston, SC
22 August 2014